Her Passionate Italian

He wanted her in his bed!

Three intense, powerful novels from bestselling Mills & Boon® Modern™ authors – irresistible!

In July 2008 Mills & Boon bring back
two of their classic collections, each
featuring three favourite romances
by our bestselling authors…

HER PASSIONATE ITALIAN
The Passion Bargain by Michelle Reid
A Sicilian Husband by Kate Walker
The Italian's Marriage Bargain
by Carol Marinelli

THE TYCOON'S MISTRESS
by Carole Mortimer
His Cinderella Mistress
The Unwilling Mistress
The Deserving Mistress

Her Passionate Italian

THE PASSION BARGAIN
by
Michelle Reid

A SICILIAN HUSBAND
by
Kate Walker

THE ITALIAN'S MARRIAGE BARGAIN
by
Carol Marinelli

MILLS & BOON
Pure reading pleasure™

Harlequin Mills & Boon Limited,
Eton House, 18-24 Paradise Road, Richmond, Surrey TW9 1SR

HER PASSIONATE ITALIAN
© by Harlequin Enterprises II B.V./S.à.r.l 2008

The Passion Bargain, A Sicilian Husband and The Italian's
Marriage Bargain were first published in Great Britain by
Harlequin Mills & Boon Limited in separate, single volumes.

The Passion Bargain © Michelle Reid 2004
A Sicilian Husband © Kate Walker 2003
The Italian's Marriage Bargain © Carol Marinelli 2004

ISBN: 978 0263 86128 0

05-0708

Printed and bound in Spain
by Litografia Rosés S.A., Barcelona

THE PASSION BARGAIN

by

Michelle Reid

100 Reasons to Celebrate

We invite you to join us in celebrating Mills & Boon's centenary. Gerald Mills and Charles Boon founded Mills & Boon Limited in 1908 and opened offices in London's Covent Garden. Since then, Mills & Boon has become a hallmark for romantic fiction, recognised around the world.

We're proud of our 100 years of publishing excellence, which wouldn't have been achieved without the loyalty and enthusiasm of our authors and readers.

Thank you!

Each month throughout the year there will be something new and exciting to mark the centenary, so watch for your favourite authors, captivating new stories, special limited edition collections…and more!

Michelle Reid grew up on the southern edges of Manchester, the youngest in a family of five lively children. But now she lives in the beautiful county of Cheshire with her busy executive husband and two grown-up daughters. She loves reading, the ballet, and playing tennis when she gets the chance. She hates cooking, cleaning, and despises ironing! Sleep she can do without and produces some of her best written work during the early hours of the morning.

Don't miss Michelle Reid's exciting new novel, *The De Santis Marriage,* out in September from Mills & Boon® Modern™.

CHAPTER ONE

FRANCESCA used gentle pressure on the brake pedal to bring the Vespa to a smooth stop at a set of red traffic lights then stretched out a long golden leg and placed a strappy-sandalled foot on the ground to maintain the motor scooter's balance while she waited for the lights to change.

It was a gorgeous morning, still early enough for the traffic on the Corso to be so light that she actually seemed to have the road almost entirely to herself.

A rare occurrence in this mad, bad, traffic-clogged city, she mused with a smile as she tossed back her head to send her tawny brown hair streaming down her back then closed her warm hazel eyes and lifted her face up to the sun to enjoy the feel of its silky warmth caressing her skin.

The air was exquisite today, clear and sharp and drenched in that unique golden light that gave Italy its famous sensual glow.

Her smile widened, her smooth rather generous mouth stretching to enhance the sheen of clear lip-gloss that along with a quick flick of mascara was the only make-up she wore.

Life, she decided, could not be more perfect. For here she was, living in one of the most beautiful cities in the world and only days away from becoming formally betrothed to the most wonderful man in the world. One very short month from now she and Angelo would be exchanging their marriage vows in a sweet little church overlooking Lake Alba before taking off for Venice to honeymoon in the most romantic city in the world.

And she was happy, happy, happy. She even sighed that happiness up at the sun while she waited for the lights to change, too engrossed in the warmth of her own sublime contentment to be aware of the sleek red sports car drawing up at her side. It was only when the driver decided to send the car's convertible top floating into its neat rear housing and the sultry sound of Puccini suddenly filled the air that she took note of his presence.

Then immediately wished that she hadn't when she took a glance sideways and saw *why* the driver had sent the car hood floating back. Her skin gave a sharp warning prickle, her soft hazel eyes quickly lost their smile—none of which had anything to do with the way she was being thoroughly scrutinised from the tips of her extended toes to the shiny flow of her freshly washed hair. Heck, it was almost obligatory for any warm-blooded Italian male to check out the female form when presented with the opportunity. No, her prickling response was due to the fact that she knew this particular Italian male. Or, to be more accurate, she had made his acquaintance once or twice when they had been thrown into the same company.

'Buon giorno, Signorina Bernard,' he greeted, the beautifully polite tones of this supremely cultured male completely belying the lazy sweep his dark eyes had just enjoyed.

'Signor,' she returned with a small acknowledging dip of her head.

If he noticed the chill she was giving off then he chose to ignore it, preferring to divert his attention away from her to guide one of his long-fingered hands out towards the car dashboard. Puccini died into a slumberous murmur. As he moved, sunlight shot across the raven's-wing quality of his satiny black hair. Signor Carlo Carlucci was a man that most people would describe as truly handsome, Francesca acknowledged with a complicated pinch of her stomach muscles that forced her to twitch restlessly. Skin the shade of ripened dark olives hugged the most superbly balanced bone structure she had ever seen on a man. Every one of his lean features quite simply fitted, even the nose that was so Roman you could not mistake his heritage. His jaw-line was square, his chin cleft, his cheekbones ever so slightly chis-elled, and the firmly moulded shape of his slender mouth was—well—perfect, she admitted with yet another restless twitch.

Dark brown eyes were set beneath a pair of almost straight, satiny black eyebrows and were shaded by eye-lashes that were almost a sin they were so long, and silky black. And as he shifted his long lean torso in the seat so he could give her his full attention Francesca would have had to be immune to the whole male species to resist notic-ing the leashed power in his muscles as they flexed beneath the bright white cloth of his shirt.

He oozed class and style and an unyielding self-possession. Everything about him was polished and smooth. He disturbed her when he shouldn't. He *antagonised* her when she knew she shouldn't let him.

Even the strictly polite smile he offered her set her nerve-ends singing as he remarked pleasantly, 'You were looking the essence of happiness as I drove up. I suppose credit for this must go to the fine weather we are enjoying today.'

If it was, now it's gone, Francesca thought resentfully. And wished she understood why she always suffered this itchy suspicion that he was taunting her whenever he spoke to her. He had been making her feel like this from the first time they'd been introduced at a party given by Angelo's parents. Even the way he had of looking at her always gave her the uncomfortable impression that he knew things about her that she did not and was amused by that.

He was doing it now, holding her gaze with his velvet dark eyes that pretended to be friendly but really were not. He mocked her—he *did*.

'Summer has arrived at last,' she agreed, willing to play the weather game that was what it took to keep this unwanted interlude neutralised long enough for the lights to change.

'Which is why you are out and about so early.' He nodded gravely, mocking her—again?

'I'm out and about early, as you put it, because this is my day off and I have things to do before I can hit the shops before the crowds arrive.'

'Ah.' He nodded. 'Now I understand the happy essence. Shopping has to be the preferred option to herding weary tourists through the Sistine Chapel or encouraging them to squat upon the Spanish Steps.'

He really had this taunting stuff down to a fine art, Francesca acknowledged as he put her right on the defensive. She had been guiding British tourists round the historical sites of Rome for months now and had learned early on that, though the city's economy might enjoy the healthy fruits of its tourist industry, the true residents of Rome did not always treat this point with the respect it deserved. They despaired of tourists, could be gruff and curt and sometimes downright rude. Especially in the high season, when they couldn't walk anywhere without bumping into camera-toting groups.

'You should be proud of your heritage,' she censured stiffly.

'Oh, I am—very proud. Why should you think that I am not? I simply object to sharing,' he said. 'It is not in my nature.'

'Which sounds very selfish.'

'Not selfish but possessive of what I believe belongs to me.'

'That still adds up to being selfish,' she insisted.

'You think so?' He took a second or two to contemplate that declaration. As he did so he shifted his body again, drawing her gaze to the white-shirted arm he lifted to rest across the black leather back of his seat. Long brown fingers with blunted fingernails uncoiled from a loose clench then rose upwards, tugging her trapped gaze with them as he brought them to rest against the smooth golden sheen of his freshly shaved cheek. He was gorgeous. Her mouth ran dry. Her tummy muscles pinched again and she became suddenly very aware of the Vespa's little engine vibrating between her spread thighs.

'No, I cannot agreed with you, *cara*.' He began speaking again, making her eyelashes flicker as her attention shifted to his moving lips. 'When I am involved in a deeply serious relationship with someone, would you still think it selfish of me to expect my lover to remain completely faithful only to me?'

Was he involved in a deeply serious relationship? For some mad reason her skin began to heat. Oh, stop it, she thought crossly. What was the matter with her? She had absolutely no excuse to get so hot and bothered over a man she didn't even like. She hardly knew him—didn't want to know him. The Carlo Carluccis of this world were way out of her league and she was happy to keep it that way.

'We were talking about Rome,' she pointed out curtly and flipped her eyes towards the set of traffic lights, willing the stupid things to hurry up and change.

'We were? I thought we had moved on to discuss my objection to sharing,' he murmured lazily. Teasing her—taunting her, she was sure—but why? 'Are you prepared to share your lovers, Francesca?' he dared to ask her. 'If I was *your* lover, for instance, would you expect me to be faithful only to you?'

This was stupid—stupid! I hate you, she told the stubborn red traffic light. 'Since there is no chance of that happening, *signor*, I don't see the use in discussing it,' she announced in her coldest, primmest English voice.

'Shame,' he sighed. 'And here I was, about to test my luck by suggesting that we continue this discussion in more congenial surroundings...'

Congenial...?

It was a clear come-on. Francesca was shocked enough to slew her widened eyes back to his face. It was a mistake. Her breath caught. Those warning prickles began racing up her spine because those dark, hooded eyes were travelling the length of her outstretched leg again. The sun-drenched air was suddenly charging up with sense-invading atoms that made the inner layers of skin covering her leg tingle as if he'd reached out with one of those hands and stroked right along its smooth golden length.

She almost gasped out loud at the electric sensation. The urge to whip her leg out of sight was almost too strong to stop. It took all of her control to keep the leg exactly where it was as she became stiflingly aware of the way her white cotton skirt was stretched taut across her slender long thighs.

Stop it! she wanted to shout at him. Stop trying to do this to me! But she found she couldn't manage a single stuttered word and those eyes were moving on; heavy-lidded, darkly lashed, they began slowly skimming her little blue sun top where her rounded breasts pushed at the finely woven cloth. Her nipples responded, tightening with piercing speed. The shock of it held her utterly transfixed as those dark eyes lifted higher until—shockingly—their gazes clashed.

He wanted her. The realisation hit her like a violent blow to the chest. Heat enveloped her from feet to hairline. Those eyes told her he knew what was happening to her and, worse, they were doing nothing to hide the fact that the same thing was happening to him. She could feel the sexual tension in his body, could see it burning in his now blacker than black eyes. Messages began leaping across the tarmac road and to her horror that place between her thighs feathered a ripple of pleasure across the sex-sensitive tissue.

It was so awful she shifted her hips with an uncontrollable jerk. In all of her twenty-four years she had never experienced anything as sexually acute as this. For a few more terrible seconds the world seemed to be closing in on her.

She couldn't breathe, couldn't think, couldn't move, couldn't—

'Have coffee with me,' he murmured suddenly. 'Meet with me at Café Milan…'

Have coffee with me, she repeated slowly to herself, her brain so sluggish that the invitation made no sense. Then it did make sense with all of its hot and spicy meaning. She grabbed at some oxygen. A car horn sounded. The real world came crashing back in. Dragging her eyes away from his, she looked blankly at the traffic lights, saw they'd turned to green and gunned the Vespa's little engine and took off down the Corso like a terrified pigeon in flight.

A top-of-the-range Lamborghini could outstrip a Vespa without any effort but, ignoring the protesting car horns behind him, Carlo remained exactly where he was.

His eyes were narrowed and fixed on the racing scooter and its beautiful rider, whose silky hair was blowing out behind her as she fled. He'd scared her out of her wits, Carlo acknowledged. Had he meant to do that? He was not entirely sure what his real motives had been, only that he had been presented with an opportunity and had used it—ruthlessly. Now pretend that I barely exist, *signorina*, he thought grimly.

The muted sound of Puccini rising to a crescendo began to infiltrate his consciousness. Reaching out, he hit the volume control to fill the air with the music then set the powerful car into motion again. There was a fine film of sweat bathing his torso beneath the fine cloth of his crisp white shirt and he grimaced. Francesca Bernard was the most excitingly sensual woman he had ever encountered and there was no way he was going to let all of that sensuality be laid to waste on a crass, mercenary fool like Angelo Batiste.

As the car built up speed along the Corso the Vespa had already turned off at a junction and by the time Carlo passed that junction neither bike nor rider were anywhere to be seen.

Francesca had pulled into a small piazza, cut the engine then climbed off the machine. She was feeling so shaken up inside that her legs felt like jelly, and she headed for the nearest café so she could sit down. A waiter appeared and she ordered fresh orange juice. She desperately needed a cup of strong coffee to calm her shattered senses but the very idea of drinking coffee was out of the question now that Carlo Carlucci had given the simple pleasure a whole new twist.

She shivered, still gripped by the shock of what had just happened. The whole incident had turned her into such a mess inside she could still feel those hot little *frissons* chasing across her skin. If he'd actually reached out and touched her she had a horrible feeling she would have gone up in a flaming orgasm. She had no idea where it had all come from. How it had gone from a simple tit-for-tat conversation at a red traffic light to—to what it did!

Her throat felt ravaged. She didn't think she'd managed to take a single breath all the way from those wretched lights until she sat down on this seat. Her hands were trembling, her legs, her arms—the tips of her stinging breasts!

It wasn't as if they even knew each other well enough to be anything more than polite nodding acquaintances! They'd met—what—twice before, maybe three times at most? And she didn't even like him. He had a way of antagonising her with that smoothly sardonic manner of his. Her orange juice arrived. She nodded her thanks to the waiter then picked it up and gulped at it. The cool drink helped to soothe her throat but the rest of her didn't feel any relief.

Putting the glass down on the table, she hunched forward to sit there frowning into it. It was just beginning to dawn on her how easily she had let him get away with what he'd done. Usually she would know exactly how to deal with a teasing Italian who was only out to fill in a few empty seconds by having a bit of fun with her.

But Carlo Carlucci was no ordinary teasing Italian. He was the thirty-five-year-old head of the famous Carlucci Electronics. That placed him more than a decade ahead of her in years and eons ahead of her in every other way she could think of. Women adored him. He was rarely seen out without some acknowledged beauty hanging on his expensive arm. Put him in a room packed full of his tall, dark, handsome peers and he still managed to overshadow them all.

He was special. Even here in super-sophisticated Rome he was the man other men wanted to emulate. In the way these things should work, a lowly tour-guide like herself should never have come into contact with him at all. But Angelo was the son of one of Signor Carlucci's business associates, which meant they'd happened to find themselves in the same company while attending the same parties over the last few weeks. Not that this placed them in the same circles because it didn't, she reminded herself with a frown. Even Angelo only received a cool nod in acknowledgement from Carlo Carlucci's sleek, dark, sophisticated head. Angelo's father's company relied on Carlucci's for the main thrust of its business and Angelo was only a few years older than herself, which made him very junior and insignificant in the pecking order at these bright and sparklingly sophisticated social events.

But at least Angelo was warm and gentle and easy-going. He preferred fun to passion. It was years since a man like Carlo Carlucci had weaned himself off anything so juvenile as *fun*.

He was way out of her league, and anyway, she loved Angelo.

Yet when it really came down to the bottom line of it, she hadn't given a single thought to Angelo while she'd been thinking of Carlo Carlucci at that wretched traffic stop sign.

'Oh.' She choked on a fresh wave of *frissons*, which were

quickly doused by a heavy blanket of guilt. How could she—how *could* she have forgotten about Angelo at that wretched set of lights?

On impulse she reached into her tote bag to fish out her cellphone with the intention of calling up the man she loved. She needed to reassure herself that what Carlo Carlucci had just made her feel was nothing more than a blip on her hormonal calendar. She needed desperately to hear his warm, loving voice!

His cellphone was switched off. It was then that she remembered that he had business in Milan today. He was catching the early flight and had predicted he would be unreachable all day.

Then, *'Milan,'* she repeated and shuddered as the name conjured up a whole new meaning that placed it like *coffee* in the realms of sin.

Oh, stop it, she thought and tossed her cellphone onto the table then sat back in her seat and closed her eyes to work very hard at building Angelo's beloved golden image over the top of the darker one that should not have found a way into her head at all!

Angelo didn't have a dark corner in him. He was all sunlight. Golden skin, golden eyes and fine golden strands streaking in his tawny hair that she so loved to trail her fingers through. When he walked into a room he didn't cast a long shadow over everyone else, he lit it up with his warm golden temperament that had not yet become hidden beneath a hard, sophisticated shell. When he looked at her she felt warm and loved and beautiful, not—invaded by dark, untrammelled lusts.

Oh, all right, so she admitted it. Sometimes she'd wondered why their relationship wasn't more passionate. In fact, they had yet to actually make love.

'Time for that when you're ready,' she could hear his gentle voice saying.

And he was right because she wasn't ready. He'd understood from the beginning that she needed time to get used to the idea of full physical love. It wasn't that she was frigid, she quickly assured herself, just—wary of the unknown.

It came from being brought up by a deeply religious and straight-laced mother who'd instilled in her daughter standards by which she expected Francesca to live her life. Those standards included the sanctity of marriage coming before any pleasures of the flesh.

Outmoded principles? Yes, of course, principles like those were so out of fashion they could appear almost laughable to some. Indeed Sonya, her best friend and flatmate, did laugh at her—often. Sonya couldn't believe that a gorgeous masculine specimen like Angelo put up with a shrinking violet from a different century.

'You must be mad to play Russian roulette with a man like him,' she'd told her. 'Aren't you terrified that he might take his sexual requirements somewhere else?'

Well, yes, sometimes. She'd even confided those concerns to Angelo. He'd just smiled and kissed her, said Sonya was jealous and she wouldn't recognise a principle if she was staring at one.

Angelo didn't like Sonya. Sonya could not stand him. They provoked each other like two enemies across a neutral zone. Francesca was the neutral zone. The old-fashioned girl with the old-fashioned principles who loved them both but—more to the point—they loved her.

A smile crossed her mouth again. It wasn't quite as sunny as the smile she had been wearing before she ran into Carlo Carlucci but at least it was a smile.

Her telephone beeped, she twisted it around to check who was calling and the smile became a rueful grin. 'Were your ears burning?' she quizzed.

'Meaning what?' Sonya demanded, then sourly before Francesca could offer an answer, 'I suppose by that you're somewhere with darling Angelo and he's slandering my character again.'

'No,' Francesca denied. 'Angelo's in Milan today so put your claws away and tell me what you're ringing me for.'

'Do I only ring you when I want something?'

'The honest answer to that is—yes,' Francesca answered drily.

'Well, not this time,' her flatmate countered. 'I got up this morning to find you'd already left the flat. Why are you out so early? This is supposed to be your day off.'

'And you should be on your way to work by now.' Francesca took a quick glance at her watch. 'What time did you crawl into bed this morning?' It was definitely long after she had fallen fast asleep.

Her answer was a mind-your-own-business tut. 'Stick to the point,' Sonya snapped. 'Where are you going and how long will you be gone for?'

'I decided to come into town and do my shopping before it gets too hot and sticky to try on clothes.'

'Oh, I forgot. It's find-the-right-dress-to-knock-dear-Angelo's-eyes-out day.'

She really was obsessing on the man. 'Oh, do stop it, Sonya,' she sighed impatiently. 'Have you any idea how wearing this war between you and Angelo is? I hope you're going to call a truce before the party on Saturday night or I might just knock your heads together in front of Rome's best.'

'Maybe you would prefer it if I stayed away altogether— then you won't have to worry.'

She was offended now. Francesca uttered another sigh. 'Now, that's plain childish.'

'And you are beginning to sound like my mother. Don't do this, don't do that. At least try to behave yourself,' Sonya chanted deridingly. 'I hoped when I came to Rome that I would leave all of that stuff behind me in London.'

She was right, Francesca realised with a start—she sounded like her *own* mother. 'I'm sorry,' she murmured heavily.

'Forget it,' Sonya said and it was her turn to sigh. 'I'm a bitch in the mornings. You know I am. Go and buy your knockout dress and I'll crawl into work like a good girl.'

The call ended a few seconds later, leaving Francesca sitting there frowning and wondering what the heck had happened to her beautiful day.

The answer to that came in the form of a pair of dark eyes and a sensually husky voice saying, 'Have coffee with me at the Café Milan.'

A sudden breeze whipped up, swirling its way around the square, flipping tablecloths and shifting lightweight chairs. Francesca's hair was whipped backwards, her skin hit by a shivery chill. Then it was gone, leaving waiters hurrying to make good the disarray the breeze had left behind it and Francesca feeling as if she had just been touched by an ill wind.

She got up, took some money from her tote bag and placed it on the table to pay for her drink. As she walked back across the square to where she'd left the Vespa her skin was still covered in goose pimples yet she was trembling not shivering. She felt the difference so deeply it was almost an omen in itself.

CHAPTER TWO

IT WAS gone lunchtime by the time she arrived back at the apartment. As she stepped in through the door she then stood for a moment just looking around her in frowning puzzlement. The place had been quite tidy when she'd left here this morning but it didn't look like that now. The cushions on the sofa were crushed and tumbled. There were two half-drunk coffee-cups sitting on the low table and an empty bottle of wine with two glasses lying on their sides on the floor. She could see through the open door to Sonya's bedroom that it looked pretty much in the same tumbled state.

She was still frowning at the mess when her cellphone beeped and, placing her shopping bags on the floor, she fished out her phone to discover the caller was Bianca, the office manager of the tour group she and Sonya worked for.

She was looking for Sonya. 'She didn't turn up to work today,' Bianca announced. 'Have you any idea where she is? She isn't answering her mobile or the phone at your flat.'

Looking around at the evidence, Francesca could only assume that Sonya had been entertaining an unexpected visitor, though her loyalty to Sonya was not going to let her tell Bianca that.

'I'm sorry,' she said, 'but I left the flat before Sonya was up this morning so I've no idea where she is,' which wasn't a lie. 'Didn't she call in to warn you she wasn't going to make it?'

'No.' The manager's voice was tight. 'And she's left me a guide short. It really isn't on, Francesca. This is the third time in two weeks she's let me down like this.'

It was? Francesca's eyes widened at this surprise piece of information. She hadn't been aware that Sonya had been skipping off work. 'I know she's been suffering with a troublesome wisdom tooth lately,' which was true. Sonya complained about it a lot but was terror-struck at the mere mention of the word dentist. 'Maybe she couldn't stand the pain any more and went to get treatment.'

'And pigs might fly,' Bianca snapped. 'It's this man she has been seeing.'

Man? 'What man?' As far as she was aware, Sonya wasn't seeing anyone special at the moment.

'Don't pull the innocent, Francesca,' Bianca scolded. 'You know all about the married man she's lost her head over. If she's any sense she will drop him before this company drops her. I can't have my guides not turning up when they should. It makes an absolute mess of my...'

Francesca stopped listening, so stunned by the turn of this conversation that she had to sit down. She'd known Sonya since they'd been at university together and—OK, she acknowledged, so she was a bit of a rebel and tended to let her heart rule her head. But she confided most things to Francesca and she did not recall her saying a thing about a new man.

A *married* man?

Bianca had to be mistaken, she decided, only to look at the evidence laid out in front of her eyes that told her Sonya was up to *something* clandestine if she was resorting to skipping work so she could entertain her man here, where there was little chance of them being seen together.

'I'll come in and cover for her if you need me.' She cut across whatever it was Bianca was saying. She glanced at her watch. 'I still have time to get there if it will help you out.'

'Are you sure you don't mind? You were supposed to be shopping for your dress today. It doesn't seem fair that you should—'

'The dress is bought,' Francesca assured, glancing across the room to where she'd placed the elegant dress box that she'd ridden back here safely trapped between her legs. 'I'll be there as soon as I can make it.'

'You truly are an angel, Francesca,' Bianca said in relief. 'Unlike your wretched friend!'

The phone call ended. Francesca continued to sit there wondering what the heck had got into today. It had begun so well. She'd been happy—everything had been perfect!

Then Carlo Carlucci had happened, she recalled with a small shiver. Since her run-in with him nothing had gone right. She'd had phone calls that irritated, ill winds blowing chills across her skin and a tiring trudge through Rome's finest fashion boutiques, looking for a dress she still wasn't sure about even though she'd bought it. Now Sonya had gone missing and it was just beginning to dawn on her that, true to her flatmate's nature, she *had* rung her this morning to ask if she would cover for her at work. Only she'd then chickened out when they'd got into an argument over Angelo.

And now she had discovered that Sonya had been lying to her! Or keeping secrets was probably a fairer way of putting it.

But she didn't want to be fair. She didn't want to be *an angel* or have her best friend sniping at Angelo and then likening her to her mother because she happened to lose her patience.

More irritation struck, slicing right down her backbone and bringing her to her feet. She bent to pick up the used coffee-cups then stopped herself. Tidying up after Sonya was something her mother would do. So was tutting and sighing all over the place, as she'd been about to do.

'Oh, damn it!' she shouted at the tiny apartment. And she *never* swore!

Because her mother would have been appalled.

'Damn it,' she said again out of sheer black cussedness and went to put her purchases away.

Then she went still, listening to herself and not liking

what she heard. Her mother was gone now and she did not want to think ill of her. She didn't want to be sniping at her inside her head! There had been too much ill feeling in Maria Bernard's life while she had been alive, she thought bleakly as she went to unpack and hang up her dress.

Her mother had once been the beautiful Maria Gianni—only child of Rinaldo Gianni, a man who ran his household with a rod of iron. He'd woven plans around his only daughter that had mapped out her entire future from the day she had been born. Then Maria had thwarted those plans by falling in love with a thankless English rake called Vincent Bernard, who had his eye firmly fixed on Maria's inheritance. It had taken a month for him to make her pregnant and another month to get her father's permission to marry her—before Rinaldo Gianni threw them out. Vincent had taken her mother to England. He'd been so sure that his father-in-law would relent and forgive once Maria produced the grandson the old man wanted so much that he was prepared to wait the whole nine months for the event to take place. A girl had not fitted either man's criteria. Vincent Bernard had cut his losses and left Maria holding a baby girl that nobody wanted by then. A year after that Vincent had divorced her to marry his next rich fool of a wife. Divorce had been the ultimate humiliation and sin in her mother's eyes. She'd never acknowledged that legal slip of paper ending her Roman Catholic marriage. She'd never forgiven her father for refusing to forgive her for going against his wishes. All three had never spoken again.

Rinaldo Gianni had died when Francesca was ten years old, having never acknowledged that he had a granddaughter. She'd never met him, just as she had never met her own father, who—and here was the irony—died around the same time. It wasn't until a year after her mother's death that she'd given in to a long-suppressed yearning to come to Rome and meet with her only surviving blood relative. And even as she'd taken that first step onto Italian soil she had still been struggling with her conscience because she'd known her mother would not approve. But it was lonely being on her own yet knowing she had a great-uncle living here who might—just might—be prepared to welcome Maria's child.

She'd wanted nothing else from Bruno Gianni. Not his money or even his love. She hadn't got them either, she mused with a wry little smile as she dried herself after a quick shower. Her great-uncle Bruno, she'd discovered, was a very old man living the life of a near recluse in his draughty old *palazzo* tucked away in the Albany Hills south of Rome. He did not receive visitors. He did not have a great-niece, she was informed by return letter when she'd made her first tentative approach. It had taken determined persistence on her part before the old man eventually gave in and reluctantly granted her an audience.

It was a strange meeting, she recalled, pausing for a moment to look back to that one and only time she'd met Bruno Gianni. He was nice. She'd liked him on sight even though he had told her straight off that if she was after his money then there was none to be had. The crumbling *palazzo* belonged to the bank, he'd said, and what bit of money he had left would go to the tax collector when he was dead.

But she'd been able to see her mother's eyes in his eyes— her own hazel eyes looking curiously at her even as he'd labelled her a fortune-hunter. She recalled how badly she'd wanted to touch him but didn't dare, how his skin wasn't at all wrinkly despite his great age and he might live in a near ruin but his grooming had been immaculate. Quite dapper.

She smiled as she began dressing again, slipping into her uniform red dress with its flashes of bright yellow and green.

She'd told him about her life and her mother's life in London, the schools she'd attended and her university degree. She'd told him that she was working as a tour guide in Rome and that she was sharing an apartment with a friend she'd met in university. He'd listened without attempting to put a stop on her eager flow. When she'd finally slithered to a stop, he'd nodded as if in approval then rung the bell. When the housekeeper arrived to see her out all he'd said was, 'Enjoy the rest of your life, *signorina*,' and she'd nodded, knowing by those words that he had no wish to see her again.

That didn't mean she'd stopped corresponding though. She'd continued to send him little notes every week, letting him know what she was doing. When she'd met and fallen in love with Angelo, besides Sonya, Great-Uncle Bruno was the first person to know. He'd never replied to a single letter and she hadn't a clue if he even bothered to read her silly, light, chatty notes. When she confided in Angelo about him he was shocked and disbelieving at first, then he'd laughed and called their first meeting fate because Bruno Gianni lived only a couple of miles away from his parents' country house.

'If your mama had been allowed to live there with you, we would have grown up together—been childhood sweethearts maybe.'

She liked that idea. It gave their love a sense of inevitability and belonging that her unforgiving grandfather could not beat.

On the few occasions she had been invited to spend the weekend at the Villa Batiste in the Frascati area of Castelli Romani she always made a point of walking the few miles to her great-uncle's *palazzo* to leave a note to let him know where she was staying—just in case he might relent and asked her to visit him while she was there. It had never happened. He hadn't even bothered to reply to the formal invitation to her betrothal party this weekend, she reminded herself.

Did that hurt? A little, she confessed. But—as Angelo said—persistence could often win in the end. 'Maybe he will relent and come to our wedding.'

And maybe he would, she thought hopefully as she shut up the apartment and stepped back out into the sunlit street.

However disappointed she was with her great-uncle, she had never regretted coming to Rome. Her Italian was fluent, her knowledge of the city's history something she'd drenched herself in from the time she had been able to read. She loved her job, loved her life and she loved—loved Angelo.

The ride down the Corso was a mad, bad bustle this time around. Francesca skimmed deftly between tight lines of traffic. The afternoon was a long one. The city was beginning to throb with people now the tourist season was in full flow—not that it eased by a huge amount at any time of the year. By the time she arrived back at the apartment she was so tired all she wanted to do was dive beneath the shower then put up her aching feet.

The first thing she noticed was the tidied apartment, the next was Sonya, curled up on the sofa wrapped in her bathrobe, looking very defiant.

'Before you start, it was the toothache,' she jumped in before Francesca could say anything. 'It flared up after I spoke to you this morning and I just had to find a dentist to do something about it.'

'Makes house-calls, does he?' Francesca didn't believe her. It took only a flick of her eyes to the empty coffee-table for Sonya to know what she meant.

'Of course not,' she snapped then winced, pushing a hand up to cover the side of her face. 'God, it's hurting more now that the anaesthetic's worn off than it did before I let him touch it!' she groaned.

'*Who* touched it?'

'The dentist, you sarcastic witch,' Sonya sliced. Then she sighed when she realised she wasn't about to get any sympathy, her gentian-blue eyes moving over Francesca's clothes. 'Sorry I spoilt your day off,' she mumbled contritely.

'You meant to do that a whole lot earlier this morning,' she drawled.

'Mm.' Sonya didn't even bother to deny it; her fingertips were now carefully testing the slight puffiness Francesca could see at her jaw.

'You look grotty,' she observed, yielding slightly. 'How bad is it?'

'Really bad.' Tears even swam into her eyes. 'He drilled it then dressed it with—something.' She dismissed that *something* with a flick of her hand. 'I'm to go back next week—ouch.' She winced again. 'I also got the full lecture on the cause and effect of neglect.'

Francesca couldn't help but smile at the last dry comment. Sonya didn't like lectures especially when she had no defence. 'Did you punch him?' she asked.

'Not likely! He had me pinned down with all these contraptions sticking out of my mouth and was holding a drill in his hand at the time.'

'Poor you,' she commiserated.

'Mm.' Sonya was in complete sympathy with that comment. 'Did you get your dress?' she then thought to enquire.

'Mm,' Francesca mimicked. 'Did you get your intriguing new man to hold your hand while you sat in the dentist's chair?'

Sonya looked up then quickly away again, a definite flush mounting her delicately pale cheeks. 'Don't ask because I'm not going to tell you,' she muttered.

'So he *is* married,' Francesca concluded.

'Who told you that?' Sonya was shocked.

'Bianca,' she supplied. 'Who seems to know a whole lot more than I do about your love-life.'

That still hurt, and she turned away to walk towards her bedroom.

'I'm sorry, Francesca, but I *can't* talk about him!' she threw after her. 'It's—complicated,' she added awkwardly. 'And Bianca only knows the bit she gleaned out of me when she caught me rowing with him on the phone in the office the other day. '

'So he is married?' She turned to look at her.

Sonya looked down and stubbornly closed her mouth.

The urge to tell her what a fool she was being leapt to the edge of her tongue—then was stopped when she remembered the 'you sound like my mother' stab from this morning. So she changed her mind about saying anything at all and turned back to her bedroom.

'I'm going to change,' she said. 'I'm meeting Angelo in a hour—'

'No, you're not.'

Once again she stopped and swung round. 'What's that supposed to mean?'

'He rang here—a few minutes ago—to say he's still in Milan and won't be coming back until tomorrow.' For some reason relaying all of that also poured hot colour into her cheeks.

Francesca's eyes narrowed in suspicion. 'Have you two been fighting again?'

'No,' Sonya denied.

'Then why the guilty face?'

'OK, so we fought a little bit,' Sonya snapped. 'Stop getting at me, Francesca! I can't help it if—'

'So, why didn't he call me on my mobile to tell me this?' Francesca cut in. She was not going to let Sonya start one of her character-assassination jobs on Angelo again. One a day of those was enough.

'He said you weren't answering.'

Francesca glanced at her bag then went to recover it. The moment she fished inside the uniform brown leather satchel she knew why he couldn't reach her. In her rush that lunchtime she must have left the phone in her tote bag.

'Idiot,' she muttered and went into the bedroom to get it so she could return his call—only to find Sonya had followed her and was standing in the doorway, wearing the oddest expression on her face. Francesca couldn't quite read it—anxiety, pleading? Or was it pain from the tooth?

'Are you feeling all right, *cara*?' she probed gently. 'You look terribly flushed.' She put a cool palm against Sonya's cheek and was surprised just how hot she felt. 'At the risk of being accused of mothering you, would you like me to tuck you into bed and bring you a nice hot chocolate drink?'

The tears arrived then, turning gentian-blue into midnight pools in a face that was so classically beautiful it was no wonder she'd been screen tested by a film director once. 'Don't be nice to me, Francesca,' she murmured.

'I love you,' she smiled, moving her fingers into the straight, glossy pelt of her friend's long, flaxen hair. 'Why shouldn't I be nice?'

'Because I don't deserve it.' Sonya stepped away from her so she could use the sleeve of her bathrobe to wipe her eyes with. 'I use your friendship dreadfully.'

'Only because I let you.'

'Yes...' Sonya agreed and looked momentarily devastated. The phone went then, breaking the moment. Sonya went into the sitting room to answer it and a few seconds later was calling Francesca to come to the phone.

'*Ciao, mi amore.*' It was Angelo, his voice sounding weary and flat. 'You don't answer your cellphone because you don't want to speak to me and I cannot blame you.'

'I didn't have my phone with me so I couldn't answer it, you sweet idiot,' she chided, her eyes flickering sideways to watch Sonya disappearing into her bedroom. The moment the door shut behind her Francesca lowered her voice into soft, loving tones. 'I'm sorry you're stuck in Milan.'

'So am I,' he agreed. 'I am about to get ready to take dinner with some business colleagues when I should be on my way to share a romantic dinner with you. Ah, *misero*,' he declared feelingly.

'Poor *caro*,' she commiserated.

Angelo heaved out a sigh. 'But enough of this.' He firmly

pulled his mood out of the doldrums. 'Tell me about your day.'

'Well, my plans fell to pieces much as yours did…' She went to explain, leaving out the incident at the traffic lights and editing some of the more contentious events involving Sonya so she didn't invite him to vent his frustrations on the one person guaranteed to earn his wrath. 'But I did manage to find a dress for Saturday,' she finished on a high note.

To her surprise he made no cruel remarks about Sonya's toothache. In fact he skimmed right over the fact that she'd even been mentioned at all and asked about her dress instead. She refused to tell him and there followed a few minutes of soft teasing that was much more like the man she loved. Then he had to go and the call ended, leaving Francesca feeling loved and filled with that golden warmth that was her Angelo.

Sonya didn't come out of her bedroom again that evening. Francesca went in to check on her a couple of times but all she could see was the crown of her head peeping out from beneath a mound of duvet and eventually left her to sleep off the ordeal with the dentist.

By the next morning she was herself again and ready to face Bianca's wrath head-on. They rode down the Corso side by side on similar Vespas and dressed in the same red uniforms. Their day was busy as always.

Angelo called at lunchtime to break the news that he was going to be stuck in Milan for another night. The next day was Saturday and they were supposed to be driving into the Alban Hills together but that plan had to be shelved. 'I have arranged with my parents for you to travel with them,' he told her.

It wasn't a prospect that filled her with delight. She had discovered quite early on in her relationship with Angelo that his parents were not the kind of people who were ever going to welcome her with open arms. She harboured a suspicion that she was not what they'd been hoping for as a wife for their precious only son and if it wasn't for her very loose connection to the Gianni name they would have been actively against Angelo marrying her. As it was, Mrs Batiste had grilled her once about her mother, then surprised her by confessing that she and Maria Gianni had attended the same convent school. 'You look very like her—apart from the hair,' she'd said, Maria's hair having been as glossy Latin black as hair could be. 'I'm sorry she had such a difficult life, Francesca. I hope your marrying my son will give you a happier one—for Maria's sake—and that Bruno Gianni relents his foolish stubbornness one day for your sake. But until then I think we will not mention him again.'

And that had basically been it. The Gianni connection was smoothly sidelined, which suited Francesca because she didn't like talking about it and was happy to keep it that way.

The journey to Frascati wasn't too bad. Angelo's parents' manner towards her might be cool but it wasn't frigid. She loved Angelo, they loved Angelo, so that was their line of communication. They were almost at their destination when Angelo's mother voiced her annoyance that her son should have been held up in Milan this week of all weeks.

'It is his own fault,' her husband returned without any sympathy. 'Angelo knows it is not good business practice to keep busy people kicking their heels while they await his late arrival.'

'It wasn't as if he intended to be late. He overslept and missed the flight,' Angelo's *mama* defended loyally.

He did? thought Francesca. It was the first she'd heard of it.

'No one else missed the flight,' the father made the succinct distinction. 'Whatever *they* had been doing the night before, they still managed to get to the airport on time.'

In the back of the car Francesca shifted slightly, catching the attention of Mr Batiste via his rear-view mirror. 'My

apologies, Francesca,' he said, 'I was not being critical of
the late hours you young people keep, only Angelo's failure
to rise from his bed when he should,' bringing a flush of
heat into her face when she realised what he was assuming.

But it wasn't true. She hadn't seen Angelo the night before he went to Milan. Because of the early time of his flight
he'd told her he was going to get an early night.

'We cannot afford to offend a man like Carlo Carlucci.
His business is too important to us,' Mr Batiste went on,
his attention back on the road ahead so he didn't see the
way Francesca's face went from hot to pale at the mention
of Carlo Carlucci's name. 'Being stuck in Milan while Carlo
puts him through business hoops is a better punishment than
to have Carlo take his business somewhere else.'

Mrs Batiste demanded her husband's attention then, with
a comment that was spoken too low for Francesca to hear.
It didn't matter because she had stopped listening anyway.
She was thinking about Carlo Carlucci and that awful morning she had met him at a set of traffic lights. He must have
been on his way to meet with Angelo at the airport yet he
hadn't bothered to mention it—nor had it stopped him from
making a play for her.

She shifted restlessly again, feeling the same hostile
prickles attacking her skin as she replayed the ease with
which he'd conducted that little scene.

What made the man tick that he felt he could do that to
her, knowing what he knew? Arrogance? A supreme belief
in his right to toy with another man's woman simply because it had amused him to do so? If she'd said yes to the
coffee thing, would he have just laughed in her face and
driven off, having got all the kicks he'd been looking for
from the interlude by successfully seducing another man's
woman? Or would he have been willing to miss *his* flight
in favour of coffee with her at Café Milan?

Oh, don't go there, she told herself, frowning out of the
car window as something low in her abdomen began to stir.

What about Angelo? She considered, firmly fixing her attention on what should be important here. Why hadn't he told her that he was stuck in Milan because he'd overslept and annoyed an important business client? Did he think that confessing he'd messed up would lose him his hero status with her?

A smile touched her mouth, amusement softening the frown from her face. He ought to know that nothing could do that. He was and always would be the wildly handsome superhero to her.

They arrived at their destination, driving between a colonnade of tall cypress trees towards the stunning white and gold frontage of Villa Batiste. It wasn't a big house by Castelli Romani standards but, standing as it did on its own raised plateau, neither the house nor its amazing gardens skimped on a single detail when it came to Renaissance extravagance.

As they climbed out of the car at the bottom of wide white marbled steps, Francesca could almost feel the Batistes filling with pride of ownership and wondered wryly—not for the first time—how that pride really dealt with Angelo wanting to marry a little nobody like her. He would inherit all of this one day, which would make her its chatelaine and her children its future heirs.

The house was already under the occupation of an army of professional caterers. A quick cup of coffee after their journey was all they had time for before they were busily helping out. Mr Batiste went off to check his wine cellar. Mrs Batiste made for the kitchen. Francesca became a willing dogsbody, helping out wherever she could. By two o'clock there was nothing more for her to do that she could see. Angelo was still stuck in Milan and his parents were resting before the next wave of activity began.

On a sudden impulse, she decided to write a note to her great-uncle then go and deliver it. You never know, she told herself as she set off, she might *just* catch him at a weak moment.

Her walk took her along narrow, winding country lanes with blossom trees shedding petals on the ground and the golden sunlight dappling through their gently waving branches. It was a beautiful place and she took her time, taking in the hills and the rolling wine-growing countryside that gave such a classic postcard image of Italy.

Half an hour later and she was standing by a pair of rustic old gates, gazing on a house and a garden that would make Angelo's mother shudder in dismay. There was nothing formal or neat about her great-uncle's garden, she mused with a smile. The whole thing seemed to merge in a rambling mix of untended creepers with the old *palazzo* struggling to hang on to some pride as its ochre-painted face peeled and its roof sagged.

She lingered for a few minutes, just looking at it all like a child forbidden to enter. She didn't think of opening the gate and stepping inside. She never intruded past this point when she came here because she knew it was only right that she respect her uncle's wishes. After a little while she heaved out a sigh then took her sealed note out of her jacket pocket and fed it into the rusted metal letter slot set into one of the stone pillars that supported the gates. As she listened to it drop she had the sorry image of the note landing on top of all the others she'd posted and a sad little smile touched the corners of her mouth as she turned slowly away.

Head down, shoulders hunched inside her fitted little denim jacket that matched the jeans she was wearing, she was about to begin the walk back to Villa Batiste when a flash of bright red caught her eye. Her chin came up then all movement was stalled on a stifled gasp of surprise and undisguised dismay when she saw an all too familiar red sports car parked up on the other side of the lane with its driver leaning casually against shiny red bodywork.

Oh, no, not him, was her first gut response as they stared at each other across the few metres of tarmac.

He was dressed in dark blue denims and cloud-blue cashmere that skimmed his tapered body like a second skin. The way he had arms folded across his chest ruched up the lip of the long-sleeved, round-necked sweater, exposing the bronze button that held his jeans in place and almost—almost—offered her a glimpse of the lean flesh beneath.

On a sharp flick of shock as to where her thoughts were taking her she dragged her eyes upwards to look at his face. He was smiling—or allowing his attractive mouth to adopt a sardonic lift. His chin was slightly lowered, his eyelashes glossing those chiselled bones in his cheeks. And he was checking her out in much the same way that she was guilty of checking him out, viewing the length of her legs encased in faded denim, then the fitted denim jacket and finally her face.

'Ciao,' he greeted softly—*intimately*—causing her next response to him, which was a shower of prickly resentment that raced across her skin.

'What are you doing here?' she demanded, not even trying to sound polite.

'We do seem to meet in the oddest of places,' he mused drily. 'Do you think, *cara*,' he added thoughtfully, 'that we might be the victims of fate?'

CHAPTER THREE

FATE, Francesca repeated to herself. She knew about the power of fate. Fate was what Angelo maintained had brought them together. She refused to accept that this…force she was being hit with here had any familiarity with Angelo's fate.

It was then that she remembered tonight's party and that this man had been invited. She'd even written the invitation herself. *Carlo Carlucci and Guest,* she'd scribed in Italian.

Which brought up another thought that sent her eyes slewing sideways to glance inside the open-top car expecting to see some raving dark beauty sitting in the passenger seat. To think of Carlo Carlucci without his usual female appendage was impossible, so she was puzzled to discover the seat was empty.

When she looked back at him he'd lifted those lashes higher and was watching her. 'I do travel light on occasion,' he said lazily, reading her like a gauche open book.

'Does the fact that you're here and not in Milan mean that you've tired of making Angelo's life a misery and let him come back too?' she threw back.

He smiled at this attempt on her part at acid sarcasm but his reply when it came was deadly serious. 'Angelo deserved everything he got from me, Francesca, and don't let him tell you otherwise.'

'I suppose you've never overslept and missed a meeting.'

'Not even after a heavy night with a beautiful woman in my bed,' he replied. 'Although…' his eyes moved over her '…I can appreciate that the cause in this case was worth the consequences…'

He was inferring that she was what had caused Angelo

to oversleep that morning, Francesca realised, and opened her mouth to deny the charge only to close it again when she realised that Angelo must have used her as his excuse for missing his flight. A frown creased her brow and she lowered her eyes to the ground while she tried to decide how she felt about that. She didn't think she liked it. It smacked too hard at the male ego conjuring up a night of erotic sex with his lover as a way of getting himself out of an awkward situation. Her mind even threw up a picture of Angelo standing in some faceless office in Milan, casually boasting to this man of all men about something that should remain private to themselves—if it had happened at all, which it hadn't.

'I've got to go.' She spun away, not wanting to continue this line of discussion. Not wanting to be here at all. She was cross now with Angelo—cross with Carlo Carlucci for placing a cloud across her golden image of the man she loved.

There was a hiss of impatience, a scraping of shoe leather on the road surface. 'Wait a minute,' he said, and began striding towards her across the lane.

Her shoulders tensed, her clenched hands jerking out of her pockets as those now familiar prickles began really asserting themselves the closer he came. A hand curved around her arm, long fingers gently crushing sun-warmed denim against the skin beneath that began to burn like a flame. She jumped in response to it, her breathing snagged. He turned her to face him and she found herself fascinated by the discovery that her eyes came level with his smooth brown throat.

'I embarrassed you. I apologise,' he murmured huskily, and she watched his throat muscles move with the words. 'It was unforgivably crass and insensitive of me to say what I just said.'

Yes, Francesca agreed. It had been crass and insensitive— but which man had been the most crass and insensitive?

'Forget it,' she said, but both of them knew she was only mouthing words she did not mean.

'If it helps, he did not mention you by name,' he offered.

'Meaning what?' she flashed. 'That he left it open to interpretation as to whether he was sleeping around or not? Great. Thanks.' She gave an angry tug at her arm.

He refused to let go. She could feel his anger, the pulse of his frustration because his bit of light teasing had gone so wrong.

'I apologise—again,' he bit out finally.

Francesca glared daggers at his chest. 'I suppose you think it's all just jolly good fun to swap sexual experiences across some office desk,' she said shakily. 'Men being men,' with lots of *phews* and *wows* and *you'd have overslept too if you'd been there.* She'd heard the men at work talking like that, having no idea how cheap they made their lovers sound. 'Egotistic cockerels crowing about their prowess,' she muttered, not realising she'd said the words out loud until he laughed as if he couldn't help himself.

'Don't laugh at me!' she snapped out hotly.

'Then don't say such comical things,' he threw back. 'You sound like some outraged virgin.'

But she was an outraged virgin—that was the whole point! 'Did you tell him all about the way you propositioned me on the Corso just to even up the score a bit?'

'No,' he denied. 'But the interesting point here is—did *you* tell him?'

'Why, are you worried that he might damage your famed sexual ego by telling him how you made a play for his woman and got turned down flat?'

It was reckless. She shouldn't have said it. His eyes turned as black as bottomless caverns and his other hand came up to capture her other arm. Hard fingers crushed the denim fabric as he drew her closer.

'Did you turn me down?' he prompted. 'Or did you run

like a frightened rabbit because you were already so turned on you didn't know how to cope with it?'

'That's not true!' she gasped in shocked horror.

'Shall we test that?'

She saw in the dark glitter of his eyes what he meant to do next and drew in a sharp breath. Suddenly something dangerous was dancing in the air, spinning silver spider webs of tension into the golden sunlight.

Then a twig snapped somewhere, bringing the whole episode clattering down as both heads turned to stare across the top of her great-uncle's wooden gates. Trapped in a trembling force field that held her breathless, Francesca searched the wilderness in some wild, weak, pathetic hope that her great-uncle was about to appear to rescue her from this.

It didn't happen. No dapper old gentleman wearing a wine-red velvet smoking jacket appeared on the twig-strewn driveway. The dappling light from the afternoon sun quivered amongst the heavily leafed branches of the tangled trees and vines and played with peeling ochre paint, but otherwise the wilderness garden remained at peace.

She sighed as she thought that, the action parting her lips to release the sad sound. He moved, she looked back at him without thinking and met head-on with a pair of dark, brooding eyes that told her things she didn't want to know—or feel the way she was feeling them.

It was better to look away. 'Please let me go,' she whispered shakily.

His fingers flexed against the denim and for a horrible moment she thought he was going to ignore her plea and just continue from where he'd been interrupted. Her throat ran dry. She tried to swallow. The promise of tears bloomed across her eyes.

Then his grip eased and slowly lifted. She stepped back— went to turn her back, desperate now to get away.

'You are acquainted with Bruno Gianni?' he asked.

'What…?' She blinked, lifting slightly unfocused eyes back to his face. 'Oh, n-no,' she denied, and quickly lowered her eyes again—not because of the lie she'd just uttered but because she didn't want him to see the threatening tears.

She shoved her hands back in her pockets, swung away and made another attempt to leave.

'Strange…' he murmured. 'I could have sworn I saw you posting a note in the letter box as I drove up.'

And she froze all over again. 'Y-you mistook what you saw,' she said stiffly. 'I was admiring the garden, that's all.'

'The garden,' he repeated and uttered a soft laugh. '*Cara*, that isn't a garden, it is a neglected mess!'

'And what would you know about a real garden?' she swung round to slice at him, not sure if she was responding to his derision or the near kiss she had just escaped. 'I bet your idea of a beautiful garden has to be something filled with straight lines and must be manicured to within an inch of its life!'

'Bruno Gianni obviously doesn't feel like that,' he pointed out.

He was laughing—*still* laughing at her! He'd even leant a shoulder against one of the gateposts—right next to *her* letter box! And he'd folded those wretched arms again, tugging that jumper up over the bronze stud at his waist. She hated him, really hated every hard, mocking inch of his sardonic, handsome—*sexy* stance!

'Well, neither do I,' she declared, uttering this next half-lie as she tried very hard to put her temper back under wraps. 'And I like this garden,' she added within a tightly suppressed breath. 'I like the way it's been left to do its own thing. It has soul and atmosphere and—and—'

'An irresistible hint of romance about it,' he inserted when she stammered then stalled. 'We could even say it possesses a kind of lost-in-time mystique about it that some may love to weave secret fantasies around. We could even imagine Sleeping Beauty lying in one of the cobweb-strewn rooms inside waiting for her prince to come and waken her with the all-important kiss.'

'Oh, very droll,' she derided. 'Next you will be telling me you believe in fairies.'

'Why not?' he quizzed. 'We should all believe there is magic out there or we would stop bothering to look for it and that would be sad, don't you think? Oh, come on, Francesca,' he sighed out impatiently when she stiffened up in offence. 'I was teasing you. Stop prickling.'

'I'm not prickling,' she snapped, prickling even as she denied it.

He uttered a short laugh. 'You remind me of a very beautiful but temperamental tabby cat,' he told her. 'Every time I look at you I can almost see the hairs on the back of your neck standing up.'

'You don't know me well enough to know anything of the sort,' she hit back, saw the amusement lurking behind those glossy eyelashes, went to stiffen up some more—then sighed heavily instead. 'You enjoy winding me up.'

'*Sì,*' he acknowledged.

So she was a game, Francesca concluded. An *easy* game.

Carlo studied her beautiful face as she stood in her own pool of sunlight and wondered grimly if she had any idea how hurt she looked by his last comment. Anger gripped him, along with a hot and bloody frustrated urge to grab for her again and impress on her *why* his barbs could hurt so much.

Easy, he thought inwardly in grinding contempt and flicked a hard glance at the crumbling Palazzo Gianni hiding inside its romantic wilderness. Sleeping Beauty she was not; Cinderella more like, so damn starved of ordinary love and affection that she left herself wide open for any no-good adventurer to take advantage of.

Damn it, he cursed to himself and straightened away from the gatepost. 'I suppose,' he started, 'if I offer you a lift, you will throw the offer back in my face.'

He was right and she would. 'Take no offence but I will enjoy the walk.'

The sound of his dry laughter brought her reluctant gaze back to his face again. 'That was so beautifully English and polite, *cara*.' The mocking man was back, she saw.

'I am English.'

'Mm,' he murmured as if even that amused him now. Then he surprised her by abruptly striding back to his car. 'Like a cool breeze on a hot summer's day,' he threw over his shoulder as he opened the door then swung his long body into the seat. 'Very—contradictory.'

'Thank you—I think.' She frowned.

Carlo just grimaced and gunned the car engine. 'I will see you later,' he said by way of a farewell.

Francesca sent him a perfectly blank look.

'Your engagement to the mistreated Angelo?' he prompted and was truly rewarded when the blank look changed to one of dismay because that look told him she had not given a thought to her wonderful Angelo beyond those first few seconds of this encounter.

Having to be satisfied with achieving that much, he put the car into gear and sped off down the lane, leaving her to stew alone on his final heart-ruthless barb.

Francesca watched him go with the sunlight clinging to his satin black hair again and his last sardonic punch making her eyes blink. How could she have become so drawn in by him that she'd completely forgotten the most important event in her life was about to take place tonight?

Another twig snapped somewhere behind her and she turned to glare at her great-uncle's wilderness as if all of this confusion she was feeling was his fault. And maybe it was, she thought as she turned away again. If he'd been a kinder man he would have accepted her hand of friendship and her pathetic need to maintain contact with him would not have driven her to walk here to post him silly little notes.

Then she would not have been standing here like a prime target for Carlo Carlucci to amuse himself with—again.

Easy, he'd called her. And she flinched, ashamed of herself—disgusted with him for playing with her as if she was a toy.

Well, she wasn't anyone's toy. She wasn't *easy* either—and it was about time that she remembered that! Her chin came up, her hazel eyes glazing over with contempt for the hateful Carlo Carlucci. What was he after all but just one man among many that believed all women were fair prey?

She began to walk, feeling better now she'd managed to snatch her shaken pride back from the brink.

Villa Batiste came into view, its white marble walls drenched in the coral warmth of the late-afternoon sun. The contrast between it and Palazzo Gianni was so pronounced that Francesca pulled to a stop for a moment, struck by the sudden realisation that she did not like this beautiful place. It was all too neat, too shiny and pampered; even the elegant gardens had been groomed to within the tips of their hard edges.

But what the heck? It was a great place to throw a party, she decided, and with a lighter step she began walking up the long, straight driveway with its ceremonial guard of cedar-tree soldiers flanking her approach. She was just walking around the circular courtyard in front of the house when she saw Angelo come through the front door and a light came on inside her that quite simply lit her up. He was wearing jeans and a loose-fitting white sweatshirt and his hair shone golden in the sun.

She began to run to him, and he opened his arms and grinned as she raced up the shallow flight of steps. She fell into those open arms—and fell into his warm, familiar kiss. Oh, she loved—loved—loved this beautiful man, she thought happily.

'You've no *idea* how much I've missed you,' she sighed when the kiss eventually ended.

'I think I got the message,' he grinned.

It was then that she noticed the tiredness around his eyes and the hint of strain tugging at his mouth. 'Bad day?' she asked softly, running a gentle finger along a newly arrived groove at the corner of his mouth.

'Bad week,' he grimaced, then added with feeling, 'I never want to get on the wrong side of Carlo Carlucci again.'

Oh, Francesca could sympathise with that. Then she remembered to be annoyed with him for what he'd said to Carlo Carlucci and was just about to tackle him about it when the sound of a car horn grabbed their attention and the embrace was broken so they could turn to watch a minibus come hurtling up the drive.

She smiled in recognition, relaxing into the warmth of Angelo's circling arms as she watched the minibus pull to a stop at the bottom of the steps. Doors were flung open. People began piling out. Francesca's friends and work colleagues had arrived, having commandeered one of the company tour buses so they could travel here *en masse*. They were staying overnight in a hotel in the town but they'd stopped here first to drop off Sonya, who, like Bianca and several others, had had to work today or she would have travelled here with Francesca and Angelo's parents.

There were fifteen people in all, and every one of them had eyes round like saucers as they scanned the magnificence of Villa Batiste, making suitably impressed comments to each other and tossing teasing ones at Francesca and Angelo.

Sonya was the last one to climb out of the bus. She was wearing a simple white shift-dress that clung to her slender figure and left a good portion of her long legs on show. As she took her time turning a full circle to view her surroundings the late-afternoon sun placed a pale copper gloss on her flaxen hair. She really was beautiful. Everyone said so— except Angelo. He said that her looks were spoiled by her own vanity. That too many compliments had given her a hard edge. The fact that Sonya held much the same views on Angelo was a classic sign that they were two people whose strong characters just did not mix.

When Sonya finally lifted that delicate, heart-shaped face to look at them, Francesca felt an instant pang of irritable despair as she read the sardonic expression in her wide-spaced baby-blue eyes because she knew Sonya was mocking the overt display of wealth here.

Angelo must have seen it too because his arms tightened around her and he uttered something nasty beneath his breath.

'Oh, wow, this place is amazing!' one of the others exclaimed. 'Why isn't it on our tour list?'

'Don't let my mother hear you say that,' Angelo responded drily. 'She will send you all back the way you have come before you have a chance to do more than gasp.'

Group laughter rippled into the late-afternoon sunlight. One of the many things Francesca loved about Angelo was his willingness to send up. He might be a fully paid-up member of Rome's wealthy set but he had never allowed that to tarnish his attitude to her less advantaged friends. He was easy-going and warm and generous. He liked to be liked.

Unlike someone Francesca knew who did not give a care what anyone thought of him. He simply strolled through his life, upsetting anyone he wanted to upset and to heck with the consequences. But then, Carlo Carlucci was a fully paid-up member of the very *upper* echelons of Rome's wealthy set. A cut above the rest in other words—a very large cut.

Oh, stop thinking about him, she told herself crossly and was glad to have her thoughts diverted when a mass migration back into the minibus began to take place. Angelo strode down the steps to take Sonya's overnight bag for her, and the two exchanged stiff if polite words then came to join Francesca to wave the minibus off.

A silence fell. Sonya was pretending a deep interest in the garden while Angelo became engrossed in his shoes. Standing between them, Francesca glanced from one to the other then uttered a heavy sigh. She'd never managed to find out exactly what it was that had started hostilities between the two of them but she did know that it was getting worse.

Angelo shifted, his square chin rising. 'Shall we go in?' he said politely then he turned and strode into the house with Sonya's bag. The atmosphere cloyed as they followed him into the sheer grandeur of the green and white marble reception hall and walked together up the imposing curve of the white marble staircase. Pushing open a door to one of the bedroom suites, Angelo stood back to allow the two women to enter a place fit for visiting royalty.

Sonya walked forward and stood with her back to them. Angelo remained standing stiffly by the door. 'If I plead very hard, will you *please* be nice to each other for tonight?' Francesca burst out.

'Excuse me,' Angelo said. 'My father is expecting me in his study.' Then he left, closing the door behind him with a quiet click.

Sonya turned to look at Francesca. 'Don't blame me for that,' she said. 'I never did a single thing!'

'I know you didn't,' Francesca agreed with her. 'I apologise for him.'

'You don't have to do that,' Sonya said irritably. 'He's just…'

Mad at me, Francesca found herself finishing the sentence and then began to frown because she didn't understand why she would think like that unless…

It hit her then, just what this war between Sonya and Angelo was all about. 'It's the married man you're seeing,' she declared suddenly. 'Angelo knows who it is, doesn't he?'

To her grim satisfaction Sonya gasped out a choking response then spun away from her in a way that all but confirmed her accusation. Things suddenly began to fit. Their barbed comments to each other, the heated exchanges they had in quiet corners that lasted less than thirty seconds but always managed to destroy a pleasant atmosphere. And more relevant was that the hostilities had only started two weeks ago, which, according to Bianca, was when Sonya's new affair began. Two weeks ago Angelo had asked her to marry him. When she said yes, he'd arranged a celebration dinner at one of his favourite restaurants. It was the first time that Sonya had come into contact with Angelo's family. She cast her mind back, searching that sea of new faces, hunting out the married ones and trying to decide which one might be willing to cheat on his wife.

How did I miss all of this before? she asked herself. But she knew how. She had spent the last two weeks so engrossed in her love for Angelo that she hadn't been able to see anything beyond it.

But there was worse to come as yet another thought hit. 'He's going to be here tonight, isn't he?' she challenged. 'He'll be coming here with his wife and you're going to think you can sneak off with him somewhere for a little while!'

'That's so much rubbish,' Sonya denied.

No, it wasn't. 'I know you, Sonya,' she said. 'I know how common sense shoots right out of the window when a new man comes into your life.'

'You sound like my mother again.'

She did, Francesca acknowledged and this time didn't care. 'Angelo is worried that you're both going to risk causing a scene tonight. I bet he even asked you both not to come.'

'You're so way off the mark, it's sad to listen to you.' Sonya bent to collect her bag.

'Then *why* is Angelo mad at you?' she demanded outright.

Sonya didn't answer but just walked across the room and threw open the first door that she came to. The fact that it happened to be the bathroom was due to luck more than anything, but as she went to slam the door shut so she didn't have to have this discussion, Francesca got in one final plea.

'Promise me you won't do anything stupid tonight, *cara*,' she begged anxiously. 'I need your assurance—please.'

For a moment she thought Sonya was going to go on protesting her innocence, then it was as if all the fight just trickled out of her and she released a heavy sigh. 'So long as you promise to keep Angelo away from me,' she bartered. 'And *don't* try to get out of me who the man is!'

The bathroom door swung shut. Francesca winced as she turned back to the main door. She was just stepping out onto the landing when she heard the sound of raised voices echoing in the hall below. She paused, her heart beginning to beat faster when she recognised Angelo's angry tones.

'Do you think I am a fool? Of course I am not going to risk everything now! Your business is safe, Papa, take my word for it,' he said bitterly. 'And don't forget which of us is paying the price for it!'

Angelo's father spoke then but she couldn't hear what he was saying because he wasn't as angry as his son. Then a door closed and she could hear nothing else, but she was left wondering if the Batiste business was in trouble.

Had Carlo Carlucci lived up to Alessandro Batiste's worst fears and threatened to remove his business and take it elsewhere?

The wretched man was beginning to cast a very long shadow over almost everything that was important in her life, she mused grimly as she stepped into her own room next to Sonya's and closed the door. If *he* was a married man she would have to start wondering if he was Sonya's new lover! Sonya's reed-slender beauty being most definitely his type!

And on that truly caustic note she took herself off to the

bathroom to indulge in a long, hot, tension-relieving soak
before she had to present herself downstairs to help welcome the other guests that Angelo's parents had invited to
stay overnight at the villa.

'I promised myself I wasn't going to do this.' She frowned
at the mirror.

'Do what?' Sonya was standing behind her, busily fixing
a beaded comb into the twisted knot she'd fashioned with
Francesca's hair that now felt as if it had left her creamy
shoulders and neck vulnerably exposed.

'Buy something that moulded.'

She was no raving beauty and had never pretended otherwise to herself. She might be tall and slender with pass-
ably attractive legs, but she possessed curves—old-
fashioned curves like a waist and hips and full, firm breasts
that sort of pouted whatever she wore. They were doing it
now, pushing up above the straight edge of the bodice as if
they were trying to escape.

'Oh, dear,' she sighed, and with a shimmy and a tug tried
to pull the bodice up a bit.

'You're too critical of yourself,' Sonya mumbled from
behind her. 'Have you any idea how many women shell out
thousands to get C cups like yours?

'They can have mine for free,' Francesca muttered.

She'd gone shopping for classic black sophistication that
would put her on a par with her super-elegant guests tonight
and come back with this sultry dark red creation that was
supposed to skim not cling to all those places she did not
want to accentuate. The silk organza skirt was its saving
grace with its ankle-length handkerchief edge. It was sin-
gularly the most expensive item of clothing she had ever
bought, and, 'I look like a lush.'

'Idiot,' Sonya chided. 'You look like the lovely belle at
your own ball, which is how it should be.' She finished

securing the hair comb then stepped back to study the over-all look. 'Gosh, that colour suits you.'

'It reminded me of the ruby setting in my ring,' she explained, which was why she'd bought it instead of nice, safe black. 'Do you think Angelo will like it?'

'I think Angelo will adore it,' Sonya replied without a single hint of her usual caustic spoiling her tone. Then she turned away to pick up the fine chiffon scarf that came with the dress. 'Here, let's drape this around your shoulders just so and—presto, we have a princess.'

'We have an overdressed Barbie doll.'

'No.' Sonya appeared beside her in the mirror wearing a short skimpy blue satin slip dress that matched the colour of her eyes. '*I'm* the Barbie doll around here, *cara*,' she pronounced. 'Complete with twenty-four-inch spiked shoes.'

They both fell into a fit of the giggles, which was nice because they hadn't done much laughing recently—not since Sonya and Angelo fell out. 'I'm going to miss having you around when I'm married,' Francesca confided softly once they'd both calmed down again.

There was a silence—a stillness, both short, both tight. Then Sonya uttered a different kind of laugh. 'You must be joking. You'll be too busy doing something else to miss me.'

She was talking about making love but the moment that Francesca tried to visualise that Rubicon moment all she saw was a deeply sardonic dark, handsome face. It shook her so badly that she actually gasped.

'What?' Sonya demanded sharply, staring at her suddenly whitened face.

'Nothing,' she dismissed because how could she confess to Sonya what she had just seen? She would laugh—and why not? To her it would be one in the eye to her favourite enemy, Angelo, to learn that another man could arouse hot visions of lust inside his sex-shy fiancée.

She frowned again. It was beginning to worry her that she could feel like this about another man when she was about to commit herself to Angelo.

There was a knock at the door then. Sonya went to answer it. It was Angelo, come to escort Francesca downstairs. With a stiff smile and a mumbled, 'See you down there,' Sonya left them alone, pulling the door shut behind her as Francesca was turning from the mirror.

The moment she looked at him all her worries faded. He was wearing a formal black dinner suit and bow-tie and he looked so handsome that she felt herself melting inside. He was smiling at her, he was warm, he was all sunlight not mocking darkness. I'm just suffering from pre-betrothal nerves, she told herself and found her own smile when he sighed and said, '*Ah, bella—bella, mi amore.* You take my breath away.'

And that was all that she wanted, she told herself as she moved towards him. She wanted to take Angelo's breath away. She wanted to bask in the warmth of his love.

Which was exactly what she did for the next few hours, as the villa slowly filled with people and Angelo rarely left her side. The official announcement of their engagement was to take place at midnight and until then everyone was encouraged to sample the banquet buffet laid out in one of the grand salons or dance to the music provided by a group of live musicians in another grand salon. By ten the villa was throbbing with music and laughter and the more elegant hum of conversation.

She noted Carlo Carlucci's arrival at around ten o'clock. Who didn't note it? she thought sourly as she watched surreptitiously the way he drew people to him without him having to do more than stand by the main salon doors. He'd arrived without the usual beauty hanging on his arm, which surprised her. And he also made no effort to come anywhere near her, which was also a surprise since it wasn't very polite of him to keep his distance.

But it was an even bigger relief. She didn't want him using one of his mocking smiles on her, or worse—letting it drop that they'd met by accident a couple of times and exposing the fact that she hadn't mentioned those meetings to Angelo.

She would do, she promised herself. Tomorrow maybe when this was all over. But for now she was happy—happy—happy again and wanted to keep it that way.

Sonya, she saw, was behaving herself and sticking close to their own friends and work colleagues. If her new lover was here tonight—and Francesca was certain that he was here somewhere—she couldn't tell from Sonya's manner who the man was.

And foolishly she relaxed enough to drop her watchful guard on her friend. She was too busy being passed from one partner to another to be whirled beneath glittering crystal chandeliers. She was showered with beautiful compliments and teased and flirted with as only the Italians could do with such stylish panache. It was such a novelty to be the centre of everyone's attention like this that she began to feel intoxicated by it—or was it the champagne?

Each time she paused for breath someone placed a long, fluted glass in her fingers and bid her a toast that demanded she sip. Her cheeks had discovered a permanent rosy hue and her eyes sparkled beneath the overhead lights. Angelo was being treated to the same kind of attention. They would whirl by each other occasionally and share a laughing comment, but that was all they were allowed.

It was as if there was a conspiracy afoot to keep the two lovers apart until the bewitching hour and when she challenged one of her partners with the suspicion he laughed and whirled her away. No one would know from observing this glitter-bright gaiety that the whole thing was about to shatter with the same spectacular force you would get if one of the huge chandeliers suddenly dropped to the floor.

Francesca was taking a moment to catch her breath when

she happened to see Sonya quietly slipping away behind one of the gold-embossed curtains that had been drawn across a wall of French windows that led outside. Her antennae began to sing, sending her eyes flickering quickly around the room to see if anyone was going to follow her out.

It had to be her misfortune that her eyes clashed with those belonging to Carlo Carlucci. He was still holding court by the salon doors, standing with his dark head slightly tilted to one side as he listened to whatever the person with him was saying to him.

But his dark eyes were fixed on her.

That prickling sensation arrived, scoring tight *frissons* down her back, and she quickly dragged her eyes away from him and began weaving her way towards the French windows, determined to put a stop to the clandestine meeting she was now absolutely certain Sonya had arranged.

Sonya had left one of the doors slightly ajar. Slipping quietly through the gap, she walked across the wide marble terrace towards the stone balustrade beyond which the garden began to drop in a series of stylised tiers. It was cold out here, the late-spring chill in the air sending her hands up to rub at her bare arms as she paused to scan the darkened gardens in search of Sonya and her new man.

She heard them before she saw them, her slender body twisting towards the sound of scuffling feet and hushed voices filtering up from the terrace below. They were standing by the lower balustrade, and she was surprised to see that it was Angelo who was gripping one of Sonya's arms while she was trying to tug herself free.

'Let go of me!' she heard Sonya hiss out angrily.

'No,' Angelo rasped. 'I won't let you ruin this, Sonya—'

'I'm still going to tell her,' Sonya lashed back. 'She deserves to know the truth before this charade goes any further. I will be doing her a favour.'

She was threatening to confess her affair to her lover's wife! Oh, dear God, Francesca thought. She couldn't let her do that! She was about to move towards the steps to go down there to add her own pleas to Angelo's—when Angelo's harsh reply stalled her feet.

'You think she will be grateful to you for your big confession, heh, *cara*? Do you think she will fall on your neck and forgive you, her closest friend, for sleeping with me, the man she is heart and soul in love with...?'

And that was the point where everything shattered, sprinkling around her like fine crystal shards that lacerated her flesh as they fell.

CHAPTER FOUR

FRANCESCA began to shake so badly she could barely stay upright, even her heart trembling, clawing at the walls of her chest as if it was trying to escape from what she was being made to face. She struggled to believe it, didn't *want* to believe it. She even closed her eyes and replayed Angelo's words inside her head in a silly, stupid, desperate attempt to find out where she had misunderstood what he'd said.

But there was no misunderstanding, Sonya's next shrill claim made it too sickeningly clear. 'You don't want her! You don't even like her that much!'

'What I want and I what I am to have are two different issues.'

'Money,' Sonya sliced at him. 'As if the Batistes haven't got enough of it locked up in this place, you're willing to marry a woman you have no feelings for just to lay your hands on the Gianni fortune! It's disgusting. '

'And none of your damn business,' Angelo rasped.

'While you can't keep your hands off me, it's my damn business.'

There was a groan—an agonised groan that brought Francesca's eyelids flickering upwards to watch as Angelo pulled Sonya against him then buried his mouth in her throat. 'I cannot get you out of my head,' he muttered. 'I close my eyes and all I see is you, naked, on top of me.'

'When your little heiress is naked on top of you, will you close your eyes and think of me then?'

The vile taunt brought Angelo's head up, set his hands moving in a tense, urgent, restless sweep over Sonya's slippery blue satin dress. 'Yes,' he said thickly.

Francesca swayed, her whole world tilting sideways as if it was trying to tip her off. A pair of arms came around her from behind and covered her shivering arms where they still folded like clamps across her front. Long brown fingers closed over her icy fingers, a solid male torso became a supporting wall to her trembling back. A dark head lowered, a pair of lips came to rest on her ear.

'Heard enough?' Carlo asked in a soft, rough voice that scraped over her cold flesh like sand across silk.

She wasn't even surprised that it was him who was holding her. In some mad, tortuous way it seemed fitting that he would be the one to witness this—as if the two of them had been building towards this devastating moment for days.

She was about to attempt a nod in answer to his question when Angelo uttered a thick groan and took fierce possession of Sonya's lips. Sonya didn't even try to stop him. The way they kissed, open-mouthed, deep and frantic, their two blond heads locked together. The way they touched, hands moving over each other in hot, tight, convulsive movements that stripped clean to the bone any lingering doubts she might have had that they'd done this many times before. A long, silken thigh was exposed to the hip bone, a small, pale breast was uncovered to receive the hungry clamp of Angelo's mouth. It only took eyes to see that Sonya was wearing nothing at all beneath the skimpy scrap of silk. She'd come prepared for this, despite all the angry threats and protests she'd just uttered, she'd had no intention of missing out on the sex.

Sickened, Francesca began to shudder. Carlo responded with a swiftness that caught her breath. The soft hiss of his anger stung her icy, quivering face as he twisted her around then tugged her against him and held her there for a moment while she shivered and shook.

Then Angelo's voice came, raw with pleasure. 'Yes, do that again,' he groaned.

For a horrible moment Francesca thought she was going to faint. Carlo Carlucci must have thought so too because the next thing she knew one of his arms had hit the backs of her knees and she was being lifted off the ground.

'I'm all right,' she choked.

His lips arrived at her ear again to utter the harsh rasp, 'Be quiet or they will hear you.'

The very thought of that happening had her curling into him. He started moving, long, swift strides taking them the full length of that side of the villa. A stunning silence arrived as they turned the corner and it was only then Francesca realised that the whole ugly thing had taken place to a background of music and laughter filtering out from the house.

He kept on going further and further down this wing, which housed the more private apartments that were not being used for the party tonight. All the windows were shrouded in darkness, the only light coming from the hazed moon hanging in the night sky. He pulled to a stop beside yet another set of French doors. The villa was ringed with them; elegantly styled and evenly spaced, they gave every room on the ground floor its own access onto the wide terraces that flanked all four sides of the house.

She felt tensile muscles flex as he reached down to try a handle. A door slid open and he swung her inside. It was dark in here too, but she did manage to register that he'd brought her to Mr Batiste's private study with its heavy, dark pieces of furniture that didn't blend in with the rest of the house.

Then she was being dumped on a leather chair by the fireplace with logs neatly laid in the grate ready to light. Still shivering, she instantly wrapped her arms back round her body as Carlo moved to close the door they'd just used. She heard a key turn and quivered, though she didn't know why she did. Then he was moving swiftly in the other direction and a second later another key turned in the door leading out to the hall.

'Don't,' she said when she saw him raise a hand towards the light switch.

The hand dropped to his side and she tried to relax some of the screaming tension from her body. It didn't happen. Too many muscles had locked and knotted and she'd never felt so cold in her entire life.

Still without comment he began to move again. He was nothing more than a shifting shadow in the darkness, and right now she was happy to keep him like that. She didn't want to see his face—she didn't want him to look into her own. She felt stripped and raped and bruised and battered.

This time she heard the chink of glass on glass.

Angelo and Sonya—Sonya and Angelo. Her eyes drifted shut as that dreadful little litany began playing itself over and over inside her head alongside frame-by-frame images of what she had just seen.

The open-mouthed kiss that devoured greedily, the slippery blue satin that was so willing to slide away from a silken thigh and hip. She heard the gasps, the groans of passionate agony, and felt sick to her stomach because all she'd ever got was quietly, calmly—briefly wrapped in a light-hearted affection, not the raging fires and animal lust.

What a perfectly choreographed act they'd put on for her benefit, she thought painfully. What a smooth blinding mask they'd pulled over her eyes as they snipped and sniped at each other the way that they had.

And what a sick—sick joke the two of them had been enjoying at her expense.

Humiliation poured through her bloodstream, the power of it grinding her bruised heart against her ribs. Dragging up her eyelids, she stared down at her dress. Angelo had not felt compelled to drag down this bodice and lay bare one of her breasts. He'd never once so much as stroked her thigh. The light touches she'd received that she'd believed were offered with love and tenderness and respect now became touches of idle contempt wrapped up in calculation and necessity.

He'd intended to marry her and take her to bed only when he had to do it and even then he was going to impose

Sonya's sylph-like image over her to help him get through the ordeal.

She quivered again, despising him for doing this to her—despising herself for being so gullible and blind.

A sound reached into her consciousness—people laughing as they walked past the closed study door. The party, she remembered. Her engagement party. Hers and Angelo's.

The Gianni heiress and the fortune-hunter, she then thought bitterly.

But she was no heiress. There was no fortune to be had if she was. And she could not understand why Angelo could believe otherwise when she'd already told him the hard truth about her connection to the Gianni name.

'Here, drink some of this…'

She hadn't realised her eyes had closed again until she was forced to open them. The dark shadow was squatting in front of her, she realised, though she hadn't noticed him arrive there. Only he wasn't quite a dark shadow any more because her eyes had adjusted to the darkness. So she could see the way he was studying her narrowly, the way he was holding his mouth thin and flat. The bright white of his shirt stood out, casting reflected light along the grim set of his chiselled jaw bone as he placed the rim of a glass to her mouth. She sipped without protest. The brandy trickled across her tongue and she forced herself to swallow, leaving warm vapours behind in her mouth.

He sipped too. She watched with unblinking absorption as he lifted the glass away from her lips to place it against his own. His throat moved as he swallowed, shifting the butterfly collar to his shirt. He held the glass between long brown fingers while her own pale fingers still clutched at her arms, her nails scoring crescents into the icy bare skin.

'H-how much did you overhear?' she whispered unsteadily.

For a moment she thought he wasn't going to answer, his mouth compressing. Then, 'Most if it,' he admitted, and rose to his full height.

She looked away from him—at the logs piled in the grate—on a sinking sense of dismay that robbed a bit more of her ravaged pride. This tall, dark, sophisticated man of Rome had stood there in the background witnessing the brutal murder of everything she cared about.

She felt stripped bare again and flayed this time.

'Why were you out there?' No one else had been out there—or at least she hoped no one else had been there!

The laughter came again, echoing around the marble hallway and sounding cruelly mocking to her oversensitised ears. It was then that a sudden thought hit that was so horrible it feathered her breathing. How many of those people out there knew the real motives behind Angelo's engagement to her? Did they all know? Did all her friends know about Sonya's affair with Angelo?

Had Carlo Carlucci known it all even before he stepped outside tonight? Her breath feathered again as she shifted her gaze back to his tense profile.

'You weren't there by accident, were you?' she charged shakily. 'You suspected that something was going to happen so you followed me outside then s-stood there like some—s-sleazy voyeur—'

His dark head turned to lance her an amused look. 'You see me as sleazy?'

No, she didn't, but... 'Don't laugh at me!' she bit out painfully. 'None of this is funny!'

'You're right.' The laughter died. 'It isn't.'

The threat of tears came then. She dragged in a deep breath, fighting to stop them, fighting to keep her mind fixed on what had started her travelling along this thread. 'H-how much of it did you know before you followed me?'

Without answering her he turned abruptly and walked away, disappearing back into the shadows at the other end of the room as if the darkness could save him from having to offer a reply.

But she needed to know. 'How much?' she launched shrilly after him.

'All of it.'

The answer hit her like a blow. Her breasts heaved behind her crossed arms, and for a moment she felt dizzy again. Then she pulled herself together and asked the next wretched question burning a hole inside her head. 'And— everyone else out there?'

She heard the fresh chink of glass on glass before the words came, felt the angry tension in him as he poured another drink. 'Your true identity became an open secret within days of you meeting Angelo,' he told her. 'The fact that you were not announcing that you are the heiress to the huge Gianni fortune only helped to fuel the fires of intrigue and speculation as to why you wanted to play the ordinary working girl and keep your identity such a closed secret.'

'I'm not the Gianni heiress,' she denied. 'There is no fortune to be had.'

He laughed like a cynic. 'You are worth so much money, Francesca, *cara*, that the figure can make Rome's wealthiest blanch.'

Which was all so much rubbish her brows snapped together. 'Stupid rumour and speculation,' she dismissed. 'Bruno Gianni lives in a ruin. He has no money to leave to anyone, never mind a great-niece he won't even see!'

'Well, you're right about Bruno's money,' Carlo drawled as he strode back into view. 'But we're not talking about Bruno Gianni's money. We are talking about *Rinaldo* Gianni's money. Your grandfather,' he extended as if she needed that clarified, and bent to prise a set of cold fingers away from her arm so he could slot a fresh glass of brandy between them. 'The fortune is his,' he continued. 'Rinaldo left everything to you. Bruno only lives in the *palazzo* at your behest because it, like everything else, belongs to you—or it will do when you marry,' he then amended, 'a man from a good Italian family, I think is near as damn it to the official working of his will. The lot to be held in a trust to be solely administered by his surviving brother until you comply. Angelo thought he'd hit gold when he seduced you into falling in love with him,' he added. 'He's the real hero of the party tonight, *cara*. The man who pulled off the perfect coup.'

She was beginning to think she was dreaming all of this. 'I don't have a clue what you're talking about,' she said.

'I know.' He used that laugh again. 'And that is the real irony of it.'

He went to lean a shoulder against the mantel, pushed his hands into his trouser pockets then studied her ashen face as he continued.

'While everyone else thinks you're being intriguingly clever and infuriatingly devious, you are merely oblivious to it all. It took me weeks to suss you out,' he confessed as if that was some kind of shock in itself. 'You are not pretending to be the wide-eyed and beautiful, naïve innocent—you *are* her. And Bruno Gianni has a lot to answer for—which he will do when I get my hands round his wicked old throat.'

'You won't go near my uncle Bruno,' she muttered dimly, feeling swamped by words that didn't make any sense.

'What—protecting the hand that robs you, Francesca?' he mocked. 'What were you—ten years old when your grandfather died? For the last fourteen years he's been sitting on your inheritance and probably praying that you never show your face in Rome.'

'Stop it,' she jerked out. 'There's just been a dreadful misunderstanding, that's all!' she cried. 'Angelo knows the truth. He knows I'm—'

His hiss of impatience snapped her lips shut. 'Get real, Francesca,' he derided. 'You heard what that mercenary bastard said out there! To start trying to defend him is bloody pathetic! He wants your money,' he lanced down at her. 'He *needs* your money! Get that into your lovesick head and deal with it!'

He was angry—why was he angry? That was her prerogative! She was the one being used and abused and talked about as if she was some kind of juicy commodity!

'There is no money!' She launched herself to her feet to spit the denial at him. 'And what makes you any better than Angelo when you actually believe all that stuff you just threw at me?'

There was a glinting flash behind narrowed eyelids, a glimpse of angry white teeth. A hand snaked out and she released a choked cry as he clamped his fingers round her wrist.

'Don't compare me with Batiste—ever,' he bit out from between those white teeth.

'I w-wasn't...' The confused words disintegrated when she began trembling all over again, shocked by the sudden eruption of violence in him. His dark face had changed out of all recognition, the clenched bones, the narrowed eyes glinting with a danger she could actually taste. Her heart was pounding, her wrist hurting where he held it in a vice-like grip.

He hated Angelo, she realised—despised him with a ferocity that had turned him primitive.

She tugged at her wrist. He held it fast. The next thing she was drawing in a sharp breath when the other hand came up. She thought he was going to slap her. Her eyes widened as the cold sweat of fear broke out on her skin. 'No...' she husked.

And was dragged even deeper into the mud of confusion when he began carefully easing the brandy glass she had forgotten she was holding out of her clenched fingers and she realised with new horror that it was aimed to empty its contents into his face.

Not just his violence but her violence. Her head began to swim. She wasn't a violent person, so how had she reached the point of wanting to throw brandy into someone's face?

The glass was removed. The wrist released. She took it in her other hand and began absently rubbing it while her insides were so shaken up she had the hysterical impression she was going to fall into little pieces any minute.

'There is no money,' she repeated, trying desperately to cling to this one safe thread.

The hard angles in his face didn't soften, the eyes still glittered in the chiselled set of his face. And his voice when it came was like cold steel slicing through silk. 'Whether there is or there isn't money, is not actually the important issue—not when you manage to remember what your friend and Batiste were doing out there, that is…'

And just like that she was devastated, the steel-like thrust of his point cutting right to the core of everything because she *had* been concentrating on the money thing instead of what really mattered here.

She'd been used and betrayed by two people she loved most. Duped like a fool because she'd been too blinded by trust to see what was happening beneath her nose.

It all came crashing down again, coiling like a tight band around her aching chest, and fresh tears began to build in her throat.

The rows, the *passion* it required to generate so much hostility. Sonya's guilty looks, the lies that had tripped so defiantly from her tongue. Money had nothing to do with Sonya's part in her betrayal. She'd just wanted Angelo with a fever that had raged out of control. So she'd had him, because the wanting had been more powerful than her loyalty to a close friend!

And the money had nothing to do with the sexual part of Angelo's betrayal because he must have known he was putting everything at risk when he gave in to his desire for Sonya. For who else was more likely to confess all in a fit of conscience than the closest friend to his future wife?

His future wife. The one he would take to bed only when he had to.

Oh, dear God… 'I've got to get away from here,' she whispered on a sudden burst of panic and reeled away to take a couple of shaky steps towards the terrace doors.

Everything happened so fast then that she was thrown into shock. There was a muttered curse followed by two hands arriving at her waist and she was being lifted bodily off the floor, turned and dumped unceremoniously back to the floor then clamped to a hard male chest.

'What are you—?'

'Shut up,' he ground out furiously. 'Someone is coming.'

And she froze like a statue as she heard the sound of Angelo's voice calling her name from the terrace just outside their door. The door handle rattled. Her heart withered in her chest and her fingers went up to clutch at the lapels to Carlo Carlucci's dinner jacket.

'I don't want to see him,' she choked. And she didn't. She never wanted to set eyes on Angelo again!

'I locked the door,' his grim voice reminded her.

'He will see us through the glass.' She moved even closer to his superior framework as if trying to blend right into him.

His arms accommodated her, a hand gently curving round her slender nape, the other splaying across the low part of her back. 'He can't see you,' he murmured in husky reassurance. 'It's dark in here. I am wearing black and my back is to the window. If he sees anything it will be the dark outline of one of his male guests enjoying a snatched moment in his father's study with one of his female guests.'

'M-me,' she pointed out.

There was a short silence. Then he said cynically, 'Did you tell him about our two meetings, *cara*? How very loyal of you.'

The cold taunt brought her eyes up to clash with his. The guilty flush that mounted her cheeks said all she needed to say.

'Well—well,' he murmured. 'It seems to me that your whole life is built on dangerous secrets, *mi amore*.'

'I don't have *any* secrets,' she snapped. 'And there was nothing dangerous about our two brief meetings!' she added, frowning at the sudden quickening she felt in her pulse.

'Liar,' he drawled. 'We connected sexually. I don't know how you kept your hands off me.'

'How did you *ever* get to be so arrogant?' she gasped, staring at him.

'It took practice,' he replied, and the weird thing about this conversation was that it was so deadly serious without a hint of mockery to be heard! In fact she could see that frightening anger simmering in his eyes. 'You want to be thankful that I am attracted to you or you would be languishing somewhere in the Batiste garden, slowly dying from a broken heart by now.'

It was like being kicked when she was already lying in a battered heap on the ground. On a stifled choke she went to step away from him. Once again he showed his superior strength to keep her still.

'I hate you,' she choked.

He didn't bother to answer. She could feel the strength in his fingers where they pressed into her lower back and the very disturbing presence of his thumbs slowly circling against her stomach wall. Tiny senses began to stir in places she didn't want them to, low in her abdomen and in the tips of her breasts. It was mad; the whole crazy evening was turning her quietly insane. She hardly knew him, she certainly didn't like him yet here she was, standing in his arms, letting him tell her that she fancied going to bed with him!

The door handle rattled again. 'Who is in there?' Angelo's glass-muffled voice questioned impatiently.

'Persistent devil,' Carlo said. 'Perhaps we should give him a taste of his own medicine.'

Alarm stiffened her backbone. 'No!' was all she could get out before he lowered his dark head.

It was the sheer, heart-stopping shock of it that held her immobile, the unfamiliar touch of his mouth against hers. He was taller than Angelo, darker than Angelo, harder and stronger and more forceful than Angelo had ever been with her. Her startled lips were ruthlessly parted, and his tongue darted through the gap. A tight rush of sensation shot from

er mouth to her breasts to low in her abdomen then poured
ike quicksilver down her legs.

She had never experienced anything like it. A shocked,
lisorientated whimper clawed at her throat as she was sud-
lenly flung into alien territory, the heat, the intrusion, the
lagrant intimacy of that invading tongue exploring the inner
issue of her mouth trapping her inside butterfly tremors of
pemused response.

He pulled his head back, glinting her a dark-eyed puzzled
rown, saw her wide-eyed startlement, the revealingly
shocked tremor of her lips. 'Did Angelo sexually starve you
nto submission?' he uttered with an oddly strained laugh.

She just continued to stare at him, too befuddled to take
n the question, and his eyes took on a hard light. He hissed
something unrepeatable about Angelo then lowered his head
again to return to where he'd left off. Only this time with
more heat, more sensual purpose, and his hands joined in,
lifting and crushing her into closer contact with his body
and holding her there while he ravaged her mouth. She felt
the burgeoning power of his passion pressing against her
then her own body responded as that place between her
thighs began to pulse then grow damp. Sensation was slith-
ering everywhere, in her bloodstream, coiling round muscles
to make them writhe into greater contact.

It was shocking, so basic and—and physical! Her crushed
breasts swelling and stinging painfully as her nipples grew
tight.

The door handle rattled. She jerked her head back against
his restraining hand and their lips parted with a disconcerting pop. Electric wires had been attached to every extremity.
She was breathless yet panting. Her tongue and lips felt
swollen and hot. He was staring down at her with glinting
black fixed eyes and a perfect stillness, his expression pe-
culiarly…

She didn't know what his face was telling her. She only
knew she'd just been somewhere very perilous and that she
did not like it—but she did.

Sex, she called it. *Lust* said it better. She'd been kissed with hot and driving passion for the first time in her life by a man who was very good at it.

Heat hit her pale cheeks. She dragged her eyes away from him and became aware of the way the flat of her hand braced painfully against the solid wall of chest. Everything about him was solid, his shoulders, his arms, the bowl of his hips where she could feel the solid column of his—

'Let me go,' she demanded hazily.

He did the opposite, pressing her closer then lowering his head again to flick his tongue across her burning lips. She almost detonated on a ball of hot static. A helpless cry keened in her throat.

Footsteps sounded as Angelo moved away from the window, bringing Carlo alive with a jolt. His eyes lost that frightening expression, his brows pushing together on a frown. His grip on her tightened and Francesca found herself being lifted again, swung around then unceremoniously dumped in the chair she had used before.

The wretched brandy glass was slotted back between her fingers. 'Drink it this time,' she was tersely instructed as he turned away.

'I'm dizzy enough,' she thought and didn't realise she'd said it out loud until his grim response came back.

'Think how you're going to feel in about five minutes. Because that is how long it will take Angelo to walk through the other door.'

Feeling as if she'd been tossed from a storm into a maelstrom, she stared at the solid wooden door which lead out to the main hallway as if it were some brooding dark monster. 'You locked it,' she breathed shakily.

He was already striding over there. To her utter consternation he turned the key to unlock the door.

'What did you do that for?' she cried out in protest.

Ignoring her, he reached up to flick the light switch next. It was like being bombarded with hot shards of glass. She screwed her eyes shut on a shrill little whimper of agony then dragged them open again almost immediately because she needed to know what he was going to do next. He was already halfway back across the room and bending down to pick something up off the floor. She'd never seen such a change in anyone. His energy levels had shot from virtually somnolent to the other extreme.

The black dinner suit barely rippled as he straightened up again, the butterfly collar to his white dress shirt still looked as crisp as it probably had when he'd first put it on. His skin wore a warm olive sheen and his satiny black hair had the merest hint of a wave that she hadn't noticed before. His head was bent slightly, eyes hooded, those thick lashes hovering a breath away from his chiselled cheekbones. He was breathtakingly attractive and his mouth wore the bloom of their recent kiss.

Fire pooled between her thighs again and she wrenched her eyes away from him. Everything about him was suddenly so physical, so—sexual!

Oh, dear, she groaned inwardly. What's happening to me?

Lifting up the glass, she took a large gulp at the brandy. Why not get drunk? she decided wildly. It had to be a better option to feeling like this.

He arrived in front of her, making her jump nervously when he bent to use one hand to take the glass from her so he could take his turn with the drink, while the other hand pulled her to her feet. She felt like a puppet—*this* man's puppet! He kept pulling and pushing her, picking her up, putting her down and *kissing* her.

Oh, dear, she thought again as her insides went haywire.

'No,' she husked in muffled protest.

'No what?' he asked, discarding the glass.

But she'd already forgotten what when he proceeded to hook long fingers beneath the lip of her bodice as if he had every right to touch her like this!

'What are you doing?' she choked out in protest as she felt the smooth backs of his nails stroke her flesh.

His answer was a demonstration. Coolly and very proficiently he gave a tug that resettled the dark fabric across the thrust of her breasts. Glancing down, she gave a gasp of horror when she realised how close she must have been to revealing too much flesh.

Like Sonya.

Like Sonya... Her eyes closed on the next dizzying wave to hit her as reality came crashing back.

He moved his attention elsewhere then, throwing her into a deeper state of confusion when he proceeded to tidy her tumbled hair. She hadn't even realised the knot had come undone.

'Now listen,' he said. 'We haven't got much time for this so you are going to have to make some quick decisions as to what happens next,' he said quietly, deciding to organise her wrecked life for her now, she noted dully.

'Lock the door again.' That was a decision.

She watched as his mouth compressed. 'The way I see it, you have several choices. You can turn a blind eye to what you saw and continue with tonight as if nothing has happened...' She winced at the word *blind*. 'Or you can brave it out and go out there of your own volition to announce that you're calling off the engagement and why you are.'

Either way she looked the fool. 'Great choices,' she muttered.

'I haven't finished yet,' he chided. 'If you really feel you can't bear to face him then we can leave through the French windows right now, before he gets here, climb into my car and just disappear.'

She glared at his chest and grimly added coward to fool and shrew.

He was using her hair comb to tame the thick silken swathe into some semblance of tidiness, surprising her with the efficiency he used to secure her hair in yet another neat twist. And her scalp was beginning to tingle—with pleasure. She couldn't bear it. It was all just too much.

'Please stop it, Carlo,' she breathed out anxiously.

'You do know my name, then,' he said lightly and she lifted her eyelids to show him dark pools of agony.

'Please lock the door again,' she pleaded. 'I'm not ready to cope with him!'

His fingers dropped to cup her shoulders, his eyes suddenly sober and dark. 'It is midnight, Francesca,' he informed her very gently.

Midnight. The witching hour. The time her engagement to Angelo was to be formally announced. Her gaze flicked the room as if a hundred glossy people were already standing here watching and waiting to bear witness as Angelo claimed his mighty prize.

She shuddered in dismay as the full weight of his betrayal returned like a flood. The hands on her shoulders moved in reflex response. 'Don't cry,' he said brusquely. 'He doesn't deserve your tears.'

She knew that, but it didn't stop what was beginning to break up inside. 'What am I going to do?' she whispered tragically.

His hands moved again, coming to frame her face so he could tilt it up to receive his next warm kiss. When she responded with a small sob he caught the sound with the lick of his tongue. Each stifled sob after it was gently robbed from her; in between he placed words, low, dark, seductive words that made her want to cling.

'Leave it to me,' he said. 'I will deal with it. Trust me to get you through this.'

'But why should you want to?' she asked, realising it was a question she should have asked a whole lot sooner than this. 'Why should it interest you at all?'

His answering smile was the cynical one. 'Come on, Francesca, the answer to that one must be perfectly clear,' he mocked as he moved one of his long thumbs to send it on a sweep of her now pulsing not quivering mouth. 'I want you for myself,' he told her grimly. 'Therefore I will do what it takes to get you.'

Then he was lowering his mouth again to show how

much he wanted her with yet another full-blooded mind-blowing kiss.

Everything he did now was laced with intimacy. Every touch, every look, every small gesture was staking claim. And the worst of it was that she let him. She felt so vulnerable and weak and drawn to his passion that she had a terrible suspicion he could spread her out on the desk across the room and have his way with her and she wouldn't try to stop him.

It was a dreadful admission. It shocked and appalled her but didn't make her pull away from him. Where was her pride, her dignity?

Not where her mouth was anyway. It clung and encouraged, like her fingers where they lifted and clung to his nape, smoothing, stroking, and her hips as they arched into the masculine bowl of his. And the whole hot, sensuous embrace was so slow and deep and intoxicatingly rousing, she moved with it, soaked in it, and didn't even hear the door flying open until a stunned voice rasped, 'What the hell do you think you are doing?'

CHAPTER FIVE

SHOCK wired her up to a live cable. She felt its electric fingers *frisson* her skin. On a choked gasp she tried to break free but Carlo was in no hurry to let that happen. He took his time easing the kiss, lingering long enough for Angelo to be in no doubt as to what he was witnessing here.

'As you can see, a great deal is going on,' he then murmured with smooth, slick—diabolical composure. And he said it without moving his eyes from Francesca's hot, kissed-hazed, dismayed face. He even dared to compound on his statement by shaping yet another warm, excruciatingly possessive kiss to her gaping mouth.

'Leave her alone!' Angelo bit out hoarsely. 'Francesca— come over here. I can't believe that you are doing this with him while everyone out there is waiting for our announcement!'

That last part really said it all, Francesca thought heavily. For here she stood, caught red-handedly wrapped in a passionate embrace with another man, and all Angelo could think about was getting his ring on her finger.

My God, that hurt.

'There will be no announcement,' Carlo declared smoothly. 'Francesca doesn't want you any more. You are out, *amico,* and I am in. You may announce that if you wish.'

It was an unbelievably cut-throat, throwaway comment, and Francesca could only stare up at the smooth, challenging face.

'I told you I would deal with it,' Carlo reminded her gently then placed a finger beneath her chin and calmly shut her still gaping mouth.

71

Angelo seemed incapable of saying anything. She could feel his confusion, his blank, bubbling bewilderment. She turned her head to look at him. He was standing two strides into the room with the door swinging wide open so he was framed by glaring white marble from the hall beyond. People were milling about, moving to or from one of the many rooms that had been opened up for tonight's party. Some halted and stared when they saw the little trio standing in Alessandro Batiste's study, making her aware suddenly of other things like the way her slender arms were still coiled around Carlo's neck and the front of her body resting intimately against his.

Culpable heat flooded up her throat and into her cheeks. 'Close the door,' she breathed on a stifled whisper.

Angelo's blue eyes flared to life and he spun about to see for himself the way they were being stared at. His arm shot out and the door slammed into its housing then he was twisting back to them again to pin her with a furious look.

'Explain to me what the hell you think you are doing with him,' he gritted.

It was like looking at a complete stranger. Nothing about him was familiar to her any more. His smooth golden features that had once looked beautiful to her now looked hard and selfish. The glitter in his eyes one of mercenary greed not tender possessiveness. How could she have missed all of that? she wondered painfully. Everything about him, from the contrived streaks in his tawny blond hair to the angrily petulant curl to his mouth, bore no resemblance to the man she'd thought she loved. An ache throbbed in her stomach; she had never felt so deceived—by herself. Blinded by smooth, deliberate lies and a pitiable desire to be loved.

A pair of hands slid around her waist. She looked back at Carlo and saw hardness and toughness and a strength of will in his face that promised to devour her if she let it. But she also saw truth. He was hiding nothing, pretending nothing. I want you, he'd said, nothing more—nothing less than that. But at least it was honest.

'Tell him, *cara*,' he prompted softly.

Her breasts heaved on a tense little breath and she looked back at Angelo. 'I'm not going to marry you,' she announced obediently then was shocked by how easily the words came out. 'You don't love me. You never even tried to.'

Then she looked back at Carlo. He didn't love her but at least he didn't say that he did. He kissed her gently. Maybe he could sense the aching threat of tears still working in her throat.

'Will you stop kissing her like that?' Angelo rasped out. 'Francesca—*amore*,' he pleaded huskily, 'of course I love you. How could you think I do not?'

A picture of an all-consuming open-mouthed kiss and an urgent hand sliding blue silk away from a slender thigh closed her eyes on a wave of thick anguish. She heard the sound of shrill words declaring, *You don't want her! You don't even like her that much!* echoing their bitter poison into her head.

'Listen,' Angelo planted into the swirling mists of that fading image, 'if this is a case of pre-engagement panic, Francesca, I can understand that. Come to me,' he urged. 'We will go somewhere private so we can talk about it...'

He was very good, Francesca acknowledged and even felt herself start to tremble inside because she was hearing that other Angelo again, the quiet and tender one she'd fallen in love with. Maybe they should discuss this without a third-party witness. Maybe she—

'Careful, *amore*,' a soft voice cautioned. 'Seduction can take many formats.'

He was right. She was being seduced by Angelo's tender charm again. How easy she must have made it all for him, she thought with a self-deprecating dismay that sent her swaying closer to this tall, dark man who was her only truly honest support right now because she certainly could not rely on herself!

Her mouth accidentally brushed the cleft in his chin, sending tight tingles of awareness skittering across her skin. She sucked in a soft gasp, shocked at how sensitised she had become to everything about him. His voice, his touch, she could even taste him—drew greedily on his subtle male scent.

Anger roared at her from across the room. *'Puttana!'*

She blinked, too dazed and disorientated by what she was feeling to really take the retort in, and she turned her head to find herself facing a man pulsing with biting contempt for her. The change from bewildered and pleading lover to this was startling. Golden eyes were flashing silver steel. A dark flush had mounted his skin. His teeth were showing, bared as if he were a riled wolf preparing to pounce.

Carlo had turned his head also. In the throes of all of this hostility it struck her that it was the first time he had bothered to look at Angelo. 'Be very careful whom you insult,' he warned with a soft-voiced snarl. 'Or I might decide to bring your house tumbling down like the flimsy pack of cards it is.'

And Francesca's skin began to prickle because if Angelo was a wolf then he was a mere puppy compared to this very dangerous man. Seeming to recognise that, Angelo instantly backed down, an unsteady sigh hissing from his lips as he ran a shaking set of fingers through his hair. He was floundering in a brain-numbing state of shock, she saw, and knew exactly what it felt like.

'But she can't to do this to me,' Angelo groaned out unsteadily.

'She can and she is.' It was so cold and brutal that she shivered, bringing his attention back to her again. Long fingers gently crushed silk chiffon against the sensitive skin at her waist as he lowered his head to brush his lips across the frown-creased bridge of her nose.

There was a sound of disgust as Angelo threw his back to them.

The door flew open. 'Angelo—Francesca, what are you doing in here? Your guests are…'

The words were cut off when she saw Carlo, her eyelashes flickering when she took in the scene. Angelina Batiste was blond and golden like Angelo but unlike Angelo it didn't take her more than a few seconds to understand what was really happening here and her face became a perfectly blank page.

'Leave us, Madre,' Angelo bit at her. 'I am dealing with this.'

But his mother was not going to leave. She was too busy seeing a terrible scandal staring her in the face and surprised everyone by turning on her son.

'What have you done?' she demanded accusingly.

'I've done nothing,' he growled, sounding like the puppy wolf again. 'Look to them for your culprits.' He tossed a hand out. 'The way they cannot stop kissing each other speaks for itself.'

'At least we do it with a lot more *finesse* than you were using on Francesca's flatmate, *amico*. And we sought privacy, not the garden, where anyone who wanted to could view your technique…'

Francesca closed her eyes as the world swayed at this next stark revelation. For a moment she thought she was going to faint. Angelina Batiste almost choked on the shocked gasp that rose in her throat.

Opening her eyes again, she saw Angelo had spun round to stare at them. He looked shattered. He'd had the high ground ripped from beneath him by a man with a lethal penchant for ruthlessness. It left him with no argument to pursue, nothing for him to say in his own defence.

He tried though, eyelashes flickering as he moved his stunned eyes to his mother's shock-whitened face then on to look at Francesca. '*Cara…*' he murmured in a huskily pleading, unsteady tone. 'For goodness' sake, don't listen to him. What he's implying isn't true.'

'Perhaps I should have explained that we *both* observed your lack of finesse,' Carlo inserted.

Angelo went white then an angry red. '*Bastardo!* Shut up!' he launched at Carlo. 'This has nothing to do with you!'

His mother jumped. Francesca blinked. Angelo took a step towards her. 'Listen to me,' he said urgently. 'What you saw tonight was a moment of madness. Your friend— she threw herself at me. She—'

A shrill gasp came from the doorway. None of them had noticed that it had been left open when Mrs Batiste came into the room. Angelo swung round—they all swivelled their eyes to find Sonya standing there with her beautiful face a study of icy anger and burning guilt.

'You lying son of a bitch,' she hissed at Angelo, causing his mother to stiffen in personal offence. 'We've been sleeping together for weeks!'

He was being attacked from all angles. He responded to that with violence. One of his arms came up and for a horrible second Francesca thought he was going to slap Sonya's face. His mother must have thought so too because she darted forward and in a mad scramble she took hold of Sonya's arm and hustled her from the room. Angelo's arm diverted to grab the door. It slammed into its housing again.

Silent hit. Singing in the turbulent atmosphere. Francesca was trembling so badly that her teeth were chattering. She tried to clench them into stillness but they just rattled inside her shocked head.

Carlo's arms folded right around her. 'It's OK,' he said then repeated it soothingly. 'It's OK…'

But it wasn't OK. His voice might be calm but the rest of him wasn't. Every muscle was clenched, pumped up and ready for whatever Angelo's anger made him do next.

What Angelo did was swing back to face them, and his

face was hard now, locked in a mould of anger and contempt. 'Let's cut to the chase,' he thrust out at Francesca. 'Looking at this little scene I interrupted, you have been behaving no better than me. So let us stop this foolishness. Come over here, Francesca,' he commanded but she noticed he didn't attempt to come and get her. 'We can talk about this later but for now we have an engagement to announce.'

He just didn't get it—or refused to get it. 'Don't you understand? It's over between us.'

'Because you think he is a better bet than me?' he sliced. 'Don't delude yourself. He doesn't want you. He's toying with you, *cara*, just for the hell of it and to get his revenge on me. Look at yourself then look at the women he usually has hanging on his arm. What do you have to compete with them?'

The cruel words flayed her already battered ego. And the contempt in his eyes flayed it some more. He might be lashing out at her in anger, but to hear and to see how much this man she'd believed loved her only an hour before actually openly disliked her was the worst blow of all.

But he was also right. A man like Carlo Carlucci had his pick where beautiful women were concerned. What could he possibly see in her?

'Don't listen,' Carlo advised in a roughened undertone. 'He wants to draw blood to salve his wounded pride.'

'He's after your money, *cara*.' Angelo fed her more poison. 'Don't kid yourself that his attention means anything more than that.'

The money. She winced. It had to come down to the wretched non-existent money. 'There isn't any money,' she sighed.

He sent her a cynically disbelieving look.

'I'm telling you the truth,' she insisted. 'I've *always* told you the truth about the money,' she added because that was just another hurt she was having to deal with—the knowledge that he'd smiled all of those careless smiles about her

Gianni connection and had been scoffing at her at the same time. 'There never has been a Gianni fortune languishing in a bank vault somewhere, waiting for me to marry before I make my claim. Whoever started that silly rumour must be rolling on the floor laughing at you by now, Angelo, because my grandfather died virtually penniless, having spent years squandering his wealth on bad investment after bad investment.' She told it more or less exactly as her great-uncle Bruno had told it to her. 'What you see at the Palazzo Gianni is basically all that's left.'

'You're lying,' he said, 'to punish me.'

'Punish you?' Her chin lifted, dusky eyebrows arching above clear hazel eyes. 'If I wanted to punish you I would be walking out of here without telling you a word of this, knowing I'd left you really festering on your loss.'

His blue eyes flicked a look at the man standing behind her. Whatever he saw in Carlo's face drained the gold out of his skin. 'You believe her,' he breathed.

'I couldn't care less if she comes dressed in rags and dragging a mountain of debts along with her so long as she does come to me,' he answered. 'And that,' Carlo added succinctly 'is the marked difference as to why you are standing where you are right now and I am standing right here...'

You had your chance and blew it, in other words. Carlo might have well said those words the way all the anger drained out of Angelo and he sank into a nearby chair then buried his face in his hands.

'What am I going to tell everyone out there?' he groaned.

Francesca could have felt a pang of sympathy for him—until he said that. Selfish to the last, he was still thinking about his own situation and wasn't showing a hint of guilt or shame for the one he'd put her in.

'Tell them the truth about your little heiress that isn't,' Carlo suggested. 'But if you can't bring yourself to do that only to be laughed at then tell them your betrothed jilted you in favour of Carlo Carlucci. At least that should win you the sympathy vote.'

Once again he was revealing his ruthlessly cutting edge. Francesca shivered as she acknowledged it. The hands at her waist tightened their grip. 'Are you ready to leave now?' He used that same edge on her next.

She hovered over giving an answer, aware that she could well be making the second biggest mistake in her life by going anywhere with him. He was ruthless to the core, easily as selfish as Angelo. And she was also aware that all that stuff about taking her in rags had been a slick cover-up to what he really believed about the Gianni fortune.

But was Carlo willing to sacrifice his freedom for it? No, the answer came back. He had too much pride in himself, too much inner strength. And he hadn't offered to marry her in Angelo's place, she reminded herself quickly. Just to get her away from here and maybe indulge in some hot sex before they parted again.

The kind of sex she'd never felt even mildly tempted to experience until she came into contact with him. That made him dangerous. She'd always known he was dangerous. Say no, she told herself. Do yourself a favour and go out there, find your friends and let them take you *safely* away from here before you drop yourself into even deeper trouble than you are already in!

'Stop thinking so much,' he rasped suddenly. 'You're no good at it right now.'

She flinched at the angry flick of his voice. He could feel her hovering indecision—feel the uncertain flutter of her heart beneath the hand he had slid up the wall of her stomach and had settled beneath the curve of her left breast. A thumb dared to move in a single light stroke against its sensitive underside and she responded with a stifled gasp.

Angelo lifted his face out of his hands, picking up the tension in the atmosphere like an animal sniffing sexual scent. 'How long have you two been two-timing me?' he demanded harshly.

It was so much like the pot calling the kettle black that she stared at him, a bubble of hysterical laughter threatening to burst in her throat.

'Not quite as long as your affair with the flatmate but long enough to know what we want.' It was Carlo who answered. He was so good at this lying business, she thought anxiously. How could she be considering putting her trust in him?

He surprised her then by lifting his hands to her shoulders, the fingers threatening to bite. She dragged her eyes away from Angelo to look into this other, darker face. He was angry, she saw. His eyes were a glitter, his mouth compressed into a grim line—not kissable, definitely not kissable right now.

'Do we leave quietly by the back way or are you up to running the gauntlet out there so you can pack your bag?'

It was both a question and a hard warning. He'd put his pride on the line here and now she was threatening to make him look a fool by wavering over going with him.

'How old are you?' she asked out of nowhere.

'Old enough to have grown out of playing games,' he said. Then he kissed her, and she learned that angry or not that mouth was indeed very kissable, hard and demanding and searingly hot—

'This is sickening.' On that muffled choke Angelo got to his feet and lurched towards the door.

'Stay where you are, *amico*,' Carlo lifted his head to toss after him. 'We still have things left to say to each other.'

Angelo froze. So did Francesca. What did they have left to say? Her skin began to prickle. She didn't like the new dark look in his eyes. 'Don't you dare discuss me with him!' she warned tautly.

'Frightened he might give your most intimate secrets away?'

She gasped, 'What's the matter with you?'

'Nothing,' he said, then on a growl of impatience lowered his mouth to her ear. 'Stop looking at him as if he's your preferred option.'

She jerked her head back to stare at him. 'But I wasn't—'

'Do we go by the back or the front?' he cut over her.

It was decision time, Francesca realised. Did she go with him or did she not? In the end it was pride that made the choice for her. What bit she had left of it was not going to let her kill it by taking the coward's way out.

So, 'The front,' she replied and wondered straight away if there was insanity in her family because, pride or not, she had to be crazy to want to go anywhere with him.

Some of the anger seeped out of him. He nodded his dark head then actually smiled. 'Brave girl,' he murmured and even kissed her for it before taking hold of her arm to lead her to the door.

He had to step around Angelo to open it for her and he did it with a smooth shift of his body that blocked the other man off from her behind the width of his wide shoulders and ignored his presence at the same time.

Ruthless, she repeated inwardly, and shivered and knew she didn't feel brave at all. The door swung open. Heaving in a deep breath, she clutched her hands into two tight fists by her sides then lifted her chin and took that first mammoth step over the threshold.

The first thing she noticed was the lack of music, then the small clutches of people dotted around the vast hall. There was a sudden drop in the hum of conversation as all faces were turned her way. What they thought they knew as fact about what was going on here and what was pure speculation was impossible to judge. That depended on which story had made the biggest impression—the one where some of them had witnessed her standing in Carlo's arms or the one where Sonya had spat out the truth about her affair with Angelo.

Her stomach muscles knotted, her throat ran sandpaper-dry. Behind her she could feel Carlo standing in the doorway as he took in their audience.

'Ten minutes long enough?' she heard him say quietly.

She swallowed and nodded, her cheeks feeling as if they would never cool down again.

'I will be here.'

It was a promise, issued loud enough for everyone to hear it. And, dangerous man or not, it was a promise she needed to hear right now.

Then she was drawing herself up, lifting her chin that bit higher and walking on legs that did not really want to support her towards the wide and sweeping marble staircase without allowing herself to make eye contact with anyone. She might not know if their expressions were vilifying her for being caught red-handed in another man's arms or if they were feeling sorry for her because she'd found out the truth about Angelo and her best friend, but one thing was certain—they would be leaning one way or the other.

It really was like walking the gauntlet. By the time she hit the stairs the low hum of conversation had begun to gather pace again. From the corner of her eye she could see Carlo's tall, dark figure still standing by the study door. No sign of Angelo. He was doing what she had been doing earlier and hiding away while he got himself together enough to face the madding crowd, or should that be buzzing crowd? she thought as she kept herself moving at a steady pace even though she wanted to run.

About halfway up, where the stairs swept around the great central chandelier, she dared to take a final peek down and saw that Angelo's parents were being ushered into the study by a grim-faced Carlo. He still didn't move from his firm stance at the door, though, watching her all the way.

Standing guard.

By the time she reached the sanctuary of her room she was almost expiring beneath the stress of it all. Closing the door behind her, she then leant back against it and closed her eyes in relief. She was trembling all over. Stupid hot tears were pricking at her eyes. She was suffering the shock and humiliation from what she had seen and overheard in the garden, she acknowledged. Was desperately confused by her own behaviour with Carlo afterwards and even more shocked by his passionately possessive behaviour towards her.

Now she was leaning here feeling frightened for the future and had the worrying suspicion that she had just committed herself to a torrid affair with the last man on earth any ordinary, sensible woman would want to become tangled up with.

Ordinary, sensible, boring, undesirable to the point where the man you intended to marry needed to supplement his passions with a real woman—a woman he'd also intended to fantasise about when he did get around to making love to her.

'Francesca…?' a wary voice murmured as if it was shooting straight out of her last bitter thought. 'Are you all right?'

She opened her eyes to see Sonya perched tensely on the end of her bed. Blue eyes big, face pale, lush mouth quivering in anxious appeal. Her heart sank like a lead weight to her stomach. 'Much you care,' she replied.

'I do care.' Sonya scrambled off the bed and began walking towards her. 'Why do you think I've been sitting here waiting for you? I needed to apologise and explain. You have to—'

'It doesn't need explaining,' Francesca cut in. 'I know what I saw, *cara*.'

The sarcastically spoken endearment earned itself a painful wince. 'I know that—don't you think I don't know that?'

Did she honestly think Francesca cared? Pushing herself away from the door, she moved at an angle that gave her the widest route around her so-called friend. Her feet took her towards the walk-in wardrobe. Sonya followed, trailing sullenly behind her.

'I need to explain to you *why* it happened,' she said pleadingly. 'You don't know the real Angelo, Francesca. He's selfish and sly. He puts on a special act for you but—'

'Not any more he doesn't.'

'No,' Sonya huskily conceded and watched as Francesca located her suitcase from where she'd stashed it just inside the room then knelt with it on the floor so she could unzip it. She had been intending to change her clothes for something more appropriate before leaving this room again but now all she wanted to do was pack her things and get out.

'You're leaving?' Sonya asked as if it was some huge surprise.

'What do you think?' It was enough to make her let loose with a strangled laugh.

She glanced up at her once closest friend to find her propping up the doorway with her arms folded defensively and looking all guilty and pale.

But she was still wearing that wretched blue satin dress, she noticed. 'You disgust me,' she said and looked away again, angry fingers unzipping the suitcase.

'I know,' Sonya surprised her by agreeing. 'I disgust myself. You know how much I hate him! I've never tried to make a secret of it but…'

They were back to the *but* Francesca didn't want to listen to. 'So how come you went out of your way to introduce this man you hate to your best friend?'

'What?' Sonya blinked her long lashes at her.

Francesca felt like slapping her face. Instead she got to her feet to go tugging clothes off hangers. 'You were living here in Rome for a whole six months before I came to join you,' she expanded, tossing clothes haphazardly down into the case. 'Your friends became my friends. You even got me my job! So how come I got no warning about the real character of this man you say you hate? How come you introduced me to him at all?'

'What was I supposed to do—ignore him when he was there with the rest?'

She had a point, Francesca conceded, though she didn't want to. She started emptying drawers. 'You wanted him for yourself even then,' she stated and only realised it was the truth as the tight words left her lips. She stopped what she was doing as full clarity began to hit. 'He wasn't interested. He already had a girlfriend. A gorgeous, dark-haired creature with amazing brown eyes...'

'Nicola,' Sonya mumbled.

Francesca nodded, and turned to look at her again. Sonya was looking at the floor now, her long hair like a heavy silk curtain hiding her face. 'You wanted to get his attention,' she went on slowly. 'So you thought you would impress him by telling him that your friend from England had some Gianni blood.'

Sonya's chin shot up. 'I didn't know he would go apoplectic at the mere mention of the Gianni name!'

'I told you that in confidence! You had no right to set that hungry wolf on to me! And once he did go apoplectic, why didn't you warn me then what you'd done?'

Sonya flushed and looked away again. Inside Francesca was beginning to seethe as each veil was scraped from her eyes. 'He took you out to pump more information out of you, didn't he? I bet he even took you to bed then!'

'As I said, I hate him.'

And she did, Francesca accepted as she stood taking in that blunt admission. Sonya hated Angelo with absolute venom but she was also so crazily in love with him she couldn't say no to him.

'He's manipulating and sly. He used me to get at you and used our friendship to stop me from telling you the truth. He said you would never forgive me—and he's right, isn't he?'

'Yes.' Francesca didn't even need to think about it. Sonya had been deeply instigative from the very beginning in setting her up for all this pain and heartache she'd had to suffer tonight because she was sure of one thing and she would not be standing here in the Batiste villa if Sonya hadn't mentioned the Gianni name.

You don't want her; you don't even like her…! Francesca sucked in a thick breath. Those cruel words were going to be etched on her soul forever now, she predicted painfully.

Bending down, she scooped up the open case with its spilling contents and pushed past Sonya to go and put the case down on the bed.

'I'm sorry,' came the husky murmur from somewhere behind her.

'You call Angelo manipulating and sly but what does that make you, Sonya?' she asked as she went about gathering up whatever other bits she'd left lying about. 'We've known each other for years. We confided everything.'

'You kept your affair with Carlo Carlucci a dark secret.' Sonya got in her own hit. 'How long has that been going on, *cara*? Don't think I missed the way you were wrapped around each other before Angelo's mother dragged me away! The room was swimming in overactive pheromones. You were both so kiss-drugged you could barely focus on anything else!'

'But at least I still had my underwear on,' Francesca retaliated with a withering slide of her eyes down the front of Sonya's dress.

She was rewarded with a choked gasp and the sight of a hand jerking down to tug guiltily at the hem of the dress. Leaving Sonya to stew on her own sluttish behaviour, she moved into the bathroom and began quickly gathering up her toiletries.

When she re-entered the bedroom she saw that Sonya was ready to go back on the attack. 'You might like to think of yourself as morally a cut above me, Francesca. But you're as guilty as I am for playing around with another woman's man.'

Was she saying that Carlo was committed to some other woman? It stopped her dead in her tracks.

'And here's the real nasty little twist, *cara*,' Sonya continued, aiming sure with her knives now. 'Nicola Mauraux—you know, the dark-haired beauty with the brown eyes you were talking about? She's Carlo Carlucci's stepsister. It was a bit of a foregone conclusion that she and Angelo would marry one day—until you came along and he turfed her out.'

Carlo was not in another relationship, was the first part of that she grabbed at with relief. Then the rest arrived like a blast, blanching the colour out of her face.

'Angelo told me it was already over,' she breathed in a stifled whisper.

'Since when has he ever spoken the truth?' Sonya asked. 'He's an incurable liar with a greedy eye for the main chance! Nicola isn't rich like you will be one day, Francesca. She isn't a Carlucci so has no claim on the Carlucci wealth. She attends this very posh university in Paris at her stepbrother's expense but that's about the sum total of what she's likely to get from him.'

'You knew all of this and didn't bother to tell me?'

'What for? I wasn't to know that you would start two-timing your beloved Angelo with Carlo Carlucci.' Oh, the knives were flying thick and fast now. This was Sonya at her cutting best. 'But if I did happen to be you right now, I would be asking if Signor Carlucci isn't using you to get back a bit of revenge on Angelo for dumping his stepsister.'

The word *revenge* hit her first. Angelo had accused Carlo of being out for revenge on him but she had been too confused to pick up on it then. He'd also said that Carlo was *using her* and she'd let that float right by her too. Then there were Carlo's displays of contempt towards Angelo and the smooth, slick, cutting way he had demolished him from the very outset—as if he'd been planning to do it—as if the whole kiss thing had been timed and rigged to happen as Angelo walked into the room!

She began to feel sick again—very sick. Her hand had to jerk up to cover her mouth. If it wasn't enough to be used by one ruthless swine, now another one had come along to do the same thing again!

Talk about being a sucker for it, she thought bitterly, and had to turn her back to Sonya so she wouldn't see the hurt tears starting in her eyes.

'I just don't want you to pile all the blame on me, that's all!' Sonya cried out. 'If you witnessed what Angelo and I were doing out there on the terrace then you must have heard me tell him that I wanted to tell you everything—and I was going to do it this time, Francesca! Only you found out before I could get to you first.'

After the sex, of course, Francesca thought bitterly. After she'd stood there on that wretched terrace and drowned herself in Angelo!

She was never going to trust a single living person, she vowed as she went to throw the last of her things into the suitcase. The tears were blurring her vision. Her fingers had developed a permanent shake. If someone had told her that she was going to spend her engagement night having her life ripped apart she would have laughed in their face!

And she still had to run the gauntlet to get out of here. She still had to face Carlo Carlucci knowing what she now knew about him!

She shut the suitcase, stuffing straggling bits of clothing inside it as she struggled to fasten the zip. Where was she going to go—what was she going to do?

'Let me come with you,' Sonya begged suddenly as if she could actually read what was going on inside her head. 'Wait for me to pack and we'll go and stay at that hotel where the rest of our group is staying.'

'Do they know about your affair with Angelo?' she asked quietly.

Silence met that—one of those stark, thick silences that screamed the answer loud and clear.

She took a final quick glance around her to see if she'd missed anything, then bent to pick up her little denim jacket and pulled it on over her dress. Next she hauled up the suitcase.

This was it. There was nothing left for her here. Mouth tight, eyes hard, she turned to walk towards the door.

'Please…' Sonya's painfully shaken cry followed her. 'Don't leave me here to face the music alone, Francesca. You're my friend—you're the only real friend I've ever had! Let me come with you—*please!*'

Francesca turned to look at this petite, flaxen-haired, sylph-like *friend* who was just too beautiful for her own good. Even the tears shining in her anxious blue eyes enhanced that beauty, as did the quiver of her lips.

'Enjoy the rest of your life, Sonya,' she said, then left with her great-uncle Bruno's chilling form of goodbye still ringing behind her like the toll of death.

CHAPTER SIX

SHE must have inherited some of the Gianni genes after all, she thought with a bitter-wry smile. Funny, she mused, but she'd always assumed she missed out on most of them. Her mother had insisted she had.

No thick and glossy raven hair, none of the Gianni bone features that had given her mother's face such a striking impact. Her mouth was too wide, her skin too pale—but that cold and unforgiving final cut she'd just used to sever her friendship with Sonya had to have come from the Gianni gene stock.

Along with her mother's propensity for falling in love with the wrong kind of man. Like lightning striking twice, or that nasty thing called fate other people liked talking about. Had it been written at her birth that she was fated to fall in love with a mercenary like Angelo then be seduced by a vengeful rat like Carlo?

She saw him then and had to pause at the top of stairs while she dealt with the way her heart dipped then shrivelled like a dried-up prune in her chest.

He was standing at the bottom of the stairs, waiting for her, looking stunning as always. The shockingly perfect profile, the smooth, olive-toned skin, the gorgeous mouth that was a mere shadowy outline from up here but could still tighten muscles all over her body on the knowledge of the way it could kiss. His black hair was making her think of ravens' wings again as it captured the overhead lights and his curling black eyelashes hovered sensuously against those chiselled cheekbones as he stood looking down at his watch.

In a rush to get this over with, *signor*? Francesca quizzed. Do you want to get the poor little fool out of here so you can finish what you started in the name of revenge?

He could have heard her for the way his dark head lifted. He smiled the most relaxed, warm smile then began walking up to meet her. 'I was just coming to get you,' he murmured in that rich, dark voice of his.

Francesca was contemplating telling him where to put his lying smile—when she noticed the people still gathered in the hall. The gauntlet, she remembered, and snapped her mouth shut again then carefully hooded her cold, glinting eyes. There was no way she was going to show herself up again while she told Carlo Carlucci what she thought of him on the Batiste staircase with the mob listening in.

The mob, she thought again, struck by her own acid turn of phrase and almost—almost found it in her to laugh. If these people were a mob they were a very exclusive kind of mob with their designer clothes and their designer jewels and their designer expressions that made her think of wax.

Carlo stopped two steps down from her and reached for her suitcase. 'Like the jacket,' he said in a husky attempt to break the tension laying whip cracks across all of them. 'It goes with the dress.'

'Can we go, please?' she responded in a voice misted with frost.

He stopped smiling, his eyes narrowing on her cold face. 'Of course,' he replied without any notable change in his rich voice tones but her senses began to scramble about inside her when they detected a change. It didn't do to return his warm overtures with ice, she realised. He was used to orchestrating the moods of others not altering his own mood to suit.

His fingers closed around her fingers where they clutched the handle to the suitcase. The suitcase changed hands within a hooded silence. Stepping to one side, he indicated that she should continue down the stairs. As she passed by him he fell into step beside her, his tall, dark bulk trying its best to hide her from most of those curious faces down in the hall.

What were they thinking? How much did they know? Was she the sinner in their eyes, caught by Angelo kissing

Carlo Carlucci on the night of his engagement to her, or the one to be pitied for falling for Angelo's smooth, slick, calculating charm at all?

Angelo—Angelo, she suddenly repeated. And felt a shaft of pain as her love for him exploded right here on this fabulous marble staircase. How could he have done this to her—treated her like this?

How could Sonya?

Delayed shock to her night of revelation really began to kick in as they made ground level. She was shaking so badly that she had a horrible suspicion she was going to further humiliate herself by falling into a sobbing huddle on the cold marble floor. Beside her, Carlo must have sensed it because his free hand came to rest against her back as if in assurance. She almost jumped out of her skin as the old warning prickles of hostility and self-defence arrived to remind her that he was not her saviour—far from it. He was as guilty as the others for trying to use her for his own ends.

'Don't touch me,' she hissed in a taut, teeth-clenched whisper.

He did the opposite. Shifting the hand until it arrived at the indent to her waist and with a single warning curl of his long fingers, he brought her into full contact with his side. Then he made the ultimate move to subdue her by stopping them walking so he could propel her around to face him, then in front of their audience he bent his dark head.

His lips arrived against her ear lobe, his breath scoring her frozen white cheek. 'Behave until we get out of here or I will kiss you stupid,' he warned very grimly.

There wasn't a split-second when she thought he might be bluffing. This was yet another man on a mission and she was just his disposable pawn. Bitterness welled, the fine tremors of dismay converting themselves into silver-shard tremors of contempt as he set them moving again.

It was then that she saw their farewell party waiting by the open front door. Mr and Mrs Batiste were standing straight-faced and soldier-like, ready to play the perfect hosts to the bitter end even as their glittering party lay in a wreck around their elegant feet. Did they know what their son had done? Had they been in on his deceit? *'Your business is safe, Papa, and don't forget who is paying the price for it.'*

Yes, they'd known from the beginning, she concluded and shuddered. Did that also mean they knew *why* she was being escorted from here by Carlo Carlucci?

Of course they did, she derided her own question. Everyone knew. Everyone knew everything but me!

'I hate you,' she hissed.

He ignored that one, the hand keeping her moving towards the open door.

'Carlo, we need to talk—' Alessandro Batiste jerked into anxious speech as they reached him.

'Next week,' Carlo Carlucci cut him off curtly, passing by him without a single pause. 'And without your son,' he added abruptly. 'If you want to hold on to my business, that is…'

'Y-yes, of course,' Angelo's father agreed in gruff obsequious Italian.

Angelina Batiste said absolutely nothing. The whole thing was a real *coup détat* for Signor Carlucci. He'd effectively cut Angelo adrift from just about everything, including the support of his own parents, it seemed.

The night air had a sharp nip to it. Carlo's car stood parked at the bottom of the steps. He guided her towards it and opened the passenger door for her and only then allowed his fingers to ease their grip on her waist when he stepped back, his expression a wall of cool politeness as he waited for her to get in the car. As she sank into luxurious black leather the door was closed with a solid click. Her eyes began to sting as she listened to him putting her case in the car boot and she had to bite down hard on her bottom lip in an effort to maintain her icy dignity as he got in beside her, folding his body like a lithe jungle cat with its killer instincts set on full alert.

It was easier to look out of the side-window than to keep him hovering even on the periphery of her vision. What she saw through that window was the door to Villa Batiste drawing shut. It was the last time she would look at that door, she vowed silently.

The car engine came to life. It kicked into gear and with a spin of wide tyres on loose gravel they moved off, the force of the acceleration pushing her back into the seat. Headlights spanned the two lines of cypress trees. They sped between them and barely paused at the junction before they were turning into the lane and accelerating away again.

She had no idea where he was taking her and at that precise moment she didn't care. Her life was in tatters. If someone had come along with a knife and cut her to ribbons she couldn't feel worse than she did right now.

Then she found that she could feel a whole lot worse when he brought the car to a sudden neck-jolting halt. She'd barely recovered from the shock of it when he was twisting towards her in his seat.

'OK,' he said. 'Tell me what your friend said to you to turn you back into the spitting cat.'

Cats and wolves were making a prominent show tonight, she thought ridiculously and almost choked on what she recognised as a lump of hysteria now blocking her throat.

'What makes you think it was Sonya?' she flashed.

'Because she was the only loose cannon out there I couldn't protect you from,' he answered.

Protect? Her eyes widened. He called this protection? She twisted her face away again, fizzing inside and refusing to answer. For a long, taut tick in time she continued to sit with her eyes still fixed on the side-window and her lips clamped tightly shut.

'Francesca!' he rasped.

'Nicola Mauraux.'

Silence. That was it. She sat there waiting for some kind of response—a guilty curse would have been enough! But nothing else happened. She wasn't breathing but he was—in and out with a calmness that set her teeth on edge. Her eyes began to sting again—she so badly wanted to break down and cry like a baby that she didn't know how much longer she could stop herself from doing it!

When he finally moved she was forced to flick another glance at him, warily unsure as to what was coming next. But all he did was settle himself back in his seat and a moment later and they were moving again as if she hadn't spoken his stepsister's wretched name.

Well—fine, she thought burningly. Let's just ignore I said it. Your silence suits me because it means I won't have to listen to you talk your slick way around the reasons why I am sitting in this car at all!

The car began to accelerate, moving very fast on the straight parts of the narrow country lane, slow and smooth through the bends with the headlights sweeping the darkness ahead of them as her grim-profiled driver put on a slick display of man versus power versus control. His timing was immaculate. He never missed a gear. The engine growled then purred then roared on acceleration then growled and purred again. And the whole thing took place beneath a heavy blanket of silence that helped to hold Francesca mesmerised even though she didn't want to be. He was the man with everything—great looks, great body and a great sense of style that utilised both to their optimum. Then there was his wealth and his power and his razor-like intellect. The way he used passion for persuasion, words like clubs to beat his opponents to death. And he drove his car with a ruthless, selfish, utter single-mindedness that dared anyone to get in his way. He reminded her of a dark, sleek, prowling predator, top of the food chain. Nothing or no one could touch him.

They sped by her great-uncle's *palazzo*. Recognising it jerked her into impulsive speech. 'You can—'

'Shut up,' he incised and made his first mistake with a gear change as if the sound of her voice was all it took to spoil his immaculate performance. The car lurched then put in a surge of power when he'd corrected the error, eating up the winding country lane with precision timing again.

And Francesca subsided in her seat as another bitter thought hit her: what was the use in demanding he take her to her uncle when the miserable old man was likely to refuse to open his door?

When disillusionment hit it stripped you of everything, she noticed, as Bruno Gianni became another name she added to her hate list. I am never going to contact him again, she vowed. He didn't care about her, hadn't even bothered to pretend that he did.

The hot ache of tears that were coming closer to bursting free by the second had her closing her eyes and huddling into her seat. As soon as this stupid journey is over I'm going home to England and I'm never going to step foot in Italy again, she promised herself. No wonder my mother never came back. No wonder she froze up whenever Italy or Rome came up in conversation. She was wise; she knew the score. *Why* hadn't she listened to her and saved herself a whole lot of grief?

They couldn't have gone more than a mile or so when the car made a sudden turn that brought her jolting back to her present situation. Her eyelids flickered upwards; she'd barely managed to focus through the tears before they were coming to another neck-jolting halt.

What now—what next? she wondered tensely.

'I w-want—'

'You don't know what you want,' he cut in tightly.

Then he was dousing the headlights and shutting down the engine with short, tight flicks of his fingers that told her he was still angry—bubbling with it. There was a click and a slither as his seat belt slid away from his body then he was opening his door and climbing into the dark night.

Her wary eyes slewed frontward, following his dark bulk as he moved around the car's long bonnet, *frissons* of uncertainty chasing across her skin. Her heart began to stutter. Was he going to eject her from his car and leave her out here in the middle of nowhere now he didn't have to bother explaining himself?

Her door came open. A waft of cold air placed a chill on her flesh. He bent down to reach across her to unlock her seat belt, and as his face arrived close to her face she saw the grim determination etched into the flat line of his mouth.

'I'm not getting out,' she informed him stubbornly.

'Does it appear that I am giving you a choice?' he asked. Then grabbed one of her hands as he straightened up again, and used it to haul her out of the car.

She arrived beside him in a state of numbing panic, sights and sounds hitting her senses at the same time as his body did. His arm came round her waist, arching her into full contact with his lean, hard length at the same time that she heard the car door shut behind her and another sound of whirring that had her twisting her head in time to see a pair of huge, thick wrought-iron gates swinging shut beneath a heavy stone arch she hadn't even been aware that they'd passed beneath.

Dizzy and disorientated, she became aware of uneven cobblestones beneath her thin-soled shoes and turned her head again in an effort to search the darkness for some hint as to where they were. Her mouth brushed his chin as she moved and his hissed sound of his tense response brought her search to a stop on his face. Then she wasn't seeing anything but the angry flame of desire leaping in his dark eyes, the savage tautening of his skin and flaring nostrils as he took in a swift breath of air. She felt a sudden tightening in his body, sucked in her own shocked gasp when she realised what the tightening meant. Her gaze dipped lower—

to his mouth…his hard, tight, angry mouth that was already advertising what was going to come next.

'No—' She managed that one breathlessly weak protest before he made full contact. After that she wasn't capable of saying or doing a single thing as his mouth moulded hers and his tongue made its first stabbing thrust. She was instantly electrified, fierce heat pouring a hot, tight sting of pleasure right down her front to gather in a sense-energising pool at her thighs.

She groaned and clutched at his shoulders, so shocked by her own response that she tried to push away from him, but it was a wasted effort because he only had to use the flat of his hand against the arching base of her spine to bring her in contact with his hard, muscular front for her to go weak at the knees.

He felt them go, felt her whole body quiver as a helpless little moan of pleasure keened in her throat. If this kiss was meant to be a punishment then it had failed in its mission, she found herself thinking dizzily as she went willingly when he pulled her even tighter up against him and she was kissing him back as she'd never kissed anyone, with a wild, deep, urgent hunger that took her over completely.

A powerful light suddenly drenched the two of them. The kiss broke abruptly, and on a curse Carlo twisted with her still wrapped against him while Francesca buried her face in his dinner jacket and quite simply lost the will to live. Her senses had shattered. She'd thought they'd done that earlier tonight when she'd watched Angelo with Sonya. But even that devastating moment could not compare with how she was dealing with the loss of that unbelievable kiss.

'My apologies, *signor*,' a deeply contrite male voice murmured in Italian from somewhere close by. 'The security lights are not functioning. I had to come myself to see—'

'Take that damn torch off my face, Lorenzo,' Carlo commanded in a harsh, rasping growl.

They were thrown into instant darkness again. Francesca managed to unclip her fingers from where they clung to Carlo's neck. From feeling virtually incandescent with pleasure she was now slowly sinking into horror and shame.

She hated him! How could she have responded like that to a man she absolutely hated?

She tried to stiffen away from him but he was having none of it, his grip only tightening warningly as he held some kind of intelligent discussion with what she presumed was a security guard though she couldn't be sure of anything right now. Her feet felt strange, as if they didn't belong to her, her legs were tingling from ankles to hips. And the dragging sensation taking place between her thighs was desperate enough to tug a thick whimper from her aching throat.

Whatever Carlo thought that whimper meant, he reacted to it with another black curse and suddenly she was being thrust beneath the power of one arm and forced to walk.

'Let me go,' she choked out. Being this close to him was beginning to take on the properties of a nightmare—the whole evening was!

'Not in the near future, *cara*,' he responded with dry, grim sarcasm that was so thick with sexual reference that she stumbled.

He kept her upright. He kept her moving over uneven cobblestones. He kept her wrapped so closely to him that she had difficulty trying to take in her surroundings though she did manage to note that they were walking across an enclosed courtyard that made her footsteps echo off the surrounding walls. She could also hear the soft sound of a fountain somewhere, saw dark blue paintwork framing long, narrow windows set into burnt-sienna-painted walls.

Then they were stopping in front of a door. Muscles flexed as he leant forward to grasp the handle, the grasp of his long fingers sliding upwards a small inch that was all it required to let her right breast know they were there. She sucked in a sharp gasp as a fresh wave of heat poured in that direction. If it hadn't been for the denim jacket helping to conceal what was happening to her she would have folded with embarrassment when she felt the nipple grow excruciatingly tight.

The door swung open with a twist of the handle, and she was being propelled through it into a fully lit long, wide hallway with faded blue walls and gold-leaf plasterwork. He didn't so much as pause as he began hustling her over a stunning blue mosaic floor towards the other end of the hall. They passed by a pair of staircases that sped off at right angles, one on either side of them, passed beautiful pieces of furniture that were in themselves priceless works of art. Everything she set her dizzy eyes on was stunningly tasteful and elegant, nothing bore so much as a vague resemblance to the Batistes' white villa with its overt grandeur and style.

Another door was flung open and once again she was being ushered firmly through it into a square-shaped room with more gold-leaf plasterwork, chalk-pale terracotta walls and yet another mosaic floor made up of brown and black marble inlaid with gold.

At last he let her go and she swayed a little as she looked for balance, then instantly spun round as the door was slotted into its frame. Eyes wide, control shot, unsure whether she should be terrified or just plain angry after that shocking kiss and the way he'd hustled her in here, 'W-what is this place?' she demanded. 'Why have you brought me here?'

His smile had a sinister cut to it. The way he folded his arms across his impressive chest, crossed his elegant black shoes at his ankles then leant those broad shoulders back against the door and even the glitter behind his narrowed eyes were displays of arrogant provocation that brought every nerve-end she had left ringing on full alert.

'Welcome, to the Palazzo del Carlucci,' he murmured smoothly. 'Home to my family for the last four centuries and now, *mi amore*, the venue for your complete ravishment—in the honourable name of *revenge*, of course.'

As a calculated heart-stopper he had certainly hit the perfect note, Carlo saw as he watched all colour drain from her face. His sarcastic tone had slid right by her and he was angry enough not to care.

No, he was more than angry—he was bloody furious! He'd put his reputation on the line for her tonight. He'd watched over her, been there to catch her when she'd fallen, found her time and the privacy to come to terms with the reality of what Batiste was really like. He'd protected, supported—smiled in the face of a hundred scandalised stares while he got her out of that situation as fast as he could. And what did she do?

She took the word of a lying tramp like her flatmate and turned him into the enemy!

'Lay a hand on me and I'll claw your eyes out,' she responded shakily to his silk-honed threat.

He sent her a smile that mocked and derided. 'Since we both know that my laying *both* hands on you is more likely to make you purr than claw, it was a rather wasted threat, don't you think?'

It was like feeding candy to a baby, he noted. She grabbed every word and swallowed it whole. In some dark corner of his anger he enjoyed watching her squirm in growing alarm. He even shifted his stance as if to come after her, just to see how she would react.

She took a step back. 'Stay right where you are!' she jerked out sharply and put out a hand to ward him off.

Some chance, he thought. The ravishment was becoming more appetising by the second. And that kiss-softened quivering mouth was just begging to be ravished again—and again. If her beautiful eyes went any darker they would be the same colour as his own eyes, which made him very curious as to how dark they were going to go in the throes of some very intense passion.

'I will be no one else's victim—especially not yours!'

'Why not mine? When you don't think twice about playing the willing victim for anyone who wants to beat you up with their lies?'

'Whose lies are you referring to?' She threw a puzzled frown at him. It hit him low in his loins like a kick. He'd never known a simple dusky frown could be so damn sexy, it sent his shoulders shifting tensely inside his dinner jacket.

'Are you saying that Nicola Mauraux *isn't* your stepsister?'

'No,' he sighed. 'I am not saying that.'

'Then what are you saying? Do you think tonight has been a ball of laughter for me, *signor*? Do you think I *want* to be standing here listening to you play stupid word-games just for the fun of it?'

He went to answer but wasn't given the chance to. 'I am not the one at fault for whatever Angelo did to your stepsister,' she told him in trembling self-defence. 'As far as I knew they'd finished their relationship when Nicola returned to her studies in Paris!' she cried. 'I do not steal other women's men from them. And I will not take the blame because your stepsister was hurt! If you want your revenge look to Angelo—and show a little class by moving away from that door so that I can leave!'

Well, well, Carlo thought curiously, narrowing his eyes on her stiff if trembling stance, and had to acknowledge that his tables had just been turned. It came as a surprise because he hadn't thought she had it in her to take him on with quite so much ego-shredding venom.

Show a little class, he repeated musingly to himself, and almost smiled at the hit that cutting remark had landed on his pride.

'And here I was, waiting for you to apologise to me for daring to believe the word of some vamped-up little tramp in really deep trouble, who thought she would stick a few knives in by telling you that I was capable of using you for the purposes of revenge!'

His voice had risen in anger; now she was staring at him through huge shocked eyes. 'I…' she began.

'From there I thought we would continue where we left off in the courtyard,' he continued ruthlessly without letting her speak. 'With some really deep, passionate sex—preferably in my very big, comfortable bed, where we would work to help clear away your quite understandable blues.'

Her chin shot up at the very deliberate way he had just casually dismissed the devastation she had to be suffering.

'*After* the sex we could then discuss Nicola and how the whole Carlucci clan is in your debt for luring Batiste into believing that the Gianni fortune would be more accessible than hers would be.'

At last she was beginning to realise that this conversation had another edge to it. He could see a slow dawning colouring her eyes.

'However,' he went on, 'if you prefer to leave then by all means do so.' He even straightened from the door to give her safe passage. 'There is a phone in the hall and a pad lying next to it with the number of a very good taxi service. If I were you I would get the driver to recommend a hotel for the night and avoid going back to your apartment—just in case you walk in on your best friend and your ex-fiancé indulging their lusts on the sitting-room carpet.'

Having watched her blanch at his final cut-throat comment, he strode across the room, arrogantly assured that he had recovered his ego—at the expense of hers.

Did that knowledge sit well on him? No, it didn't, he admitted with a grimace. But one of them had to climb off their high horse and, since he had no intention of doing it, it had to be Francesca.

He was a full-blooded Carlucci after all. She was only half a Gianni.

And anyway, he was still angry despite his smooth, careless speech. There were a million things he could have been doing out there if he hadn't been devoting his full and undivided attention to Francesca Bernard and her Cinderella plight!

Cinderella, he scathed as he approached the antique French armoire almost dominating one wall. Well, if that made him her Prince Charming then he wasn't doing a very good job of it, he conceded as he glared at the armoire his stepmother had brought with her from Paris when she married his father.

As he opened the doors he smelled the age of the solid old wood. Inside had been converted into a comprehensive drinks cabinet, which had always seemed a desecration to him but—he offered another grimace. Nanette had been proud of it and in the end that was all that mattered. This single piece of furniture had been her one and only heirloom and she'd loved to see it sitting here in this great house that groaned beneath centuries of Carlucci statements to wealth and good taste. What else she brought into this house had always been far more valuable.

It was called love and happiness. And for those gifts alone the armoire would remain exactly where it stood for as long as he held power of decision over the house.

Reaching for the bottle of cognac and a deep-bowled glass, he was aware that Francesca still hadn't made that move towards the door. Placing the bowl of the glass in his palm to warm it while he uncapped the bottle of cognac, he dared a sideways glance at her.

She looked like a pale and bewildered ghost, he observed. Her eyes were too wide and rimmed by the stinging threat of tears that placed a fine quiver on her mouth. She was trying to control it, trying her best to maintain some pride and dignity. But she wasn't standing where he was standing and seeing what he was seeing. She looked vulnerable, exhausted, so damn shattered he was amazed she was still in one piece.

Her skin looked so strained it was waxen. And her hair was trying its best to escape again, the beaded comb barely clinging to the twisted silken knot.

But not for long, he promised himself as he turned away again. He was going to help the hair out in a minute. He was going to remove the silly comb and let the whole tawny mass tumble free. And he was going to heat that waxen flesh until it melted. He was going to remove that silly denim jacket then that silly dress with its romantic layers of chiffon that did nothing for her and yelled 'bought to please Angelo Batiste!'.

Anger growled like a snarling dog inside him; his lips bit together to stop the sound from coming out.

He was going to strip her down to her wonderful skin and bin the whole bloody outfit. Then he was going to begin the task of rebuilding her from the inside out. He was going to turn her into what he perceived she would be if she hadn't had her self-confidence beaten to a pulp by inadequate selfish swines like Bruno Gianni and Batiste.

But for now he was going to have to continue to play it tough here, because she also looked like a trapped bird trying to sum up the courage to make a bolt for escape. If she did then he was going to have to stop her—and cornered, trapped birds had a nasty habit of flying at your face.

He poured a generous splash of cognac into the glass then swirled it around while deftly recapping the bottle with his free hand. By the time he turned back to her he was relieved to find that she'd moved at last and was no longer staring vacantly into space but was looking up at the gilt-framed portrait hanging above the huge stone fireplace, in which his father stood with his arms linked around the slender frame of the beautiful dark-haired Nanette. Nanette was looking up, his father was gazing down, and only a blind idiot would miss the wealth of love and affection that poured from every brushstroke.

'You look like him,' she said.

'Mm,' he acknowledged with a small wry smile. 'Nanette Mauraux was my father's second wife,' he explained as he walked towards her. 'My mother died when I was—quite young.'

He offered her the glass. Francesca shook her head, her attention still fixed on the portrait. 'That could be Nicola standing with him,' she said.

'Does Nanette look so young?' Turning to view the portrait for himself, 'Yes, she does,' he answered his own question. 'My father managed to shock all of Rome when he went to Paris on a business trip and came back with a child bride clinging to his arm...'

He took a sip of the brandy, remembering. Then offered a soft laugh. 'He was fifty-four and she was twenty-three. Nicola was a tiny replica of her *mama* and I was a brooding, dark, resentful youth of nineteen who was appalled to be presented with a stepmother I would probably have made a play for if I'd met her first.'

'Did you?' she looked at him. 'Make a play for her, I mean.'

It took him a few seconds to understand why she dared think such a thing of him. Then, 'Ah,' he smiled. 'I forgot—I have no scruples.'

It was the wrong thing to say. He knew it the moment the comment left his sardonic mouth. She stared at him for a second—then on a small choke she turned and ran.

On a thick black curse he went after her, having to pause to divert to the armoire to lose the brandy glass before continuing on. She'd already thrown the door open and was disappearing into the hall. He uttered another terse curse in Italian. His trapped bird had flown but in her eagerness to get away from him she'd turned the wrong way.

CHAPTER SEVEN

FRANCESCA knew what she'd done two flying steps along the hallway but there was no way she was turning around and risking passing that door just as he came out of it.

She'd had enough. She just couldn't take any more of his cruel sarcasm and anyway, she'd already spied a pair of doors standing shut ahead of her so she just kept going, not caring where those doors led to as long as she managed to put a distance between herself and the hateful Carlo Carlucci before she finally gave in and fell apart.

What she didn't expect was to drag open those two doors and take two more flying steps, only to come to a perfect standstill, held breathless, feeling as if she'd stepped out of that door and straight into a completely different world.

Lake Alba was floating right in front of her, its smooth surface wearing a moonlit glaze like a sheet of frosted white silk. She had never seen anything quite like it. She forgot she was supposed to be running away from Carlo's taunting as she stared through a stone archway supported by twin slender pillars that framed the lake like a painting, its base trimmed by a low stone latticework balustrade that seemed to form an edge to the end of the world.

It was the most magical scene she had ever encountered; nothing had prepared her for it on the swift journey here through the winding lanes. Villa Batiste claimed a view of the lake but nothing to compare with this one. They were so close—yet not very close at all. It was a strange very disorientating sensation to stand here and feel as if you could reach out and touch those silver silk waters yet be aware at the same time that acres of layered garden lay in between.

Her feet took her across the wide stone terrace, drawing her like a magnet to stand beneath the arch. She was so enchanted she didn't notice that she was shivering so badly that her arms had wrapped around her in an instinctive attempt to ward off the cold.

'The lake changes with every hour,' a deep voice murmured levelly. 'She will pull on her shimmering silver cloak in the early morning, a burnished gold one in the late afternoon. In the middle of the day she wears a sensational azure-blue cloak and invites you to come and play...'

'So you framed it,' she said softly.

'One of my ancestors was inspired by that particular vision,' he replied in a lazy tone that reluctantly refused to take the praise. Then she heard the slow, even pace of his steps bringing him closer as he continued, 'We are in fact standing in a colonnade of arches, each one carefully placed to form the same framework of the lake whichever door or window you happen to step through in this wing.'

A fleeting glance sideways confirmed that she was indeed standing in the middle of a line of arches that attached to the house by long, gracefully arching ribs on which the moonlight placed more frosted silk.

'It's beautiful—the whole thing.' She turned her head frontward again as he came to a halt directly behind her.

'*Gratzi,*' he replied at the same time as his jacket settled across her shoulders and was held there by a pair of hands that curled around her slender upper arms. She shivered compulsively as her chilled flesh grabbed at the warmth the jacket offered. 'No, *cara*, don't prickle.' He'd misread the shiver. 'I am not about to renew hostilities.'

Then what does come next—the ravishment? she heard herself thinking. And this time the shiver was a prickle.

'I'm sorry if I hurt your stepsister,' she felt compelled to say.

'You didn't—*he* did.' His grip on her arms altered fractionally so he could turn her round to face him. She found herself staring at the bright white front to his shirt. 'All I could do was support her through her heartache. While I was doing that I became curious as to who this new woman in his life was, who could make him dare to hurt one of mine.'

'So whose wounded pride were you out to salve when you went looking for a way to punish him—your stepsister's or your own?'

This time it was the cleft in his chin that captured her attention when it flexed with his brief, dry smile. 'Try—both,' he said and moved his fingers, causing her breathing to feather as he ran them lightly beneath the silk lapel to his jacket, lifting the fabric so it hugged her chilly nape. 'And you have a novel way of making subtle stabs at a man's ego, *cara*,' he said softly. 'But I advise you to drop such tactics with me. You see, I *like* my arrogance. It gives me leave to do anything I want to do even when I know the moment is not appropriate.'

And that was the point when alarm bells began to ring. She managed only to lift wary eyes to his face and note the warning gleam of what was to come before he gave a firm tug on his jacket collar and she was arriving with a breathless gasp against his chest. She felt the heat of him, his sheer physical power, wanted to push away but only found herself raising her chin.

Their eyes connected, almost black consuming anxious hazel with promises that robbed her of the ability to breathe.

'No,' she said, 'don't…'

And to her hopeless confusion he didn't do anything but hold her trapped between his body and his jacket and a tense, tingling limbo world between heaven and hell. She couldn't even tell which the hell belonged to—the kiss or no kiss.

'Sure?' he said softly.

She nodded, lips parted and trembling like wicked liars. He was too much—of everything. He overwhelmed in every way there was. 'I'm out of my depth with you,' she heard herself whisper and though she wished the words back the moment she'd said them she knew they were telling the utter truth.

His response was one of those sardonic tilts to his mouth. 'I am wading in pretty deep myself, *cara*,' he responded huskily. 'So don't let yourself think that those pale cheeks and that frightened expression is going to save you. We *will* come together sooner or later.'

Then he dropped his head, capturing her lips in a single swift, hard kiss that fused them together with its heat. 'Again and again and again…' he murmured with sensual promise as he lifted his mouth away.

Why? Because she'd responded. He knew it. She knew it. She'd even been the one to taste him with the moist, tingling tip of her tongue and placed that gloss on his lips she could see. And the worst of it was she wanted to do it again. She wanted to curl a hand around his nape and bring that mouth back to her. She wanted to…

His chest heaved on a tense intake of air, dark eyes glittering now as he took in the helpless expression colouring her eyes. 'Come on,' he said with a low gruffness. 'It's too damn cold out here for this…'

This being that she had just committed herself. *This* being that she couldn't even pretend to herself that she didn't want him. Letting go of his jacket lapels, Carlo placed an arm round her shoulders and turned them back to the house.

The door closed behind them; centuries-old blue mosaic caught the tap of her delicate heels. She wanted to say something—anything to break the grim, sexual resolve she could feel pulsing in him. But there wasn't a single word that came to mind that could halt what was now in flow.

He led her up the left-hand staircase, his arm still keeping her close to his side. They emerged from the stairs into another long corridor flanked by long, narrow windows she saw looked out on the courtyard below. He paused at a door, pushed it open and took her through it. She found herself standing in a bedroom like no other bedroom she had ever been in.

The floor was an ocean of polished dark wood that led her eyes to the huge stone fireplace opposite where logs blazed in a black iron grate. The flames flickered across the floor, the dark terracotta-painted walls and crawled like fingers up the swathes of dark red silk festooning a huge canopied four-poster bed.

The bed dominated the room above everything. It dominated her—grabbed her eyes and fixed the senses exactly where it intended to fix them. If she'd ever wondered what a room designed to pull all the right sensual strings looked like then this would have been it. She even captured an image of herself lying there naked like a wanton on the red silk coverlet. She saw him with his dark golden flesh touched by the flames as he lay at her side.

The vision alone was enough to put her right back into a panic. She turned on him. 'I don't...'

Want this, she had been going to say but the words became lost in the feel of his light touch as he plucked the comb from her hair. The heavy twist quivered as it uncoiled its way to her shoulders. He stood observing the effect through dark, unfathomable eyes for a long moment then abruptly turned away.

'I'll go and get your case,' he said. 'Relax, take a look around, I won't be more than a few minutes...'

Threat or reassurance? Francesca wondered as she watched him disappear. Then she shivered and turned back to her new surroundings. Her gaze was instantly drawn to the four-poster bed, where those unnerving images still played with her head.

Shame on you, she tried telling herself and tugged her eyes away then moved restlessly across the room towards a long window draped with more red silk. The window showed her a different view of the lake. Its surface wasn't quite as frosted now, the moon having already continued on its way.

What am I doing here? she asked herself.

An answering tug on certain sensitive folds of flesh made her draw in air on a sharp catch of breath.

'Oh,' she choked, and dropped down onto the polished wood window seat, lost her shoes then pulled her knees up to her chin and dragged Carlo's jacket tightly around her before she lowered her face to her knees.

To hide.

From what she was.

From what she was beginning to turn into.

A betrayed woman with the terrible—terrible desire for another man.

She shuddered, despising herself for feeling like this. Still hurting in so many ways and clearly so darn desperate to prove she was worthy of the title ''woman'' that she was sitting here having to squeeze her thighs together in an attempt to cut off these tight little tugs that were so much a pleasure as well as a sin.

Sin.

She picked out the word and looked at it. What sin? Whose sin? Where was the sin in wanting to make love?

Her mother's sin. Her mother's cold assessment of what sexual desire could do to you. It could turn you into a slave to your own body cravings and the faceless property of the man who took those cravings and used them to slake his own.

Why him though? If she had to turn into this sex-needy person, why did it have to be for Carlo Carlucci of all men? Why couldn't it have been Angelo? Maybe their relationship could have stood a better chance if she'd been more forthcoming on the physical side. Maybe he would not have gone looking elsewhere and the rest of this dreadful night would only exist in some far-off nightmare and she would be in bed by now—with Angelo—sublimely content in her blindness to what his true character really was like.

Is that what she wanted? she then asked herself. To be lied to so long as she didn't have to face the miserable truth?

She heard his step in the half-open doorway, felt him pause when he saw the way she was sitting here. Tears burned. Her heart burned. That place between her thighs grew hot on a fresh flurry of excitement because she wanted him.

She wanted him.

Not Angelo. She had never wanted Angelo. Not like this, she groaned silently. Blind didn't begin to excuse the way she had been behaving around Angelo in the name of that thing called love.

'I've brought your case.'

She nodded. Love was nothing but an illusion anyway, she thought as she listened to his footsteps taking him across to the bed. Love was nothing but a word invented for women to use to justify giving in to this hot sexual ache and for men to use to give them the right to tap into that ache.

Her head twisted at the sound of his footsteps. Heat gathered in her cheeks this time, her eyes glued to him as she followed his approach. Tall, dark, breathtakingly alluring to her newly awoken senses, they drank in the width of broad shoulders and long, lean torso covered in white shirting that did nothing to hide the promise of what she envisioned lurked beneath. The butterfly collar of the shirt had been unfastened and the bow-tie now rested in two loose black strips against the shirt.

He looked relaxed; he even offered her one of his tilted smiles as he bent to take hold of her hands to break the clasp they held on her knees.

'Come on,' he said quietly. 'You've had enough. It's time to go to bed.'

He pulled and she uncoiled to land on her feet in front

of him. Removing the jacket from her shoulders, he tossed it onto the window seat then turned his attention to the line of bronze studs holding her denim jacket in place.

The word bed made her throw a hooded glance at him, the way he was casually removing her clothes tingled her spine—and he smiled again at those two very revealing actions. 'It's OK. The ravishment of Francesca Bernard has been put on hold for the time being,' he assured her lazily.

'Shame,' she heard herself say—then caught her top lip between her teeth and wished the floor would open up and swallow her when he went perfectly still. She attempted a weak smile. 'Joke,' she said.

He went back to what he'd been doing but his mouth had a grim look of disapproval about it now.

Disapproval? she repeated inwardly and uttered a thick laugh. The person who disapproved of her around here was herself!

'Why the laugh?'

'Don't ask,' she advised a little wildly. Because the cool backs of his fingers were brushing against her breasts and making them tingle and if anyone wanted the ravishment of Francesca Bernard then it was Francesca Bernard!

Denim parted and was eased from her shoulders. She shivered as the fabric trailed down her arms, exposing her flesh to the cooler air seeping in through the window behind. The jacket landed on the window seat on top of his jacket then, with the touch of a master at undressing women, he slid his hand to the side of her ribcage to locate unerringly the concealed zip that held the dress in place.

'I can do the rest myself,' she told him stiffly.

'Why rob me of the pleasure?' he mocked—silkily—bringing her eyes up to clash with his.

He knew what she was thinking, what was happening to her, what she *wanted* to happen. And the look in his eyes was daring her to just come out and say it.

Ask! that look challenged.

She looked away again—moved away. His hand pulled her back again. She came into full contact with his full length. Her senses took flight on a mad ride of desire, she shivered and shook and sparked up like a firework. Her breathing fractured, her breasts heaved a gasp. His free hand lifted to burrow beneath her hair and his fingers clenched, imprisoning a thick swathe of her hair to use it to pull her head back.

She couldn't tell if his eyes were angry or on fire with desire. His mouth still looked hard, his cheekbones taut. 'What do you want from me, Francesca?' he demanded on a low, dark growl.

The impact of the question quivered its way right down to her toes because she knew exactly what she wanted from him. She wanted him to give her sensual escape. She wanted to lose herself in him and become that other person she had just seen lying in naked abandon on that bed.

And she wanted to emerge the other end of this dreadful night a completely different woman, a sexually liberated woman who could state with confidence—to hell with you, Angelo, I know what I am now and you will never know what you missed out on!

'I want everything,' she whispered.

There, she'd said it. She didn't even regret saying it, she told herself defiantly as his eyes narrowed on her flushed face. Now it was up to him whether he took what she was offering or rejected it.

He didn't reject it. He took with a swift, dark passion that blew her apart. Her mouth was taken, its inner recesses invaded by the urgent probe of his tongue. She joined in this electric-charged fire dance with an eagerness that could have suggested she always kissed like this, when the opposite was the truth. It didn't matter, she was with that kiss all the way—totally committed to it, totally committed to greedily learning anything he could teach her that would fuel the fires of what was happening to her. The side zip to her dress gave suddenly, the tight bodice springing free so the dress fell without stopping to the floor, leaving him free to explore new areas of exposed flesh with one hand while the other maintained its fierce grip on her hair to keep her face turned up to the kiss.

It was a very potent display of masculine domination—she knew that even as she surrendered to it. He stroked her waist, her back, her shoulders, he ran his fingers beneath the thin back strap to her flimsy strapless bra—testing its tension before trailing those fingers down the indent of her spine to the edge of her very brief high-leg panties to test their tension as his hand slid beneath.

She'd never felt a man's hand against the smooth, rounded flesh of her bottom before. She'd never been touched like this at all. It felt strange but so exquisitely sensual she wriggled. He gripped and lifted her into contact with what was happening to him.

The movement tangled her feet in silk organza. On a curse he released her mouth so he could glance down. She was panting and clinging to his neck, too delirious to notice the way his eyes paused to linger blackly on the rise and fall of her breasts cupped in blood-red silk that was losing the battle to keep the tight thrust of her nipples covered. On a soft growl he clamped an arm around her waist and lifted her off the floor to swing her free of the dress—then he held her there, trapped against him, and closed his mouth around one of her breasts. The hot lick of his tongue sliced an arcing sense of tight pleasure across the tight nipple. She gasped out a thick breath, shaken and shuddering, her fingers clutching at his shoulders, and he tugged on her hair again to arch her backwards to bring the other breast pointing invitingly upwards for the delivery of the same experience.

Then they were kissing again, and he was turning with her still clamped against him as he walked towards the bed. That was not all he did on that short journey. With the strength of his hands he lifted her higher, somehow guiding her legs around his hips. The pulsing centre of all this madness made contact with the bulging hardness of his penis and her hips lurched in shock then writhed as a new pulsing wave of pleasure caught fire.

As he let her slide slowly down his length her bra sprang free. Two full, rounded breasts fell out of their bra cups, and she looked down to watch with a kind of fascination as their stinging tips settled against his shirt front.

He muttered something. She looked up into blazing black eyes and an oddly pale complexion. 'Are you sure you want this?'

She gave him his answer by capturing his mouth with a reckless hunger. When he broke away from her she felt bereft.

Then not so bereft when he began stripping his clothes off, watching her as she stood watching him with a strange mix of fascination and shyness flickering across her expressive face. His shirt was peeled off and tossed away to reveal broad shoulders that gleamed like satin in the fire glow, and a taut, bronzed torso matted with dark hair. His shoes were heeled off and kicked to one side then his fingers went to deal with the fastener and zip to his trousers—and that was the moment when she had to look away.

Her eyes went straight to the bed with its red silk coverlet and its flame-licking promise of what was to come. She dragged in a breath, her senses fluttering on the beginnings of uncertainty, but that was all the time she was given to doubt this because his hand snaked out to cup her chin and he was making her look back at him. He was naked—naked, and so utterly beautiful it was no wonder he could strip with such ease.

His mouth closed over hers again, not fierce but gentle and soft. His other arm coiled around her waist and slowly drew her in. Nothing had prepared her for what it felt like to be held against a naked man. The warmth of him, the intoxicating differences between smooth and rough textures, the heady power of his scent, the unyielding strength in him, the uncompromising evidence of his manhood pressing against her abdomen and the way he moved against her leaving her in no doubt as to how much he wanted this. She released a shaken little breath in response to that knowledge and he stole it from her with a flick from his tongue.

He kissed the heat burning in her cheeks, her shyly lowered eyelids—he drew her that bit closer to him then pressed moist kisses to her shoulder, her neck, then her mouth again while she stood absorbing each tiny pleasure without being aware of how still she was.

'If you've changed your mind and want to stop, this is the moment to say so,' he said gently.

She frowned, not understanding why he kept asking that question. 'I don't want to stop.'

'Then why are your hands clenched into fists at your sides?'

They were…?

They were, she realised as she tried to move her fingers, only to find they'd locked in two tension fists.

'I will not make love to a sacrifice, *cara*. If you're standing here like this, hoping to God I will wipe Batiste's loving into oblivion, then you are wasting your time because neither do I play substitute for another man.'

The fact that she'd believed he'd understood, from what he'd overheard Angelo say to Sonya, that she had never been with Angelo like this made her frown as she stared fixedly at the crisp dark coils of hair on his chest. Now she knew he must have misunderstood, there was no way she was going to expose just how little Angelo had wanted her, by telling him the truth.

'I w-wasn't thinking anything of the kind,' seemed a fair compromise.

'Then why the tension?'

Her lips quivered; she tugged in a breath. 'Y-you,' she

told him shakily. 'You're so…' She ran the nervous tip of her tongue around her lips.

If she'd conjured up the excuse just to flatter him she could not have found a better one. He laughed, low and throatily, then moved against her in a way that left her in no doubt as to how her little confession was affecting him.

Then he wasn't laughing, he was dipping his dark head, and suddenly the whole thing became intense again. The deep, drugging kisses, the caressing sweep of his hands. The gentle, pulsing movement of his hips that slowly—slowly began to draw answering movements from her. When he hooked an arm around her waist and used it so he could feed her onto the bed he did it with such smooth control that she wasn't even aware of what was happening until she felt cool cotton beneath her and opened her eyes to stare in surprise.

The red coverlet had been tossed aside without her noticing, the rest of the covers folded back. And Carlo's lean, dark golden length was caught by the fire again as he stretched out beside her, then came to lean above her, his dark eyes languid now, sensually engrossed as he sent a hand stroking the length of her body, then began touching light, soft, tantalising kisses in a delicate line along her mouth then across her cheek to her temple and down along her jaw line before returning to her mouth again. Her tongue made its first shy stab between his teeth, her fingers curling into his hair in an effort to hold him still. He let her keep him, he let her trace the moist inner recesses of his mouth and play with the kiss as she'd never played before.

His hand came to cup her breast, the pad of his thumb gently circling the dusky aureole in a slow, breathtaking caress. His mouth moved on again, planting soft kisses along her throat and across the pale slopes of her breast before it closed a tight pink rosebud nipple inside a warm, moist, gently sucking mouth. Sensation became a low deep throbbing ache that spread its sensual fingers to every part of her, quickening her pulses and dragging on her breath. He gave the other breast the same slow, sensual pleasure, his hand gently kneading in tune with his lips until she groaned in sweet agony to it all.

As if the little sound was a sign that stirred his blood his mouth suddenly was back on hers again, taking with driving, hungry passion at the same time his hand trailed a caressing passage down her ribcage to the flat of her stomach before moving on, smooth fingertips slipping beneath the flimsy triangle of raspberry silk and spearing through the dusky mound of curls on a seeking quest.

Shock turned her limbs to liquid, her shaken choke broke their kiss. She opened her eyes and found herself staring directly into naked desire burning molten in the fire glow as his fingers discovered the heart of her. Alien though it was, she squirmed on a wave of white-hot pleasure, her heart pounding at a thundering pace, her fingers clawing at his shoulders as he dipped, withdrew, caressed then dipped again with the smooth, sure touch of a man who knew exactly how to make a woman feel like this. Wild, she felt wild, caught in a slipstream of scintillating pleasure that flowed through her blood. She arched against him, quivering, her breathing reduced to tight, aching little gasps. He captured one of her breasts and she leapt, she shuddered, she sank beneath the rolling surface of shattering sensation and fought him like a mad woman but clung to him desperately at the same time.

And he was hot, his breathing thick and tense, each lithe movement of his body such a sensual act she didn't know which part of him was going to inflame her next. He murmured something in Italian but she was way beyond being able to translate. The sensual, soothing sound of his voice impinged, though; the gentle brush of his hand across her cheek.

She opened her eyes to find he was frowning—at her naive lack of control no doubt. 'I'm not...' used to this, she was about to confess, but he hushed her into silence with the warm crush of his mouth.

Then she was losing herself again in a world made up of pure feeling. He trailed kisses across her breasts, catching each distended nipple and rolling it with his tongue. He kissed her all over. He explored her like a master and she responded with a writhing and whimpering then groaning in protest when his trailing mouth moved to the singing sensitivity of her groin. He kissed her hip, her waist and finally her breasts again, then recaptured her mouth at the same time as he reached for one of her hands and gently curled it around his sex.

It was a shock, a mind-rocking shock to feel the smooth, thick length of a man's sexual power then experience its surge of pleasure to her touch. As he moved she found herself curling towards him with an instinctive need to be closer than close. Her mouth found his throat and fastened there, her breasts pressed against his chest. Her untutored hand clasped him as he moved with small, slow, delicate thrusts. She could feel his heart pounding and the tautness grow in his body as the sensual fever grew. And through it all his fingers sustained their gentle, knowing caresses with an expertise that sank her deeper and deeper into a place she had never been before.

'Carlo…' she said on a breathless whimper but didn't know why she needed to say his name like that.

He responded with a surge of energy that sent her hand fluttering away from him in shocked surprise. He bit out something—a muttered curse, then the last scrap of silk was being taken away, trailing down pale, slender thighs that received the sharp, stinging touch of his kisses, kisses that began to work their way towards the one place they hadn't tasted yet.

'No,' she said. 'No.'

He didn't hear her. The first touch of his tongue lost her the will to protest. She groaned, she gasped, she shook and quivered. She clawed at his hair in a desperate effort to pull him away, then she wasn't pulling, she was stretching each wire-tight muscle as a new tension began to sing in her blood.

Hot, she felt hot. She felt bathed in static, the careful thrust of his fingers and the moist caress of his tongue dragging her on a silent scream towards a pinnacle she knew about but had never experienced.

'Oh, Carlo,' she whispered.

He moved over her in a single lithe, swift stretch of his body, claimed her mouth with a deep, hot, dark eroticism and at the same time made that first deep, penetrating thrust, seeking passage with a power that drove him through the fine barrier and locked her muscles on a pinprick cry of pain.

Stillness followed, a terrible silence. Her eyes flew open to stare up at him, he stared down, eyes turned black with shock. Between them the silken shaft of his penetration pulsated against the shock-contracted walls of her sheath and she waited, breath held, not sure if there was more pain to come or even if he was so appalled by his discovery that he was going to withdraw.

He didn't withdraw. He hissed out her name like a curse, flexed his tight buttocks then drove that bit deeper. Pain lost out to a scorching trail of agonising pleasure. His mouth trapped her aching gasps and her fingernails dug deep crescents into his chest. With each powerful, fiery thrust he possessed her that bit more, filled her, drove her towards a blank wall that she knew was going to burst apart and send her crashing into a devastating place. She was sobbing in fear of it yet desperate to get there. As if he understood, Carlo wrapped both arms beneath her and pressed his cheek to hers.

'Let go,' he said. That was all—let go—and she did, held tightly against him with his heated breath in her hair and his heartbeat pounding against her breasts, her sobs changing to gasps as she broke through the restraints holding her trapped to explode into a maelstrom of blistering ecstasy that jerked at her body and ripped at her breath and made Carlo lock her more tightly to him as he absorbed each quivering shockwave that dragged him shuddering into the same frenzied place.

She didn't think she was going to survive it. She really believed she was going to die. She closed her eyes and tried to decide whether that had been the most frightening experience of her life or the most beautiful. Nothing—nothing she'd ever heard or seen about the act of love with its culminate orgasm had prepared her for the devastating reality of it.

In a state of near complete shutdown, she actually had to tell herself to breathe. Carlo was breathing; he was heaving in breaths like a man who'd just completed a mile-long sprint. His body was wet with perspiration, hers was the same, and the heat the two of them were generating as he continued to hold her clamped to him was enough to turn to steam.

And the aftershocks were still attacking his body, his possession still an aggressive entity she could feel, while she was so weak and limp she couldn't move a single thing. Eventually he recovered enough to relax his grip and allowed her to sink back into cool cotton. But even when he stayed heavy on top of her and began layering soft kisses on her face she could not find the energy to respond.

I'm not real any more, she thought hazily. I've left my body and I'm floating somewhere up there.

'You are wonderful,' Carlo's husky voice murmured. 'You are the most beautiful creature living on this earth.'

She tried a weak smile, but that was all she managed.

The brush of his lips feathered that smile. 'I am one lucky guy to be lying here with you now and you are one lucky woman to have me as your first lover...'

Ah, she mused sleepily, he wanted some feedback. He

wanted her to confirm what a great lover he was. 'You're
wonderful,' she returned lazily.

'Mm,' he said, and moved just enough to remind her that
the wonder of him wasn't over yet. 'So,' he said lightly,
'when are you going to marry me?'

CHAPTER EIGHT

MARRIAGE...? Francesca came alert as if someone had thrown a light switch. Her eyes shot open to stare into a smooth, dark, slightly mocking face.

'Since when did marriage come into this?' she tremored disbelievingly.

'Since the first time I set eyes on you.' He leant down to kiss her protruding bottom lip.

Heat seared a passage right down to her abdomen. To her shock she realised he still possessed her and with a stifled gasp she wriggled herself free and instantly discovered that when you detached yourself from an aroused man the sensations it caused were as life-grabbing as the sex!

'I'm not marrying you,' she declared in a husky, shivering voice she hoped he read as anger and not what it actually was. 'You must be joking.' Why would a man like him want to marry her? 'No way,' she added for good measure and wriggled the rest of herself free before he got different ideas about what happened next.

'You mean I am being jilted already? But this means I did not last as long as Batiste! I am stricken,' he announced. 'My ego is fatally wounded.'

'Not your heart, I notice,' Francesca muttered as she scrambled off the bed. 'And you can't jilt someone when there was never a relationship in the first place.'

'Ah, so you prefer to be romanced as you were by Batiste than overwhelmed by my unabated passion. You should have said, *cara*,' he drawled as she looked anxiously around for something to cover up her nakedness. 'I would have brought you champagne and flowers instead of simply my amazing prowess.'

125

She saw the red silk coverlet draping the corner of the bed and reached for it, trailing it from around a heavy wood bedpost. 'Is there no limit to your arrogance?'

'Not after what we just shared.'

He moved on the bed, stretching like a long, sleek, well-pampered and very satisfied cat. Francesca wrapped herself in exotic silk and hoped to goodness he hadn't seen the hectic flush that had mounted her skin.

'You were amazing,' he murmured as he relaxed again. 'To respond to me with such wonderful generosity and passion when it was your first time made two precious gifts you gave to me. I will cherish them always—*gratzi tanto amore…*'

'*Prego,*' she said, moving slender shoulders in response to the ripple of feeling that arrived with the husky intimacy in his voice. She had never been so aware of her own sexuality—never would have believed that she had it in her to respond the way that she had.

'It was special—take my word for it…'

'Is—is there a bathroom in here?' she quavered, sending her eyes on a hunted scan of the walls, looking for a door that would offer her some kind of escape.

'…Because my word is all you will ever have to go on,' he continued as if she hadn't spoken. 'I think I've told you before that I am very possessive of what belongs to me.'

'I do not belong to you!' she turned to flash at him then and just stared as the firelight struck a flame down the length of his body and licked the aggressive length of his penis.

She looked away—wildly as tiny muscles between her thighs began to pulse. This had to stop. It *had* to! What am I doing here? she asked herself, trembling and tingling and… 'I think I w-want to go h-home,' she heard herself stammer.

'Sorry, *cara*, but, like me, you are committed. *This* is your new home. Next week we will marry and make it official.'

'I'm in love with another man!' she threw at him in the

shrill voice of panic. 'Why would you want to marry me knowing that?'

'What has love got to do with it?' He thoroughly mocked the word. 'I want you here, in my bed. The fact that you have just shown how much you want to be in my bed makes your so-called love for another man pretty useless here, *cara*. So I advise you not to bother mentioning it again.'

'I do *not* want you!' she denied furiously, which was really stupid of her after what they'd just shared. 'Again...' she added as a weak tag-on.

Sardonic eyes studied the hectic flush in her face then slowly, lazily drifted all the way down her front. She trembled from tumbled hair to toenails. 'Those two tight little nipples pushing against the silk are talking to me,' he taunted softly.

Francesca looked down. 'Oh,' she gasped in horror when she saw what he was seeing and crossed her arms over her tingling breasts and turned to make a dash for the bedroom door, tripping over trailing silk in her haste to get away.

'Oh, no, you don't...'

He came off the bed like a striking cobra, moving so fast that she'd barely reached for the door handle when he'd closed his hands on her shoulders and spun her around.

'You will not run away this time, Francesca,' he said grimly. 'Your chance to escape from what is now set in stone is long gone.'

His eyes were glittering down at her and there was nothing languid about his grim stance now. He was all tense and cruel-looking—exciting as— 'I don't know what you're talking about,' she mumbled distractedly and she wished he would go and put on some clothes.

No chance. His grip tightened on her shoulders. 'I put my pride and my reputation on the line for you tonight in front of my business colleagues and my friends,' he explained.

'I didn't ask you to.'

'You didn't stop me either,' he countered. 'Do you honestly think that I went to that much trouble just for a hot night of sex with you?'

Francesca shrugged, lowering her eyes because that was more or less exactly what she'd thought.

His breath hissed out from between his teeth. 'This may come as a surprise to you, *cara*, but I don't need to work that hard to get a woman in my bed. They usually line up to wait their turn—and that is not my arrogance talking,' he said before she did. 'It is simply the truth. The fact that I rarely choose to avail myself of what is on offer is due to a healthy respect for myself and who I share my body with!'

He shared it with her—all of it with her.

'There was not a person there tonight that did not assume my motives were strictly honourable—or that plans for our marriage would be announced soon. The moment you stepped out of the Batistes' villa with me you made an agreement on those terms and you are not going to make me look a fool in front of all of Rome, by ducking out of it!'

'I did not agree to become your wife—or your lover for that matter!'

'You can also stop lying to yourself!' he rasped. 'You have been wanting me as your lover from the moment our eyes met at a set of traffic lights. I knew it. You refused to acknowledge it. Now, my sensational Francesca, you have no choice but to admit that we *both* are crazy with desire for each other!'

'That's not—'

His mouth came down, crushing the lie from her lips and sending a rush of feeling shooting down her quivered length. Her legs suddenly felt like electrified wire. She didn't know what she was doing; the kiss took her over so completely she even threw off the silk cover so she could wind her arms around his neck and press herself into the sense-savaging heat of his naked length. He accommodated her standing rock-solid on long bare feet and holding her against him while she arched and stretched and moved as she kissed him back in a turmoil of sensuous greed.

'Angelo had no idea what he passed on,' he muttered as he lifted his head. Glinting eyes shot a narrowed look into her dazed, desire-shot eyes. 'Or maybe he did,' he then added grimly. 'Maybe he knew you would be too hot for him to handle. Is that why he turned to your much more predictable flatmate, do you think?'

It was a cruel comment too far. Francesca responded by instinct, feeling as stunned as he was when her arm made a slicing arc through the air to land the flat of her palm against his face. She had never done anything like it in her entire life before. She didn't even know where it had come from. And now she was heaving and gasping and quivering for a different reason, because he was furious. It pulsed all around him like a physical thing. She stood with her spine pressing back against the door and her palm tingling accusingly while she awaited his response. The silence thundered—or was it her heartbeat? And while she waited, eyes wide, lips parted and trembling, she had to watch the marks of her fingers begin to slowly stand out on his lean cheek.

Then it came, and she let out a small cry as his hands arrived on her shoulders. With a jerk she found herself flattened against him again and this time his mouth came crashing down on hers with no wish to make the kiss anything but a punishment. She supposed she deserved it. In some small, floundering part of her head she knew she should not have hit him, but still this angry kiss that ground the inner tissue of her lips against her teeth was brutal by comparison.

Then she was released, thrust away so her spine made contact with the door again while he turned his back and stepped away. 'Thank your lucky stars that I am not the kind of man that slaps back,' he said harshly.

No, it would be beneath his dignity to slap a woman. He preferred to use a fierce ravaging as revenge. Lifting tentative fingers to her bruised lips, she found them hot and swollen. To her wary consternation he swung around to look at her. He lifted a hand. For a horrible moment she thought he was going to change his mind and slap her anyway.

'Please don't,' she whispered.

He released a tense sigh. The hand took hold of her hand, gently removing it from her lips so he could inspect the results for himself while she stared up at him through huge, helpless eyes and trembled and shook and felt her throat start to sting.

'I deserved the slap,' he said.

And as a final humiliation, she burst into tears. She had been fighting them off all evening, and now they swept through her on an unrestrained flood that made her give way so thoroughly she dropped into a puddle of flaming red silk, covered her face with her hands and sobbed for all she was worth.

Carlo felt as if he had been sliced open and gutted. He just had not expected it. Why had he not expected it? he demanded of himself as he stood in frozen stillness, watching her fall apart in front of him. She had taken so many blows tonight that it was inevitable that one of them had to be the final blow.

The fact that it was his ruthless blow that had caused her breakdown dragged out his conscience so he had to stare it full in the face. He felt his mouth work in a tense quiver. A thick lump arrived in his throat. On a self-condemning curse he bent to lift her back to her feet, bringing the red cover up with her and engulfing her in it before wrapping her against him.

'Francesca—*amore*, I'm sorry,' he murmured huskily. 'Don't.'

'I h-hate you,' she sobbed.

'*Sì*,' he agreed with a touch of unsteadiness. 'I am a monster. Shout at me. Slap my face. But don't weep; I'm not worth it.'

For some reason this low opinion of himself made her

weep all the harder. 'I don't know what's happening to me!' she cried against his throat.

'No.' He could understand that. The whole evening had run like a black comedy for her. If she hadn't had enough to deal with tonight with the betrayal of both her fiancé and her best friend, she'd had to deal with his anger, his vile-humoured mockery, his bloody single-minded seduction that robbed her of her innocence, and finally—his contempt.

What did that say about him?

He didn't want to hear the answer to that—he didn't think his ego could take it right now.

She was trembling and sobbing against him; the scent permeating from her body smelled of him. He went to utter yet another apology then pinned his lips together because he couldn't trust them to say the right thing. So he went for the practical gesture of contrition, bent to place an arm behind her knees and scooped her up in his arms.

The bed looked tempting but he bypassed it, carrying her into the bathroom, where he set her down on the bath stool then left her there to weep while he turned and with a touch to a hi-tech switch set water gushing into the spa bathtub that took up almost half the space in the room. Next he hooked up a towel and draped it around his hips—hiding, he mused with a grimace.

Francesca was still weeping softly into her exotic silk shroud, her hair a tumble of loose, dark golden spirals that covered her face. He went to squat down in front of her then silently handed her a cloth for her tears. Taking it required her to expose a delicate pale shoulder to set free an arm and a hand. Her slender fingers were trembling as she took the cloth from him and her muffled, 'Thank you,' twisted his heart.

She used the cloth to mop up her eyes. 'Sorry,' she said though he didn't know why she did.

'Don't apologise to me, Francesca,' he said soberly. 'I think the tears were well overdue.'

'You've tied m-me in knots.'

'*Sì*,' he accepted.

'You've pl-played me like a puppet on strings.'

'*Sì*,' he agreed again, but this time it came with a wry smile. 'Great strings though, *cara*,' he could not resist saying. 'Wonderfully passionate and responsive strings.'

She heaved in a shaky breath of air. 'Stop talking like that,' she said, and pressed the cloth to her eyes. 'H-have you no guilty conscience?'

'About making love with you? None at all.' Which was the truth.

'Well, you should.'

'Because I want you?' he said, watching the careful way she kept her face averted from him. 'Because I am willing to do anything to keep you here with me?'

'Which says what you want—n-not what I want.'

'And what do you want?' he questioned gently.

How was she supposed to answer that when the whole point was that she didn't know? Francesca thought painfully. She was so confused and fearful because she didn't feel in control of herself any more. Shocked too, because she'd discovered that she had the ability to turn into an absolute raving sex wanton and—more awful—loved feeling that way.

How was it possible that she could feel anything like this when she was supposed to be breaking her heart over another man?

Oh, God, she groaned silently, feeling the light touch of his hand brush her tumbled hair from her damp cheek, and made the big mistake of lifting her face to look at him.

It was like walking head-on into the answer to everything.

Him. Signor Carlo Carlucci—her lover. The rush of feeling the title evoked robbed her of the ability to breathe. His hair was tousled and his cheek still wore the remnants of her fingers against it. The anger had gone from his eyes but not the passion; that still lingered in the low burn she could just see glimmering behind the dark.

His shoulders were bare, as was his long torso, and the rest of him was hidden by a towel that was doing so little to stop a rush of awareness from attacking her because of the way he was squatting with his thighs spread, parting the towel enough for her to be aware of what was lurking there.

'Don't start weeping again,' he said as he watched her eyes begin to fill. 'Tears will gain you no sympathy from me because I have discovered I like them.' He even reached out to brush a teardrop from the corner of her eye as it spilled onto her cheek. 'They may make you feel vulnerable and weak but they make me feel very protective and tough.'

'Mr Macho,' she mocked, making a play of using the cloth to wipe her eyes again but really she was trying to wipe away the tingling his gentle touch had left behind.

'*Sì,*' he agreed. 'You cry like a baby yet I don't see a single unsightly red blemish spoiling your beautiful pale face.'

'What has that got to do with anything?'

'It makes you special,' he said. 'I have never seen a woman cry without ruining her looks. I might decide to make you cry often because I love the huge pools of ocean-green your eyes have become.'

'My eyes aren't green, they're hazel.'

He ignored the correction. 'They make me want to drown in them. They make me want to gather you in my arms and kiss your worries away.'

And he was doing it again, seducing her with the honeyed tone of his voice, using passion for persuasion and words with which to beat her defences to death.

'You're my major worry.'

'Why?'

'Because you make me want you when I don't want to want you!'

There, she'd said it. Put the whole wretched problem in one neat sentence. She wanted him but didn't want to want him! Good grief, but it felt good to have a sensible label she could stick on all of this.

'Ah,' was all he said and climbed to his feet.

But the way he said that made her look up to study his smooth, handsome face. 'What was that supposed to mean?' she asked warily.

'Nothing,' he said and turned to switch off the flood of water pouring into the huge bath. Another switch was hit. A bubbling sound burst into life. Subtle aromas began teasing her nostrils with the sensual hint of aromatic oils captured in spirals of steam that rose up against a background of sumptuous red and black-grained marble surrounding the biggest spa bathtub she had ever seen in her life.

Then her attention was quickly grabbed back by him when the towel around his hips was dropped. She caught a glimpse of a lean, tanned, muscle-tight behind just before he turned around and faced her with the full force of the man she had met in the bedroom.

He was fully aroused. Her senses gave a shuddering throb, her eyes leaping up to the savage beauty of his face—as her alerted senses were now seeing him anyway.

'N-no,' she gasped.

It was the only protest she managed before he bent, kissed her mouth and deftly robbed her of the silk cover then lifted her back into his arms. Her second protest was ignored when he turned, stepped into the bath then sat down and repositioned her to sit between his spread thighs. Delicately fragranced blood-hot water bubbled up all around her; she felt the gloss of aromatic oils cling to her skin. With the movements of a man possessed of supreme self-confidence, he eased her rigid spine to curve into him.

'Relax,' he lowered his mouth to her ear to murmur. 'Enjoy your second new experience of the night.'

'You can't—'

'Oh, I can,' he assured her lazily. 'But I won't—not yet anyway. I was referring to the water, *cara*, and what it feels like to be washed by a man...'

He did in the end. It was inevitable, Francesca thought hours later as she lay watching the dawn break the night sky. What had begun as his determined assault on her senses while he was supposed to remain sublimely in control, ended up with her straddling his lap, making love with a man who didn't mind that she saw how deeply she could affect him.

Their third experience took place in bed—only not the bed they had first shared but—his bed. His bed. The one he had brought her to after the bath. It came as a shock to realise that he hadn't deliberately set out to seduce her that night.

'I do have scruples,' he'd smiled at the expressive look on her face. 'I did intend to give you a few days to recover from your ordeal by Batiste, but events overtook scruples.' He'd shrugged.

So here she lay in a room with soft cream walls and a huge, very modern divan bed with its snowy white cotton coverlet sliding off the corner of the bed. Everything in the room was either cream or white, though the floor was the same beautifully polished wood.

She preferred him in the red-room setting, she decided as she lay there. All the fire and passion the room evoked suited his temperament.

Or had the other room been chosen because he'd thought it suited her temperament? It did strange things to her to think that he saw her as the exotic wanton she'd become in his arms.

Turning her head on the pillow, she looked at him. He was lying on his stomach and sound asleep, but had an arm curved possessively around her as if he was making sure she didn't go anywhere while he snatched a few hours' respite.

He had, in a few short hours, shattered every principle by which she'd lived and the awful part was that she no longer cared, so maybe he was the perceptive one and she the closet wanton who'd spent years of adulthood lying to herself.

Or hiding from herself, she then amended, thinking of all those other men she'd held off with ease as if some inner instinct had held her back from allowing the real Francesca to reveal herself—until this man came along.

This strong, dark, beautiful man with the kind of passions her instincts had recognised would match her own. So they'd unlocked their restraints and set the real Francesca free to indulge every sensual desire she possessed.

She'd told herself that she wanted to wake this morning as a different woman and she had. His woman. She didn't even bother to argue with that any more.

He stirred in his sleep, his mouth brushing against her shoulder as he moved. She looked at his mouth, traced its shape with her eyes and felt the impact of its passion on just about every inch of her skin. A sigh whispered from her. It sounded sensuously languorous. But then everything about her was like that now. She looked, felt and was sensuously languorous. She liked it. She even turned carefully so as not to waken him and brushed her kiss against his shoulder before she curled against him, closed her eyes and drifted into sensual sleep.

Lying beside her, propped up on an elbow, Carlo watched her come slowly awake. He was helping the gentle swim up from her little dream world, of course, by the slow, light circling of her nipple with a finger. The rosebud tip was already invitingly erect and he was going to lower his head and enjoy it in a moment. But for now he was content to enjoy watching her respond without being aware that she was doing it with her soft, feathered breathing that turned on his senses and the way the rest of her body was making some very seductive undulating movements.

He watched as her lips parted, felt the heavy tow of desire begin to creep through his blood. He'd never known a woman like her. If asked, until last night, he would have stated that virginity was nothing more than an obstacle that must be surmounted before the real enjoyment could begin. Not so, he knew now. Virginity meant innocence—for Francesca anyway. And her innocence was a like a blank canvas on which he was free to paint whatever colourful impressions he wished to create.

Her breathtaking willingness to trust his guidance through all things to do with sensual pleasure being the richest colour he was painting with. It was an empowering experience, and yet another gift she had given him.

Dangerous, he thought. Very dangerous if entrusted to the wrong man. Batiste, for instance—how would he have treated this precious gift if she had given it to him?

Then—no. He shut that thought away when his senses began to tighten just thinking of Batiste touching her like this. Any other man, he then expanded jealously. Francesca belonged to him and the sooner she came to terms with that the better it was going to be for both of them.

She didn't want to want him.

He smiled as he recalled those telling words. Well, *cara*, he told her silently, by the time the next few days are over I am going to turn that statement on its head.

He began by closing his mouth around his prepared prize, his eyes still fixed on her face to watch her response. Her eyelashes fluttered. He moved his tongue. She released a small, very sexy sigh. He sucked delicately. She arched her slender spine towards the source of her pleasure and relaxed again then slowly opened her eyes.

'*Ciao*,' he said softly and snaked up to steal a kiss from her sleep-softened, beautiful mouth. She clung very satisfyingly but when he lifted his head again he saw the wariness was already creeping in.

'I...'

'*We* are going to enjoy an—interesting day today,' he layered lightly over whatever she had been going to say.

'You…'

'And *we* are going to begin it as all perfect days should begin, with some very slow loving.'

He grinned rakishly then lowered his head again—to the inviting nipple waiting for him.

And so continued the ravishment of Francesca Bernard, Francesca acknowledged as she fell into his honeyed trap without putting up much resistance at all. He ravished her with his body and with his easy charm. When they eventually went down to find some breakfast he ravished her on the terrace with warm, needy looks across a sunny breakfast table overlooking a sparkling lake.

She discovered that Lorenzo had a wife called Caprice and between the two of them they looked after the house. They didn't live in. They had a villa of their own situated in a sunny corner of the grounds and had two sons that looked after the extensive gardens that curled horseshoe-like around the *palazzo*.

Carlo showed her the *palazzo*, and ravished her with the rich, melodious tones of his voice as he displayed his intimate knowledge of the *palazzo*'s amazing history and of his ancestors, each of whom had left their mark here over the centuries. She hung on every warmly informative word like a mesmerised cat and let him make love to her in the humid warmth of the solarium, on a chaise tucked inside a jungle of exotic tropical foliage.

'Trust me,' was his favourite answer to any hesitation she might reveal in the process of making love. 'Trust me, you will love this. Trust me, I can make this wonderful for you.'

And he did, every time. She learnt things about herself— and things about him that could swamp her mind when she allowed herself to think about them afterwards. He touched her at every given opportunity. If he couldn't touch he made love to her with his eyes. He kept her balanced on a needle-sharp tip of sensual awareness that never let up—even when she slept.

If she slept. One day drifted into two then three, and sleep had become a snatched thing she did between sensual assaults. He was insatiable, devastatingly inventive and—shocking.

Sometimes.

Sometimes he fell so thoroughly into her power that she became the shocking one.

They didn't leave the *palazzo*. They didn't talk about the things that they should. If she tried to broach the subject of reality he stalled her with, 'Don't spoil it, *cara*. Trust me, it will turn into a fight.'

Living in this unreal, cloistered little world he had carefully wrapped her in was foolish. In those few moments before sleep she'd sometimes find herself wondering if this was a deliberate campaign he was waging to soften her up for a ruthless kill.

Sometimes. Most of the time she didn't want to think at all. Especially if thinking meant facing head-on the issues they'd both pushed to one side.

Like his marriage proposal for instance; that still made no sense to her whatever way he chose to dress it up. And, as with each new experience another veil of innocence was taken from her, she had to question why she was letting this happen at all.

She'd even said out loud to him, 'I don't know why I'm letting you do this to me.'

'Why think at all?' had come his light response. 'Why not just enjoy?'

Because it wasn't that easy, she thought with a frown as she sat on one of the lichen-dressed stone benches against a high stone wall that formed one of the many terraces which swept the garden down towards the lake.

For once she'd escaped his almost constant presence while he dealt with a business call in his study-cum-office inside the house. The respite was giving her a chance to do the one thing he'd advised against her doing—and that was to think.

She'd gone from loving one man to becoming sexually obsessed with another in the same time it took to think the words. She didn't think she liked what that said about her. In fact she knew that she didn't. Putting her life on hold like this was solving nothing and they couldn't go on much longer without the world trying to intrude on their sensual retreat. He was already receiving a string of business calls that demanded his attention and reminded them both that he had a multinational business to run, while she had...

Nothing.

No life left out there to make her want to return to it. No friends left she felt she could trust. Not even a great-uncle she wanted to go on hoping would soften his hard stance towards her.

All she had left to cling to, in other words, was—him.

As if he knew what she was thinking he suddenly appeared, striding along the pathway between the wall and the spread of freshly mown turf, which led to the edge of the next terrace drop. It was like watching sheer poetry in motion, she thought as she followed the long, graceful stretch of his stride and the way the sun on his hair was making her think of ravens' wings again. She looked away—quickly—and began frowning out at the lake again.

He sat down beside her and stretched out those long legs in front of him. 'Calculating how quickly these gardens could be turned into a wilderness?' he said lightly.

CHAPTER NINE

'THE gardens are lovely as they are and you know it,' she answered quietly.

'But they do not inspire you to defend them with passion like the Palazzo Gianni,' he sighed with teasing regret.

Mention of her great-uncle's home froze her up so quickly that she even shivered. 'The Palazzo Gianni is a dump and a ruin.'

'But a dump and a ruin with soul and atmosphere,' he promptly extended. 'Perhaps we could allow the west terrace to revert back to nature so you can feel the same blood rush of passion...'

'I would rather not be reminded of what I said back then when I was blind and stupid, thank you,' she cut in with a snap and got up to walk a few tense steps away, aware that her abrupt change in mood had left him sitting there frowning at her in surprise.

'Would you like to explain the reason for this little outburst?' he requested eventually.

'I just don't want to be reminded of the Palazzo Gianni,' she supplied.

'But your great-uncle—'

'Has gone on my special discarded heap of people I no longer wish to associate with.'

The space behind her was filled with grim silence. She was already regretting her irritable snap but did not seem able to push this new restlessness away again. She turned to glance at him. She was wearing her denims and her hair was up. He was wearing denims too but the outfit looked a whole lot more sexy on him. The black hair, the olive-toned skin, the way he was sitting with his legs stretched out and

his arms resting along the back of the stone seat. He was
still frowning and even that was sexy.

'Who else is on this heap?' he questioned.

'Angelo; Sonya.' She effected a shrug. 'Anyone else from
now on who thinks they can play around with my feelings
and get away with it.'

'Growing tough, hm?'

'Yes.' She frowned at her black-booted feet. 'I've discovered I have more Gianni blood than I thought I had,' she
then added bleakly. 'There wasn't a forgiving bone in any
Gianni I've ever heard about. They just severed connection
with those people that let them down and that's it, problem
solved, you can't be hurt by those who don't exist any more.
Great way to deal with life.' She tossed up her head to stare
bleakly at the lake. 'I'm going to cultivate it.'

'And Bruno Gianni deserves this brutal—severing?'

'Oh, yes.' She nodded, then took in a deep breath and
explained to him about her one and only meeting with
Bruno Gianni. She told him what she'd said, what he'd said
and about all her ensuing letters to him that had been coldly
ignored. 'He sees me as Maria Bernard's shame-child. Like
my mother, I don't exist, in other words. Well, that's fine
by me because he doesn't exist for me any more.'

'But Bruno is your only living relative, Francesca. You
cannot really want to cut him out of your life without giving
him a chance to—'

'To what?' she challenged. 'Come round? Soften his miserable stance and condescend to accept me? Be careful,
Carlo,' she cautioned acidly, 'or I might start to wonder if
you're no better than Angelo.'

Her eyes gave a bitter flash. His narrowed, glinting at her
in the afternoon sun. 'Meaning what?' he demanded.

He hadn't moved a single muscle but Francesca suddenly
felt as if she was treading on unstable ground.

'Nothing,' she said, backing down from the brewing fight.

But Carlo was not going to let her do that. 'Oh, don't

stop with nothing, *cara*,' he drawled. 'I am now totally riveted by the conversation. In what way am I being compared to Batiste?'

Defiance made her lift her chin to him. 'You might think you have me all wrapped up and labelled—yours for the taking—but you're wrong, Carlo. I still have enough brain left to question why you are doing all of this.'

'We've been through that.' He frowned.

'Have we?' she disputed. 'The way I recall it, you did a lot of telling me what we were going to do and I did a lot of protesting, which you arrogantly ignored. Since then we have hidden away here like a pair of clandestine lovers doing lots of sex but nothing much else—while Rome, I presume, waits with bated breath to see what Carlo Carlucci does next with the Gianni heiress.'

She came to a teeth-snapping silence, inwardly stunned by how much she'd needed to say all of that. Carlo did nothing. He just continued to sit there staring at her with his thoughts locked away behind those narrowed eyes.

'All of Rome, hm?' he murmured then. 'Interesting, *cara*, but it avoids the question as to what way I am being compared to Batiste.'

Lips pinned shut, she refused to answer. The silence gnawed like teeth on bone. In the end he said what she refused to say out loud—was too scared to say in case speaking the words filled them with a wretched ring of truth.

'You think I am just another fortune-hunter like Batiste, solely after your family's secret stash.'

'Well—are you?' she flashed.

He moved at last and her heart took on a hectic flurry as he folded his arms across his chest, crossed his long stretched-out legs and proceeded to study her with a smooth, sleek, unfathomable assessment of a man taking his time considering his answer before he spoke.

Was he angry? She couldn't tell but she knew suddenly that she was looking at the tough businessman she'd heard about but never seen before with her own eyes. She didn't think she liked him. In fact she was sure that she didn't—so much so that she thought about running again before he made up his mind how to answer…then changed her mind.

No, she thought. It was time that they dealt with this. And there was no way she was going to let him intimidate her with that look. So she folded her own arms beneath her breasts and lifted her chin that bit higher to give him back glinting look for look. Something new filtered into the atmosphere—a taste for a fight. It had a rather sexy hint to it that tingled through her blood—more so when he opened his mouth to speak.

'For every Gianni euro you put on the table I will match it with a million euro,' he announced.

It was a smooth, slick throwing-down of the gauntlet. But more than that, it had taken her by surprise. A million? she was reluctantly impressed. His remarks the other evening about the Gianni fortune being able to buy out half of Rome made his fortune obscenely large indeed. 'Now, that's an awful lot of money,' she conceded.

He smiled—thinly. 'Nothing multiplied by nothing is—nothing, *cara*. So don't start counting it quite yet.' Then he smiled. 'Though I will allow you to be impressed.'

'I am,' she admitted. 'So why do these very impressive millions want to attach themselves to me?'

'Billions,' he corrected. 'I am a fabulously wealthy man, my sweet-tongued angel. Look around you and check out the Carlucci credentials if you don't believe me. Though I was hoping that my—charm alone would have been enough to say I am worthy husband material for a *half* Gianni with nothing but her suspicious self to offer me.'

He was—a billion times more than enough for her. And that, she thought bleakly, was the crux of the problem she was struggling with. Four nights ago she had been in love with Angelo; today, as she stood here in the bright sunlight looking into his handsome face, she knew—almost knew—that today she was in love with Carlo.

Fickle didn't come close to describing how that made her view herself. She just had to start mistrusting her ability to know how she felt about anything any more. And while she felt like this…

'I feel as if Francesca Bernard died that night of her betrothal party and this—person I've become is such a complete stranger to me that she needs a new name,' she murmured helplessly.

'I can give you a new name. Marry me and become Francesca Carlucci.'

Just like that. He made it sound so simple but—she shook her head. 'I won't marry you, Carlo,' she told him huskily.

He responded with—nothing.

She twitched restlessly. 'Why bother with marriage at all?' she asked. 'You don't need to marry me; I'll stay around without the ring.'

She could hardly say otherwise after the way she'd been responding to him. She was in too deep and that worried her too.

'As my mistress.'

'As your *anything*!' She rounded on him agitatedly. 'Except your wife.'

He stared at her for a few moments longer, no smile, no noticeable change in him anywhere to give her fair warning of what was about to come.

'Then it's nothing,' he announced, got up and walked away, leaving her standing there frozen in shock at the clean, cold way he had made that decision!

But her heart wasn't frozen, it began to beat wildly, a sudden deep, thick ball of stark panic rising up in her throat. He didn't mean it, she told herself. He was just trying to pay her back for turning his offer down the way she had.

Thinking that didn't stop her from suddenly taking off after him though. *Believing* it didn't stop her from racing up the shallow layers of wide steps with the anxious intent to seek him out.

He was already inside the house by the time she shot beneath one of the elegant archways that framed the lake. Entering the house at a run she took the stairs, and was running down the upper corridor when a sound outside the windows brought her to a shuddering halt.

Glancing out of the window, she saw Carlo standing in the courtyard talking to Lorenzo. He looked his usual cool self, supremely relaxed, the sunlight catching his hair again and the olive sheen of his skin as he talked. There was no sign at all that he had just made the most momentous decision of their very brief relationship.

It's OK, she calmed herself. He had just been bluffing her—playing the smooth, slick manipulator to the wretched hilt.

She took in a deep breath, let it out again, blamed the breathless feeling on her mad run and was about to turn away and walk *calmly* into their bedroom—when he raised a hand to make a gesture as he talked, and she saw a flash of something metallic glint in his hand.

Car keys.

The panic rose again and so swiftly she didn't even have to think before it had enveloped her.

He was going to go.

He was going to get in his car and drive away.

He was probably telling Lorenzo to get rid of her while he was gone!

He was ruthless, heartless. She'd probably let what bit of conscience he had off the hook when she'd turned his proposal down and now he was striding towards his car as if a huge great weight had been lifted from his shoulders!

And she should let him go.

But she didn't let him go. She hit the stairs at a sprint and all but slithered her way down them to the ground floor.

She couldn't breathe, yet she was panting like a maniac. She ran along the hall and pulled open the front door.

The car was just reversing from beneath its shady parking spot beneath an old olive tree. Her head was spinning; she didn't even know what she was doing as she sprinted at an angle across uneven cobblestones and reached the car as it paused in its manoeuvre, facing the gates, waiting for them to open.

Her fingers fumbled with the door catch. She tugged open the door and sent it flying wide. 'No, don't go,' she said in a dark, thick, husky tremor. 'Don't leave me here.'

Then was launching herself into the car and onto his surprised lap. Her ribs grazed painfully against the steering wheel but she didn't care; her arms flew tightly around his neck.

'I'll marry you. I'll do anything—h-hide in your bed! Just don't—'

At which point she burst into sobbing tears.

Carlo had never been more stunned by anything than to have her weep all over him again. Reaching out with a hand, he switched off the car's ignition then sat back. Her arms were gripping his neck like a vice, her body heaving, her hot tears drenching his throat.

'This is very innovative of you, *cara*, he murmured, 'but the tears are a bit over-the-top.'

'Y-you don't understand,' she sobbed. 'I don't like m-myself any more.'

'No.' He was beginning to see that.

'Y-you use me—*they* u-used me and I just let you all do it!'

'We will leave other people out of this, I think.' His hands went up to frame her face so he could lift it out of its hiding place; she looked so pathetic he wanted to kiss her so badly he ached. 'But how do I use you?' he challenged sternly. 'And don't dare quote the sex at me,' he warned, 'because

I am the sex slave around here. Your every sensual wish has been my command!'

'That's not true!' Her eyes were so big and tear-soaked he wanted to drown in them again. He did the next best thing and kissed her hard. She responded as she always did, with heat and verve and some heart-rending sobs thrown in.

'The born sensualist and the sex slave—the perfect combination,' he muttered as he drew away again. 'Forget the marriage thing, Francesca. I think we are perfect as we are. So, come on…'

Before she could respond he tipped her off his lap and out of the car onto the courtyard so that he could get out of the car.

'But…' She'd changed her mind. Well, tough, *cara*, he thought.

'The offer,' he incised, 'has been closed.'

She looked so wounded he wanted to hit something—the car was closest. He slammed the door then took her hand.

'Where were you going?' she asked as he began pulling her behind him back to the house.

'It is of no importance now,' he answered blandly, feeling as ruthless as hell. Why tell her that he had been on his way to deal with the whole Gianni situation once and for all? 'What does matter now is that we are going to play this your way. We will go inside and pack then get back to Rome, where you will hide in my bed and I will indulge your every fantasy because that, *cara*, is my role…'

He drove them to Rome with the same single-minded, typically Italian daring and panache that he'd driven her away from Villa Batiste a few nights before. He didn't speak and neither did Francesca. She wasn't happy but she didn't know why she wasn't happy when he'd conceded to her every wish.

Contrary is what you are, she told herself glumly. You

want one thing then when you are given it you start wondering if you prefer what it is you turned down!

Maybe it was Carlo Carlucci, the whole package, that was her real problem. Maybe she should have let him leave when he was going to do it without her, instead of falling on him like the plague.

Oh… She shuddered, shifting restlessly at her own awful description.

'Almost there,' his quiet voice murmured as if she was a restless child that needed soothing—and that irritated her too.

He turned beneath an archway, which opened up into another enclosed courtyard, and slotted the car into a parking space between lines of cars that wore their wealth as much as the three-storey buildings that said exclusive city living to her. As she got out of the car she recognised her Vespa parked neatly against a wall.

'I had it delivered,' he explained, following her gaze then arching a challenging smile at her when she frowned.

They entered through a door and climbed the stairs to the top floor. The apartment was huge, spreading across two corners of the building. She wandered aimlessly from room to room while Carlo dealt with a stack of mail that had been waiting for him on a table in the foyer. His eyes followed her though, flicking her lowered glances as she wandered out of one room to move to the next. She spied all her stuff from her flat stacked in what looked like a spare bedroom by its small size—in comparison to the two other large, luxurious bedrooms she'd already checked out, along with the luxurious sitting room, a fabulous formal dining room, a very male study and a kitchen that was bigger than the whole area of her apartment.

'How did these get here?' she asked him.

'Your—friend packed them for you,' he replied.

'When did she pack them?'

He made a play of slotting a letter back in its envelope before saying casually, 'The day after we left Villa Batiste.'

He was that sure she was going to end up here with him at some point? 'I suppose my nightdress is already laid out on your bed,' she said.

'Since you know you won't be wearing such a garment in my bed, *cara*, you can quit the sarcasm and tell me what you think.'

'Are you joking? It's gorgeous and you know it.' The city apartment for the city-slick sophisticate. 'Is that Canaletto hanging in the sitting room the original or a fake?'

He lost interest in the letters. 'What's the matter with you?' He frowned.

Besides feeling as if I'd won the battle but lost the war? 'I wish I knew.' She shrugged. 'I feel as if I've stepped out of fairy-tale history straight into the perfect example of its modern-day equivalent.'

'But the handsome rake who intends to ravish you is still the same guy, *mi amante*...'

Her skin began to prickle, sending warning signals to her legs as the letters slipped from his open fingers to land on the table and the gleam in his eyes said—

With a shriek of protest she turned and made a bolt for it. It was her misfortune that she chose to run into the room that she did. His flying tackle carried her with ease onto the middle of the big, downy, soft bed. After that she didn't care where they were as they fought and tumbled and made love until the sky began to darken and hunger pangs began to strike.

It was after they'd showered and he'd suggested that they get dressed and go out to find something to eat that she remembered she didn't have anything to wear because all her clothes were stuffed away in boxes or in the suitcase still languishing in his car boot.

With his usual casual manner he strode naked across the bedroom, pulled open a door and silently gestured her to ake a look inside. What she saw was rail upon rail of the most fantastic clothes she had ever seen in her life.

'For me?' she gasped in disbelief.

'Who else shares my bedroom with me?' he mocked lightly.

'But I will never wear all of these!'

'Try,' he suggested, kissed her cheek and strode off to the opposite side of the room towards a door.

'Carlo…' The call of his name stayed him as he reached for the door handle and he half turned to look at her. 'Thank you,' she said softly. 'But you don't have to buy me things. I can—'

'I know,' he cut in gently. 'It gave me pleasure, *cara mia*. Accept, enjoy—and choose something to drive me crazy while we eat!' was his last comment before he disappeared from view.

She chose a pale, misty purple wrap-over dress that scooped low between her breasts and was held together by nothing more than a couple of strategically placed hooks and eyes. And because she wasn't quite brave enough to go out wearing such a wickedly sexy creation she added a long-sleeved sheer chiffon blouse in the same misty colour patterned with scrolls of cloud-grey. She put her hair up, slipped her feet into a pair of backless shoes then stepped out of her exotic new dressing room to find the man of her dreams waiting for her.

He was wearing a casual suit made of taupe linen and a dark blue open-necked shirt and he looked so attractive her breathing stilled. His eyes darkened as they drifted over her, the sensual curve of his eyelids touching his chiselled cheeks.

'Now, that is most definitely risky,' he drawled lazily and made her blush, which made him grin.

They walked the short way to a local restaurant he told her was a favourite of his and seduced each other beneath soft lighting across the dinner table while they ate food neither of them noticed. It was all very bewitching. Francesca began to see them truly as lovers for the first time since their intimacy had begun.

Then two couples came in, saw Carlo and came over to their table to say hello. Francesca could not have repeated their names afterwards, only the way Carlo introduced her as 'my lover, Francesca', and the curious looks she received which made her aware of her name and her notoriety.

They were nice people though, too well brought up and refined to stare for too long or ask awkward questions. They joined them for a glass of wine and she actually found herself relaxing with them. And all the time that they sat there talking and laughing, Carlo's hand never relinquished its hold on hers.

As he watched the wary tension slowly seeping out of her, Carlo wondered if she had any idea how beautiful and beguiling she looked when she used that shy and tentative smile on his friends.

When they left the others to enjoy their meal and began the walk back to his apartment, he drew her beneath the wrap of his arm and felt her hand slide up beneath his jacket to come to rest between his shoulder blades. They fitted each other in every way a pair of lovers could do, he noted. Then frowned because *lovers*, was not the label he wanted them to share. It was all such a damn mess, he thought grimly. But how the hell he was going to sort it out without hurting her he had no idea at the present moment.

'Why the sigh?' She lifted her face to look up at him.

He lowered his to steal a kiss. 'You're too beautiful,' he replied. 'I was considering whether to keep you hidden in my bed in future as we agreed instead of risking you out here, where there are other men to turn your head.'

She laughed, it was a gorgeous sound, soft and light yet unbelievably sensual. 'Modesty isn't your thing, *caro*,' she told him drily. 'You know that I know I'm already with the best.'

'*Gratzi.*'

'*Prego.*'

He pulled her into a darkened shop doorway. 'You are becoming too big for your dainty shoes,' he scolded. 'I think it is time you were reminded who is the boss around this relationship.'

Then he kissed her until she begged him to stop. Until she agreed—breathlessly, 'OK, you're the boss,' and he took her home to substantiate it with more—physical methods.

It was a role he filled to its optimum capacity, Francesca mused as she walked through the apartment that had come to feel like home to her after living here with Carlo for several wonderful weeks.

In fact the only cloud on their sunny horizon was her insistence that she was going back to work and his disapproval of her doing it. They'd had a really big row about it when the subject came up. She had won—mainly because, having gone into the office to hand in her resignation, she'd ended up giving in to Bianca's pleading. It was high season and the tourist industry was at the height of its flood. Sonya had apparently returned to England, which had left Bianca short of two guides. She'd apologised for not telling Francesca that she'd suspected that Angelo was Sonya's other man.

'How do you break that kind of news to someone when it is only a suspicion?' she'd said.

With a bit more cajoling and the knowledge that Francesca was already bored, kicking her heels on her own throughout the day while Carlo went about his high-powered business, Bianca had gleaned a promise out of her that she would continue with her job.

So she spent her days back in her red uniform, being the efficient tour guide, and came home in the evenings to change into the clothes Carlo had bought to become his attentive lover.

No man could have it any better. No woman could want for more. Carlo eased them gently into socialising by carefully picking those close friends and associates who did not move in the same social circles as the Batistes.

He continued to introduce her as 'my lover, Francesca', and in a tone that demanded she be judged on the value he placed on her in that role. And, since it was well known that he'd literally scythed her away from Angelo on the night of their engagement, that value meant a great deal— or so she let herself believe.

He rarely left her side on these occasions; he made no effort to conceal she did things for him that kept him faithfully at heel. She blossomed under this kind of devotion, and even learned to tease him by flirting once or twice just to watch his eyes darken and read the threat of what her punishment would be.

She also learned to value herself again—learned slowly to trust him.

Then she met Angelo.

They were attending a charity function in one of the big city hotels and had been there for about an hour when she detached herself from Carlo's side to go and find the ladies' room. It was as she was walking back into the main reception room that she walked straight into Angelo. If she'd known he was here she would have been on her guard and therefore avoided this kind of face-to-face confrontation but the way it happened the two of them just stood staring at each other in a surprised and discomforted silence.

He looked as he always did—the beautifully turned-out, handsome guy, still with that golden glow about him which had blinded her to the real man. The charm was missing though, she noticed as she looked into his blue eyes and saw no false warmth or perpetual smile lurking around his mouth.

A nerve twitched in his jaw as he skimmed his eyes over her tight little strapless dress made of pale peach satin that moulded her figure like a second skin. Her hair had been cut to highlight the natural streaks of gold in the light brown, and expertly styled to float around her heart-shaped face and slender shoulders. She knew she looked good because Carlo had told her so—in more ways than one.

But she did not need Angelo confirming that judgement. 'You look amazing,' he said curtly. 'I will give it to Carlucci—he has managed to bring out the best in you.'

Tension spun a steely case around her throat because she didn't want him looking at her like that—with lying eyes that pretended to desire what they saw.

'I have nothing to say to you—excuse me,' she said and went to walk past him.

His hand captured hers, bringing her to a halt shoulder to shoulder with him. She fixed her eyes on the milling throng, anxiously checking out how many people had noticed them standing here.

'Let me go,' she insisted.

'Not until you have heard me out.' His grip tightened on her fingers. 'What you overheard me say to Sonya that night about not wanting you was all lies, Francesca. The kind of lies any aroused man will utter without conscience to keep the woman in his arms sweet.'

'Is telling me that supposed to make me feel better about you?' she asked.

'No,' he said. 'But it does me a lot of good to let you know that I was never blind to your attractions, *cara*. I wanted you. It was you who tied my hands with your shy confessions of innocence and old-fashioned views on marriage before sex. I can't tell you how bloody annoying it is to know that if I'd pushed the issue as Carlucci obviously has, then Sonya would not have got a look-in and we would be standing here as a happily married couple now.'

'You believe a marriage based on your desire to get your

hands on Gianni money could be happy?' She pushed out a derogatory laugh. 'By now, *caro,* you would know there is no money and be as unhappy as a greedy man with no fortune to spend could be.'

'So you are still sticking to the no-fortune story,' he murmured softly. 'Good for you, *cara.* Keep the bastard dancing on his toes for as long as you can. He'll break some time and tell you the truth about the Gianni—Carlucci union.' His mouth arrived close to her ear. 'Unless you already know about it, of course, and you keep him dancing as you did me—just for the hell of it.'

She tugged her hand free; he let it go. He was poison, she reminded herself as on a wave of sickness she walked shakily away, weaving through the clutches of people without daring to make eye contact—just in case they'd seen her talking to Angelo.

She made a beeline for the one place she felt safe. He was still talking business with the same two people she'd left him with when she went to find the loo. Coming up beside him, she slipped her hand into his and felt his fingers close instantly. She was trembling. Could he feel she was trembling? He made no sign of it as he talked in velvet dark undertones, which held his audience captivated. She didn't hear a single word. She was too busy trying to filter Angelo's poison from her blood. After a few minutes, Carlo excused them and swapped her hand for her waist to lead her into the adjoining room then onto the dance floor. Music was playing, soft and slow.

His fingertips feathered lightly down her sides and came to settle at the indentation at her waist then he drew her against him. Relieved to be in the arms of the only man she ever wanted to be with, her hands came to rest against his wide shoulders, her unsteady breath warming his throat.

'OK,' he said quietly. 'What did he say to you?'

It was a shock. She hadn't thought he'd seen her talking to Angelo because he'd had his back turned towards the doorway. 'I—you—I didn't know he was going to be here tonight.'

'Neither did I,' he said in a tone that made her blood chill.

'H-he took me by surprise…'

'I can see that,' he drawled. 'You're as white as a sheet and trembling like a leaf.' And he was not happy about it. 'So, what did he say?' he prompted again.

She fixed her eyes on the cleft in his chin and tried another steadying breath. 'Poison,' she said. 'He's made up of pure poison.'

'Is that it?' he said after waiting a minute for her to explain.

'Yes.' She moved that bit closer to his strong, dark frame. 'If I talk about it, Carlo, he will have achieved what he wanted to achieve. And I won't let him.'

'Fair enough.' He didn't push the issue and they left not long after the dance.

But he was silent on the journey back to the apartment and there was a new intensity about his lovemaking that night. He took her swimming close to the edge, only to pull her back from the brink time after time. In the end she had to plead with him before he relented and let her topple into the fierce and furied waterfall of release.

Exhausted afterwards, too weak and boneless to do anything other than breathe, she fell asleep, only to be woken in the dark depths of the night to be pulled through the same intense journey all over again.

CHAPTER TEN

THE next morning she woke up late to find the place beside her in the bed empty and with a hangover that had nothing to do with the few sips of wine she'd had the evening before. Her body ached—inside and out. Her head felt as if it was trying to swim and as she moved sluggishly into the bathroom she felt so dizzy she thought for a few minutes that she was going to be sick.

It took all her energy to get dressed and go to work, feeling the way that she did. The day passed like any other day. She trailed people round the sites of Rome and managed to sound interesting and enthusiastic as she went through her usual routine. But the headache hadn't eased and the sickness lay like a knot in her stomach she couldn't seem to release.

By the time she got back to the apartment she felt so wrecked it was all she could do to strip and shower then crawl between cool cotton sheets.

Carlo found her like that, nothing more than a tumble of dark golden curls lost in a mound of white. He stood looking at her for a long time, his expression made stern by the way he frowned. Then he too stripped off his clothes and went to take a shower. When he came back she heard him moving about and stirred.

'You're back,' she mumbled.

'Mm,' he said. He was pulling on a pair of jeans. 'Too tired to talk to me?' he asked lightly.

'Mm,' she echoed, burrowing deeper into the covers. 'Headache,' she explained. 'Feel a bit sick. Just want to sleep.'

It was the last thing she remembered until she awoke the

next morning feeling a whole lot better. Carlo, the perpetual early riser, was already up. She showered, dressed for work then left the bedroom to go in search of sustenance—starving after her queasy fast of the day before.

But she didn't get as far as the kitchen. Passing his study, she saw Carlo standing behind his desk.

'Morning,' she smiled from the doorway.

'*Ciao*,' he responded—without a returning smile.

He was dressed for the office in a pale blue shirt, grey trousers and a dark tie. His jacket, she saw, was draped over the back of the chair behind him. Freshly shaven, hair neat, he was holding a stack of papers in his hands, which he was in the process of lining up in a neat column on the desk.

And if she had to epitomise man at his most dynamic then Carlo was it at that moment. 'Sorry about last night,' she murmured. 'I had a headache.'

'So you said.' She watched him select a few more sheets of paper then put them down on the long row.

The atmosphere was strange—cool—and the lack of a smile from him was making her frown. Was he cross with her about last night? He'd barely offered her a glance and his mouth had a flatness about it that suggested he was annoyed about something. He'd slept beside her last night; she had a vague memory of his soothing 'shh' as he'd gathered her close.

'I'm disturbing you,' she said, deciding his preoccupation was with those papers not annoyance with her, and went to turn away.

'No—wait,' he said. 'I need you to sign these for me.'

'Me?' She frowned as she walked forward, looking down at the column of documents and recognised the Carlucci business logo on the top one, but after that she could only see the bottom two inches of each set, bearing the bold scrawl of his own signature. 'What are they?' she asked.

'Mostly bank and store accounts I've opened for you that require your signature,' he answered coolly.

'But I thought you understood I don't want—'

'The point of this particular exercise is not what you want but what I want,' he cut in.

'And you want the Carlucci mistress to have all the right-coloured cards in her purse as befitting her exalted title?' she responded with tart.

'The Carlucci bride would be receiving a lot more.'

She stared at the smooth dark planes of his unsmiling face. Marriage hadn't come up in conversation once since they'd left Castelli Romani. Now here it was being filtered back in beneath the guise of loaded grim sarcasm.

'Neither are you my mistress,' he added curtly, 'so I would prefer you did not refer to yourself in such a way.'

'I will be your mistress if I sign those papers, Carlo,' she stated heavily. 'At the moment I keep myself while I'm living here…'

'Unless, of course, you are forced to come to me like a guilty thief about to rob me because you need extra money to get you through the rest of the month.'

She looked up, blushing at the reminder. Within a few short weeks of living with him here in Rome she'd come to realise how expensive it was to be a wealthy man's lover. Only last week she'd been forced to ask him to lend her some money to get her through the rest of the month until her next salary cheque because she'd blown all she had on haircuts and manicures—and that dress she'd bought on a wicked whim because it promised to raise his temperature gauge.

'It was a one-off loan and I do mean to pay you back,' she insisted defensively. 'And I never meant to prompt you to—'

'This way you don't have to pay me back.' He held out a pen. 'Accept with grace, *cara*,' he advised smoothly.

'You don't look too happy about having to do it.' She folded her arms instead of taking the pen.

'That is because I knew I was in for a fight.'

'H-how much money are we talking about?' she asked warily. He named a monthly allowance that made her gasp. 'But I'll never spend that in a hundred years!'

'You will when you get used to it,' he assured with a touch of cynicism.

'I don't want to get used to it!'

He didn't budge a small inch. 'Sign,' he instructed.

She looked down at the column of documents. There were a dozen of them at least. 'And...' she prompted. 'You said these papers were *mostly* bank and store accounts, what else is there that requires my signature?'

'Some legal stuff to do with you living with me.' He effected a shrug. 'Call it protection against—'

'The mistress with avarice.'

'No.' He leant forward, looking her directly in the eyes for the first time since this strange interview began. 'To protect you if I decide to throw you out in only the clothes you stand up in—which might just happen quite soon if you don't stop being so stubborn,' he threatened darkly.

'I don't need protecting from y-you or anyone.'

'Trust me, *cara*, you should be standing behind bullet-proof glass right now.'

His eyes took on a familiar glitter. She saw seduction as the next form of persuasion being promised to her and felt her senses begin to sting. Would she be able to hold out under one of his sensual onslaughts? No, of course she wouldn't be able to hold out, she informed herself—and snatched the pen from his fingers.

There was little grace or gratitude in the way she penned her name in the appropriate place he indicated with a long finger. The atmosphere hissed and spat with each full stop she stabbed at the end of each signature and each grimly pointed indication of his finger as it moved down the column.

When it was over she threw down the pen and straightened. 'Just think,' she said tartly, 'I get to swan around

Rome playing the pampered bitch that gets doors opened for her and a suitable amount of grovelling because I now possess the appropriate clout.'

'You also get to give up your job,' he included as he gathered in the signed papers with the deft slide of his fingers. 'And instead of coming home to me dead on your feet, you will be here,' he stated, 'rested, beautiful and waiting for me.'

Francesca felt her eyes widen to the fullest in utter incredulity. Was that what this was really all about? She'd spent one measly night neglecting him due to a headache and he responded with—this?

'I'm not giving up my job just because you say so,' she told him. 'No way,' she added as the papers were neatly slotted into a folder then shut away in a drawer. It was one thing letting him dictate just about every other facet of her life but she was not going to let him take away the one small thing she had left that gave her some independence from him!

His hands arrived flat on the cleared desk surface. He ignored the angrily lifted chin and the warning flash from her eyes. 'Not negotiable, *cara*.'

'Then you can keep your money and your—other stuff,' she responded. 'We will continue as we are or not at all!'

With that she turned and walked out of the door then out of the whole apartment with a very satisfying slam of the outer door.

Carlo moved to the window to watch as she appeared in the sunny courtyard. Each tense move she made as she wheeled her scooter between parked cars then climbed onto it told him she was angry enough to drive straight at him if he dared to walk in front of her.

Red dress, red Vespa, red flags in her cheeks…he watched her drive off then uttered a thick, black, bloody curse and turned back to his desk. The folder reappeared with its neatly signed documents. Next he picked up his mobile and began making calls. Ten minutes later he was following her out onto the Corso but where she would have turned into the city he turned out of it with the kind of grim resolve about his driving that left no room for him to worry if she was concentrating properly negotiating the mad traffic that was Rome.

Francesca was too angry to concentrate—and she'd slammed out of the apartment without so much as a cup of coffee to help kick start her day!

He'd done that—Mr Arrogant, who thought he could dictate to her and get away with it.

She glowered at a motorist who cut right in front of her. He—it had to be a man—hit his horn and blew her a kiss. 'Bella—bella!' he called out then looped his way into the stream of traffic. Men were all the same, she thought as she watched him go. They were all pushy egotists that liked to get their own way.

She parked the Vespa at the rear of the hotel she was to collect her tour group from and because she was a half-hour earlier than she should be, due to storming out without breakfast, she walked to the nearest patisserie and bought a chocolate croissant and a coffee to go. The moment she bit into the croissant she knew she wasn't going to be able to eat it. Even the coffee tasted sour.

His fault, she blamed, dumped the croissant and coffee in the nearest bin and walked back to the hotel. An hour later she was in full professional mode, two hours further on and they'd reached the Trevi Fountain, where she left her group to toss coins and take photographs, while she bought a bottle of chilled water from one of the kiosks and sank down on a nearby bench.

The sun was hot and the crowds were thick; drawing a decent breath was an effort and she was beginning to feel dizzy and sick again.

Maybe she'd caught a bug, she mused as she sat sipping water. It was a big relief to know that this was the last stop on this morning's tour, which meant she had a whole two hours to herself before the afternoon tour began.

She was just considering whether to go back to the apartment to take some painkillers and lie down for a while, when a shadow fell across her. She glanced up—it was instinctive—then instantly wished she hadn't when she saw who it was.

'Ciao,' Angelo greeted sombrely. 'I hoped I would find you here today.'

Her heart sank like a stranded whale to her hollow stomach. 'Why did you hope that?' she demanded heavily.

'We need to talk.'

'We've already done that.'

'I know.' He shrugged. It was oddly diffident for him.

Then he seemed to make some monumental decision and sat himself down next to her. Two young girls sharing the same bench were staring at him in open-mouthed awe. He had it all, Francesca observed ruefully, the amazing good looks, the long, lean body perfectly turned out in a lightweight grey suit. The gold streaks in his hair were catching the sunlight and warming his golden skin. He even smelled good, and if he decided to turn his head and offer them an afternoon's wild sex then his two man-struck observers would be his for the taking—it was that obvious.

But he didn't turn his head. With an art taught to any Roman in its cradle he completely ignored that they were sitting there at all. In fact he just sat staring at the Trevi Fountain with his eyes hidden behind the glasses and the relaxed pose he'd adopted doing nothing to hide his tension from her.

Francesca took another sip at the water. Her head was beginning to ache, bright balls of pain propelling themselves at the backs of her eyelids. She really did have a bug of some kind, she told herself wearily and wished she were back in bed.

'Don't marry him,' he said suddenly.

'What?' she gasped, turning to stare at him, not believing she'd heard what he'd just said.

'I know I messed up, and I know I messed you up, but don't make another mistake by marrying him, Francesca.'

'What business is it of yours what I do, Angelo?'

'None.' He grimaced. 'But I could not just turn my back on this, knowing what I do.'

'You don't know anything,' she denied huskily. 'And I'm not marrying anyone, so just leave it alone and go away.'

'Don't lie, *cara*, It is not in your nature. He rang me this morning to tell me,' he added before she could speak. 'You plan to marry next week in the small chapel attached to his *palazzo*.'

She didn't even know there was a chapel attached to the *palazzo*! 'Carlo—told you that?' She gasped in disbelief then felt a funny little flutter gather pace in her stomach as her head threw up a vision of the bad-tempered brute as he'd looked this morning while he bullied her into signing his precious documents.

Had he been planning a surprise wedding for them? Was that what the papers had really been about? Did he intend dragging her off by her hair and forcing her to wear his ring because he knew she would put up a fight otherwise? The flutter altered to a warm glow of humour. The headache began to ease. She even smiled to herself.

'He then went on to warn me off,' Angelo was saying. 'If he sees me in the same room as you again he suggests I will not like the consequences.'

'Then what are you doing sitting here?' she asked him. 'Batistes discovered they can survive without his business, have they?'

'I don't think he was referring to the business side, *cara*; he was meaning my skin.'

So Carlo was jealous of Angelo? Oh, this was getting better and better. Just wait until I get alone with him and I will...

'And I'm sitting here because I've discovered I have a conscience that is overriding my common sense.'

Angelo stole her attention again and dragged off his glasses, revealing those amazing blue eyes that still had the ability to startle when you first looked into them. 'You're so beautiful these days you take my breath away,' he said tensely. 'I regret losing you, *mi amore*. I cannot tell you how much I regret being such a fool. But this isn't about me, it's about you. Don't marry him, Francesca,' he begged urgently. 'He means to hurt you just as badly as I did.'

'No.' She stood up. 'I'm not going to listen to any more of your poison, Angelo.'

He stood up too. 'I might speak poison but I also speak the truth!' he insisted in a harsh undertone. 'He warned me off coming near you because he is scared of what I know!'

'And what do you think you know?' she challenged fiercely. 'That there really is a Gianni fortune stashed away somewhere waiting for me to marry to claim it, and now Carlo is the mercenary rat trying to get his greedy hands on it?'

'Yes,' he hissed. 'I'm sorry, but that's exactly how it is.'

'There is *no* fortune!' She sighed. 'How many times do I have to repeat that to you before you will believe?'

'How many times do I have to tell you there is a fortune for you to inherit before *you* believe?'

'Oh, stop this.' She sighed. 'Even if there was money, unlike you, Carlo doesn't need any more—he has enough of the stuff as it is!'

'Not money,' Angelo conceded. 'But a large block of Carlucci stock has been locked away in your grandfather's estate since he died. Carlo wants it back. He certainly does not want any other man getting control of it.'

'As in—you?'

'As in any other man but himself!' He released a harsh sigh.

She turned away, not wanting to listen any longer but—

'No, don't turn your back on this, Francesca.' Angelo grabbed her arm and spun her back again. 'On my mother's life I am telling you the truth! I don't want your unhappiness on my conscience any longer. I don't want to see you hurt again!'

The headache was getting worse by the second and their two observers were still watching avidly. By their expression they could not understand a word of Italian so had no idea what they were talking about, but that did not stop this from turning into a very public scene!

'But if you cannot bring yourself to believe me then speak to your great-uncle,' Angelo persisted. 'Demand he tell you the truth. Ask him *why* your grandfather's estate has Carlucci stock locked up in it,' he urged huskily. 'Ask him about the Carlucci-Gianni feud that has been going on since your mother jilted his father at the church altar to marry her English gigolo!'

Her head began to spin dizzily. She had no option but to sit down again. Angelo joined her. 'I am not toying with you just for the hell of it,' he continued hurriedly. 'I am in fact risking a great deal by telling you this because Carlo can ruin my family with a single blow.'

She looked up, some hazy part of her professional instinct making her search out her tour group. Eyes barely focusing, she managed to detect them dispersed around the small square, shopping for souvenirs.

'Then why are you doing it?'

'Because I discovered I'm in love with you,' he declared with a self-deprecating grimace. 'Though I had to lose you before I knew it.'

Oddly enough, she actually believed him. She had never heard Angelo sound so grimly sincere. The thing was, did she believe everything else he'd said?

She didn't have an answer to that. She couldn't seem to think of anything clearly right now. Even trying to take the cap off her bottle of water was beyond her. Angelo took it and did it for her while she swallowed thickly on the nausea she could feel building inside. She took a few sips, felt the cool water slide down her throat and into her empty stomach. No warm glow there now, she noticed bleakly.

And she knew at that precise moment that, whether she believed him or not, she was going to have to check his story out.

Pushing herself back to her feet, she swayed a little.

Angelo rose also. 'What are you going to do?' he asked.

'Go and see my great-uncle.' What other choice was there?

'I'll take you,' he offered. 'You cannot want to do that journey on your Vespa and the train station is miles away from your great-uncle's *palazzo*. Let me drive you,' he begged. 'You don't look too good, *cara*,' he added gently when she went to refuse him.

Gentle did it. Gentle made her eyes swim with weak tears and her heart swim with other things—pending agony, she named it. It was preparing itself for what was about to hit. 'OK,' she agreed. 'I h-have to take my tour group back to their hotel first.'

There wasn't a hint of smug triumph about him and if there had been she would have changed her mind about going anywhere with him. 'Tell me which hotel and I'll collect my car and meet you there,' was all he said.

Two hours later Angelo was pulling the car to a stop by her great-uncle's wilderness driveway, after having completed the whole journey in near silence after Angelo's main attempt of, 'Let me explain about—' had been stalled before it got started, by her muted,

'How is it you know so much about the Giannis and me?'

There had been a moment of silence, a flat-line grimace that attacked his mouth. Then, 'Your great-uncle's housekeeper talks to my mother's housekeeper,' he said.

She had nodded, seeing—feeling the import in that reply

like an extra weight trying to suffocate hope. 'I will hear the rest from my uncle,' she told him. And Angelo had respected that.

The gates were shut as always. He was about to climb out of the car to open them but Francesca stopped him.

'Thank you for bringing me, but I want to go on alone from here,' she said.

He turned a frowning look on her. The fact that she was as pale as a ghost didn't pass him by and her mouth was trembling—though she wished that it wouldn't.

'You know I am telling you the truth, don't you?' he murmured.

What could she say? He would have to possess a really twisted sense of humour to go to this amount of trouble on the back of a few lies. But there was one small, tiny glimmer of hope left in her that what he thought he knew was nothing more than rumour getting out of control.

She went to climb out of the car without answering.

'I will wait for you,' he said.

Francesca flashed him a glance. 'You don't have—'

'I said I will wait, *cara*,' he insisted. 'You never know,' he smiled then, 'you might actually be glad to see me by the time you leave here.'

Not in the way she suspected he meant, she thought as he left it at that and climbed out of the car. She could feel his eyes following her as she stepped up to the gates and pushed one of them open. As she closed it behind her again her eyes grazed over the rusty old letterbox that looked as if it hadn't been opened in a hundred years.

The whole place still had that look about it, she thought as she began walking up the vine-strewn driveway beneath the overhanging branches of gnarled old trees. Even the quiet heat of the afternoon had a hushed, undisturbed quality about it, the cracked and peeling frontage of the house wearing the patina of neglect.

Her nerves began to knot as she walked around a huge

rhododendron bush, which kept more than half of the house hidden from the drive. What if her great-uncle refused to see her? What if he refused to answer her questions even if he did condescend to grant her a meeting?

Then she saw the red car parked at the bottom of the crumbling steps that led up to the front door and she knew then—knew that whatever happened next she was going to walk away the loser.

It took her a few moments to come to terms with that, and a few more moments to get anger to override the growing throb of her aching heart. Then she walked around the car and up the steps to use the heavy brass door knocker, grained and pitted with age.

The housekeeper opened the door to her. One glance at Francesca's face and she was lowering her eyes and stepping aside.

'Where are they?' she demanded as she stepped past her.

'The main *sala, signorina*. Where you met with your great-uncle the last time you were here.'

Moving on legs that did not feel very stable, she walked along a threadbare carpet runner and paused outside the *sala* door. Deep breath, she instructed herself. Be ready for what you see. Then she pressed her lips together and opened the door.

They were sitting in cracked leather wing-back chairs by an open fire. The heat in the room was oppressive, though the chill covering her skin kept Francesca feeling like ice. The remains of a lunch of crusty bread and pasta lay spread on a small table and if she was expecting to find two feudal lords confronting each other then she was disappointed. They were sharing a bottle of crisp dry Frascati wine and could not appear more at ease with each other as they sat there talking as if they'd been close friends for a lifetime.

Carlo was the first one to see her standing there. He shot to his feet, looking everything she wished that he wasn't, which was tall and dark and so unbearably handsome her heart tilted over and gave a squeeze of quiet agony.

'Francesca,' he breathed in surprise.

Don't speak to me, she wanted to shout but didn't dare say anything to him while she was feeling so raw. So she turned to look to her great-uncle Bruno, whose silver head took its time turning and the eyes—so like her own—remained calm as they looked back at her.

Why couldn't you like me? she thought helplessly and had to curl her fingers into her palms before she could utter a word. 'I believe you have something to tell me,' she prompted.

'I do?' Silver eyebrows rose in a typical Latin gesture. 'As far as I am aware, *signorina,* I have nothing of importance to say to you.'

'Francesca—'

No, *don't*! She flashed Carlo a wild, bright, silencing look—then looked back at her great-uncle. 'Just tell me,' she demanded. 'Am I or am I not the sole beneficiary to my grandfather's fortune?'

'Not as you stand here now, *signorina,*' he replied ambiguously.

'When I marry, then,' she said tensely.

'Are you married?'

'No, I am not married and not planning to be,' she flashed out. 'And why can't you just answer me without turning it into a—?'

Carlo shifted on a sigh. '*Cara*, don't turn this into a drama. There is an explanation as to why—'

'You're here?' She turned on him tensely. 'As to why you—and all of Rome—know more about me than I know about myself? Tell me, Carlo, how long did it take your father to recover from my mother's desertion before he went to Paris and married his child bride?'

'Who has been talking to you?' He frowned suddenly.

Francesca tugged in an unsteady breath of air. 'What does

it matter who's been talking when I only need to ask any stranger on the Corso to find out that my mother jilted your father to marry my father and that Bruno Gianni is a nasty, sneaky, miserable old man!'

'Hah,' Bruno Gianni laughed. 'She has spirit, that one, just like a Gianni. You have trouble on your hands, Carlo, if you mean to tame the child.'

'I am not a child,' she flung at him next. 'And Signor Carlucci is dead in my eyes. Is that Gianni enough for you?'

'*Sì,*' the old man nodded seriously. 'Your grandfather would be proud of you.'

'Why won't you tell me what I need to know?' she quavered suddenly and knew she was about to lose control.

'Because his hands are tied by your grandfather's will,' Carlo provided. 'He is not allowed to discuss it with you until you comply with its terms.'

'How can I comply when I don't know what those terms are?' she cried.

'Precisely,' Carlo said. 'The Giannis are not known for making life easy for anyone, *cara.*'

'Have we moved on to discuss Carlucci stock now?'

Carlo cursed. 'Who *has* been talking to you?'

'Batiste?' her great-uncle suggested helpfully.

'He would not dare,' Carlo said narrowly. 'I warned him off this…'

Francesca's face gave her away. And that was the point when Carlo's mood changed. 'How did you get here, *cara*?' he demanded thinly. 'You don't look as if you rode ninety kilometres on a Vespa.'

She looked as pristine and neat as she had when she stormed out on him this morning—except for her face, Carlo saw. Her skin was pale and her eyes looked bruised. Pining for her lost love? Or was the look down to guilt because the lost love had returned? he wondered cynically, and felt his teeth grind together behind his taut lips.

'You've been with him,' he rasped in accusation. 'You came here with him!'

'Maybe he loves me after all,' she said defiantly. 'Maybe we stopped on the way here to indulge in some—'

He moved like streaked lightning. She didn't even see him coming until his hands landed on her shoulders. 'Carlo—*amico*,' Bruno murmured in protest but he barely registered the words.

'Take that back or I will kill you both,' he growled furiously.

She was trembling all over but her chin went up, her eyes bright with both anger and tears. 'Vendettas all round, *caro*?' she taunted.

'There are no vendettas!' he rasped. 'But if you don't withdraw what you just said to me I will turn this into one!'

'Why don't you confess your sins to me then I will confess mine?'

'I don't have any sins to confess to!'

'You've been lying to me. You've been making love to me for weeks and weeks as if I meant something special to you but all you really wanted was—this!'

Her voice had risen to a shrill pitch by the time she'd finished. 'You are getting me mixed up with Batiste,' he gritted.

'Are you saying there is no Carlucci stock locked up in my grandfather's estate?'

He breathed and let go of her before he did something stupid. Then had to watch her quiver and sway then put a pale hand up to cover her eyes. Had he hurt her? Had his fingers bitten too hard? *'Cara…'* he murmured roughly.

'No, don't come near me.' She held up her free hand to ward against him. 'I need to…' pull myself together and finish this, Francesca thought desperately. Because she'd just remembered something else and it was making her feel sick to her stomach.

She looked up at him through the bruised eyes of pain. 'What did you really get me to sign this morning?'

He turned away. She saw attention caught by her great-uncle Bruno, who had sat through it all, listening with interest. There was an exchange of glances. She couldn't see what Carlo's look was saying but she read her great-uncle's get-out-of-this-one expression.

'Tell me,' she whispered.

'You signed your life away,' he informed her sardonically. 'You can marry who the hell you want to but your fortune will be controlled by me.'

The air in the room suddenly felt oppressive, the heat from the fire and the intensity of Carlo's silence weighing on her aching head. The walls tried to close in. Grimly she pushed them back again. I've got to get out of here before I completely humiliate myself by fainting at his feet, she thought hazily.

'OK.' She nodded then had to swallow thickly when the foolish head movement sent her dizzy. 'Then I won't marry.'

'Oh, don't restrict yourself so, *signorina*,' her great-uncle Bruno lazily put in. 'If you don't want your grandfather's fortune then you only need to stay away from Italian men from good families.'

'Stay out of this, Bruno!' Carlo raked at the old man. 'You are not supposed to speak about it!'

'Seems futile to remain silent if Francesca has no wish to inherit,' the old man pointed out.

'Which pleases you because you get to go on living here for free.'

'True,' Bruno agreed. 'Until I die, when the money goes to charity.'

Charity, Francesca repeated to herself and almost found a bleak little smile. This whole set-up was one huge, self-seeking charity.

'Well, good luck to you, *signor*,' she murmured politely.

'I hope you enjoy the lonely comfort of the rest of your life.'

With that she turned and walked back into the hallway. She heard Carlo angrily hiss her name but didn't stop her from walking away. She'd had it with Rome. She was going to go home—to England—and never set foot on Italian soil again.

CHAPTER ELEVEN

CARLO didn't come after her. She didn't know if that made her hurt all the more or if she was just aching with relief. Whichever, there were tears in her eyes as she stepped outside into the dappled sunlight and she felt as though she was floating as she walked down the drive.

Angelo was leaning against his car when she stepped through the gate again. He took one look at her face and was leaping into action, striding round the car to open the passenger door for her then grimly watching her as she slipped silently into the seat.

'Where to now?' he asked as he got in beside her.

He wasn't even going to ask if everything he'd said had been confirmed in there, she realised. But then he didn't need to. For once Angelo felt secure in his truth.

'Back to Rome,' she said. 'I—need to pack my things.'

'Then what?'

She shrugged, not wanting to think that far ahead.

'Why don't we go to the villa?' he suggested huskily. 'It's only a couple of miles from here and you look as if you need—'

'Rome, please, Angelo,' she put in firmly. 'Or you can drop me off at the train station if you don't want to drive back there tonight.'

He didn't even bother to answer that. Grimly firing the car engine, he fed it into gear and turned them around to go back the way they had come. Within minutes the smooth motion of the car sent her sleepy, the headache, stress and now a throbbing heartache dragging her down into a dark place that kept her huddled and motionless in the seat beside Angelo while he drove.

She didn't stir again until her senses picked up the scents and sounds of the city. Sliding upright in her seat, she looked out on the half-light of the summer evening to discover they were moving down the river embankment.

Pulling in through the archway to Carlo's apartment building, Angelo stopped and killed the engine then glanced outside.

'His car isn't here.'

'No.' Even Carlo couldn't be in two places at the same time, she thought bleakly.

'Thanks for giving up half your day for me.' She reached for the door lock.

'Look,' he turned in his seat. 'I can't just drop you here and drive away without knowing you're OK, *cara*. Go and pack a bag. I'll wait here for you. Then you can come and stay with me while you decide what—'

'Sorry, Angelo,' she cut in. 'But whatever you're hoping to gain from today, it isn't going to be me.'

'I never meant—'

'I know exactly what you meant, *caro*,' she said gently, then climbed out of the car. His side-window came down as she walked past it. An arm appeared with a set of long golden fingers that gently caught her hand. Her beautiful golden man, she thought sadly as she paused to look down at him—and felt nothing.

Nothing.

'You're in love with him, aren't you?'

'Surprise, surprise,' she mocked then felt the tears fill her eyes.

'I'm sorry.'

'What for—opening my eyes for me…again?'

His sigh was accompanied by a wince. 'I messed up big time.'

So did I. 'Thanks for driving me.' Slipping her hand free, she walked on, and didn't look back again even though she knew he watched her all the way until she'd disappeared inside the building.

The first thing she did on entering the apartment was go straight to the bathroom to take a couple of painkillers.

The second thing she did was strip off her clothes and stand beneath the shower for ages, just emptying her mind of everything.

The third thing she did was wrap herself in a long white terry bathrobe, then went to find her small suitcase, threw it down on the bed, sat down beside it—and burst into tears.

Carlo arrived in the open bedroom door after the crying fit was over and she was packing her case. His jacket had gone, as had his tie, and he was looking just a bit worn round the edges, she noticed in the one very brief glance she allowed herself to offer him before turning away. His hair was ruffled and he looked tired and grim but not particularly bothered to find her packing to leave him.

That hurt, but then everything was hurting—throbbing head, aching heart, painful—

'Where are you going to go?' he questioned levelly.

'A hotel for now,' she replied coolly. 'Then back to England, where I intend to get on with my life.'

'Starting it by finding a strictly English man to marry just to get back at me?'

'You said it.' She shrugged and walked away into her dressing room, where she spent a few minutes carefully selecting only the clothes she had bought herself.

When she came back into the bedroom he was still standing there with a shoulder resting casually against the door jamb, arms folded, feet crossed in classical Carlo Carlucci look-how-relaxed-I-am-about-this pose.

'I won't stop you from leaving, you know,' he told her.

'I don't want you to stop me.' She sent him a false smile and dropped an armload of clothes onto the bed.

'But I will not allow it to finish like this.'

'Because you want your Carlucci stock back.' She packed two skirts and a jacket without even knowing it.

'The stock is incidental.'

'Like the control of it you got me to sign away?' Several other items of clothing went the same way.

'You needed protecting.'

'From whom, for goodness' sake?' she turned to flash at him, then spun away again because it still hurt too much to look at him and the tears were trying to come back but—not this time, she told them fiercely. I will not cry in front of him ever again! 'The only person I need protecting from around here is you,' she declared huskily. 'I trusted you, Carlo. In spite of everything I went through with Angelo, I trusted you to be honest with me.'

'I was honest,' he snapped. 'As far as I could be,' he added. 'Would you like to know how it was that I became involved with you in the first place?'

Shoes, she'd forgotten shoes, she realised, and walked back into the dressing room, ignoring his offer of an explanation as if hadn't spoken at all. Then she just stood there with her hands clenched and her eyes tightly closed, trembling like a pathetic, weak-minded idiot because she wanted to hear his explanation more than anything if it was going to justify what he'd done.

But how could he justify it? her cynical side put in. He was just another taker like Angelo, probably willing to say anything if it got him what he wanted from her.

Which was a block of measly stock with a bit of revenge thrown in because her mother had jilted his father twenty-four years ago. She felt sick again.

No, she didn't, she then told her dipping stomach and grimly forced open her eyes and selected two pairs of shoes at random.

When she went back to the bedroom her case had gone. She stopped dead in her tracks. The bedroom door had been open before but it was now firmly shut and the brass key had disappeared from the lock. Her eyes flickered to where Carlo was now standing by the bed, casually feeding his wrist-watch into the bedside-cabinet drawer.

Her turned a glance on her, her skin began to prickle, her pulse dropping to a low, slow throb. Provocation was written into every single challenging pore of him. She glanced around the room. The suitcase was nowhere. She looked back at him.

'You said you weren't going to stop me from leaving,' she murmured warily.

'I changed my mind.' He began to unbutton his shirt.

'Any reason worth hearing?' She tried for sarcasm but didn't quite pull it off.

'Sex is a good enough reason for me, *cara*,' he drawled lazily. 'But I think you might need a bit of convincing before you will agree.'

She stared at him, hovering like an idiot because she wasn't quite sure what to do next. The shirt was slowly revealing a long male torso, rich in the sensually masculine sweep of crisp dark hair.

'Please don't do that,' she tremored.

The shirt landed like a challenge on the floor by his feet.

'I'm going to take a shower before we finish this,' he announced and turned towards the bathroom, tanned muscles glossed with the sweat of a long day and flexing with a tension he was trying to pretend he didn't have.

'Carlo, please don't—'

He turned on her like a panther on the attack. Even the snap of his white teeth scared the life out of her as he covered the space between them, snatched the shoes from her hands, dropped them then picked her up by the waist.

She landed on the bed without really knowing how she'd got there. 'What do you think—?'

He arrived then, one hard, angry male accompanied by one hard, angry kiss. She groaned beneath the pressure of it, then whimpered because she knew she was going to respond.

He saved her that indignity by lifting his dark head to glare at her. 'Now, listen to me, you broken-hearted idiot,' he ground out. 'I am not your enemy and I never have been.'

'Y-you plotted against me.'

'I plotted *for* you!' he amended fiercely. 'Bruno called me in as soon as you wrote to tell him you were going to marry Batiste.'

'He's as bad as you are!'

'Who? Bruno or Batiste?'

'Both!' she cried and tried to wriggle herself free.

His eyes darkened. 'You don't want to do that, *amore*, if you don't want this to move on to its inevitable conclusion just yet.'

Sheer fury at his confidence made her hit out with her fists. Both were caught and pinned above her head with a hand while the other hand firmly cupped her chin.

'The Batistes are in serious financial trouble,' he told her. 'That huge white marble museum of a villa they own has been a drain on their resources since they inherited it. The last time Alessandro came to me for a loan I advised him to give the house away to the country and let them open it to the public—which would mean the Batiste name would keep its damn kudos and they would not be such slaves to the place. No,' he rasped when she tried to speak, 'you don't say anything—you just listen.'

Then he kissed her again just to punctuate which of them was in control here. 'I hate you,' she managed.

'Don't you just,' he mocked, adding a smile because her mouth was still quivering with pleasure from the kiss.

'Angelina Batiste loves that house more than she loves her husband and son,' he went on. 'She would sell them before she would sell it, which is basically what she did. When your name came up in conversation between her and Angelo, she leapt at the opportunity to do a bit of matchmaking—with some subtle blackmail thrown in to keep Angelo in line. He's like Villa Batiste, Francesca. He consumes money faster than he can earn it. He drives a top-of-the-range car and lives in a top-of-the-range apartment—all bought on credit, of course. He's handsome but vain, which makes him very high maintenance. The designer stores rub their hands together when they see him coming.'

'I suppose you're not high maintenance?'

'I can afford to be. I do not spend above my means!'

'But your stock still languishes in my grandfather's bank vault! We all crave what we can't have.'

'And what do you crave, *mi amore*—the man you have spent half the day with or the man who pins you to this bed?'

'What do you care?' She glared at him. 'You couldn't even make the effort to stop me driving away with him!'

'Ah,' he said and rolled away from her.

She should have got up while she had the chance—but she didn't.

'He drives like a maniac. You are lucky he got you here in one piece.'

She turned her head to stare at him. 'You mean you followed us?'

He turned to look at her. 'Two cars behind you all the way,' he said.

She frowned as she studied the half-mocking gleam in his rich, dark eyes. 'Then why didn't you follow us into the courtyard?'

'Because,' he answered softly, 'I wanted to see what you were going to do next.'

'Do next in what way?'

'As in whether you packed a bag then left with him or you gave him short shrift and sent him on his way,' he explained.

'I don't understand.'

'No, I can see that you don't.' Closing the gap between

their mouths, he stole a quick kiss from her then sat up, leaving her lying there with her lips tingling and what was beginning to feel like a permanent puzzled frown.

He moved then, stretching and flexing those wonderful back muscles like a body builder putting on a show. Her mouth ran dry, her tongue snaked out to coil a lick around her lips.

'Explain,' she said.

'Later,' he said and got to his feet. 'I need that shower—'

'No!' Sitting up, she scrambled to her feet too. 'Explain now!' she insisted.

He swung round to look at her, his dark eyes brooding on her tense, challenging pose. Sudden tension in his face made the bones in his cheeks stand out, not with anger but with—

'You are still in love with him,' he grated.

Her eyes widened. 'I am not!' she denied.

'Don't lie to me,' he said harshly. ' I saw what it did to you when you met him the other night.'

'Shocked—disgusted me?' she suggested.

He flashed her a bitter look. 'Enough for you to whisper his name while you were sleeping in my arms?'

'I couldn't have,' she gasped.

'Well, you did,' he declared. 'You let me make love to you but you fell asleep afterwards with his name on your lips—and if you thought, *cara*, that I was going to stand by and let you swap from me back to him without doing something to protect you from the bastard, then you don't know me at all!'

'You mean you…?' she stopped, tried to think then swallowed before beginning again. 'You mean you tricked me into signing those papers because you thought I was going to go back to him?'

'I told him this morning he would not be touching a penny belonging to you. Clearly, he did not believe me.'

'Y-you also told him you and I were getting married.'

'Why not?' he challenged. 'Would you expect me to hand you over without a fight?'

'I don't know.' She blinked. 'I don't think I know anything of any certainty right now. You've been twisting me in knots since the first time I met you.'

'Knots?' he repeated. 'You want to know about being tied in knots, Francesca, then try being me for a moment or two,' he ground out cynically. 'Because the first time we met I only needed to take one look at you to fall in love so fast I didn't know what had hit me, but you were so starry-eyed over that bastard that you didn't even notice! And that is what I call being *twisted* in knots, which is a hell of a lot worse than just being tied!'

With that he turned and slammed into the bathroom, leaving her standing there frozen by what he'd said. She stood unmoving while she listened to the shower running, remained exactly where she was through every sound that seeped through the bathroom door until he reappeared again, hair wet, clean-shaven, droplets of water clinging to his skin now and a towel clinging to his lean hips.

'I noticed you,' she pushed out, bringing him to a stop. 'I noticed and noticed you!' she extended on a helpless choke. 'I dreamed about you and felt so guilty about doing it that I used to push my head beneath the pillow to hide in shame!'

'You don't have to say this.' He frowned impatiently. 'I don't need pacifying.'

'But it's the truth!' she swore. 'I w-wanted you in a way I never wanted Angelo. I used to hate you being in the same room because I sometimes couldn't cope! You were up there,' she flung a hand out. 'Way beyond me in every way I could think of. And I was committed to another man I was supposed to be in love with, so how could I go home at night and ache for you? S-so I pretended to myself that I didn't like you, that what I was feeling was hostility, that was all. Then we met at those traffic lights and I couldn't pretend anything any more!'

'Don't,' he warned gruffly, 'turn the tears on.'

'But I don't know what else to do!' she cried. 'You say I twisted you in knots but how do you think it felt for me to find out I was falling in love with you? And you *did* play me like a puppet!' she accused him. 'You're still doing it now by standing there waiting for me to grovel when I don't want to grovel! Because I still think you—'

'That's it,' he said and reached out with a hand to grab a chunk of white towelling at her throat then used it to yank her close. 'No need to grovel, Francesca; just shut up and kiss me.'

So she did. She kissed him until they had no clothes on and she kissed him as they tumbled on the bed. She kissed him as she rode him with a fierce, desperate, hungry passion that held him utterly her captive then he reversed their positions and gave back to her what she had given him.

'We marry next week,' he informed her lazily much later.

'In the chapel I don't know about on your *palazzo*?'

He was silent for a moment, then, 'I am going to have to make Batiste keep his nose out of my business,' he said.

'Would my mother have married your father there too?'

He wasn't slow, he knew what she was prompting here. 'OK,' he rolled to lie beside her, 'this is it, the final explanation, so listen carefully because I have better things I want to do with you than talk about other people,' he warned. 'Our parents came together in a business arrangement that revolved around the Carlucci company needing an urgent injection of cash and your grandfather wanting a husband for his daughter. Your mother was never happy with the arrangement so when she met and fell in love with your father she refused to marry anyone else but Vincent Bernard. It caused one hell of a scandal at the time, especially when she fell pregnant. By then our company stock was already in your grandfather's possession. Being a contrary devil, he blamed my father for not getting in there first and making your mother pregnant. Yes,' he nodded when Francesca gasped, 'you can be shocked. My father was shocked too. He told your grandfather a few home truths about his morals, to which your grandfather responded by refusing to sell us back our stock. We have remained on the Gianni black list ever since then—until you came along and frightened Bruno by telling him you were going to marry Angelo Batiste. Suddenly a Carlucci was useful to a Gianni and Bruno thought he had the perfect bargaining tool with our block of stock.'

'So you came hunting me because of a business arrangement with Bruno.'

'No, you suspicious little witch,' he chided. 'I came hunting because I had *already* seen you and already wanted what I saw! You can keep the Carlucci stock locked up forever if it pleases you, *cara*; I don't care.' He rolled again to arrive back on top of her to add lazily, 'So long as you keep me locked up with it.'

'Like a slave?'

'Mm,' he murmured with seductive promise.

'OK,' she agreed. 'Then consider yourself locked up.'

'Good,' he said. 'Great,' he added. 'Then that brings an end to it all.'

'Just like that?'

'*Sì*, just like that.' He nodded. 'I love you. You love me. Your great-uncle Bruno is very happy because I promised not to throw him out of your house. Angelo will be happy because I will promise not to ruin his family business so long as he forgets he knows your name. Now, do you want me to run you a bath so you can relax and recuperate before I ravish you again, or do I get to do more ravishing first?'

Francesca pushed her head back into the pillows so she could look into his handsome, sardonic face and wondered how she was going to live the rest of her life with so much arrogance?

Easy, she told herself. 'Oh, why wait?' she said to him. 'Let's do the ravishing. You know you'll only do it anyway the moment I hit the bath.'

'I knew you were on my wavelength from the moment I set eyes on you.' He smiled in satisfaction, and the ravishing began.

A SICILIAN
HUSBAND

by

Kate Walker

Kate Walker was born in Nottinghamshire, but as she grew up in Yorkshire she has always felt that her roots were there. She met her husband at university and she originally worked as a children's librarian, but after the birth of her son she returned to her old childhood love of writing. When she's not working, she divides her time between her family, their three cats, and her interests of embroidery, antiques, film and theatre, and, of course, reading.

You can visit Kate at http://www.kate-walker.com

CHAPTER ONE

THE man at the other side of the bar was beautiful.

Beautiful.

Terrie could find no other word to describe him that fitted those devastating looks quite so well. And she had tried. Because *beautiful* didn't seem like quite the right word to use about someone so masculine, so totally male. And yet it was the only one that worked.

She'd tried *handsome* and it was too weak, too 'pretty' somehow. It didn't allow for the straight, firm slash of a nose, the sharply defined cheekbones. And *good-looking* was way too bland. This man was more than good-looking—he was superb!

Attractive didn't even come near the truth, and, although *gorgeous* fitted with the lush warmth of his mouth, the stunning deep, deep brown of his eyes, the sleek olive skin that gave away the fact that he was most definitely not English, both *attractive* and *gorgeous* lacked the hard edge that this man wore like a suit of armour, the hint of danger that lurked in those deep-set eyes. And she suspected that that mouth, although apparently sensual, could soon harden to a dangerously cruel line.

His disturbing blend of supreme confidence, bordering on arrogance, and an aura of total ease in his surroundings and himself made him stand out in the crowded room as clearly as if a spotlight had been switched on, its beam centring on the glossy mane of jet-black hair.

No, *beautiful* was the only word that was right. He had a starkly masculine beauty that had caught and held her attention from the moment she had walked into the room. And now she couldn't drag her eyes away, even though she suspected that the intensity of her gaze must soon get through to him. Surely he would sense that someone was staring at him, feel it like a faint touch on his skin—and then he would look up.

And even as she thought it, the heavy-hooded lids that had been lowered suddenly lifted, and the burning golden-bronze eyes blazed into hers through lush black lashes.

And the look of cold disdain, the molten glare he turned on her, the obvious distance that he clearly wanted to put between them, was so clear, so sharply cutting that it made Terrie actually jump in her seat. Hastily she looked away again as quickly as possible. Heat screamed along the nerve paths of her body, searing a sense of burning embarrassment and humiliation at being caught staring like that. It was the behaviour of some lust-smitten adolescent confronted by the boy-band focus of her latest crush. She had never done anything quite so crass in her life before.

Stop it! she told herself in furious but silent reproof. Stop this nonsense right now!

The woman at the other side of the bar was staring straight at him, Giovanni Cardella realised. Staring straight at him with a mindless, dumbstruck expression on her face that made it look as if she had never seen a man before in her life. Sliding another glance in her direction through the concealment of thick, dark lashes, he frowned deeply, and dropped his eyes again to stare down into his glass.

Another woman.

Another woman who wasn't Lucia.

Another woman who was making it plain that she found

him attractive when that was the last thing on God's earth that he wanted.

He was no fool. He knew that he had the sort of looks, the colouring, the height, the build that drew female eyes his way. And that when their gaze rested on him, it lingered. As soon as it had become known that he was alone, they had been there. The female vultures had gathered, all seeking to 'comfort' the rich widower.

But he had no time, no inclination for other women. There had only ever been one woman in his life—Lucia. And Lucia had been all he had ever wanted.

And this woman was no Lucia. For one thing, she was a pale ash blonde with the sort of delicate complexion that came with the impossible weather on this rain-soaked island. And she was tall; even though she was sitting down he could tell that. Lucia had been petite; slight, dark and stunning. This woman, with her blue-grey eyes and fair hair, was like the opposite. The negative to Lucia's positive.

And she was still looking, damn her!

Today of all days, her bold stare felt like an invasion. It pushed into the privacy of his thoughts, intruded into his memories. And he hated that.

'Madre di Dio!'

Hot fury washed over him, driving him to lift his eyes again, when he would far rather have kept them fixed on the ground. His gaze swinging to her face in a rush, he turned on her a blazing glare that held all the force of the rejection of her unsubtle approach that burned in his soul.

'Oh, damn!' Terrie muttered under her breath, horrified by the response her unthinking reaction had caused. 'Damn, damn, damn!'

And the trouble was that even looking swiftly away and down at the table did nothing to ease the sensation of embarrassment and unease. She could still feel the scorch of his contempt searing over her skin, stripping her of a much-needed layer of protection.

'Well, it's time we got back.'

Beside her, Claire and Anna drained their glasses and made moves to get to their feet, picking up handbags, pushing back their chairs.

'You coming, Terrie?'

'What? No—I think I'll give this last session a miss.'

What was she doing? This was the perfect opportunity to sneak out of there, disappear before she made an even greater fool of herself. If she went now, then she and this man, the stranger she had been caught staring at, would probably—hopefully—never catch sight of each other again. If she could hide herself in the bustle and crowds of the conference she had come here to attend then hopefully he would forget about her and her *faux pas* would be overlooked as well.

But the truth was that she really didn't want to go. Even before she had come into the bar with her friends she had determined that the last session of the sales conference was more trouble than it was worth.

'Are you sure?'

Terrie nodded emphatically, shaking loose some of the blonde locks that she had forced into a hopefully disciplined chignon at the start of the day so that they fell in disordered tendrils around her oval face.

'Absolutely. I've been bored out of my skull from the start, and I really can't take any more. Before I came here, I was beginning to suspect that a career in selling baby clothes just wasn't for me—and now I'm absolutely positive that it's not. As soon as I get back to Netherton, I'm handing in my notice and looking for something else. So there's no point at all in my going back to hear the MD spouting about quotas and new lines.'

It sounded totally rational, clearly thought through. Nothing whatsoever to do with the fact that her sense of reality had just been severely rocked as a result of being confronted by the most devastating specimen of manhood she had ever seen. It had *nothing* to do with that, she told herself fiercely. Nothing at all.

'Well, if you've made up your mind.'

Claire still looked uncertain, but Anna was pulling at her sleeve, tugging her away towards the door through which the other conference delegates were already streaming, heading back to the ballroom.

'Definitely. I'm going to finish this drink and then go to my room and pack, ready for an early getaway tomorrow.'

'Then we'll see you at dinner?'

Terrie nodded abstractedly, her attention elsewhere. Until she had heard herself speak the words aloud, she hadn't really been aware that she planned to say them. But now that she had, she knew that she meant everything she'd said.

She *was* bored. If the truth was told, she hated her job. Hated the long hours and the travelling involved in it. Hated trying to persuade people to buy overpriced, second-rate items. She didn't know how she'd stuck it this long.

Well, from now on everything was going to change!

And for a start she wasn't going up to her room to pack after all. She was going to stay here and have another drink and relax. Recover from the endurance test that had been the sales conference.

And she wasn't even going to so much as *glance* in the direction of the wretched man on the other side of the

room, she told herself as she got slowly to her feet. There
was no way on earth that she wanted to risk another of
those glares. She was still smarting from the scorching
effect of the one she had already received.

Despite his determination not even to look in her direction again, Gio found that the woman's movement
drew his attention once more. She uncoiled her slim body
like a cat, he couldn't help reflecting, fascinated in spite
of himself. Her movements were slow and sensual, the
short stroll from her table to the bar making her slender
hips sway underneath the deep red suit with its fitted
jacket and narrow pencil skirt. The blonde hair was clearly
fighting against the restraints of the too-severe knot she
had twisted it up into, and feathery strands of it were
blowing about her face, wafting onto her neck.

With a sigh of impatience that he caught even where
he sat, she paused, reached up, pulled out a couple of
strategically placed pins, and shook her head determinedly. The result caught Gio totally by surprise.

As the pale blonde swathe of hair came loose and tumbled down her back, flowing over her shoulders like a
golden wave, he found himself suddenly a prey to an urgent, twisting pull of sensual demand low down in his
body.

It had the force of a kick in his gut, hitting with the
sort of intensity that he had thought that he would never
experience again in his life.

'*Inferno!*' he swore under his breath, struggling to force
his attention away and onto the narrow gold watch that
encircled one wrist. Though even as he concentrated
fiercely on its square face, he knew that every male instinct he possessed was still in a state of heightened
awareness of the woman at the bar.

Where the devil *was* Chris Macdonald?

Drinks and a meal, and a chance to discuss how the day's events had gone in court, he had suggested, and the prospect had seemed like a lifesaver to Gio, who had been dreading spending the time on his own. Once he'd talked to Paolo on the phone and wished his little son sweet dreams, the evening had stretched ahead empty and dark, filled with bad memories. He had snatched at the opportunity to have company on this, the anniversary of the worst night ever in his life.

But Chris showed no sign at all of putting in an appearance. Their meeting had been arranged for six, and it was now half past.

The realisation had barely crossed his mind when his mobile phone rang sharply. As if summoned by his thoughts, there was Chris Macdonald's number on the screen.

Flicking the case open with an impatient hand, Gio lifted it to his mouth.

'*Sì?*'

A few seconds later he snapped the phone off again and tossed it down onto the table, glaring at it as if the inoffensive gadget were in fact Macdonald himself.

Chris was not coming. He had to stay at home, he had said. His young daughter was ill and they had just called the doctor.

'*Non c'e problema!*' he had assured him. 'Don't worry about it.'

But he had been lying through his teeth. There *was* a problem. The problem of the long, lonely night that lay ahead of him.

He should be used to long, lonely nights. He'd lived through enough of them since he had lost Lucia. Lying awake, staring blank-eyed into the darkness, in the big, empty bed that had suddenly seemed so cold and uncomfortable without the warmth of her softly curvaceous body beside him.

And if he managed to fall asleep then it was even worse. Because then he woke to a moment of forgetfulness, a brief, merciful spell of believing that it had never happened. That she was still there, with him. Until he reached out and felt the coldness of the empty space beside him, and the reality all came flooding back.

'*Dio—no!*' he muttered savagely, both hands clenching into fists as he tried to push away the black thoughts that flooded his mind.

Tonight he had thought that he would escape them. That with friendly company, a meal, and perhaps a glass or two too many of a fine wine, he might find some relief from the emptiness that was always there, like a dark, dangerous chasm in his mind, just waiting for him to fall into it. But Chris's phone call had just shattered that hope.

'And what can I get for you, Miss Hayden?'

'Dry white wine, please.'

Behind him, Gio heard the bartender's question, the soft, feminine tones of the reply, and knew without a moment's hesitation that it was the blonde who had spoken. The blonde who had been eyeing him up so blatantly.

'Your friends not with you tonight, then?' The bartender almost echoed Gio's own thoughts.

'No, they've gone into the final session of the conference. I'll be joining them later for dinner, I suppose.'

'You didn't fancy going with them?'

'No.'

He could almost hear the shudder in her voice.

'I've had more than enough of sales figures and targets. I've been bored stupid the past two days; I couldn't take any more. In fact, I've decided to chuck the job in.'

Bored, huh?

The word seemed to echo inside Gio's head. She was bored, and she had been eyeing him—and she had deliberately stayed behind when her friends had left.

Coincidence or invitation?

The clamour in his body wasn't easing. If anything, the sound of her voice had made it worse. It was soft, musical, and faintly husky. The sort of voice that made him think of murmurs in the darkness of the night, the heat of a sensual bed, the whisper of her breath across his skin as she spoke.

And it had been so long. Too long for any red-blooded male.

'This conference has been no fun at all. I've decided I need some other way of making a living. So I think I'll just hang around here for a while and see what happens.'

The thread of laughter through the words was the last straw. It seemed to carry an electrical charge with it, sparking off hot little arrows of hunger that ran along every nerve, bringing them so stingingly awake that he had to bite his lip to keep back the groan of reaction.

So she wanted *fun*, did she? And he…he wanted anything, *anything* other than to be alone for another long, dark night. He wanted a warm, living, breathing, responding body in his bed after far, far too long.

He hadn't felt this interested, this alert, this *alive* in years. And he wasn't going to turn his back on the chance to let this feeling continue for as long as he could.

He was on his feet before he had actually finished the thought, turning and heading for the tall, slender figure at the bar.

Terrie rested her elbows on the polished wood, stared down into the cool, clear liquid in her glass and wondered just what she had done.

Burned her boats, the answer came back from the sensible, rational part of her mind. She had well and truly burned her boats, or her bridges, cut off her nose to spite her face,... Insert whatever other clichéd sayings described her uncharacteristically rash and unthinking gesture.

She was probably in trouble with her job, for one. James Richmond, her immediate manager, would have noticed her absence from the MD's speech and she had no doubt that he would haul her into his office as a result. He was that sort of man. And people just did *not* skip what he considered to be vital parts of this conference— at least, not with impunity. The last time that had happened, the offending person had been shown the door pretty fast.

So even if she didn't resign herself, she was almost certainly unemployed. And, as a result, in financial difficulties, owing rent on her flat, and with no way to keep up payments on her car. OK, so her job had been a bore and a grind. But it had been a job. One that paid her way at least. And she had put it at risk on some foolish, impossible impulse that she couldn't even explain to herself.

That man. The thought rushed into her mind, driving everything else before it.

It had been the sight of the beautiful man at the other side of the bar that had somehow pushed her into this crazily impulsive mood. The sort of stupid, irrational mood in which she threw up a perfectly decent job and behaved in a way that meant she just didn't recognise herself.

For example—just *what* was she doing standing here, propping up this bar, when everyone else was completing the schedule of the conference before the final dinner and going home? What was she waiting for? Hoping for?

Did she really think—was she actually *hoping* that the

stunning and exotic-looking stranger was going to come up to her and change her life?

Fat chance!

Terrie actually snorted cynically at the idiotic path of her own thoughts. She really couldn't believe *that!*

Picking up her glass, she twisted on her heel, turning so that she was half facing the rest of the bar, but at an angle so that if the intriguing stranger was looking again she wouldn't risk being seen by him. Just one experience of that furiously cold-eyed glare was bad enough. She didn't want to go through a repeat performance.

The wretched man had actually gone!

'Well, thanks a bunch!' Terrie muttered against the rim of her glass as she lifted it to sip at her wine. 'Thank you so very much!'

Foolishly, she felt as if he was responsible for the pickle she was in. She had made this crazy, impulsive gesture of throwing in her job in some non-typical response to his presence. Had stayed in the bar when she would have been far better to stick with her friends and go to the final session, however boring. Had even...

Admit it! she declared to herself. She had even hung around in the bar in the hope of meeting up with and discovering more about this man who had had such an impact on her.

And the so-and-so had got up and made his way out of the bar while her back was turned, without so much as a second look. He must have walked within inches of her and she hadn't even noticed!

So much for changing her life at a stroke!

Scowling as much at her own foolishness as at the absent stranger, Terrie lifted her drink in a bleak parody of a toast, inclining it in the direction of the stranger's now empty seat.

'To ships that pass in the night,' she muttered.

And froze as, from her right-hand side, another hand reached out, deliberately clinking the glass it held against hers in acknowledgement of the toast.

'*Salute, signorina!*' a deep, lyrically accented voice murmured in her ear.

CHAPTER TWO

'WHAT?'

The shaken exclamation was pushed from her lips as her nerveless fingers lost their grip on her glass. Slipping from her grasp, it tumbled downwards, spilling its contents on the way, and crashed onto the floor, splintering into a thousand tiny pieces.

'Oh, look what you've done now!'

Even as the words escaped her, she was acknowledging how irrational they were. It was her own disturbed feelings that had twisted her nerves so tight she was ready to jump like a startled cat at the slightest thing. And as for feeling that seeing him had somehow pushed her into making rash decisions about her life, well, that was just nonsense. She had been ready to make a move long before she had ever set eyes on him.

But acknowledging that fact and reacting accordingly were two totally different things. Especially when she was now up so close to him that she could see that his eyes were closer to bronze than ebony and that fascinating little gold flecks burned like slivers of flame at the heart of their irises.

'Perdone, signorina.'

The voice was even more devastating close up, too. Pure warm, liquid honey, with just the tiniest touch of gravel in its husky undertone.

'Forgive me…your skirt…'

A long tanned hand lifted in an autocratic summons to the bartender, and before Terrie even had time to realise

17

just what he had in mind a clean, damp cloth had been provided without a word having to be spoken. The next moment she found herself looking at the top of the stranger's downbent head, staring fascinated at the sheen on the night-dark strands, as he set himself to wiping away the splashes of wine from her skirt.

And this was worse than ever. The stroke of the cloth over the lower part of her body, even with the linen of her skirt acting as a buffer, made her heart thud unevenly, her breath catch in her throat. And when he moved lower, wiping away a few glistening droplets that were clinging to the fine nylon of her stockings, she shifted uneasily, uncomfortably.

He was too close. Far, far too close. If she inhaled she could breathe in some shockingly sensual scent. The tang of bergamot and lemon, mixed with the other, more intensely personal aroma of his skin.

'No—it's all right… Please…'

Her skin was prickling with sensation, heat racing through her veins. And when the side of his hand brushed her leg, skin almost touching skin, she had to clamp her mouth tightly shut, teeth digging into her lower lip, against the moan of response that almost escaped her.

'It will dry!' she declared with more emphasis than was necessary. Anything to stop him, to distract him from these disturbingly intimate attentions. 'And it's only a cheap suit.'

'Then let me at least buy you another drink.'

Terrie was so relieved by the way he straightened up, tossing the cloth onto a nearby table, that she would have agreed to anything. She didn't spot the look or gesture with which he summoned the bartender, barely heard the swift commanding notes of his order. Yet somehow he had manoeuvred her into a seat at the far side of the room, settling her on the burgundy velvet chair before taking the one opposite her in the privacy of the booth. And the next moment a full glass was brought and placed carefully in front of her.

'It was dry white wine, wasn't it?'

'Oh—yes…'

Her response was even more distracted because as he lounged back in his seat and stretched out his long legs in front of him, crossed at the ankles, she discovered to her horror that her skirt had not been the only victim of the accident with the glass. The smart silver-grey trousers that were now in her view were liberally splashed with wine too—and his was only too clearly *not* a cheap suit. In fact, if the perfect fit, immaculate tailoring and fabulous material were anything to go by, it was an extremely expensive item of clothing.

'But there's no need… You don't have to go to any trouble.'

'It is no trouble,' he assured her, his voice low and as intent as the gleaming eyes that were fixed on her face. 'On the contrary, it's a pleasure.'

The words should have been reassuring, but to Terrie's total consternation they had precisely the opposite effect. She felt uncomfortably as if someone had scraped away a vital protective layer from her skin, leaving her nerves raw and uncomfortable, and that unnervingly direct stare made her shift uneasily on the velvet-covered chair.

Up close, he was just *too much*. Too beautiful, too big, too sexually disturbing, too *male*, for any female with the normal amount of hormones to be able to cope. And every single one of Terrie's feminine instincts was on buzzing red alert at simply being faced with him.

'I really think…'

'What are you afraid of?'

'I'm not *afraid*!'

Her tone of voice belied it, starting high-pitched and rising even further until it ended in an inelegant squawk at the end of the sentence.

'Then drink your wine.'

Softly spoken as it was, it was clearly a command, and one he intended to have obeyed at once and without question. Just for a second Terrie was tempted to argue. But the impulse to rebellion died as soon as she looked into his dark face and met the forceful blaze of those tawny eyes head-on.

'Thank you,' she managed, reaching for the glass.

But with the drink halfway to her lips she suddenly paused again.

'I wouldn't want you to think…I mean—I don't normally let…'

To her embarrassment, the faint lift of one black eyebrow mocked the struggle she was having to get her words out.

'I don't normally talk to strange men in bars.'

Was she truly as nervous as she sounded? Gio wondered. Or was it just an act? Surely the woman who had given him such a deliberate and unashamed appraisal couldn't now be feeling uncertain and ill at ease.

Wasn't it more likely that, having won his interest, she had now decided to change tactics, preferring to act as the prey rather than the hunter? Well, he would play along for the moment, though he wasn't in the mood for subtlety or games. And as they were both only after one thing, then quite frankly he didn't see the need for them.

'And I don't normally talk to women I don't know either,' he returned smoothly.

If he had had any doubts about the way he was going to handle this, then they had evaporated as soon as he had seated himself opposite her. This woman had class. The slim, elegant body, the fall of pale blonde hair, the porcelain-pale complexion, all had a touch of exoticism to a man used to being surrounded by women with a much darker natural colouring. The faint scent of her body mixed with a light, floral perfume to send a sensual message straight to his brain, making his body harden in hungry demand. But rushing things would be a mistake. The evening would be much more enjoyable if he took his time, enjoyed the journey as well as the final arrival at his destination.

And the final conquest would be all the sweeter as a result.

'So why don't we introduce ourselves and then neither of us will be complete strangers?'

One long, powerful hand was held out over the table, the fingers elegant and square-tipped.

'My name is Giovanni Cardella. But most of my friends call me Gio.'

He pronounced the name like a softened version of 'Joe', though in his beautiful accent it had nothing like the ordinary solidity of the English form.

'Terrie Hayden…'

Did she really have to touch that hand? She had reacted badly enough to the brief, faint brush of it against her leg. How much worse would she feel if she had to grasp those strong-boned fingers, feel the heat of that satin olive skin against her own?

But it seemed she had no choice. Taking a deep breath, she put her own hand into his, sharp white teeth digging into her lower lip as his strength closed around her. The sensation of grasping a live electrical wire sent a powerful, burning reaction zigzagging up her arm, making her head swim so that she missed Gio's murmured response.

'I'm sorry?'

'Terry?' he repeated, frowning faintly. 'But that is a man's name—no?'

'It's Terrie—with an i and an e, not a y.'

Carefully she eased her hand away from his, struggling to resist the impulse to cradle it against her, as if his touch had actually burned her skin.

'It's short for Teresa actually. But, like you, no one ever calls me by my proper name.'

'I would. Terrie is not right for you—but Teresa...'

He made it sound so very different, Terrie registered with a sense of shock. After so many years of being called *Tereesa*, then his lyrical pronunciation of *Terayza* had a lovely, musical sound that made her smile unconsciously.

'I will call you Teresa.'

He could call her anything he liked, if he would just continue to speak to her in that wonderful voice; if he would smile into her eyes in that enticing way. The effect of that smile was to make her feel as if she was bathed in the warm sun of some Mediterranean country, which was obviously where he had been born.

'What part of Italy are you from?' she asked impulsively.

'I am a Sicilian. My home is in Palermo.'

It fitted. Italy would have given him the smooth sophistication that he wore with the sleek ease of an elegant cat. And Sicily had added the dangerous, untamed streak that burned in the tawny eyes, the curl of his mouth. Knowing he came from Sicily was like opening the door to the family pet cat, only to find that in its place a dark, dangerous, predatory jaguar had prowled into the room.

'I'd love to visit Sicily! I've never been further abroad than a weekend trip to Bruges, and I'd really like to travel more.'

'Well, perhaps now that you've decided to "chuck the job in" you'll get the chance to do just that.'

At first Terrie thought that it was just the way that the slang phrase sounded strange on his tongue that made her pause, considering it thoughtfully. But next moment came the stunning realisation that he was quoting her own words directly, making her head whirl in shock.

'Chuck the—you heard that! You were listening!'

'You weren't exactly quiet. I wasn't aware that what you were saying was a state secret. If you hadn't wanted anyone else to hear then you should have kept your voice lower.'

Was she really trying to pretend that she hadn't meant him to 'overhear'? After that openly interested look, the way that she had announced that she was bored and looking for some fun was a deliberate come-on if ever he'd heard one. It was too late for her to back down now.

And, if the truth was told, he would be disappointed if she did. He had no time for games, for the two steps forward, one step back dance of seduction. For the flirtatious pretence of needing to be wooed in order to be won. He knew what he wanted out of this—and, he was sure, so did she. So why were they playing around?

'Have dinner with me.'

'What?'

The question came so sharply, so unexpectedly that it caught Terrie totally off guard. It also caught her mid-swallow of another sip of wine and she had to close her mouth hurriedly and gulp it down hard so as not to choke.

'What did you say?' she asked, lavender eyes opening wide in apparent shock.

Was this not what she wanted, then? Of course it was, so why did she look so startled, as if the invitation was a total surprise? Or was it that he had acted too fast, cut through some of the expected moves, the polite chat, the 'getting to know you' that she had been anticipating?

Hadn't she expected him to be quite so forthright?

Well, he wasn't in the mood for observing convention, even if waiting increased the pleasure for her.

'Have dinner with me. Oh, come on, *mia bella*! Don't look so shocked! It's not as if I've asked you to come to bed with me right here and now. It's only dinner.'

Only dinner! Terrie's head was spinning with the suddenness and the shock of it all. It was only—what?—less than half an hour since she had first spotted this man on the opposite side of the room. No more than twenty minutes since he had caught her eye and given her the most furiously off-putting glare it had ever been her misfortune to encounter. Then he had sneaked up on her, frightened her into dropping her glass, and now...

'You want me to have dinner with you?'

'And is that so hard to understand?'

The beautiful voice had developed a hard edge that reminded her unnervingly of the glare he had turned on her earlier.

'I know English is not my first language, but I would have thought...'

'Your English is perfect and you damn well know it! But after the look you gave me a while ago—when you were sitting over there...' Terrie waved a hand in the direction of the Sicilian's previous seat. 'I would have thought that you couldn't wait to see the back of me.'

'Ah, that...'

Gio had the grace to look a little shamefaced. The sensual shape of his mouth twisted slightly as he swirled the last drops of his wine round and round in the bottom of his glass.

'That wasn't meant for you,' he murmured, his attention apparently fixed on the rich red liquid. 'I was angry with someone else—someone I had expected to meet.'

'Another woman?'

Of course. It figured. He had been stood up and now he wanted to fill the unexpectedly empty hours with someone else.

'Well, you certainly know how to make a girl feel second best.'

'*Come?*'

Those heavy lids flew up, stunning eyes fixing on her face, his confusion apparently genuine.

'No—you have it totally wrong. The man I was supposed to meet was someone I work with—it was a business meeting. He rang a short time ago to say that he couldn't make it.'

'So you're all on your own?'

She tried to make it sound grudging, as if she was not fully mollified, but only succeeded in coming across as making a hasty reassessment and coming close to conceding.

'All on my own—a stranger lost in London... You don't believe me?'

Her expression had given her away.

'You're no more lost than I am! Less, in fact. You look more at home here than I do. In fact I'd be willing to bet that you know your way around London as well as you do Palermo.'

'I'll concede you that.'

The admission was accompanied by another of those smiles that had the force of a thousand-watt electrical charge, the effect of it sizzling straight through every single nerve in her body and making her toes curl in instant reaction inside her elegant court shoes.

'But I *am* still on my own. And I'm hungry. And I

would prefer to have company while I eat rather than spend the rest of the evening alone. I have a table booked for two. It would seem a waste not to use it, when you are looking for company too.'

Something about that 'looking for company' snagged on a raw edge in Terrie's mind, making her hesitate sharply. But even as she was rethinking hastily he leaned forward and looked straight into her eyes, fixing her with the hypnotic force of his deep, dark gaze.

'*Per piacere,*' he said softly, huskily. 'Please have dinner with me.'

She *should* say that she was having dinner with her friends—with the rest of the conference. She was *going* to say exactly that. She actually opened her mouth to form the words, only to hear herself say exactly the opposite.

'Yes,' she managed a touch breathlessly. 'Thank you.'

If he had put one foot wrong in his reaction... If he had so much as looked in the least bit self-satisfied or triumphant, then she would have retracted immediately. She would have rushed to her feet, told him that no, she'd changed her mind, she was already booked for this evening. She would have rejoined Claire and Anna and eaten the buffet meal that came as part of the conference package. And, although she would have probably always regretted not accepting his invitation, she would have told herself that it was safer this way—that she wasn't putting herself at any sort of risk.

But Giovanni Cardella did nothing of the sort.

Instead he simply reached out one long, elegant hand. The bronzed fingers touched hers where they lay on the polished wood table-top, rested lightly, warmly, briefly— just for a moment—and then lifted and moved to pick up his glass once again.

'Thank you,' he said, lifting it to his lips and draining

the last of his wine. 'Shall we go through to the restaurant?'

And as she nodded silently Terrie admitted to herself that it had been the brevity of that touch that had been her undoing. Delicate and swift, it had been like the feel of a butterfly alighting and then flying away again. And it had left her feeling lost and unsatisfied. It had just been enough to awaken those electric feelings that had fizzed over her skin. Awaken them and then leave them—and she wanted more. Much, much more.

She didn't know whether it was those feelings, or simply coincidence, but as she got up from her chair to follow him she caught her foot on something and stumbled awkwardly.

At once Gio was at her side, hands coming out to support her, powerful arms taking her full weight with only the faintest tensing of muscle to reveal any effort. And as he held her close, her cloud-coloured eyes flew to his and locked with ebony darkness.

'Careful!' The single word shivered over her skin.

Would he kiss her now? Terrie wondered, the question flaring so swiftly in her mind, burning so fiercely that she felt sure that Gio must see it in her eyes and recognise her need in an instant. And it was that need that stunned her, shaking her rigid because she had never felt anything like it before in her life.

Oh, she had been attracted to men, obviously, in her past. She had even come close to wondering if she was in love. But nothing had lasted. Nothing had taken root and settled and flowered into something greater, something stronger, something...

Something *permanent*?

Just the thought shocked her rigid.

No, she had to be kidding. Had to be fooling herself.

Jumping in feet first where someone wiser and more thoughtful would hold well back. Feelings like that didn't just hit home and set in the space of a couple of seconds. They took time to grow, to develop and become a vital part of you. They came with knowledge and understanding and she knew little enough about this Giovanni Cardella—and understood less.

'Th-thank you.'

She didn't know if it was the stumble or the realisation of what she was feeling that put the tremor into her voice. She only knew that she needed to touch him—really touch him! Feel that smooth olive skin without the barrier of his jacket or hers in between.

And so she lifted her hand, raising it to his face. And let her fingers rest against his cheek, lying along the hard line of his jaw, supremely sensitive to the warmth of his flesh, the power of bone, the faint roughness where the hairs of his beard lay just below the surface of his skin.

'Thank you,' she said again, amazed that this time her voice sounded stronger when inside her stomach the nerves were twisting themselves into tight, painful knots, squeezing harder and harder with each breath she took.

'*Di niente*. No problem.'

His hand touched hers again, pressing it softly against his cheek. Then his fingers closed around hers, lifting them, turning them so that he was looking straight down on to the delicate tips, the oval-shaped, shell-pink painted nails.

'No problem,' he murmured again, but with a very different intonation this time. One that Terrie struggled to interpret.

But, even as she was reaching mentally for the indecipherable note in his voice, he moved again, and this time he blew her thought process right out of focus. He lifted the hand he held; lowered his head towards it. And when his mouth and her fingers met he pressed a long, lingering kiss first on their tips and then, slowly and sensually, all the way to the back of her hand.

'Gio...'

His name was just a sigh from her lips, faint as a breath, and she was stunned and bewildered to find that sudden tears stung her eyes. Tears of confusion and delight. Of almost fearful sensitivity to each and every movement that this man made.

Did he know what he was doing to her? Did he realise that, when she was used to the fumbling, clumsy, grabbing advances of men closer to her own twenty-four years, his gentleness, his gallantry—his *courtship*—were infinitely more seductive than any more passionate approach?

A moment before, she had longed for his kiss. The image of him taking her mouth in passion had flared in her mind like the blaze of lightning. But he had kissed her hand, and the delicacy of the gesture, the gentleness of his touch, had had so much more power over her feelings than any more overt approach.

'I'd love to have dinner with you,' she managed, needing to say something to show him a touch of what she was feeling, and yet afraid to let him in fully. To reveal just how deeply he had affected her.

His smile was swift, flashing on and off with the speed of a neon sign.

'I thought we'd already agreed on that.'

This was going exactly the way he wanted it, Gio reflected as he took her arm to lead her out of the bar and towards the ornate glass doors into the restaurant. At least now Terrie—*Terrie!* What sort of a name was that for a woman? Now that Terrie had stopped pretending that she needed to be persuaded to spend time with him, they both understood what the evening was all about.

She had wanted him to kiss her a moment ago. It had shown in her face. But a kiss was not what he had in mind. At least not a kiss on the mouth. The only woman he had kissed on the lips since Lucia had been Megan. Gio let a brief, fleeting smile cross his lips at the thought of his new and hugely pregnant sister-in-law. She had brought some much-needed warmth into his half-brother's life and, he admitted, into his own. Megan he would kiss and hug willingly. And his mother. No one else.

And certainly not this woman. Not some passing stranger he had picked up in a bar purely at the prompting of his most basic masculine urgings. A one-night stand was all it was. All it could ever be. And Teresa understood that. For a moment there he had had his doubts, but the way she had accepted his invitation to dinner, the carefully staged stumble so that he would be forced to take her in his arms, had reassured him of the facts. She knew exactly what was going on; how to play this game.

It should be plain sailing from now on. A meal. Some social chat. A touch of flattery, some light flirtation across a candlelit table. A shared bottle of wine—a nightcap...

And they would share that nightcap in her room. Her room, not his. Taking her to his room implied more than he meant her to take away from this encounter. And, after the nightcap, they would share a bed.

For tonight. And for tonight only.

And tomorrow he would go on his way—alone.

CHAPTER THREE

'SO WHAT are you doing in England? You don't look like a tourist and you said you'd planned on meeting someone from work. A business meeting?'

Gio nodded slowly, dark eyes shadowed in the candle-light.

'I'm a lawyer—and we were to discuss how the case went in court today. A post-mortem if you like.'

'And how did the case go?'

'We won.' It was said with total calm; no hint of any false modesty.

Of course he'd won. Gio didn't look as if he had ever known failure or defeat in his life.

A faint touch of wary apprehension slid coldly down her spine just at the thought. She wouldn't like to come up against Giovanni Cardella in court. He would have to be counsel for the prosecution, and she just knew that his approach would be deadly, his questions swift and lethal as a cobra's strike. In fact she wouldn't want to come up against Gio in any situation. He would be a formidable opponent, whatever the circumstances.

'Was it an—an important case?'

She stumbled over the question because her treacherous mind chose just that moment to throw at her the image of another, totally different way she could possibly be *against* Gio. For a few, feverish seconds, her imagination ran riot at the thought of how it might feel to be held close to that lean, hard body, crushed against the wall of his chest in the grip of those powerful arms that the sleek tailoring of his jacket did nothing to disguise.

'Important enough. International fraud—a man who's been making millions… What are you smiling at?'

'Nothing—I mean—I didn't know I was…'

The pictures her wayward thoughts had been conjuring up of the way the devastating man opposite her might look with the sophisticated elegance of the jacket and shirt stripped away vanished in a second as the bubble of her fantasy was popped by his probing question. For a moment her hands wavered uncertainly in front of her face while she struggled with the temptation to cover her burning cheeks and hide behind them, away from his searching gaze. But then she forced them down again, reaching instead for her wine glass and taking a much-needed restorative sip.

'If you must know I was feeling like Cinderella at the ball. I mean—all this…'

The hand that held her glass waved rather wildly as she used it to indicate her luxurious surroundings, the heavy linen tablecloths, the silverware and crystal glasses, the immaculately uniformed waiters, their footsteps hushed on the thick, rich pile of the red and gold carpet.

'It's hardly how I was expecting to spend my evening.'

A sudden memory slid into her mind. The image of Claire and Anna, just emerging from the doors of the conference room, their mouths agape and a look of total consternation and disbelief on their faces as they had seen her crossing the foyer with Gio at her side. By rights she should be with them now, sharing the cold buffet, thinking about packing, about leaving tomorrow morning.

She could only pray that Gio hadn't seen them too. That he hadn't caught the way they'd stopped dead, giggled, nudged each other, and then, most embarrassingly of all, given her a blatant 'thumbs up' sign of approval.

'I was thinking that if I pinched myself I might suddenly wake up and find it was all a dream.'

'And that I had turned into a pumpkin, hmm? Isn't that how the story goes?'

'Oh, no. Not at all! Prince Charming wasn't transformed into anything. He stayed a prince all the way through.'

'And is that how you see me?' His tone was casual enough but there was an unexpected light in his eyes, one that made every tiny hair on the back of her neck suddenly lift in nervous apprehension. 'Am I truly Prince Charming?'

Was he? Was he really the person he seemed? The delightful, easy-going dinner companion, the man who was politeness personified. Who had told her to order whatever she wanted from the menu, who made sure that her every need was attended to—her meal served, her glass filled, her plate cleared, even before she had realised that she wanted anything herself. Was this the real Giovanni Cardella or was there another side to him? What about the man who appeared in court?

'You certainly can be charming when you choose,' she said carefully.

'Choose?'

'Well—I get the feeling that you've deliberately set out to be this way. That you mean to be nice to me. That you—'

'And why would I not?' Gio cut in with a touch of sharpness. 'You are a woman—and a beautiful one at that. Wouldn't any man want to treat you like this? Wouldn't any sane male want to ''charm'' you, to please you? To see you smile?'

'I have to admit that it's not exactly what I'm used to,' Terrie murmured, totally thrown off balance by that softly emphasised 'beautiful'. 'The men that I've dated haven't had your...flair—your skill—at this. Or the money to bring me here, for that matter.'

'And the money is important?'

Gio recognised his mistake as soon as the words were out. Those soft grey eyes flew to his face, narrowing sharply as she caught the note of cynicism in his voice. So the lady didn't want the truth being stated too openly? Well, he could go along with that. Part of his attraction for her might be that he obviously had the wealth to give her a good time, but she clearly preferred to pretend that it went deeper than that.

'I'm not—' Terrie began indignantly.

'You're the one who described yourself as Cinderella at the ball,' Gio pointed out with calm reasonableness. 'I got the impression that you weren't used to being in a place like this. Was I wrong?'

'Well—no...' Terrie was forced to admit. 'I don't normally end up in posh restaurants—or hotels for that matter. It's only because I was at this conference and the company's paying that I'm here at all.'

'The company that you have now decided you no longer want to work for?'

'The same.' Terrie nodded, her expression rueful. 'So I expect that this will be my one and only taste of such luxury for a long, long time. I can't expect fairy godfathers to come along every day of the week, can I?'

She looked deep into his eyes as she spoke, her lavender-coloured gaze wide and intent above the soft, full mouth. Watching her, Gio felt desire give him such a hard, demanding kick that he shifted uncomfortably in his chair.

'A moment ago I was Prince Charming, now you've cast me in the role of Fairy Godfather.'

Or she'd like to put him in that role. Well, if a long-term sugar daddy was what she was after then she was doomed to disappointment.

'Perhaps you're both?'

Though of course there was no way that the 'Fairy' part of the description fitted, Terrie reflected, her whole body tingling in sensual awareness of the strength and power of the hard masculine body seated opposite her. One lean brown hand rested on the starched tablecloth, the tanned skin standing out sharply against the crisp white damask, and, having dropped her gaze to it for a moment, she suddenly found herself unable to drag her eyes or her thoughts away again.

What would it feel like to have those long, strong fingers caress her skin? How would his touch move over her sensitive flesh? Would it be soft and tantalising or hard and demanding? Every female instinct told her that he was a man who would know how to love a woman. How to arouse her, to stir her senses until she was barely conscious with longing, to set her whole body quivering...

Oh, lord, what *was* she doing? Just to think like this was turning her on, making heated passion uncoil in yearning demand in the pit of her stomach. Clumsily she reached for her glass, swallowing down some of the wine in an attempt to ease the sudden dryness of her throat.

'Of course, I suppose to you this is quite commonplace,' she blurted out, desperate to move the conversation along and so distract herself from her wanton thoughts. 'You must always be in places like this.'

'My legal work takes me all over the world.'

'That must be exciting—working in so many different countries.'

'Not really.'

Gio shrugged off her comment.

'When you've seen one hotel room, you've seen them all. And usually I'm working so hard that I don't get to see anything of the places where I'm staying.'

And that was how he liked it. The truth was that he didn't *need* to work; not financially at least. Thanks to the huge corporation owned by their joint families, both he and his half-brother Cesare were independently wealthy enough never to have to work again if they didn't feel like it.

But working filled the long, empty hours of the day. It tired him so that at least he had some hope of sleeping at night and it stopped him from thinking—from remembering.

'That's a terrible pity! Such a waste. I'd love to see all those—'

'I'm there to work,' Gio interrupted crushingly. 'And at the end of a long day in court I'm hardly in the mood for sightseeing.'

Perhaps now she'd get the message that he wasn't prepared to listen to her unsubtle hints.

Leaning back in his chair, he too reached for his wine glass and sipped at his drink slowly, all the while watching the woman before him. Did he care that she was so obviously attracted by his wealth? he asked himself. And that she was trying to insinuate that maybe they could spend some time together?

No. Quite frankly, he didn't give a damn. He was in the mood for some female company tonight—and for tonight only. And because of that he couldn't care less what she found attractive about him. Only that she did find him attractive. Because with those huge, soft eyes, the tumble of pale hair, the moist, inviting mouth, she was the sexiest thing he'd seen in a long time.

Did she know the way the candlelight caught on her hair, raising sparks of brilliant gold in the ash-blonde strands? Was she aware of the way that it gave her skin a softly luminous sheen, like the glow on a string of the finest freshwater pearls? And had she sensed that when she leaned forward to talk to him the low V-neck of the white cotton top she wore gaped slightly, giving him a tantalisingly erotic glimpse of the shadowed, perfumed valley of her cleavage?

Of course she had! In fact, he suspected her of making that movement quite deliberately, knowing it had to intrigue him, set his pulses racing.

She was doing it again now, coming partway across the table, her arms resting on the cloth as she leaned on them. He just wished she'd take the jacket off to give him a better view.

'I wasn't hinting!' she protested, actually managing to sound sincere.

'Of course not.'

His response didn't seem genuine, even in his own ears, but he didn't care. If she thought he didn't believe her, well, tough!

He reached for the bottle in the centre of the table.

'More wine?'

'No, thanks.'

Terrie was beginning to suspect that she'd already had more than enough. The alcohol was warming her blood, which, together with the heat in the room, made her whole body glow uncomfortably. Perhaps she'd feel better without the suit jacket.

'Have you finished your meal?'

He might as well have asked if she could read his mind,

because it seemed she could. No sooner had the thought that he would like her to remove her jacket crossed his mind than she had promptly obliged. And the effect of her actions, the way that her shoulders went back, pushing her small, high breasts forward, the small, sensually wriggling movements she made as she inched the linen sleeves down her arms, was like a neat shot of brandy in his veins, flooding him with heat.

'Yes—thank you. I couldn't eat another thing.'

'Nothing sweet?'

'I'd love something but I don't think my figure could take it.'

The protest was accompanied by a smoothing movement of her hands from her ribcage, down and over her waist.

'Don't tempt me!'

If anyone was *tempting*, then it was her. That gesture had been designed to draw attention to the feminine curves of her shape, the swell of her breasts and the hips that were just barely visible before the flow of the tablecloth covered them. And just the thought of his own hands tracing the path that her fingers had taken made his body clench in cruelly hungry desire.

'Your figure is quite perfect, and you know it.'

He had given up on any attempt to pretend that he was interested in eating. Even the rich red wine was ignored, his half-full glass abandoned, his attention wholly on her.

'You don't have to fish for compliments.'

'I wasn't…'

'Of course not.'

There was something about his smile that caught on her nerves, but she couldn't focus her thinking enough to try and decide just what it was. She felt as if that dark-eyed gaze, his irises more black than brown in the shadowy candlelight, was an intangible force, holding her mesmerised and unable to move.

'But it doesn't matter. You can have all the compliments you want.'

'I—I can?'

His proud head nodded slowly, black eyes locking with grey-blue.

'What would you like me to say? That you are beautiful? Believe me, you are. That your skin has the delicate softness of a perfect peach?'

That he couldn't wait to strip the clinging top from her body, expose the creamy flesh it covered, feast his eyes and his hands, his mouth...?

'That your eyes are the colour of a dove's wing and every bit as—'

'Oh, stop! Stop it!' Terrie cried, mortified into leaning forward and catching hold of his hand in order to shut him up. 'You're going way over the top.'

'You don't believe me?'

Embarrassed beyond speech, she could only shake her head emphatically, sending the pale cloud of hair flying.

'You're flattering—'

'I never flatter.'

His tone stopped her dead, making her blink in confusion.

A single strand of wheat-coloured hair had caught at the corner of her soft pink mouth and, leaning across the table, he reached out and eased it free again. But once he had the silky lock in his hand he didn't release it but lingered, slowly twisting the delicate strands round and round his finger until she was forced to incline her head even closer to him, to avoid him tugging on her scalp.

'Never...' he murmured, his mouth seeming only inches away from her own. And the look in his eyes, the unconcealed passion that burned there, was positively indecent in such a public place.

Twice Terrie swallowed hard, vainly struggling to ease the dryness in her throat. Twice she opened her lips, trying to speak, but no sound would come out.

The rest of the room seemed to have faded into a buzzing haze, the murmured voices of the diners, the faint clatter of plates, the clink of glasses all blurring into one indecipherable mass. But in Terrie's mind, or at least the part of it that would focus, there was only herself and this sensually devastating man before her.

Releasing the pale strand of hair, Gio tucked it back behind her ear with a gentleness that wrenched at something in her heart. And the path that his hand had traced burned against her skin like a mark he had left there, a brand that said she was his and his alone. It would be totally invisible to the naked eye, but she would always know it was there—and so would he.

'Remember that…I never flatter.'

His dark gaze dropped to where her hand still lay on his, looking pale and delicate in contrast to the tanned power of his fingers. Twisting his hand in hers so that they were palm to palm, he linked his fingers with hers, smoothing his thumb softly over her skin.

'So, no sweet,' he said, reverting to the conversation of moments before. 'Coffee? A liqueur?'

'C-coffee would be nice.'

Somehow she forced her tongue to work, wincing inwardly when she heard the way that it croaked and fractured at the end of the sentence.

'We'll take it in the lounge.'

It was a command, not a suggestion, and she could only nod a silent acquiescence to the tone of his voice.

He didn't release her hand as they stood up, but kept

his fingers locked with hers, pulling her to his side as soon as she had moved clear of the table. With his free hand he scooped up the discarded red jacket, tossing it over his arm, barely waiting for her to collect her handbag before he headed towards the door out of the restaurant.

She knew how he felt, Terrie reflected shakenly. She shared that sudden need to be somewhere quieter, less public—more intimate. The thoughts that were in her head, the feelings that his words and his touch had triggered off, were not at all appropriate for the public rooms of a big London hotel. She felt sure that the sensual inferno raging in her blood must be etched onto her face, stamped onto her forehead in letters of fire for all to read. Even if they found the darkest, the most secluded corner of the lounge, she suspected that the heat of the yearning that had her in its grip must radiate from her, scorching anyone who passed.

But if they had wanted peace and quiet, as soon as they entered the lounge she saw that they would be disappointed. The comfortable chairs and cushioned settees dotted around the huge room were all occupied. Almost all the guests who had eaten in the restaurant had chosen to take their coffee here, and they looked as if they planned to linger late into the evening.

'We're out of luck.' Gio's tone was flat, unrevealing of what he was thinking.

Perhaps they were *in* luck. Terrie swallowed, made herself speak before her nerve broke completely.

'Do you think they would bring the coffee to our—to my—your room?'

Such simple words but she almost felt the reverberations that followed from them echoing through the room, making the floor suddenly unsteady beneath her feet. And Gio's sudden silence, the total stillness of his long body beside her, made it clear that he was thinking much the same thing.

'It would be quieter—more private.'

'Is that what you want?'

He was watching her again, waiting for her reply. But all Terrie's strength had deserted her, along with her ability to speak. She could only nod silently, unable to put into words the way she was feeling.

She didn't care if it was foolish, if it was the craziest, the most rash decision she had ever made. Ruthlessly she pushed aside the protesting cries of her offended sense of self-preservation, the promptings of innate caution. It didn't matter what the end result would be, what risks she was running. She only knew that she couldn't let this evening end now, here, in this public room. She couldn't let this man go, walk out of her life, without seeing just how far this unexpected relationship might go.

She knew she would regret it for the rest of her life if she did.

So she nodded again, more firmly this time, and wetted her painfully dry lips, praying that her voice would obey her this time.

'Yes,' she said rawly, thankful that at least she could speak even if the word sounded horribly rough round the edges. 'Yes, that's exactly what I want.'

CHAPTER FOUR

THE lift doors had barely closed before he reached for her.

Terrie could still hear the rumble of the heavy metal moving across the empty space, the sound of the engine starting up, as Gio's hands closed about her arms, pulling her to him. And the slight jolting of the enclosed compartment as it lurched into motion threw her even harder up against his strong frame, her face buried in his shoulder.

'*Bellezza... Mia bella...*'

The rough sound of his muttered words was blurred by the heavy pounding of his heart under her cheek, a throbbing that was echoed in her own veins as she surrendered willingly to his embrace.

Earlier in the evening she had dreamed, wondered—fantasised—about the way his touch would feel, the sensations that being in his arms might produce. And she hadn't even managed to come close. The reality was so much more—more intense, more sensual, more arousing—more than she had ever imagined it could be.

The heat of his body enclosed her. The scent of his skin was in her nostrils. The sound of his breathing filled her ears at the same time that the warm current of his breath whispered over her sensitive skin, making the delicate nerves tingle all the way down to her toes.

'Teresa...'

Once again that delightful accent turned her name into

something new and exotic, something special only to him, and simply hearing it made her heart turn over in delight.

From the moment that she had made her decision it had been simply a matter of seconds to find a waiter, put in the order for the coffee to be taken to her room.

'Of course, Signor Cardella,' the man had said, clearly knowing only too well just who Gio was. 'Shall I bring it to your suite?'

'No.'

An abrupt shake of his head had emphasised the crispness of his answer.

'To…' Ebony eyes had been turned on Terrie, a question and a prompt combined in the one glance.

'Room five three four.'

Five three four. Her room was on the fifth floor of the hotel, which meant that, even in the speedy, efficient lift, it inevitably took some time to reach their destination.

Some time in which Gio laced his hands around the fine bones of her skull, lifting her face to his, hard fingers massaging her scalp. Time in which his kisses drifted over the surface of her hair, the warmth of his mouth touched her forehead, her closed eyelids, her temples, but never reached her mouth. And most of all time in which the hard, hot pressure of his body revealed forcefully and dramatically the potent power of his desire for her, the swollen force of his erection up against her stomach triggering off a near-delirium of yearning that made her head spin wildly.

'Gio…'

Her fingers clenched in the fine material of his shirt, pulling it loose at his narrow waist. She could no longer wait for the sanctuary of her room and the privacy it would afford them. She wanted to—needed to—touch his skin, feel him properly *now*.

Her hands shook as she ran them up the ridged strength of his ribcage, stroking the warm satin of his skin, brushing across the scattering of crisp hairs that her fingertips encountered. She felt him shudder violently in reaction to her touch and with a muffled curse he rammed her into the far corner of the lift, opposite the door, with her back against the cold metal of the compartment.

His body was against every inch of hers now. Chest to breast, thigh to thigh, his heat and desire crushed into the cradle of her pelvis. And his hands were urgent on her flesh, stroking down her face, along her arms, roughly tugging the white top up to expose more of her skin to his knowing fingers. Moaning aloud, Terrie writhed against his imprisoning strength, throwing her head up and back to allow for more of the hard, snatched kisses that plundered her face and neck.

But still he hadn't kissed her mouth. And she felt that she had never known what it was to feel deprived until this moment, when he continued to deny her that basic intimacy.

'Gio!' she gasped again. 'Gio—kiss me!'

But still his mouth eluded hers. Even though his hands roamed higher and wilder. Even though he caught and cupped the soft swell of her breasts in his hard fingers, sensually tormenting her by rolling her aching nipples in a touch that was such a devastating form of pleasure it came so very near to pain, still he didn't kiss her.

'Gio, damn you! *Please!*'

Driven beyond endurance, she pulled her hands out from under his shirt, hearing something rip faintly as she did so. Ignoring it, she reached up and fastened wildly clutching fingers in the midnight-dark silk of his hair, forcing his head down to meet her own upturned face.

At first she felt his resistance, thought she would never

overcome it, but just when she was convinced that he had won and a faint whimper of defeat almost escaped her, she made one desperate, final effort, and at last his mouth touched hers.

For a second or two Terrie thought she might actually faint in sensual delight. That the warm, firm caress of Gio's lips would actually send her tumbling into an oblivion of pleasure, a world in which nothing mattered but herself and this man and the union between them. But then two things happened at once to jolt her back to the present, reality intruding on her with a jarring shock.

At first she was aware only of Gio's sudden stillness, the swift, disturbing stiffening of his powerful body, the way that his mouth hardened on hers, not in desire, but in a rejection that tore at her heart, slashing a deep wound into it. The other, more mundane event was the creak of the lift, its slowing to a halt, juddering faintly as it reached the fifth floor and stopped.

It was a moment or two before Terrie had collected the composure to realise where they were, drawn in enough breath to mutter, 'I think this is our floor.' And even then she realised that she had recovered well before Gio; that he was not anything like as alert as she had been. When she looked into his face he seemed to be only barely conscious, his eyes glazed and unfocused, two vivid flares of colour scoring along the high, wide cheekbones, his breathing raw and uneven.

'Gio,' she said again carefully, uncertainly. 'We're here. This is my floor.'

Her words invaded his head only slowly, hazily, through the buzzing, burning haze that had invaded his thoughts.

'*Sì,*' he muttered thickly, his voice still rough with the passion that had taken possession of him. 'Of course.'

Somehow they managed to make their way out of the lift and down the corridor to her room. It seemed that Terrie was as shocked and bewildered by the storm of passion that had assailed them in the lift, certainly if the way that her hand shook when she tried to push her key card into the slot was anything to go by. She tried to manage it twice, failing both times, and on the third attempt actually dropped the card to the floor, giving a cry of frustrated annoyance as she did so.

'Let me.'

Gio stooped, snatched up the card, taking a much-needed moment to draw breath, still his whirling thoughts, before he straightened up again. But even so he was only marginally more successful when he tried to unlock the door, cursing himself under his breath as his hand wavered betrayingly, and having to grip the card tightly as he rammed it into the slot with unnecessary force.

The size of the bedroom was a shock like a blow in the face. Or, rather, the *lack* of size of it. He didn't think he had ever seen such a tiny hotel room in his life.

'*This* is it?' he exclaimed, too stunned to keep the words back. The truth was that he was grateful for some distraction, anything that would divert his mind from the discomfort of his memories of that kiss.

'This is it,' Terrie confirmed, an edge of shaken laughter to her voice. 'What is it, Gio? Are you surprised to see how the other half live?'

'You paid for this!'

'We can't all afford private suites! There is a bathroom...' Terrie added. 'Well—of sorts.'

Flicking on the light to demonstrate, she caught sight of their reflection in the large wall mirror and a muffled gasp that was part horror, part giggle escaped her.

'Would you look at us! Gio—we look... Oh, thank

heaven we didn't meet anyone in the corridor! What would they have thought?'

'That we'd just escaped from a brawl—or an orgy...'

He could only pray that she would take the unevenness of his voice as evidence that he shared her amusement and not as what it really was.

Which was *what*?

If he was honest, then he knew he couldn't actually put a name to the way he was feeling. His emotions were all to pieces, seeming to be on a violent roller coaster plunging down, down, down one moment, only to swing right up again the next.

And all because of one kiss.

Just one kiss.

No. Not 'just' a kiss. Not 'just' anything. It was the first time he had kissed a woman in passion other than his wife.

Dio, the first kiss he had ever known hadn't affected him like this. In fact, the experience had been so long ago, when he was barely in his teens, that the memory had blurred and become so vague that he could hardly remember the girl's name now. But the first time he had kissed Lucia was etched onto his brain, never to be erased. It had felt like coming home; as if all his dreams had finally materialised, centring in the small, delicate shape of the woman he had loved from that moment on.

But *this*. This was so very different. Light-years away from the youthful, innocent experience of the first kiss he had shared with Lucia. It had been a kiss like no other he had ever experienced. And, although he had refused to let it show, it had been a kiss of the fiercest passion he had ever known.

At that first touch of her lips on his, a violent response had seared through him, singeing his nerves, exploding in his brain, making his head swim shockingly. He had known what she wanted, how she had tried to draw his head down to hers, and had set himself to fight against it. And in that first split-second when their mouths had touched the shock had frozen him, held him still. Another heartbeat later and it had all been completely different. Then the fuse that had been lighted at that first contact had burned away, detonating the powder keg of his physical reaction, and blasting his thoughts away with it.

Only the realisation that the lift had come to a halt and Terrie's hasty warning that someone might come had stopped him from making a complete and utter fool of himself.

'The coffee!'

'What?'

He really couldn't take in what Terrie was talking about. If the sight of himself in the mirror, shirt pulled out, tie askew, hair distinctly ruffled, wasn't bad enough, then the sensations throbbing through his body were only aggravating the situation. He still had the taste of her on his lips. The tang of red wine mixed intoxicatingly with the intimate flavour of Terrie herself. He pressed his fingers hard against his mouth, not knowing whether he wanted to rub the back of his hand against his lips to wipe away the taste or hold it, keep it there, lingering, tantalising, arousing, nagging at him with the memory of how he had felt.

And the thought of how very much he wanted to experience it again.

'The coffee?' He shook his dark head slightly, trying to pull himself back into functioning in the present. 'What the hell are you talking about?'

'We ordered coffee,' Terrie reminded him. 'They were

bringing it up to our room. They'll be here any minute. We'd better make ourselves respectable.'

Already she had straightened her top, was reaching for the brush on the dressing table to smooth down her tangled hair. Restoring order and calm where he wanted turmoil and the upheaval of passion, loss of control and the total oblivion of losing his mind to the sensation of ecstasy.

'No.'

It stunned Terrie, stopped her dead, the brush stilling in mid-stroke. Her eyes were wide and startled, clouded with confusion, as she looked up at him.

'What…?' she began but had to swallow the words hastily as she was grabbed, hauled up against him, and they were crushed back down her throat by the sudden violent pressure of his mouth on hers.

And in the blink of an eye her thoughts were swirling again, whirling off into the sensual kaleidoscope of colour and sensation that had assailed her in the lift. She was incapable of thought, wouldn't have cared if a whole army of waiters, laden down with trays of coffee, had marched through her bedroom, gaping openly at every move she made. She was only conscious of this man's touch, this man's lips on hers, the hunger that was thundering in her head, throbbing between her legs—a hunger that he had created and only he could appease.

This time his mouth was a devastating combination of hard and soft, starting off fiercely demanding and then suddenly and unexpectedly gentling into an enticing sweetness that eased open her lips, allowing him more intimate access to her mouth. The play of his tongue was an erotic caress, and the tangle of his hands in her hair, holding her exactly where he wanted and at what angle, was an arousing indication of his strength and the ease with which he could use it either to excite or control.

Her own hands went up, her fingers closing over the hard muscles of his shoulders and clinging, needing the support because her legs were unsteady beneath her, suddenly feeling as if they were made of nothing but cotton wool. She was lost, adrift on a heated sea of sensation, and could only abandon herself to the waves and the direction they wanted to take her.

The rap at the door she had been anticipating came while her heart was still pounding, so that for a second she was only aware of it as another, sharper, note in the crescendo of passion that was building inside her. But then it was repeated and at the same moment another sound blended with it, a shrill, higher pitched note that intruded into the moment, disrupting the mood.

Against her lips, Gio muttered something dark and furious in rough Italian. But when the summons came again he moved sharply, releasing Terrie abruptly and turning towards the door.

Abandoned so unexpectedly, she found herself staggering for a moment before dropping down awkwardly onto the bed, unable to remain standing. Her eyes were hazed, barely focused as she watched Gio cross the room in two swift strides, pull open the door with one hand, while hunting in his pocket for his phone with the other.

She was still trying to collect her thoughts as he waved an autocratic gesture towards the coffee-table, indicating that the tray of coffee-pot and cups should be placed there, pushed an obviously generous tip into the waiter's hand, and ushered him back out the door all in one fluid movement. And then he turned his attention to the still-ringing phone.

'Scusi... Sì?'

Whoever was on the phone was someone he wanted to talk to, Terrie reflected, stunned by the sudden transformation of his face. The hard lines and planes seemed to soften. Between the thick black lashes she could see a new light in the deep, dark eyes, and a dancing little smile curled the hard line of his mouth into something that made her heart kick sharply, stealing her breath away.

The conversation was in Italian too fast and too accented for her to be able to catch any more than a single word here or there. But there was one word she did hear, and it stuck in her mind like a burr, stinging sharply.

Cara, he said, his tone warming and gentling. *Cara mia.* And the words were like a hard, brutal slap in her face, cold as ice after the heat of her reaction just moments earlier.

Once more her eyes fastened on Gio's face, watching, reinterpreting the new expression on his face. The sense of devastation in the pit of her stomach, the feeling of being so close to something very sweet and very special, only to have it snatched right away from her, was like a raw bruise, aching and sore.

'*Buona notte,*' Gio finished. '*Ben dorme.*'

She couldn't wait until he had put the phone away.

'Are you married?'

It froze him in the middle of closing the case.

'Married?'

There was something disturbing in the way that he had reacted, the look in his eyes. Something that set her heart racing, jolting unevenly in distress.

'I heard you! You called—you said "*cara*". I might not understand much Italian, but I do know that word and I know what it means! *Cara*—darling—*darling*!' she repeated emphatically when he simply sat there, dark eyes unreadable. 'Who were you calling *darling*?'

'Is it any of your…?'

The silver phone case closed with a dangerous snap and Gio obviously changed his mind about what he had been about to say.

'My sister-in-law,' he conceded unexpectedly, but the words were still coldly clipped, falling like shards of ice into the rapidly cooling atmosphere. 'Signora Megan Santorino. The wife of my half-brother Cesare. You don't believe me? Here…'

The phone was tossed down onto the bed, sliding across the blue and white bedspread to just within reach of Terrie's fingers.

'Ring back—hear for yourself. The redial button is—'

'I don't need the redial button!' Terrie spat, painfully embarrassed by unnecessary instruction, the over-elaborate pretence at concern for her to get it right. 'I don't need to ring back! I—I believe you!'

How could she think anything else when she saw the flaring fury in his eyes, the tension that held his long body taut? She'd blundered badly somewhere.

'Gio—I believe you. Please—I'm sorry. Forgive me.'

For the space of several distinctly uneven heartbeats, he simply glared into her eyes, his jaw set tight, his mouth clamped into a thin line. But then at last, to her infinite relief, he raked both hands through the raven darkness of his hair and nodded slowly.

'OK,' he said, his tone losing just a touch of that attacking quality. 'Fine.'

And that was it? Terrie wondered. Topic closed? Continue as before? She didn't know if she could.

The sharply heated little exchange had taught her something. A lesson she had more than needed. It had shown her just how little she knew about this man, other than the most basic facts.

It had also revealed another side to Gio Cardella. A very different, very disturbing side that was in total contrast to the urbane, courteous, charming man who had been her dinner companion this evening. It had shown her Giovanni Cardella, the hotshot international lawyer, the man who had been in court today prosecuting an important fraud case—and won. In those few, unnervingly uncomfortable moments she had come up against Giovanni Cardella, counsel for the prosecution—and quite frankly it had unnerved her.

'She's seven months pregnant.'

The comment caught her unawares, all the more so because of the casually conversational way that Gio delivered it. It was as if the disturbing confrontation hadn't happened, or he had dismissed it from his mind at once.

'Who?'

'Megan. She's expecting her first baby in May and she's already as big as a house. She rang to complain about the heat.'

'The heat!'

Terrie's eyes went to the windows beyond which, with the typical unreliability of an English spring, the rain had suddenly started to fall, great drops darkening the paving stones in the courtyard outside.

'Sicily has a very different climate from England.'

'Of—of course.'

The trace of amusement warming his voice was her undoing. She could feel it heating the blood in her veins, making it throb its way around her body. And if she glanced up she could see the way that a hint of laughter had lit up his eyes, melting the ice that had been in them moments before.

And she wanted that. Needed that change of mood. Because, terrifying as she found it to admit, she now realised that in the few short hours since she had met Giovanni Cardella things had moved on at a pace that she had neither anticipated nor, if she was honest, genuinely wanted. She wouldn't have believed it possible, but she was already in so deep that it was going to devastate her if she had to back out now.

Or if Gio left her in anger, or some foolish mistake on her part drove him away from her.

'Well, they brought the coffee,' Gio muttered drily.

His gesture indicated the tray on the table, the fine china cups and saucers, the silver coffee-pot. The waiter had brought brandy too, the amber-coloured liquid glowing fierily in delicate crystal balloon glasses.

'So do you *want* coffee, Teresa?'

She was thrilled to hear a new softness in his voice, the husky note of invitation that held the promise of a future, a beginning, rather than an end.

'No,' she whispered, her voice very low but firm with conviction. 'I can't say I do.'

What she *did* want was clear in her eyes, written deep in the clouded pools of her irises, burning in the apprehensive but unwavering gaze she turned on his dark, watchful face.

Gio drew in a long, deep, faintly ragged breath and nodded slowly. And when he moved it was to hold out his arm, his hand slightly curved to beckon her to him.

'Then come here,' he said sharply, huskily, the musical intonation of his accent deepening on each word he spoke. 'Come here to me, *belleza*, and let's finish what we've started.'

CHAPTER FIVE

'COME here…and let's finish what we've started.'

Gio found that his words echoed inside his head as he watched Terrie lever herself up off the bed and then stand, hesitating, clearly undecided whether to obey him or not.

Finish what we've started.

What *had* they started? And, more to the point, how was it going to end? Was he going to be able to leave it as the one-night stand he had planned on, the 'fun' that Terrie had indicated she wanted? He didn't know and quite frankly at this moment he simply didn't care.

Tomorrow morning he might be able to walk away without a backward glance. He might be happy to say goodbye and let her go out of his life without a second thought; he didn't know. The only certainty in his mind was that *now* he couldn't do any such thing. He couldn't leave not having made love to this woman. He couldn't go without having known the full experience of sleeping with her, having her, of seeing whether the reality of her lived up to the fantasy, the promise, the hunger that her kisses had awoken in him.

After two long years of shutting away his sexual feelings, keeping them out of his life with a blockade of loneliness and working until he dropped from sheer exhaustion, it now seemed that the dam had been breached. The barriers were down once and for all and the floodtide of sensations could not be held back. Instead it was flowing fierce and wild and free, sweeping aside all restraint, all trace of anything like thought or hesitation or self-control.

He wanted this tonight; and for tonight at least he was going to have it.

'Teresa?'

She would have travelled far further and overcome far greater obstacles if it meant that she could hear him use her name in that soft, that tender way. But even so, the short distance across the deep blue carpet to where Gio stood, still with his hand outstretched, seemed to take an age. Forever.

She could hardly make her feet move. Her legs had no strength at all beneath her, and she could only step hesitantly and uncertainly, her eyes fixed on his face.

But in his face she found her strength. In those deep, dark eyes, so intently fixed on her, was all the encouragement she needed. He was there for her, and that was all that mattered, all that she wanted.

This was just a beginning. It was stepping out into the unknown, and that needed courage. She didn't know what might happen days down the line; she only knew that for now she had to close her eyes and jump, and take it on trust that he wouldn't let her fall.

And as it had been in the lift, so now his arms were there, ready and waiting for her. They gathered her close, collected her in, and drew her up to him. And when she lifted her face to him his mouth came down on hers, hard and hot and hungry and passionate. It crushed her own mouth open, parting it to the sweep of his tongue, the deepening of the caress.

And she gave herself up to that caress openly and willingly, all trace of hesitation gone, all fear swept aside in the floodtide of passionate hunger that took possession of her. She couldn't get close enough, couldn't feel enough of him pressed up against her, her senses swooning in intoxication as she inhaled the clean, potent scent of his body and felt its heat surround her.

Hard hands tangled in her hair, twisting the fine blonde strands around the long, tanned fingers, holding her head exactly where he wanted it so that he could kiss her in just the way that he wanted. And what he wanted was what she wanted too. All that she wanted was here in this one small room. The rest of the world, the past, the worries of the future, all faded away into an indecipherable blur. There was only the present and this man and the flames they had lit between them.

And those flames had her totally in their grip now. They were licking along every nerve, searing every inch of skin. Gio seemed to sense unerringly just what she was feeling and where as he freed his right hand from her hair, leaving the other one to hold her head captive, and let his other hand roam wilfully over her body. Somehow he touched unerringly on every most sensitive spot, every yearning pleasure point that pulsed just below the surface of her flesh. And in the same instant that his touch appeased one hunger, it also awoke another, deeper, more primitive one. One that demanded a satisfaction as wild and potent and as primal as its own forceful nature.

'Gio…'

His name was a muttered sound of encouragement mixed with protest on her lips. She wanted more than this exploratory touch on her body, through her clothes. She wanted the feel of his hands on her skin, the warmth of flesh on flesh. She wanted to feel his hands demand, and her body respond. Every inch, every sense, every nerve rising to meet this, the most basic claim of all that a man could make on a woman.

'Gio…'

And yet at the same time she wanted to prolong this

moment into infinity. She wanted this first coming together to go on and on forever. For a lifetime. Because
only a lifetime would be long enough for her to fully
experience, to fully *know* this first stage of making love
with Giovanni Cardella.

Never again would it be so new, so unknown, so *fresh*.
And she wanted to linger in that freshness, even as some
deeper, inner claim of her female nature was throbbing
hard and wild at the joining of her legs. And much as she
wanted to delay, to savour, to enjoy, she knew that that
demand would soon grow too strong to be ignored. It
would have to be appeased or it would tear her apart.

'Oh, Gio…'

This time the impatience was uppermost in her tone,
and in the moment of hearing it she also felt Gio's silent
laughter against her face.

'*Calma, bella mia. Calma,*' he whispered into her
mouth. 'We have all night.'

But even as he said the words, he knew that they were
a lie. There was no way that he could wait, or delay this
much longer. It was the difference that had kept him on
a tight rein so far—the stunning, shocking differences between the woman in his arms and the wife he had made
love to before. The only woman in his life for so many
years.

And the differences had seemed so important in the first
moments that he had touched her. The colour and length
of her hair. The pale cloud of blonde that fell around her
face and shoulders where Lucia's had been short and dark.
The long, slender limbs; the way her face was so much
closer to his when she stood next to him. The intensely
personal scent of her skin.

In those first seconds of touching her, holding her, she
seemed so very, very different. And the kick that his

senses gave, the way that his heart clenched painfully, made him wonder, just for an instant, whether he could go through with this. But then Terrie stirred against him, and he knew that his mind, his senses, were no longer in the past. That what mattered was here and now.

And she was here, now.

And she was what he wanted.

What he desired—so much.

And so he kissed her again, losing himself in the feel of her lush mouth beneath his. The warm, moist delicacy of her kiss seemed to melt his bones, turning his blood to white heat in his veins. He wanted to rush, to grab and snatch at the pleasure offered, yet at the same moment he wanted to delay, to linger and stretch it out as long as possible.

He wished that her white top had button fastenings. The thought of the slow, sensual delight of slipping each one through its hole, sliding apart the two delicate sides of the garment, appealed to his sense of anticipation, the thrill of waiting, building excitement on excitement. But in the moment that he tugged the stretchy cotton up and over her head, his fingers brushing over the heated skin of her torso, his already hungrily aroused body hardened and tightened even more. His hopes of delaying, of waiting flew out the window in the space of a heartbeat. And as he looked down onto the soft, creamy mounds of her breasts, lifted and displayed in voluptuous enticement by the silk and lace of her pale pink bra, he knew that he was lost.

'Teresa,' he muttered, his voice raw and thick with desire. '*Teresa, cara mia, bella mia…*'

Terrie was lost in sensation, and the sound of Gio's voice, the exotic traces of his accent deepened and roughened by the passion that burned deep in his eyes, made her shiver with excited anticipation. The stroke of his hands over her upper body, the fine lines of her ribcage, made her writhe in uncontrolled response. But the moment when those knowing fingers trailed upwards, drifted for sweet, tormenting moments over the silk of her bra, awakening the sensitive flesh beneath, made her freeze in sudden delighted anticipation, her breath catching sharply in her throat.

That felt *so* good. And it set up a stinging, burning response of hunger that radiated throughout her body, centring in a molten pool at the junction of her legs.

'I want this...' she muttered, her voice almost as rough as his. 'Gio...I *want*...'

The sound of his slightly shaken laughter filled the space where the words had deserted her and she felt the hot pressure of his mouth on her, and then again on her cheekbone, the delicate pulse at her temple.

'Do you think I don't know that, *angelina*?' he muttered against her skin. 'I know what you want—and you will get it...'

Once more he kissed her softly, his hands stilling on her breasts, and a whimper of frustrated protest escaped her lips at his abandonment of the cruelly arousing caresses.

'Don't...' she began, only to have her mouth captured again, the words of complaint pushed back down her throat.

'I know what you want, *cara*,' he repeated huskily. 'It is what I want too. But I am trying to be considerate here.'

'Con...siderate?'

It was the last thing she had expected.

'I want to take this steady—make it good for you...'

There was a raw edge to the words that made it sound as if his control was unravelling fast, his ability to keep himself on a tight rein slipping away from him. The pulse of electrical excitement that shot through her in response made her shift against him sharply, the swell of her pelvis coming up hard against the heated shaft of his erection.

Gio's breath hissed in sharply through his clenched teeth and one hand dropped from her breast to cup and hold her bottom, crushing her into even closer contact with the potent sign of his arousal.

'But if you keep rubbing yourself up against me like that, then steady is not what I can be.'

'And did I ask for *steady*?'

Terrie's mouth formed into a mock-pout, smoky eyes gleaming provocatively as she looked up into his tense face.

'Did I ask for consideration? Did I—?'

The end of her question vanished into a gasp of unexpected delight as she was grabbed, hauled into his arms, and lifted high into the air.

'No consideration, huh?'

He swung her over towards the bed, dropping her down onto the mattress with a suddenness that brought the breath from her lungs in an 'oof' of surprise.

'No steadiness...'

He was down beside her before she had recovered her breath, taking her mouth again in an almost brutal, searing kiss.

'You asked for it, lady...'

Hands as restless as his voice tugged the delicate straps of her bra down, imprisoning her arms against her sides in the same moment that he exposed the tender flesh of her breasts. His mouth took the sensitive skin by storm, kissing, licking, even nibbling gently, along the creamy curves until he reached the swollen pink nipple. When the heat of his lips closed over the aching bud and he suckled hard, Terrie felt that she would swoon with the torment of the blend of pleasure and pain that laid siege to every nerve in her body.

'Gio—oh, *Gio*…!'

His name was an incoherent litany of need and submission, tumbling from her lips in the same moment that her hands communicated another, very different mood. Urgent and demanding, they wrenched at the buttons on his shirt, tugging them apart in a flurry of hungry need.

Gio helped her by shrugging the fine linen from his shoulders, tossing the discarded garment to the floor before turning his attention to the now rumpled and disordered skirt that was pushed up around her slender hips.

'*Stockings*,' he growled on a note of purely predatory satisfaction as his efficient actions exposed the delicate lacy tops that clung to her pale thighs. 'Do you know what stockings do to me?'

Terrie could only shake her head, sending her blonde hair flying in a wheat-coloured halo. She didn't know, but she could certainly guess. And the rough, crooning sound he made low in his throat, the fierce glitter of his eyes, the raw unevenness of his breathing told their own tale.

The one flimsy barrier between him and the hot, moist centre of her need of him was easily stripped away. Clever, knowing fingers found just the right spot and stroked, caressed, tormented until she was gasping for breath, head tossing on the pillows, her own hands clenching over the hard muscles in his shoulders and clinging on desperately for support.

'*Gio!*'

'I know, *cara*. I know…'

Between them they disposed of his remaining clothing, the sensation of heated skin against skin adding further fuel to the inferno already raging in every sensitised inch of Terrie's body. She was so close now—so close to the moment of ultimate union, ultimate intimacy, that she couldn't bear to wait. And when he seemed to hesitate, just for a second, she almost panicked, clutching at him and bringing him closer to her, only now aware of how he had momentarily backed away.

'Teresa…'

Her name was a moan of protest on his lips.

'I have—nothing… Do you…?'

She didn't understand what he was saying. Couldn't understand why he had hesitated. Didn't *want* him to pause, to think, to do *anything* now but take her, love her, make her his.

'No, no, no,' she muttered. 'It doesn't matter—really, it's not important, not… Gio—*please*!'

The final word was a cry of desperation, of longing. And in the same moment that she let it escape her she lifted her hips from the bed, pressing herself invitingly against him, mutely encouraging his final possession.

Through the roaring in her head she heard Gio give a faint sigh of surrender, sensed all resistance seep from him like air from a punctured balloon. And the next moment he had curved hard, hot hands around her hips, holding her just where he wanted her as he thrust his powerful body into hers in one long, forceful movement.

Almost immediately whatever control he had been exerting broke totally. His movements, hard and fast and fierce, took possession of her, took control of her, lifting her up and up, riding the waves of demanding passion, cresting each one. Going higher and higher and higher…until there was nowhere else to go but over the edge into an explosion of ecstasy and oblivion that totally engulfed them both.

* * *

It was the first, faint fingers of light from the dawn that crept through the uncurtained window and fell onto his face that gradually penetrated the heavy, exhausted sleep into which Gio had fallen, making him stir and frown slightly, wondering where he was.

Outside in the street below, the sound of cars, a noise that never stopped in this city that never seemed to sleep, reminded him that he was in London. But this was not his room. Not the elegant suite he had woken in every other morning of his stay...

Even as his thoughts were sorting and deciphering the information, a small, soft sigh, like the murmur of a sleeping kitten, broke through his confusion, waking him fully and sharply.

Teresa.

Memory hit home with the force of a lethal bullet, driving away the last traces of sleep and blasting him awake in a moment of pure shock.

Teresa. *Terrie.* The woman called herself Terrie.

She had told him her surname, but it hadn't registered in his mind. To him she was just Teresa. Nothing more.

The woman whose bed he had shared all night long. The woman whose body had opened to him, welcomed him in. And in whose arms he had lost himself, forgotten, for a few hours at least, the loneliness and emptiness of his life. With her he had shared a blazing passion that had somehow made him hungry in the very same moment that it had satisfied him. He hadn't been able to sleep, had known no rest, until he had taken her again and again and again, in an exhausting outpouring of need that he hadn't believed he would ever experience again. In her bed he had found the oblivion he had been looking for. And in this woman he had found some of the deepest, most sensual satisfaction he had ever experienced.

The woman with whom he had betrayed the memory of his beloved wife.

'Oh, Lucia!'

With an effort he swallowed down the groan of pain and guilt that almost escaped his lips, clamping his mouth tight shut against it. Beside him Terrie sighed again and nestled deeper into the pillows, the long, tangled mane of her hair obscuring her face from his sight.

Levering himself up onto his side, Gio rested his weight on one elbow as he turned to study her sleeping form. His fingers itched to sweep the blonde locks away from her face and expose the delicate cheekbones, the full softness of her mouth, but caution and common sense warned him sharply to hold back. To touch her was to risk waking her. And waking her would have the sort of consequences he wasn't prepared to risk.

If she woke then he would be tempted all over again. If she stirred, turned to him, still warm and relaxed from sleep, then he would want her with the hunger that was still lingering just below the surface of his mind, the raw passion that had had him in its grip all through the night.

'If she *wakes*…!' he muttered, low and rough. '*If*… Oh, *Madre de Dio*!' Who was he trying to fool?

He wasn't even convincing himself. Even as the thoughts crossed his mind, his body was waking, hardening in savagely demanding response simply to her closeness, to the warmth of her skin reaching his, the scent of her flesh coiling round his senses like a drug.

Face facts, he told himself with furious reproach. He wanted her again. Even the passion-soaked night that they had shared had done nothing to appease his clamouring senses. If anything he was hungrier than before. He wanted her, and he wanted her *now*, with a yearning that all the guilt and the regret could do nothing to suppress.

'*Inferno!*' he swore savagely under his breath, throwing back the bedclothes and pushing himself from the bed, careless of whether he disturbed the sleeping woman or not.

But it seemed that she was even more exhausted than he had been. For an instant she stirred slightly, seeming to sense his movement away from her side. But the next moment she had cuddled down again, once more giving that gentle sigh that tugged at something in his heart.

No! He wouldn't let her reach him, touch him again, either physically or mentally. One night he had told himself. One night and that was all. There was no room in his life for anything more.

His clothes were scattered all around the room—the shirt hanging half on and half off a chair, his trousers in an appallingly crumpled heap on the blue patterned carpet. Brown eyes clouding in disbelief and distaste, he forced himself to collect them up, shake them out into some sort of order at least.

What he really longed for was a shower. A long, hot, ruthlessly scouring shower.

Or did he mean a long, cold, ruthlessly icy one? The sort of shower that might just suppress the wanton longings that his weakened flesh was still subjected to. That would freeze his molten blood so effectively it would leave him shuddering and gasping in total shock.

Because it seemed that only that would drive away the lingering memories of the pleasures of this woman's body, erase the knowledge of how it had felt to possess her soft femininity, destroy the longing to experience it all over again.

But a shower was a risk he couldn't take. The sound of the rushing water would wake the sleeping Terrie. She would stir, and, finding him gone, his side of the bed empty and cold, would come in search of him. And if she found him in the shower…

'*Dio*, no!'

The thudding of his heart set the blood throbbing inside his skull, blotting out the possibility of rational thought. Just to imagine himself and Terrie close together in the shower cubicle, naked and relaxed, the flow of the warm water over already heated skin, was more than he could endure. Unable to withstand the beguilingly erotic pictures that were flooding through his mind, he snatched up his disordered clothing and escaped into the bathroom, shutting the door behind him as firmly as the need for quiet allowed.

Dear God, but he looked like hell!

The man who stared back at him from the mirror over the basin had heavy, hooded eyes with deep, dark shadows underneath them. His jawline was rough with a night's growth of beard, and his hair was in wild disorder, making him remember Terrie's urgent, clutching fingers closing over his scalp as her orgasm shook her slender body in wave after wave of ecstasy.

'No!'

He must stop thinking like that. Must stop remembering.

Bending over the sink, he ran the cold tap until the water was icy and then scooped it up into his hands, splashing it fiercely into his still sleep-softened face. He had to wake up. Had to get out of here as he had always planned.

By the time he had dried his face, pulled on his clothes, and forced his wayward hair into some degree of order again, he felt much more awake. Awake and in control of himself at last. Ready to return to the way of life that had been the norm before the blonde land-mine that was

Teresa Something had exploded right in his face, throwing him totally off balance.

She was still asleep when he made his way back into the bedroom. Still lying on her side, slightly curled up into a vulnerable ball, her face still hidden by the pale mass of her hair.

He could leave now. He could get out of here, get away before she even surfaced, and she would never know. He could simply walk out that door and...

But even as he thought it, he knew he could never act on the impulse. Their time together was over and, even though his greedy body was urging him to have second, and even third thoughts about the decision he had made, he was determined to stick with his resolve. But he couldn't just walk out the door without a word. He'd have to stay and say something to her. Even if that something was only goodbye.

With a sigh he flung himself into the room's single chair, raking both his hands through his newly smoothed hair, ruffling it into total disorder once again. If it had to be done then he wished she would wake. She was just too tempting lying there, sleeping. Too innocent. Too vulnerable.

Too watchable.

Some sound he had made must have disturbed her, penetrating at last the deep, deep sleep that had her in its grip. As he watched, he saw her stir, saw the faint change in her breathing as she swam to the surface of her consciousness. She stretched slightly, tensed a little as she felt the space beside her, and then turned over, her hand going out to where she had expected him to be.

'Gio?'

It was a sleepy little murmur, softly puzzled, only halfway conscious.

'Gio?'

He watched in silence as she blinked, frowned, half opened her eyes, then let them drift shut again as if rousing herself was just too much effort.

He knew exactly how she felt. Knew that heavy, almost drugged sense of disorientation on waking to find that nothing was quite as you expected it. That the scene you had anticipated finding had altered subtly and disturbingly.

'Gio?'

This time she came round more fully. Lifting her head from the pillow, she peered, puzzled, at the vacant side of the bed, her light brown brows drawing together in a frown of incomprehension, her lavender gaze still slightly unfocused.

'Where…?'

'Here,' he inserted quickly, drawing her eyes to where he sat with his back to the window. 'I'm here.'

'Oh, yes. There you are!'

To his horror she smiled straight at him. A smile that was still clouded by sleep, that made her already gentle expression even softer, twisting something that felt painfully like regret deep inside.

'What are you doing there? And why are you dressed? Do you have somewhere to go?'

'No—nowhere important.'

'Good.'

The smile grew, and so did his discomfort.

'In that case, take those clothes off again and come back to bed.'

'That won't be possible.'

The words were clipped and curt, cold as ice.

'Won't be…?'

Her confusion made her look even more vulnerable, even more young and childlike and...

'Teresa, don't! Stop it right now.'

'Stop what? Don't what?'

'Don't *look* like that! Don't look at me like that. Oh, hell, *belleza*...'

Once more he raked impatient fingers through his hair, the gesture more expressive of his unease even than the ragged edge to his voice.

'How in God's name am I supposed to leave you when you look at me like that?'

CHAPTER SIX

LEAVE you.

How am I supposed to leave you?

The words didn't make any sense to Terrie's still sleep-fuddled brain. What was Gio talking about?

She had finally fallen into a deep sleep of total exhaustion at some point well into the early hours of the morning. For some hours her oblivion had been absolute, but then, slowly and gradually, she had come awake. And, stirring slightly under the soft quilted duvet, she had felt the faint stiffness in her limbs, the tiny aches and bruises that reminded her instantly of how she had spent so much of the night.

And she had smiled to herself at the memories.

She had never woken to so good a feeling before. Never felt so totally satisfied, so relaxed, so deeply, contentedly at one with the world. Last night she had met a very special man, and she had spent a deliriously sensual, a gloriously happy night with him.

And she was firmly convinced that, after such a special night, today could only be the start of a whole new life. A life that she hoped, prayed, dreamed would include the presence of Giovanni Cardella in it for a long, long time.

On that thought she had stirred, swimming up slowly, close to the surface of waking. And in that state she had reached out a hand to the spot where, as sleep had finally closed over her, the warm, vital, wonderful body of Gio had been lying, satiated and relaxed at her side.

Which was when the first tiny flaw had entered the

perfect beginning to her day. The space was empty, the sheets already cooling rapidly as if the man who had slept there had been gone for some time.

'Gio?'

Frowning faintly, she had stirred again, struggling to make herself wake up a little more.

'Here…' She heard his voice, coming vaguely to her through the thick, clinging strands of sleep as she forced her eyes open.

He was sitting in the chair, with his back to the window. His head was silhouetted against the faint grey light, his face half in shadow as a result. What she could see looked wonderful. More than wonderful.

He no longer had the sleek, groomed perfection of the night before. His hair was only partly combed, his cheeks and jaw unshaven, roughened with the dark shadow of stubble. His eyes were heavy and hooded, and his clothes were only pulled on, some buttons still not fastened, his shirt only roughly pushed into the waistband of the grey trousers.

But in Terrie's mind he looked all the more wonderful because of that. Because she knew what had put that sleepily sensual look into his eyes. Whose hands had ruffled the sleek, jet-black perfection of his hair. The memories of the night they had shared still coloured everything in a rich, golden glow, so she was incapable of seeing anything wrong in it.

But a couple of moments later, as each unexpectedly cool response to her attempts to entice him back into her bed fell onto her exposed nerves like icy drops of rain, she was forced into a radical and uncomfortable rethink.

'Gio, what do you mean? Why are you leaving? Where are you going?'

The suspicion and the fear that had her heart in an icy

grip began to deepen when he didn't answer, but simply sat there, dark eyes levelled on her face. With a struggle she forced herself to wake properly, rousing herself to open her eyes, pull herself upright on her pillows.

A second later, a hasty, instinctive rethink had her pulling the covers up too, covering her exposed shoulders and breasts. Still not entirely sure why, she only knew she felt too exposed, too vulnerable like that.

'Wh-when are you coming back?'

'Never.' It was cold and flat and totally unyielding.

'Never? But why? What have I done…?'

'It's not what you've done, Teresa. It's what I didn't do. Or, rather, what I didn't say.'

'I don't understand.'

He was speaking in riddles, making her mind whirl in confusion. But all the same her blood ran cold simply at the sound of his words, her heart filling with dread at the prospect of what might be to come.

'I never said there would be any tomorrow. Or any sort of future, come to that. I never promised you anything beyond one night. We had that night. Now it's time to say goodbye.'

'But…'

Terrie's eyes would not focus and when she looked at his face it was just a blur. Blinking hard, she forced them back into clarity and immediately wished she hadn't. She had seen more emotion on the carved stone face of the Sphinx, and her blood ran so cold in fear that she shivered in spite of the cosy quilt.

'Goodbye?' It was just a low, desolate murmur.

'Goodbye.'

To her horror she realised that he had taken it as agreement. As if she was saying farewell to him.

And it seemed that that was exactly what he wanted.

He was getting to his feet, reaching for his shoes, stamping his feet into them.

He truly hadn't expected it to be quite that easy, Gio reflected thankfully. She must have known it was coming, but all the same he had anticipated some sort of protest, a touch of complaint at her swift dismissal. She *had* tried to cajole him back into bed at first, he recalled, thankful that the need to fasten his shoes meant he had to bend his head, so avoiding looking into her face, and hiding his own expression from her.

If she tried again he wasn't totally sure he would be able to resist her. He hadn't been prepared for how difficult it had been the first time. The struggle he had had with his most basic instincts not to toss off his clothes again, fling back the covers and join her once more in the indolent warmth of the big double bed. Even now, in spite of the fact that he couldn't see her, his body was recalling the sensual delights of the night, hardening in nagging demand and yearning for a repeat indulgence. The clutch of hunger deep in his gut made his hands disturbingly unsteady on his laces.

The sooner he was out of here the better. All he had to do was to get out the door—close it between them...

'No!'

The cry came unexpectedly, shocking him into stillness just as he caught up his jacket from the chair.

'Che?'

'I said no!'

Terrie didn't know what had brought this on; what had made him suddenly so determined to leave. She only knew that she wasn't going to stand by and let it happen.

Launching herself out of the bed, heedless now of her total nudity, she flung herself at Gio as he turned towards the door. His arm was beyond her reach, no matter how hard she stretched, but she did manage to catch hold of his trailing jacket, her fingers tangling in the fine material and clutching hard.

'You're not going anywhere!'

Her gasping protest, and the sudden catch on his jacket forced Gio to halt abruptly. Whirling round, he directed a furious glare into her uneasy face. One that shook her right to the roots of her soul and almost had her releasing her hold on the jacket again, fearful of possible retribution.

But a moment later she had collected herself, drawing in some sort of courage with the rough, unsteady breath that she struggled for.

'You're not going,' she repeated stubbornly. 'Not without some sort of explanation.'

If that glare had been terrible, then the look of pure contempt that raked her from the dishevelled, tangled cloud of blonde hair and down over every exposed and vulnerable inch of her naked body was even worse. It seemed to scour her sensitive skin, stripping away a vital protective layer, and leaving her raw and bleeding, emotionally if not actually physically.

'And who,' he enquired in tones of pure ice, 'is going to stop me?'

'I am…'

She had to force herself to say it, but somehow the fact that it came out through closely gritted teeth as she tightened her uncertain grip on the jacket seemed to give the words an added force, a determination that she was far from actually feeling.

'Oh, are you?'

It was even more condescending than before and the arrogant look that he directed at her down the long, straight line of his nose threatened to shrivel her into ashes right where she stood. It took every ounce of courage to stay where she was, though her toes curled in nervous reaction, digging into the soft pile of the carpet.

'Sì?'

The softness of the question took her almost by surprise so that she was unprepared for his sudden movement as he tried to snatch his coat away from her briefly loosened grasp. But she managed to grab at it just in time, setting up a brief and ungainly contest as each of them fought for possession of the item.

'Teresa…'

Never before had she heard her name spoken with such ferocity, such venom.

'You will rip my jacket.'

'No, you will!' she flung at him defiantly. 'But only if you keep up this ridiculous tug of war. Oh, come on, Gio…is it asking so much? Just tell me why…'

He drew himself up, taller, darker and more imposing than ever before. Dangerously so.

'I don't have to explain myself to you.'

He exerted a little extra force, pulling the jacket a few inches nearer to his side.

'And I say you do!'

With a rough little movement she tugged it right back.

For a couple of moments the garment seesawed between them, then with one final jerk Gio wrenched it out of her hands and fully into his. But Terrie barely saw it go. The movement had jolted the jacket roughly, shaking a couple of items free from the pockets, one of them a black leather wallet. And as she watched, fascinated, it tumbled to the ground, landing with a faint, soft thud, and falling open right at her feet.

'Inferno!'

With barely half her mind she was aware of Gio's furious curse, his dart forwards, his hand coming out. But that was enough for instinct to come into play, warning her that something was wrong. Something he didn't want her to see or know about.

Totally abandoning the disputed jacket, she turned her attention instead to the wallet, grabbing it up in the same swift movement that took her partway across the room, and into the comparative safety of the other side of the bed.

'Teresa!'

Her name was both a threat and a warning.

'Give that back to me—now!'

'No chance...'

She wanted to defy him totally. To challenge him to do something about her actions. But her mind chose just that most inopportune moment to push her into glancing across the room, catching sight of her reflection in the mirror on the front of the wardrobe.

It was just the wrong time to bring home to her the fact that she was totally naked, her pale skin faintly flushed from her recent exertions.

'Oh, no!'

Horrified beyond embarrassment, she clasped her arms across her exposed breasts, whirling in a frantic circle as she hunted for, found and yanked on her pale pink towelling robe, forcing the hand that held the wallet down the sleeve. It was impossible to fasten the tie belt, so she had to content herself with pulling the two sides together, clutching them close to cover as much as possible.

'Teresa... Give me back that wallet!'

'Wrong move, Gio! If you'd really wanted me to give it back without looking, then you should have pretended it just wasn't important! All you've done is to pique my curiosity. Now, let me see...'

One-handed, she caught the wallet by a corner, shook it over the rumpled bed, watching as several items fell out and tumbled down onto the quilt.

Credit and cheque cards, some English notes, and others she supposed must be Italian lira, a book of stamps…some photographs.

And in an instant, without needing to think or to ask questions, she knew that the photographs were what he had wanted to hide from her. They fell in a bundle, some totally hidden, others partly exposed, and as they did so one single, harshly explosive curse broke from Gio's lips. But when Terrie glanced up at him, suspicion in her eyes, he made no further move to stop her. Instead, he lifted both his hands, flinging them outwards in a supremely Italian gesture of defeat.

'Be my guest…' The ironical inflexion he gave the words was so sharp, so bitter that Terrie actually flinched as it stung like the lash of a whip.

Well, what did it matter now? Gio asked himself. What did any of it matter?

He didn't even know why he'd been so determined that she shouldn't find out. Why it had mattered so much that she didn't discover the truth about Lucia. About his wife.

No. Even as he formed the thought, he realised that that wasn't the point. He didn't understand why it wasn't; he simply knew that Teresa learning that he had once been married wasn't what troubled him. It was the thought of her finding out *like this*. He didn't want her to find out in this way.

Which was mad. Totally crazy. He hadn't planned on telling her anyway. Hadn't thought of telling her *anything*, if he was honest. She was just a one-night stand. Someone with whom he had enjoyed a night of passion, a brief, purely sexual interlude, and nothing more. And if she hadn't woken up before he had left this morning, then she would never have known anything other than that. Never have brought him—and herself—to this uncomfortable moment of revelation.

But that wasn't true either. She hadn't woken by accident. He had deliberately waited for her to wake. He had stayed in the room, sitting in that chair by the window, delaying until she stirred. He could have walked out of the room in any one of a dozen minutes before that, but he hadn't. Something had held him back, kept him there.

And for the life of him he didn't know what.

'Take a look, *cara*,' he drawled now, knowing she must find out and careless of the possible consequences. 'You know you've been dying to, so go right ahead.'

Perversely, now that she had his concession, Terrie found she had lost her nerve, no longer wanting to know what it was that had disturbed him so much. She looked into the darkness of his eyes and felt an icy chill creep through her veins, slowly sliding towards her heart. She was suddenly desperately, bitterly afraid.

'Oh, don't stop now, *belleza*,' Gio goaded her when she hesitated, unable to go any further. 'You fought like a tiger for this—don't turn coward on me now.'

And that 'coward' taunted her into action where nothing else would. Anything less deliberately provocative might have made her hesitate, decide she didn't really want to know, but not this. This deliberate sneer pushed her into doing exactly as he wanted, without even pausing to wonder why he had now decided not to stop her.

But first one tiny, practical part of her mind urged her into protective action, making her take a vital two seconds to pull the tie belt tight about her waist, fasten the robe firmly around her. Only when that was secure did she dare reach for the photographs.

The first one was of a little boy. A beautiful little boy. Quite the most beautiful child Terrie had ever seen. With jet-black hair and deep, dark brown eyes, he was perhaps two years old. He was wearing an oversized T-shirt, white with multicoloured flags on the front, below which just peeped a pair of neat blue shorts. His mouth was stretched in a wide, mischievous grin, and he was clutching a black and white spotted blanket firmly to him.

And Gio didn't have to say a word to explain who the child was, or the man's relationship to him. It was stamped all over the little boy's face, the way it was a perfect, scaled-down replica of Gio's own features.

'Paolo.' Clearly Gio didn't think there was any need of explanation either. 'His name is Paolo.'

'And he's your son.'

He didn't speak to acknowledge her words, which in any case had been a statement, not a question, but his dark head moved in silent agreement anyway.

Which gave her due warning of just what the other photos might show. But all the same it was still a devastating shock, dangerous as a blow to the heart, and potentially as lethal too, as she turned over the next picture and found herself staring into the smiling face of…

'Paolo's mother?' Her voice was just a raw croak as if it had been forced from a desperately sore and infected throat.

'Yes…and my wife.'

CHAPTER SEVEN

TERRIE supposed she should be thankful that at least he had been honest with her, but thankful was the last thing she felt. She wanted to rage at him, to scream and shout, to express her savage feelings in violent language. She was even sorely tempted to launch herself straight at him, hands flying, to pummel angry fists against his hard, unyielding form.

But although the thoughts were there, although the need was like an explosion inside her head, she found that, disturbingly, it was impossible to move. She could only stand there, frozen, her fingers clenched tight on the revealing photograph, her glazed eyes staring unseeingly into the woman's—Gio's *wife's*—face.

What was surprising was that the woman wasn't, in the conventional sense, at all pretty. She was petite and dark, and she had her son's wide, brilliant smile. But no one would ever have called her stunning. She didn't possess a slim, model-like figure either, but was surprisingly rounded at breasts and hips, something that her lack of height accentuated.

'Wha—what's she called?'

And *why* had she asked that? Why did she want to know such a small, but such an intimate detail? Would it make the woman any the more alive, any more *real* if she knew?

How could it? How could anything make this terrible thing more real, more true? If she knew everything about this woman, where and when Gio had met her, how long they'd been married, exactly when the little boy Paolo had been born—when he had been *conceived*—would it make things any easier to bear? Would the pain be any the less because she *knew*—or wouldn't it in fact be impossible to make it any worse?

'Her name is Lucia.'

Why phrase it like that? Gio was forced to wonder. Why not spill out the whole truth and then it would all be out in the open? Why not be strictly accurate, use the correct tense, say 'Her name *was* Lucia'? Because that, after all, was the fact.

But he hated the thought of actually framing the words. Of hearing them spoken out loud like this in this room, in this situation. His clouded gaze went to the wildly ruffled bed where to his astonishment the pillow on the side where he had slept still bore the vague imprint of his head in evidence of the night he had spent there.

OK, so he hadn't been *unfaithful* to Lucia in the strictest sense of the term, but it still felt that way in his heart.

But the problem was that his feelings for Lucia were now further complicated by the present situation.

Porca miseria! He should have gone when he had had the chance!

Or, rather, he should never have acted last night. Never have let his most basic desires, his most primitive needs, cloud his normally cool-headed thinking.

Thinking! The word was like an explosion inside his head. Face it. He hadn't been thinking at all. He had simply been *reacting*. And reacting to the tug of his sexuality, every instinct below the waist, and nothing in his head at all.

And that was what had got him into this mess in the first place.

'Lucia Paolina Cardella.'

'Thank you.'

The ice in her voice stung none the less for being deserved. And the burning glare from those soft-coloured eyes was a bitter reproach to him. Unsettlingly so. Because she had known from the start that it had only been for the night—hadn't she? 'Fun' was what she had said that she was after. She couldn't have expected anything more.

'I'm so glad you finally decided to tell me.'

Her tone said the exact opposite; and the hand that held the photograph tightened convulsively on the picture, threatening to crush it badly.

'Scusi…'

Leaning across the bed, he took hold of her hand, trying to lever her clutching fingers free, earning himself another furious glare.

'You are creasing it…'

'So I am!'

For a second she was tempted to rip the photo in two but then, rethinking, decided against it. It wasn't this Lucia's fault that she had an unfaithful rat for a husband. That she was married to a man who couldn't keep his trousers zipped up.

'Here…'

She flung the photograph in Gio's general direction, watching with burning, dry eyes as it flew a little way then floated down to the bed. The way he picked it up, concerned for its appearance, was another cruel twist of the knife in her already desperately wounded heart.

'Don't you think it's rather too late to be concerned?' she questioned bitterly, swallowing down the burning taste of acid in her mouth. 'Last night would have been a better bet if you'd wanted to pretend to have a guilty conscience. Or you could at least have the face to try the old "my wife doesn't understand me" routine.'

'It wouldn't be true.'

Gio was looking down at the picture, his concentration intense.

'If you want to know the truth, then Lucia always understood me perfectly.'

'Poor thing…'

The words slipped out before she could catch them back.

'I feel sorry for her. Being married to someone like you. It must be a hell of a life.'

To her horror, her mouth quivered on the last sentence, the words breaking painfully in the middle. And when she looked into Gio's stunning face, saw once again the stony, opaque-eyed look that had settled over his features, it was more than she could do to keep her control. The tears that she had been fighting from the moment that he had headed for the door after telling her he was leaving were now swimming revealingly in her eyes and she set her jaw, swallowing hard, refusing to let them fall.

'Or does she have her—bits on the side as well? Is that it, Gio? Do you have some sort of an open marriage?'

'No!'

The opaque look vanished in an instant. He looked horrified at the thought, shocked right through to the depths of his heart.

No, that was wrong. Not the depths of his *heart*. Giovanni Cardella didn't possess a heart. He couldn't or he wouldn't have behaved in this callous, unfeeling way.

'Lucia would never do any such thing. She has standards…'

That brought her head up sharply, brilliant eyes burning into his in defiance.

'And so do I!'

He had the nerve to look doubtful. Or something. She wasn't at all sure how to interpret the look that flashed across his face, made his gaze suddenly unsteady, but it obviously wasn't total agreement with what she had said.

'I do! I don't sleep with married men, Signor Cardella—at least not when I *know* they are married! But you didn't even have the honesty to tell me! You lied!'

'No...'

'No,' she repeated, her voice dulled by pain. 'No, you never actually lied to me. You just never answered the question, did you? Instead you distracted me with details about your sister-in-law and her pregnancy and the fact that she—she lives in Sicily. With your br-brother. And, I presume—with your *wife*!'

'No.'

'No? Then where...?' Hastily she caught herself up. 'No—don't tell me! I don't want to know! I don't want to know anything about her—or about you—or about your son...'

Liar! her heart reproached her in anguish. Liar, liar, liar!

She *did* want to know—though she would rather have died than to ask him. She wanted to know what had been in his mind when he had approached. Why he had picked on her. Had he truly only wanted a quick sexual fix, a one-night stand, nothing more?

'Teresa...' Gio began.

But the sound of her name on his lips, the wonderful sound of those lyrically accented syllables that had set her heart soaring just a few short hours before, was more than she could bear. It brought her to the edge of her rapidly crumbling control and threatened to push her over.

'Don't say it!' she flung at him. 'Whatever you were

going to say—whatever sort of an excuse you were going
to come up with—then don't do it! I told you, I don't
want to hear a word! I don't want to know!'

Suddenly too restless with pain to stand still, unable to
bear the burn of his watchful ebony eyes, she set up a
restless pacing, moving from her side of the bed to the
opposite wall of the room in swift, slightly unsteady
strides. But there wasn't enough space in the small room
to walk as far and as fast as she wanted. Nowhere she
could go at the pace that might ease the tearing anguish
in her heart, distract her from the bitter burn of the feeling
of being used.

'Why did you do it?' she demanded, whirling to face
him, blue eyes blazing. 'How could you?'

No, looking into his face had been a mistake. A terrible
mistake.

Because just in the second that she had met his eyes
once again she had seen something that looked dangerously, appallingly like—like *compassion*. And that was
the last thing that she needed from him. Because it would
destroy her. She was barely clinging on to her control as
it was.

It couldn't be compassion! She doubted he was capable
of feeling any such thing.

'Are you saying you had no part in this?'

Oh, that was better. That was more what she had expected. That was the Giovanni Cardella he had revealed
himself to be.

'Of course not!'

She'd be a fool to even try. After all, she'd been the
perfect willing victim, just ready and waiting to fall into
his greedy, grasping hands like the perfect, ripe plum. She
could just imagine how he had felt. As if all his birthdays
had come at once. He could never have imagined that

she'd be so damn easy that she'd do half the work for him—more than half.

'But at least I never told anything but the truth! I never lied!'

'And neither did I!'

'Oh, no!' Terrie scorned. 'Not half! So you didn't say you *weren't* married—but you dodged the issue quite nicely. And you...you...'

'I what?'

'You called me *cara*! And I told you that that is one Italian word I do understand. *Cara*! You said—'

'I would have said anything at the time. And I'm sure you would too. We all say things we don't mean in the heat of the moment.'

'And if we think it will get us just what we want! Oh—don't look at me like that!' she flung at him when he turned a sidelong glare of reproof on her. 'That's what men do, isn't it? They'll say anything, anything at all if it will get some poor gullible fool into bed with them!'

'I—'

'Oh, don't start backtracking now! Don't try and wriggle out of it! It was all a lie from start to finish. All of it—even—even...'

The knot in her throat threatened to close up completely, making her choke on the words.

'Even when you called me *belleza*.'

'No!'

He shook his head violently in furious rejection.

'No. That was no lie. You are beautiful. Amazing.' He actually sounded as if he meant it. 'You must know that.'

Just for a second Terrie let the words touch her. Let that vehement 'beautiful', that 'amazing' sink in, appease her, soothe the raw wounds he had inflicted on her.

But almost immediately she realised what she was doing, what was happening to her, and pulled herself up sharp.

Was she really going to listen to any more of his lies? Was she going to let him get to her again, reach her, touch her, when she knew that every word he spoke was totally untrue, purely calculated to get what he wanted? Get what he could out of her?

'Oh, no, you don't,' she said, taking a couple of steps backwards, away from him, putting as much distance between them as she could possibly manage in the tiny room.

The movement brought her up against the small table on which the long-cold pot of coffee still stood, the untouched brandy glasses from the previous night.

'You can't think I'd listen to a word you said ever again.'

'Oh, come on!' Gio declared, clearly losing his grip on the temper that had been smouldering dangerously for some time. 'Don't play the outraged virgin in all this! You were as keen for it as I was—more! You brought me up here! You—'

'I what? Threw myself at you? Seduced you?'

'You weren't exactly saying no. And we both knew why you brought me up here. Why you suggested that we have coffee in your room and not in the lounge. "It would be quieter..."' he said suddenly, dropping his voice, softening it, until it was an uncanny and disturbingly accurate copy of her own tones the night before. '"More private". Anyone would have seen what you were up to.'

'So I invited you up for coffee—and you thought that you were in there. That I was yours for the cost of a posh meal and an after-dinner brandy?'

'And you weren't?' he came back at her with the deadly

swiftness of a striking snake as his dark eyes dropped to the tray, resting thoughtfully on the still-full glasses.

'No! No, I wasn't!'

He might have thought she had come cheap, but he couldn't be more wrong. Last night had cost her much, much more than he imagined, and she was only just beginning to realise how expensive it had actually been. But she was damned if she was going to let him see the payment she had made to him in her emotions.

In her heart.

'I'm not that cheap!'

'Forgive me if I beg to differ...'

His tone spoke of anything *but* an apology.

'But neither of us was exactly particular last night. We both saw an opportunity and went for it.'

An opportunity for a quick lay. Terrie didn't know which hurt most. The implication that she hadn't been exactly picky about choosing him. Or the reverse—that if he had had more choice, he might not have wanted to be with her.

But she had been available. Oh, so available. She had been totally bowled over by him and as such had been easy prey for him to take that 'opportunity' he had spoken of.

'Well, in that case...'

Deliberately she kept her voice quiet, calm, hiding the true turmoil of her feelings behind a careful, apparently controlled mask.

'You must be sorry that you didn't have your brandy last night. Something of a waste, don't you think?'

Just as she had planned, hoped, his gaze went to the tray, then back up to her face, a faint frown drawing those straight black brows close together.

And somehow she managed to force a bright, vivid and

totally fake smile right into the darkness of his eyes. One
so brilliant that it totally distracted him from just what her
hand was doing.

'Perhaps you'd like to have it now?'

The glass was in her grip. She brought it up and out,
swiftly, tossing the contents straight into Gio's watchful,
puzzled face.

'Enjoy!' she laughed, almost meaning the amusement
as she watched him gasp and splutter, wiping the liquid
from his face. 'Oh, and while you're at it—you paid for
this one too!'

Before he had recovered, the second brandy had followed the first, hitting his chest this time and soaking
rapidly into the fine linen of his shirt.

'*Dannazione!*' Gio swore savagely, still wiping the
back of his hand across his face, blinking the stinging
liquid from his eyes. 'You—'

'Oh, spare me the insults!' Terrie broke in furiously,
the pain and the bitterness welling up and overflowing like
lava down the sides of a volcano, impossible to stop. 'We
both know what you think of me and I don't care to hear
it again! We both made a mistake—a big mistake—coming together last night. If I had my time again then believe
me I'd have done things totally differently.'

If she'd known what was coming then she'd have run,
in the opposite direction, as far and as fast as she could.

'We both would,' Gio inserted drily, uncannily seeming
to sense her thoughts.

'Well, we can't put the clock back, it's too late for that.
But I'd prefer it if you'd go—right now...'

'Teresa...'

She hadn't expected him to protest and it shook her,
weakening her so that the tears she had managed to fight

against until now flooded her eyes and threatened to spill over.

'Right *now*!' she flung at him, hiding desperation behind fury. 'I want you to go—get out—leave me in peace.'

Still he hesitated, and she couldn't bear it. She wanted to be left totally alone, to hide and lick her wounds in private. And she was determined that there was no way she was going to break down in front of him.

'Not had enough?' she asked, her voice low and deadly with warning. 'There's always the coffee...'

Her hand had actually reached for the coffee-pot, was curling round the handle, when Gio finally decided to move. Throwing up his hands and muttering something dark and vicious in incomprehensible Italian, he whirled away from her, snatched up his jacket, the wallet and its tumbled contents from the bed, and strode towards the door.

'And don't come back!' Terrie flung at his retreating back.

'You need have no worries on that score,' he tossed right back. 'I'd sooner put my head into the jaws of a hungry lion than ever come up against you again. What is it you say? Good riddance...?'

'To bad rubbish,' Terrie completed for him. 'And believe me, the feeling is totally mutual!'

They were the last words she could manage. The last thing she was capable of saying before weakness totally overwhelmed her and the tears finally started to flow. But she had just enough time. The retort seemed to bounce off the strong, upright line of his back just as he yanked open the door. And he was already out in the corridor by the time that her misery overwhelmed her and she sank down onto the bed.

The sound of the door slamming to behind him was like a sound of release. A signal that at last she was alone. Alone and free to express the volatile combination of anger, betrayal and pain that had been threatening to blow her apart for some time now. Ever since that hateful, that appalling 'and my wife'.

Throwing herself down onto the bed, she pummelled the pillows hard, pounding them in a fury of distress, wishing all the time that they were Giovanni Cardella's hard, lean ribcage. The bones that protected his hard, mean heart.

'I hate you!' she muttered. 'Hate, hate, *hate* you!'

Out in the corridor, Gio didn't even wait for the door to close behind him before he set off at an angry march, heading for the lift. There was just enough room in his buzzing, whirling brain to note, and send up a brief thank-you for, the fact that at this hour of the morning the long, characterless stretches of carpets between the door-lined walls were totally empty. He would have a hard time explaining just what he was doing in such a dishevelled state and reeking of brandy.

Just what *was* he doing?

The question hit home as he punched the call button for the lift, stabbing at it with repressed fury.

How had he managed to make such a complete mess of things?

If he had told Terrie that Lucia was dead, that although he had once been married he was now, in the eyes of society, the church, anyone, a totally free man, then she would not have felt so hurt, so betrayed—so bitterly furious with him.

And she had had every right to feel that way, he admitted to himself as the lift lurched to a halt in front of him and the heavy metal doors slid open. She was completely justified in feeling that hurt, the betrayal, while she thought that he was still married and had simply been playing around, having—what was it the English said? A bit on the side.

But he had *wanted* her to believe that. Preferred her to think that he was an unfaithful husband. That he had deceived both his wife and Teresa, rather than have her know the truth.

And the truth was *what*?

The question was emphasised, underlined in his mind, by the lift doors banging shut again, making him realise that he had been standing still, staring into empty space for who knew how long. Hastily he jabbed one long finger on the call button again, hurrying inside the lift and selecting the penthouse floor before subsiding back into thought once more.

The *truth* was that none of his calculated plans, the coolly thought-up timetable for how things were to go, had actually worked when it had come down to it.

Last night was supposed to have been quick, easy—and above all simple. It was supposed to have been just the swift and temporary sensual indulgence of a one-night stand, no emotions, no commitment involved on either side.

'*Madre de Dio!*'

Gio raked both hands through the darkness of his hair, noting with a grim touch of amusement that his action did nothing to approve his appearance in the mirror-lined walls of the lift compartment. Instead, he remained as dishevelled-looking as ever, the ruffled hair only adding to the effect of the crumpled, brandy-stained clothes.

He smelled like a drunk, too, he thought, wrinkling his nose in fastidious distaste. Anyone seeing him now would never believe that he and the suave, controlled, articulate counsel for the prosecution in court yesterday were one and the same man.

'Counsel for the prosecution!'

The phrase left his lips on a slightly shaken laugh. He'd certainly been that this morning. He'd condemned *himself* by his silence more effectively than if he'd offered any sort of evidence.

When Terrie had found out that he had a wife, he had deliberately kept back the important detail that Lucia was dead because something had stopped him from speaking. And that something had been that he had wanted her to hate him. Wanted her to throw him out of her room and never have any regrets about her actions afterwards. It would hurt her less that way, he had told himself. She would be able to shake off the memories of the previous night and go on with her life without any afterthoughts.

And he had wanted to ensure that he had no way back. That even if he tried to find his way into her life again, she would slam the door in his face hard and fast.

It had worked perfectly. It couldn't have worked out any better. Terrie had rejected him with all the speed and determination he had expected. He was free. No ties, no commitments.

And he didn't like it.

'*Dannazione!*' he swore under his breath as the lift came to a halt and the doors rumbled open just by the door to his suite. 'What the hell is wrong with me?'

Wielding his key card like a lethal weapon, he pushed it into the slot and snatched it back out again, wrenching open the door with a force that expressed the disturbed state of his feelings.

What was wrong with him was that he had planned on fixing things so that there was no way back. And now that he'd done just that, he realised it was not what he wanted. Not deep down.

Deep down, what he wanted was more of what he had experienced last night and this morning. He wanted more of Terrie's own special brand of intensely feminine sensuality. More of the deep warmth and passion he had found in her arms. More of the dreamless sleep of satiety that had followed their lovemaking.

And it was a black irony in his mind at the thought that now, finally, he had got exactly what he had set out to achieve last night. Only to find that it was the last thing he truly wanted.

CHAPTER EIGHT

SATURDAY was usually the best day of the week. A day when the prospect of a lie-in, followed by forty-eight hours away from work, gave even the prospect of the most mundane tasks, carried out in the most miserable weather, a glow of anticipation like any other.

But this Saturday was different, Terrie reflected as she pulled on faded denim jeans and a well-worn bright pink T-shirt. Or, rather, it looked set to be almost exactly like every other day this week, and that was what made it a problem.

This time last week, she had had a job. Not the best job in the world, admittedly, but at least it had been *something*. Something that had meant that she was able to support herself, pay the rent on her flat, and maintain a degree of self-esteem.

She no longer had that job. After her absence from two 'vital' elements of the conference her services had been abruptly dispensed with, a decision she hadn't even felt up to arguing about. She had already decided that employment at Addisons had totally lost any of the fragile appeal it had ever held for her. And, as a result of Giovanni Cardella's intervention in her life, self-esteem was something she was totally lacking. He had seen to that, removing all her confidence and leaving her feeling lower than a snail's behind.

'So now what do I do?'

Even the question seemed totally redundant. There was nothing to do.

Free of her job, she had spent the past week cleaning and tidying every inch of her flat. But, as it was basically a living-room-cum-kitchenette plus a single bedroom, with shared bathroom, that hadn't exactly taken long. She had done the basic grocery shopping she could afford, and now the weekend stretched ahead, empty and unappealing.

As a result, the sound of the knock at her door was a more than welcome relief from the prospect, sending her hurrying to respond to it without a second thought as to who might be there. After all, the main entrance into the hall downstairs was always locked, so only someone who shared the house with her could reach the actual door to her flat.

'Is that you, Barbara?'

Expecting to see the woman who lived across from her, the one with whom she shared her bathroom, she was totally unprepared for the tall, dark, dangerously imposing and supremely *male* figure standing on the landing outside.

'*Buon giorno, Teresa,*' drawled a lyrically accented voice that she had thought never, ever to hear again.

'Oh, no, you don't!'

Swift as she was to react, moving instantly to slam the door closed, Gio's responses were even swifter. A large, elegantly booted foot was inserted into the gap between door and frame before she had time to close it properly. A second later a powerful shoulder made contact with the side of the door, wrenching it out of her disturbingly weakened grip, and pushing it wide open once again.

'Good morning, Teresa,' he repeated with a smile that would have melted icebergs. 'It's a pleasure to see you again.'

'And you surely don't expect me to say that the feeling

is in any way mutual,' Terrie flung back, blinking be-
musedly in the wake of the brilliance of that smile. 'I
thought I told you that I never wanted to see you again?
And I meant it!'

'I'm quite sure you did—at the time. But I had hoped
that the passage of time would have given you a chance
to reconsider and to—'

'Not a hope! I meant what I said and all the reconsid-
ering in the world couldn't make me change my mind! I
thought I made my feelings perfectly clear last time!'

'And I thought you might like a chance to express them
differently— No?' he questioned when he saw the mulish
way her jaw set, the stubborn lift to her chin. 'Then it's
just as well I came prepared.'

'Prepared?'

Terrie's mouth literally fell open in shocked surprise as
Gio lifted the large carrier bag that stood on the floor at
his feet, and pushed it into her hands.

'I brought you a gift.'

'A gift—what…?'

In spite of herself she was curious, pulling away the
wrapping and revealing what it held inside. An enormous
bottle of cognac, the largest she had ever seen, together
with a huge balloon-shaped brandy glass made of superb,
delicate crystal.

'But…'

'I thought I'd bring you some extra ammunition, just
in case you felt you hadn't done enough damage already…'

The wicked smile that tugged at the corners of his
mouth, gleaming in the brilliant, dark eyes, was almost
irresistible. To her consternation, Terrie actually found
herself responding, her own lips curving upwards. Hastily

she caught herself just in time, forcing on an expression of stern disapproval that was worryingly hard to maintain.

'After all, those hotel measures are not exactly generous.'

'True,' Terrie was forced to concede.

'And I really felt that you hadn't fully—expressed your feelings last time.'

'True again.'

This was impossible! She wanted to feel anger, hatred, disgust. Wanted to retreat behind the whirlwind of emotion that had assailed her the last time she had seen him. That had been so much safer, a protective shield that protected her from her unwanted feelings for this man. But somehow she couldn't find the same force of reaction that had come to her in her hotel room, much as she longed to.

And she certainly didn't want to feel anything else. But somehow Gio's appearance had sneaked in under her careful defences, aiming straight at a worryingly vulnerable spot in her heart. And he had done it using the unexpected approach of humour, one she hadn't anticipated and so hadn't been able to shield herself against.

'I promise not even to duck.'

His resigned tone, the instinctive squaring of his shoulders was positively the last straw. Terrie fought a swift, hard battle with the amusement bubbling up inside her, trying desperately to force it down—and lost. In spite of herself the laughter she couldn't suppress escaped her on a gasping sigh of defeat.

'Very noble of you, I'm sure. Tell me,' she went on, curiosity getting the better of any sort of sense of self-protection, 'is this supposed to be an apology?'

Gio seemed to consider, dark eyes locking with her interrogative gaze.

'I think I owe you one,' he conceded at last.

Which was so totally unexpected that it actually rocked Terrie back on her heels, depriving her of the ability to speak.

Was this the same Giovanni Cardella she had met in the hotel a week ago? Or had some alien body snatcher taken over his body and replaced him with a very different sort of personality?

'An—an apology for what?' she managed at last when her tongue finally loosened enough to allow her to speak, no longer feeling like a lifeless block of wood in her mouth.

'For not telling you the full truth. Look…'

Gio's tone changed abruptly, the contrition, if that was what it had truly been, vanishing swiftly to be replaced by a note of controlled impatience that was one Terrie recognised much more easily. This was the Gio she knew and recognised only too well.

'Don't you think it would be easier to talk inside? Less public—more private? Anyone might come past here and—'

'You've got a nerve!'

Thankfully Terrie welcomed the rush of irritation, the saving heat of temper that pushed the words from her mouth. Taken aback by the shock of his appearance, the unexpected softness of his words, the nicely calculated humour of his gift, she had come close to a perilous weakness that had left her frighteningly vulnerable to his approaches. She had actually even taken a step backwards, preparing to do just as he suggested, and let him into the flat.

Let him into the privacy of her flat—into the intimate surroundings of her home.

And *privacy* and *intimacy* were two words she didn't

want to consider in connection with Giovanni Cardella. Not if she valued her peace of mind and her emotional safety.

'Turning up here like this—letting yourself into my h… How *did* you get in here?' she demanded when the question she should have asked from the start returned to nag at her brain, this time refusing to be distracted into going away.

'A lady I met at the front door let me in. She said she lived here—flat number two…'

Barbara, Terrie reflected wryly. Of course. It would be. At forty-three and twice divorced, Barbara Roberts was definitely still a sucker for a handsome male face—and she would have been totally unable to resist Gio. If he had turned on the charm—and she had no doubt at all that he *had* done just that—then the older woman would have been putty in his hands from the moment that he had first switched on that wide, bone-melting smile. And if he had treated her to the low-toned, seductive intonation of his wonderful accent, then she would practically have lain down right there on the doorstep and let him walk right over her in order to get what he wanted.

But she wasn't so easily won over, she resolved, pushing aside her momentary weakness of a few minutes before.

'Well, you can just turn right round and walk out again,' she told Gio tartly, mentally promising herself that she would tell Barbara exactly what she thought of her weakness the next time they met. 'I have nothing to say to you—and there is nothing I want to hear—'

'My wife is dead,' Gio broke in on her in a raw-voiced rush. 'Lucia is no longer alive. She died.'

'She…'

For a dreadful moment the room swung around Terrie

sickeningly so that she closed her eyes against the sensation, reaching out and clutching at what she believed was the door for support. But instead of the hardness of wood, her fingers closed over the fine silk of his jacket, clenching over the bone and sinew beneath. And that was every bit as hard as the door, she admitted. Hard, but not cold and unyielding as the wooden panels would have been. She could feel the warmth of his skin, and the flex and play of firm muscle under her grip as he adjusted to her hold, took the full weight of her body and supported it effortlessly.

With a struggle Terrie forced her eyes open again, trying to focus on the hard planes and angles of his stunning face so close to hers, the dark depths of his eyes.

'She's...' she tried again and heard him draw in his breath in a rough-edged hiss between his teeth.

'Dear God, Teresa, no, not that. I did not mean that she had died since that night.'

The rush of relief almost destroyed what little was left of Teresa's already precarious self-control. She hadn't been able to bear even *considering* the possibility that Gio's wife might have died since the night they had spent together in the hotel. Her already uncomfortable conscience couldn't have coped with the thought that they had betrayed the poor woman in the last days of her life.

That *Gio* had betrayed her, she corrected fiercely. He had been the guilty party. The liar, the manipulator, the deceiver.

'Then what did you mean?'

She would have thought that it was impossible for Gio's eyes to grow any darker, for the ebony pools to take her any deeper into his soul. But the shadows that had now surfaced in his gaze clouded their brilliance, dulling it and taking the edge off its clarity.

'I think you should sit down...'

His tone held nothing but concern, almost shocking in its unexpected gentleness, as he guided her carefully towards a chair.

Too late, she realised what he had done; how he had manipulated her yet again. The slam of the door closing behind him told its own tale—of how Gio had seized his opportunity, taking advantage of the way that she was totally distracted, knocked off balance by his shocking statement. He had ignored her obvious determination not to let him into her flat, and had moved forward, coming into the room on the pretext of taking care of her, gaining his own objective without any trouble.

'I don't want to sit down. And I think that *you* should explain!'

He was making a real mess of this, Gio reflected grimly. He had never meant to blurt out the truth about Lucia in quite that way, but when it had come to the point there had been no other way. He wanted Terrie to know the truth, but actually saying the words 'My wife is dead' was still so difficult, so painful, that his throat had almost closed over the words, blocking them off. In the end he had had either to force them out, rough and devastatingly blunt as they were, or play the coward and leave them unsaid once more.

And he had vowed to himself that he would never do that.

'I'll explain,' he growled roughly. 'Just tell me what you want to know.'

'I want to know everything...'

As she spoke she twisted away from his grasp and he didn't know whether he was glad to let her go or if what he really wanted was to hold her tighter, pull her closer to him, feel her warmth and the scent of her skin enclose him once more. The loss of the physical contact felt as though something vital had been ripped away from him, and yet at the same time it was a relief to be freed from the temptation that her body offered.

For the past week without her he had been trying to convince himself that it had all been a delusion. That the night he had spent with her had been a fleeting sexual pleasure, nothing more. He had told himself that no woman could have had such an effect on him, that he couldn't have been so instantly smitten by her. That he was exaggerating the concentrated, mind-blowing effect she had had on him.

It was only his hunger remembering, he had told himself. The hunger that was the result of two years' abstinence, two years' celibacy since he had lost Lucia. She couldn't have been so devastating. So unforgettable. So irresistible.

But now that he was here with her, he knew that by denying the effect she had on him he had been deceiving himself. She was everything he remembered—and more. When she had opened the door to him, just the sight of her had had an effect like a blow in his face, making his thoughts reel in instant response. His body had tightened, hardened, clamoured in protest at the restraint he had had to impose on himself. And now, being in the same room with her and not touching her, not kissing her...and more was a physical torment that made his yearning senses scream in agonising demand.

But he had to keep his distance. Had to hold himself together and not give in to hunger that was like an ache in every cell. At least until he had told her the truth.

'So where do you want me to begin?'

The withering glare she turned on him from those beautiful eyes might have quelled a lesser man. As it was, he felt the ice in it seem to penetrate his flesh, chilling, if only for a second, the heated rush of his blood.

'They say that the beginning is a good place to start.'

The beginning. The beginning was when he and Lucia had been so young, so innocent. Little more than children when they had first met. Barely in their teens when they had known that they were right for each other—meant to be together. But those were his memories, and his alone. She had no right to any part of them.

'Gio…'

Terrie's tone warned that he had hesitated too long.

'Either tell me or…'

She didn't have to finish the sentence. The swift flicker of her eyes towards the door, the stubborn set of her jaw, the defiance in her gaze, all made her meaning more than plain. Drawing in his breath on a rough, uneven hiss, Gio raked one hand forcefully through his hair.

'Lucia and I were married for over ten years…'

'Ten!' She hadn't expected that. 'You must have been…'

'Childhood sweethearts.'

Gio's confirmation was grim.

'She was all I had ever wanted in a woman—in a wife. I loved her from the start—and I never stopped loving her.'

His tone defied her to question the stark assurance of the declaration. But Terrie had no thought of doing any such thing.

He had *loved* his wife. She could have no doubt about that. It was there in the clouded depths of his eyes, the tautness of his jaw, the raw, roughened note in his words.

And it brought both a glorious excitement to her mind and in the same instant a terrible chill to her heart to see it there and recognise it for what it was.

What Gio had felt for Lucia had been true love. Total love. The sort of love that she had only ever dreamed a man could feel. The sort of love that she had prayed she might one day find for herself, if she was truly lucky.

But Gio hadn't felt that love for her. His heart had been given to another woman long ago, and she was beginning to doubt if there was anything left in it for anyone else.

'What happened?'

'We were married. We planned on the whole happy-ever-after—home, kids, everything. For a while we had everything, even the baby she dreamed of.'

'Paolo.'

'Yes, Paolo.'

Something changed in Gio's expression, his jaw clenching, his gaze losing focus. On an abrupt movement he swung away from her, pacing across the room to stand and stare out of the window, hands pushed deep into the pockets of his expensively tailored jacket. He assumed an intense interest in the traffic going past in the street, but Terrie had caught the betraying sheen filming his eyes, and the stiff, defensive set of those broad shoulders told its own story.

The need to touch him, to try to reach him, to communicate her understanding was almost overwhelming, but a terrible sense of uncertainty held her back. If she went to him now he might reject her, repulse her tentative gesture with an angry impatience or worse. And, feeling as she did right now, she knew she couldn't bear that.

Since the moment that he had appeared at her door again, her emotions had been on a roller-coaster ride of reaction. Shooting up in the simple delight of seeing him one moment, only to plunge down into the depths of despair at the knowledge of how little she meant to him the next.

She wanted to hate him. Hate him for the way he had treated her. The way he had used her and discarded her without a second thought. Hate was simple and easy and it precluded all other, more dangerous emotions. But hatred wasn't what she felt for him. She'd tried and, in spite of everything, had found that that wasn't what was in her heart.

And that was the truly scary thing.

'So you had Paolo…'

She had to force herself to speak. The broad, unyielding wall of his back couldn't have been any more off-putting if it had had notices pinned to it. *Go away! Keep out! Trespassers will most definitely be prosecuted.* The words didn't have to be spoken. They hung in the air like a deep grey cloud all around him.

'Was there a problem?'

'No.'

Gio's voice sounded as if it came from a long, long way away.

'No problem. The birth was fine. The baby was fine. Lucia…was fine. Or so everyone thought. We brought the baby home…'

Without warning he swung round, and, having hoped that he would no longer turn his back on her, Terrie now desperately wished the opposite. His face was almost unbearable to see. It seemed impossible that the deep lines of pain and distress etched around his nose and mouth, the bruised shadows in his eyes, could have appeared in such a short space of time.

'What happened?'

'Ten days before Paolo's first birthday, Lucia was alone in the kitchen and she collapsed. Suddenly and unexpectedly—there had been no sign of anything wrong. She'd complained of a faint headache, but that was all.'

He drew in a long, rawly rasping breath before he could go on.

'She died that night. There was nothing they could do for her. A brain haemorrhage, the doctors said. Something that could never have been predicted.'

'Oh…'

It was all that Terrie was capable of managing. She wanted to hold him. To weep for him. To do anything that she thought might help. But at the same time she didn't dare.

Her hands went to her face, covering her eyes for a second, then her mouth. Then she half extended them towards him, but almost immediately rethought and pulled them back. As long as she didn't know how Gio was going to react, she wasn't going to open herself to an attack or a rejection that would destroy her. She couldn't take any more of that.

'And every day since then I've never gone to sleep without wishing that I could tell her how much I loved her just one more time.'

'I'm—'

'No!' he cut in savagely, eyes blazing dangerously. 'Don't say you're sorry! I never want to hear that word again, at least not in this context. I had a bellyful of ''sorry''s in the months after it happened—after Lucia died. Everyone I met said they were sorry—how sorry they were…'

'They were only trying to help.'

'Maybe they were—but it doesn't help. Nothing helps at a time like that. What makes them think that ''sorry'' will somehow put it right?'

'I don't know,' Terrie admitted. 'I've never been through a loss like that.'

Somehow her words got through to him. She saw his

head go back, a tiny hint of the tension leaving his long body, a calmer light coming into his eyes.

'Well, that's honest at least. You wouldn't believe how many people will say that they know how you feel.'

'I couldn't begin to *imagine* how you feel. I wouldn't even try.'

It would hurt too much, even to feel it *for* him, never mind to have to go through it herself.

She wished there was something—anything she could do that would help. But all that her numbed, bruised mind could come up with was the simple, practical matters that would ease the here and now, because they could do nothing about the past.

'You look as if you could do with a drink. Why don't you sit down while I get you something?'

'Do you mean to say that I get to drink the brandy this time?'

As an attempt at humour it was weak and disturbingly shaky, twisting in Terrie's vulnerable heart. And the obvious effort that it had cost him to say it spoke much more of the way he was feeling than any outpouring of words could ever do, so that she struggled to raise even the faintest glimmer of the smile that she felt he had been aiming for.

'Perhaps it's a little early for the hard stuff. How about a coffee? I've only instant, I'm afraid.'

'Coffee would be fine—instant—anything.'

Did he know how grateful she was for the excuse to get away from him, escape into the kitchen just for a minute? Terrie wondered. Would he realise how much she needed to gather herself, collect her scattered thoughts, recoup her shattered defences? Or would he just think she was so totally switched off from him that she didn't care one way or another and she was simply going through the motions, using politeness and courtesy to cover a difficult situation?

Quite frankly, right now, she didn't care! She no longer even felt like the same person who had opened the door to find Gio standing outside at the start of the morning. She just needed a little time…time to focus on the tiny practical matters that seemed like such a refuge from the storm of emotions that assailed her. Concentrating fiercely, as if what she was doing was a matter of life and death, she filled the kettle, switched it on, collected mugs…

She was reaching for the coffee from the cupboard when Gio spoke behind her unexpectedly.

'I take it black.'

With an effort, Terrie managed not to drop the coffee jar as she nodded, grateful for the fact that he couldn't see her face, or the shock of reaction that must be her expression, giving away far more than was truly safe.

'OK. That's probably just as well. To tell the truth, I'm not exactly sure about the milk situation. I haven't bought any fresh for a couple of days.'

She was talking to fill the silence, she knew. Saying something, anything, that might distract her from the fact that he was there, just behind her, so close she could almost hear the soft sound of his breathing, feel the heat of his body reach out to enclose her.

'Sugar?'

'No, thanks.'

She had no choice but to turn now. No choice but to face him. Not unless she was going to stand here forever, looking like a total idiot, frozen in mid-action, unable to decide whether to move or not.

'Good. I'm not sure whether I have any of that either.'

She'd whirled round as quickly as she could, taken the

few steps across the room to the kettle, desperately trying to avoid looking at him, but it was no use. The kitchen was tiny enough on an ordinary day, and today, with Gio's tall, dark, lethally sexy presence filling it, it seemed to have shrunk to mouse-hole proportions.

'Why don't you ask me, Teresa?'

'Ask you what? I—I don't have…'

His arrogantly impatient flick of his hand, the way his tongue clicked against his teeth dismissed her protest as the prevarication that it was.

'You know perfectly well what I mean. The problem that's been nagging at you ever since you opened the door to me. The question you've been dying to ask…'

'I have?'

His dark head moved in a nod of agreement. And although deep inside she knew just what he meant, she also knew that she couldn't bring herself to say it. Couldn't just blurt it out in a rush, without hesitation, straight into his face. Her throat would close up against the words if she even tried.

'You want to know why I'm here. What I want of you. So why don't you just go ahead and ask me?'

CHAPTER NINE

'I KNOW why you came.'

Terrie knew she was dodging the issue and she suspected that Gio realised it too. Once again there had been another of those subtle shifts in the atmosphere in the room; a tightening of the pressure up a couple of notches. And because of the confined space in the microscopic kitchen it felt as if the tension had permeated the actual air around them so that it was thick and heavy, making it difficult to breathe.

'You came to apologise.'

Dumping coffee granules into a mug, she slopped on boiling water and stirred it with unnecessary ferocity.

'At least that's what you said.'

He had also said, 'You want to know why I'm here. What I want of you.' But she wasn't going to go down that road. It was too dangerous, totally uncharted territory. She had no idea what threats, what risks lay hidden along it.

'But you haven't exactly *apologised*, have you?'

She couldn't stir the coffee any longer without looking a complete fool. She must be close to scraping a hole in the bottom of the mug as it was.

Turning, she pushed the mug at Gio, heedless of the way that some of the hot liquid spilled over the side and onto the floor.

'*Have* you?'

'I said I regretted not having told you the whole truth.'

He took the mug she held out, his long fingers brushing

against hers as he did so, making her want to flinch and start backwards as if she had brushed against an exposed live electrical wire, burning her skin.

'What else did you want?'

There was a definite challenge in the dark eyes now, almost, but not quite driving away the deep shadows of just moments before. Had he truly recovered so bewilderingly fast? Or was he just dangerously skilled at hiding his true feelings behind a careful, emotionless mask? The answer to that question was one that Terrie was not at all sure she wanted to know.

'I...'

'I'm not going to apologise for something we both consented to.'

Eyes the colour of the rich coffee in his mug seared over her face, probing like a dark laser under the black brows that drew together sharply in an ominous frown.

'Or are you going to try and claim that I forced you?'

'Oh, no!'

She wouldn't dare! She *couldn't*. It was impossible even to think of it when she knew that denying his claim would be the worst lie she had ever told.

'No. I'm not saying that.'

'*Bene.*'

His nod was curt to the point of dismissive.

'Because I feel no guilt for something we both wanted...'

Dark eyes skimmed over her again, lingering appreciatively on her mouth, her throat, the swell of her breasts as they rose and fell with her uneven, nervous breathing.

'Something we'd both like to do again.'

But that was too much.

'Something *you* might like to do again!' Terrie protested. 'I don't remember having said any such thing.'

'Not *said*,' was Gio's drawling agreement. 'But then sometimes there is no need for anyone to say anything. The signs are there, clear to read. In the glance of an eye, a smile…'

Slowly he leaned forward and trailed the back of his free hand softly down her cheek and under her jaw.

'In a glow you can't hide…'

The pad of his thumb smoothed across the fullness of her lips, awakening a deep inner hunger just with the single caress.

'A softness of the mouth…'

'Don't!'

With a fierce movement that was totally unnecessary, considering the gentleness of his hold, she wrenched her head away from his grasp. The struggle to ignore the fizzing sensation along every nerve made her voice hard and tight as she rounded on him.

'You're reading the signs all wrong if that's what you think!'

It was almost impossible to hear the words through the wild pounding of her heart.

'Or perhaps you're simply finding what you want to see, because I'll tell you that your sordid fantasies are just not true!'

'Is that a fact?'

Gio's slow, faintly mocking smile almost undid her totally, sending shivers of reaction running down her spine, though for the life of her she couldn't decide whether they were of fear or tingling excitement.

'Well, you can protest all you like, *carina*, but just remember that I am the one who can see your face, look into your eyes… And I assure you that there is nothing *sordid* about my fantasies—nothing at all!'

'I—' Terrie began, but he swept on, ignoring the fact that she had even tried to speak.

'They are simply that I wish to repeat the pleasures of our night together, over and over again. And I know that you do not consider those pleasures in any way sordid. How could you, when you were the one who instigated most of them—and who actively encouraged the ones I contributed?'

Expertly manoeuvred into a corner, mentally if not physically, Terrie admitted to cowardice and didn't even try to respond, resorting only to turning a fulminating glare on his wickedly smiling face, a scornful, but inarticulate, 'Huh!' the only sound that escaped her.

But inside her mind was buzzing, replaying unwanted memories, projecting dangerously erotic scenes from their night together onto the screen of her thoughts. Just that brush of his thumb across her mouth had reminded her of the taste of his skin, the scent of his hand, the way that his touch made her feel. She felt unnervingly on edge, frighteningly restless and close to veering out of control.

All the secret, intimate places on her body seemed to wake, clamouring for more of that touch. Her mouth hungered to know again the deeply personal taste of his flesh. And the reason for all those feelings was right there beside her, his height and strength dominating the small space of her kitchen, making her feel as if it had suddenly shrunk to a quarter of its size.

Swallowing hard, she forced herself to speak with a degree of control that she was far from feeling.

'I think we'd both be more comfortable if we went through into the living room and sat down.'

Her voice was cool and tight, obviously intended to be quelling. But Gio knew that it would take more than a few words to crush down the heavy throb of desire that his whole body was a prey to.

Comfortable! he reflected on a twist of cynicism. Feeling *comfortable* was the last thing possible when he was so close to this woman. In fact, he doubted whether even moving into the other room and sitting further away from her would help. Every cell in his body was on red alert to the sight, the sound, the scent of her.

And touching her had been a mistake.

A *bad* mistake!

As soon as his thumb had brushed across her mouth, her lips had softened under his touch, reminding him of how it had felt to take them in the heat of a passionate kiss. His skin had touched the warm, moist interior, reminding him of the heated slickness of the feminine warmth that had closed around him countless times during their night together, and the urge to grab her, haul her hard up against him and kiss her senseless had almost got the better of him.

Almost. But at the last moment what little sanity he had left had prevailed—thankfully!

Grabbing Teresa Hayden was quite the wrong way to go about things, at least this time. Last time he had grabbed—and so had she—and they had both ended up in a situation that was quite out of their control. They had been caught up in a maelstrom of passion that had obliterated any hope of sensible thought, whirling them up out of the rational world and into a fierce, blazing inferno of need that would allow for no resistance.

And tonight he had promised himself that he would think—or at least try to think—with what was inside his head, not what was below his belt, and he was damned well going to stick to that resolve if it killed him. Which was what it looked likely to do if he didn't pull back and put some distance between the two of them—fast!

'After you…'

Even as he spoke the words he felt the sense of shock at his own stupid mistake. To allow her to go first meant that he would have to let her squeeze past him in the confined space of the doorway, coming closer than ever before.

The soft brush of her pert buttocks against his already hardened groin was a source of delicious agony that had him biting down hard on his lower lip so as not to groan aloud in uncontrollable response. Her silky blonde hair wafted against his face, the scent of it combining with the intimate, deeply personal aroma of her skin tormenting his hotly aroused body with its sensual caress. And he had to clench his fingers hard on the handle of his coffee mug so that the tremor in his grip didn't betray him by spilling some of the liquid onto the floor.

Dio—sucurro! he thought on a wave of despair, closing his eyes and letting his head fall back against the hard wood of the doorjamb. How had he ever let this woman reduce him to such a state of sexual slavery so fast? How had she brought him to this point where every movement she made, every glance from those lavender-coloured eyes, every sound of her voice was pure intoxication, total seduction?

'Gio?'

Terrie was clearly puzzled by the fact that he hadn't moved.

'Are you coming?'

Oh, yes…

Hastily he caught himself up, shaking his dark head hard, blinking as he forced away the last clinging strands of the erotic daydream that had had him in its grip.

'*Sì,*' he said in a very different tone, the crisp, cool note totally erasing the husky fervency of his thoughts of just moments before. 'Yes, of course I am.'

He might move into the room, but he couldn't sit down. He felt restless, edgy, a cat on hot bricks. And unknowingly Terrie only made matters worse by the way she curled up in her chair, depositing her coffee mug on the tiled hearth to her left before turning to face him.

She looked like an innocent young girl with her legs tucked up under her like that, the blonde hair tumbling about her face, falling onto the slender shoulders in the bright pink T-shirt. But the body outlined by the clinging soft cotton was all woman, the thrust of her breasts proclaiming her femininity for anyone to see. The position of her legs meant that the worn, faded denim had tightened around the sweet curves of her hips and buttocks, clinging to the length of her thighs, adding to the sensual provocation that had tormented him only moments before.

'So why did you come here today?'

And how did he answer that? Gio took a swallow of his coffee to ease a suddenly dry throat, and grab at some last-minute thinking time, then set his mug down on the mantelpiece as he turned to her.

To hell with thinking. He would just tell her the truth.

'I came because I couldn't stay away.'

'Oh, sure!'

The look she turned on him was frankly sceptical, darkening the soft eyes to a deep, opaque grey.

'Sure! I'll be honest with you—'

'I wish you would.'

'I will! I'll tell you the truth if you'll only shut up and listen for once! Do you ever let anyone speak without arguing?'

'As a matter of fact I do—most of the time,' Terrie

returned stiffly. 'It's just that you seem to have this bad effect on me.'

'And you on me,' Gio retorted. 'But all the same, this time I am telling the truth—the whole truth...'

And nothing but the truth. The words echoed ominously inside Terrie's head, giving her the unwelcome reminder that the man before her was a renowned international lawyer, at the very top of the ladder. It seemed that ever since she had met him in the hotel last week the papers had been full of accounts of his skills, his prowess in the courts. She couldn't imagine how she had ever come to miss him before.

'Go on,' she managed stiffly, the thought suddenly draining all the fight from her so that she slumped down in her seat, not daring to look him straight in the eye.

'As I said, I came here today because I couldn't stay away. Last week, I thought I could. I thought that was what I wanted. I thought that was what you wanted too.'

'What was what I wanted?'

'A one-night stand. Some fun—nothing more.'

'*Fun!*'

The single syllable was a strangled sound in Terrie's throat.

'You thought...'

Hastily she swallowed down the rest of her retort, knowing that to say what she really thought could only make matters so much worse.

'Go on,' she said stiffly.

Gio was pacing around the room, hands pushed deep into the pockets of his trousers, his restlessness as unnerving as having a tiger caged up with her, watching its hungry prowling.

'I thought I could walk away and forget about you, but

it didn't work out that way. I couldn't get you out of my mind.'

For the first time Terrie actually sat up a little straighter, her interest piqued. She had been sure that what he was going to say was simply another put-down, something that would make her feel worse than ever. Now, at last, there was a tiny spark of hope that perhaps it could be different.

'I couldn't stop thinking about you. I couldn't eat; I couldn't sleep. I couldn't concentrate on my work.'

And his tone said that *that* was unusual. That in the past his work had always been able to hold him.

'I had to see you again. I couldn't leave without seeing you once more…'

'Leave!'

There was that word again, but this time it sounded different.

'You're going away?'

Her sudden interjection had stopped his restless pacing, brought him swinging round to face her.

'I'm flying out tomorrow.'

'But where…?'

'I'm going back home—to Sicily.'

'I'm going…' Terrie noted; not 'I was going' or 'thinking of going.'

Which was worse? she couldn't help asking herself. If he had left without saying a word, without ever coming back, so that she had never, ever seen him again? Or the fact that he was here now, giving her foolish, vulnerable heart the chance to think, to dream for a moment? The opportunity to allow it to form the impossible fantasy that he might want more than he had said that first night? That there might be the tiniest possibility of a future, however brief, for them together?

And as soon as she had allowed the thought into her

mind she knew, on a painful clench of her heart, just how much that hope had come to mean to her.

'So this is goodbye?'

'It doesn't have to be.'

'But that's what you came to say? That you were leaving.'

'Teresa…'

Gio pulled both strong hands from his pockets and raked them through the dark sleekness of his hair in a gesture that revealed the ruthless control he was struggling to impose on himself.

'I *have* to go. I have to be there. It's my son's third birthday on Tuesday. I promised him I'd be home for that.'

Of course. Paolo.

'Who's looking after him now?'

She asked the inconsequential question simply in order to say something. Anything, to fill the silence that had descended as soon as Gio had stopped speaking. Because the truth was that she had no idea what else to say. There was nothing she *could* say. Gio had made up his mind. His plans were fixed, and he was determined to go and there was nothing she could say to stop him.

And did she want to stop him? The sudden rush of anguish that wrenched at her heart at the thought of watching Gio turn his back and walk out on her once more, for good this time, told her the answer to that. But it was an answer that solved no problems. Instead it only seemed to make matters immeasurably worse.

'…in Taormina,' Gio finished and to her horror she realised she hadn't heard a word of what else he had said.

'I'm sorry…' she stumbled, past caring how foolish it made her look. 'Who lives in Taormina?'

'Paolo's grandparents.'

His searching, probing glance made it plain that he wanted to know the reason for her distraction, her lack of concentration, but to Terrie's relief he didn't question her about it but answered her question equally enough.

'My mother and stepfather. And sometimes he spends time with Cesare and Megan.'

'Oh, yes, Megan—your sister-in-law.'

Terrie flinched inwardly as the name reminded her of the conversation she had had with Gio on that first night in the hotel. Just before he had turned to her and held out his hand.

'Come here to me, *belleza*,' he had said. 'Come here… and let's finish what we've started.'

'S-so Cesare is your brother?'

She spoke hastily in an effort to erase the painful memories, to crush down the bitter acid that was rising in her throat.

'Half-brother. My father died before I was a year old and my mother married again. Cesare is her son with her second husband, Roberto Santorino.'

'And how long have you been away—from Paolo?'

'Three weeks.'

Gio's quick frown told her that this wasn't the sort of conversation he wanted to be having, the topic he had planned to discuss, but she didn't care. Each ordinary word that she spoke, each matter-of-fact statement or question, seemed like another brick inserted carefully into the wall with which she hoped to surround herself. The barriers that would serve as her defence against the moment when he said that he was leaving—and that he wasn't coming back.

'He'll have missed you.'

'He'll be glad to see me again.' Gio nodded. 'I've talked to him every night on the phone, but it just isn't the same. There's no substitute for being able to hold someone in your arms.'

'No...'

It was as much as she could manage and she had to gulp the words down in the same moment as she fiercely swallowed the tears she wouldn't let fall. *Couldn't* let flow in spite of the way they burned in her eyes, forcing her to blink back the stinging liquid. If she had so much as a phone call to look forward to from Gio, then it would be something, but this time with him, such as it was, was all there would be. Once he was back in Sicily, he wouldn't contact her again. Probably wouldn't even spare her a thought, in spite of all his protestations that he hadn't been able to get her out of his mind. Once he was home, and back with his family, he would forget all about her.

While she would have nothing but memories. Memories that, if this past week was anything to go by, would come back to haunt her in the darkness of the night, in the silence and the stillness, when she was at her lowest possible ebb and totally incapable of holding them back.

'He—he must be counting the hours.'

'He's also looking forward to seeing my new friend.'

'He—he *what*?'

The sudden realisation of just what he had said had her sitting forward, blue-grey eyes locking with deepest brown.

'My son is looking forward to meeting my new friend,' Gio repeated, coolly and clearly and elaborately slowly. 'He wants to see you.'

'I don't understand.'

She was leaning forward as she spoke, reaching for the coffee mug on the hearth, needing something to do—anything—to distract her from the look in his eyes, the buzzing confusion in her head.

'It's quite straightforward, Teresa. I am returning to Sicily. I have to go back for Paolo—and I want you to come with me.'

'You...'

Hastily Terrie put her half-raised mug back down onto the tiles before she let it fall completely. She felt as if his words had caused her heart to stop abruptly then jolt back into action with an uneven judder.

Had he really said what she believed he had?

'I'm flying back to Sicily tonight. I want you to come with me.'

Even when he had said the actual words, Terrie still couldn't quite bring herself to believe them.

'Why?' she croaked.

Gio's sigh was a perfectly calculated blend of resignation and exasperation.

'Teresa, *cara*, we have been through this before. I told you—'

'I know what you told me but I don't believe it!'

Didn't dare believe it. Couldn't let the possibility that his outrageous claims might be the truth into her head because if she did then she was only opening herself to a more devastating hurt than before because she had allowed herself to hope.

'Believe it!'

Gio's voice was harsh, deep, vibrating with the emphasis on the words as he came to stand in front of her, placing one hand on each arm of the chair and leaning over her to stare deep into her face.

'Believe it, *belleza*, because it is the truth! I want you to come to Sicily with me, because this last week I have thought I am going crazy without you. Because I spend my days thinking of you when I should be working.'

'You do?'

'All the time,' he assured her.

Terrie gazed up into his dark, set face, unable to think beyond the small excited voice that was repeating over and over in her head, He wants me with him! He wants me with him! And, seeing the bemused, still not totally convinced expression on her face, Gio held out a hand to her. Like a hypnotist's mindless victim, she put her own fingers into it and let his strength draw her upwards, out of her seat, until she was standing so close to him that she felt her body melting into the heat of his.

'I want you with me because at night I dream of holding you close…'

He suited the action to the words, drawing her into the circle of his embrace, folding his arms around her.

'Of running my hands through your hair…kissing your soft mouth.'

Long fingers fastened in her hair, bringing her face to his, and his lips closed over hers in a long, demanding kiss that made her senses swim wildly. On a tiny murmur of surrender, she abandoned all pretence at keeping her distance and gave herself up to the seductive spell he was weaving around her. Her hands went up and around his neck, her mouth softening, opening under his.

Her body was curved against the lean, hard length of him, the wild demand of sexual hunger uncoiling low down in her body in the space of a heartbeat. And when one of those exploring hands left her hair and slid down her spine, closing over her hip to press her even closer into contact with the potent force of his erection, she caught in her breath on a swift, choking sigh of mindless yearning.

His kiss was stealing away her soul, taking with it all hope of thinking rationally, of being able to reason in any way at all. She could only respond, only surrender to the

forceful, primitive tug of sexual attraction that would always bind this man and her together.

'I can't sleep for thoughts of kissing you...touching
you, possessing you,' Gio murmured against her mouth.
'My whole body aches with wanting you. I couldn't leave
without seeing you again. That's why I came here today—
to ask you to come home with me.'

Come home. The words had such a wonderful sound.
They seemed to hold the very essence of her dreams, the
core of the unspoken hopes that had shimmered in her
mind on the night they had met. They whispered of togetherness and sharing, of the possibility of a future.

He wanted her to go home with him. To meet his child.
His family. Her heart clenched on a pleasure that was
sharp as a pain. Her mind was just a red-gold haze, blurring under the assault, both physical and mental, on all
her senses.

'So, what do you say, *cara*?' Gio whispered, his lips
against her hair. 'What's your answer? Will you come?
Will you—?'

'Yes!'

She couldn't wait for him to finish. Didn't need him to
complete the question when already she knew in her heart
that she had decided and that there was no going back.
The long, lonely hours of the past week, the tears she had
shed in the darkness of the night, had taught her one thing.

If there was a chance, even the tiniest hope, that they
could start again then she would reach out with both hands
and grab it, holding on tight.

'Yes!' she said again, even more emphatically than before. 'Yes, I'll come with you. I'd love to! I can't wait!
It won't take me a minute to pack and—'

'And what about your job?' Gio inserted the question

into the excited flow of her response, the ardent lover suddenly submerged beneath cool practicality.

His abrupt change of mood was rather disconcerting, the sudden stillness of his powerful body, the sharp scrutiny in his eyes bringing a sensation like the slow scraping of sandpaper over uneasily raw nerves.

'My job? Oh, that doesn't matter!'

Why did it have to happen now? Gio wondered. Why, when it was the last thing he wanted, did he have to remember moments from that evening they had spent together? Moments that hinted at another side to Terrie, a colder, more grasping side than the warm and willing woman he held in his arms.

'I can't expect fairy godfathers to come along every day of the week, can I?' she had said, and he had wondered whether she had hoped to cast him in the role of that 'fairy godfather' long-term.

'You said you planned on "chucking" it.'

'If you want the truth then no, I don't have a job any more. Not that I got a chance to chuck it. My employment at Addisons only lasted long enough for me to be interviewed by the boss on Monday and decide that it would be mutually beneficial if I left at once. In fact, if you'd not turned up here tonight you might not have found me. I was already beginning to wonder how I could afford to keep this place on, and I would probably have rung my parents and asked if I could come home.'

Instead of which, he had turned up just in time.

For a second, Gio was tempted to revoke his invitation. To say that he had made a mistake, changed his mind. He no longer wanted her to come to Sicily with him.

But that would be nothing but a lie. And a total denial of the way he was feeling. The needs he had been fighting against all week, only to know that he could hold out no longer. To admit that he could not just turn his back and walk away as he had once planned. That he had to have her once more or he would go insane with wanting.

He had told her the truth about the hunger, the emptiness he had felt all week. But until he had heard the words come out of his mouth, he had never known that he had even thought of inviting her to come back to Sicily with him. But perhaps now that he had said it, it would be the best way to work things. This way he could both have his cake and eat it, as the English saying went.

And it would serve one other, vitally important function too. It would solve another concern that had been nagging at him since his uncharacteristic loss of any sort of sense—except one—during the night they had spent together.

'Then you'll welcome a chance for four weeks in the sun?'

There it was again, that disturbingly controlled edge to his voice, Terrie recognised on a shiver of apprehension. And if she had been asked to define the look in his eyes then 'calculating' would have been the word that came to mind. The passionate, seductive Gio had evaporated like mist before the sun, and in his place was a cold-eyed analyst. A man who made her feel uncomfortably like some carefully prepared specimen on a laboratory slab, ready for dissection.

'Four weeks?'

Foolishly, she hadn't thought in terms of a set span of time. She knew that Gio wasn't promising a lifetime's commitment, but she hadn't quite expected that their time together would be so clearly defined.

'Why four weeks?'

'I think that should be long enough to be sure.'

Sure? This time she swallowed the question down,

afraid to voice it. A few moments ago she might have been naïve enough to think that Gio was talking about being sure of the way he felt about her, but now the sudden change in his demeanour, the subtle shift in his whole attitude to her was setting off warning bells inside her brain. Suddenly disturbingly ill at ease, she stiffened in Gio's embrace, holding her body away from him.

'Don't you think?'

It was asked with such total calm, such a complete lack of any emotion that it made her blood run cold just to hear it.

'And what precisely do you need to be sure about?'

'Don't play the fool, Teresa!' Gio's tone was a chilling mixture of cynical amusement and curt dismissal. 'You're not a complete innocent, so don't pretend that you are. You know what happened that night we spent together. We didn't take any precautions—at any time. You know—precisely—what might have happened. What the result of our affair might be.'

If Terrie's blood had chilled a few moments before, now it felt as if it was turning to ice in her veins. And the cold seemed to have reached her brain, destroying any chance of thinking clearly enough to answer Gio in this form—once more Giovanni Cardella, counsel for the prosecution.

'Nothing happened!' she flung at him in a nervous rush, twisting against his loosened hold and freeing herself with a jolt that took her partway across the room away from him. 'Don't honour what we had with the title of an affair—it was nothing like! It was a sordid little one-night stand in a hotel bedroom after you picked me up in a bar, nothing more! And there won't be any result!'

'And you can swear to that, can you? Am I to take it that—?'

'No!'

Even to outface him, she found she couldn't lie to him about this. But all the same she couldn't stop herself from taking several nervous backward steps, away from him. He was too big, too dangerous-looking to have towering over her like this.

'If you're trying to ask if I've had a period since last Saturday, then the answer's no—no, I haven't! But it's nothing for you to worry about! It'll be fine! I know it will!'

'So you were on the Pill?'

He read the answer in her face before she managed to find the words to say it and his beautiful mouth twisted cynically.

'No...' he said grimly. 'No Pill—no protection of any sort. And you still think you won't be pregnant.'

Pregnant. The word seemed to hang in the air between them like an insurmountable barrier that had to be dealt with, got out of the way, before anything else could be said or even considered.

'I'll be fine...'

Terrie knew she was stumbling over the words, struggling to dodge the issue that had been preying on her mind all week. Time and time again she had reproached herself for her foolishness, her unthinking impulsiveness, the sexual irresponsibility that could have landed her in the worst mess she had ever experienced in her life—but never as much as she was doing now. And all the reproofs she had thrown at herself in the darkness of the night were as nothing when compared to the dark scorn, the bitter contempt that burned in Gio's dark eyes as he fixed them on her flushed and uneasy face.

'It was only one night.'

'*Madre de Dio!*' The words seemed to be torn from

Gio's lips, his exclamation a sound of such deep disgust that it ripped into her already vulnerable heart like a deadly sharp stiletto. The wound that it left behind was so deep, so cruel, that she was desperately afraid it would ultimately prove fatal, even though right now the shock and the savagery of it had caused the blessed oblivion of numbness.

'It only takes one *time*.'

'I know that! I'm not a fool!'

The blazingly scathing glare he turned on her told her that a fool was the least insulting thing he wanted to call her, the heat of his contempt searing dangerously over her exposed skin.

'Then don't act like one! Face facts! You might be pregnant—and if you are then we have to decide what to do about it!'

'*I* have to decide what to do about it!'

'It would be my child!'

'Only half yours!'

But even as she flung the words into his dark face, she knew them for the mistake they were. To Giovanni Cardella, pure, unreformed Sicilian male, any child he fathered was *his* and no one else's. The woman who was given the honour of being impregnated by his seed might just get some consideration while she was carrying and nurturing the precious child, but once it was born it would be pure Cardella and nothing else. Then she might be lucky enough to be allowed a look-in on its upbringing, but little more. Unless, of course, she was the saintly Lucia.

'But I would take care of it. I would make sure it had everything it needed growing up. I—'

'I could do that as well!'

'How? Where?'

Flinging his hands up in a supremely Italian gesture, Gio spun on his heel, dark eyes surveying the small, scruffy room with its well-worn furniture.

'In some other shabby, run-down mouse hole like this? Where there's no garden, nowhere for a child to play? No space to run around? And how would you support it? You don't even have enough money to keep yourself—or were you expecting your parents to take care of your child as well as you?'

'No! Never!'

'Then what did you plan to do?'

'I don't know...' It was low and miserable, just a whisper of defeat. How could she claim she'd made any plans when the truth was that the fear she might be pregnant had run round and round in her head during the past week? And each time it had haunted her thoughts she had struggled to think what to do if she was, but never, ever come to any conclusions.

'I don't know. I didn't think.'

'You didn't think,' Gio echoed darkly. 'You can say that again. Well, will you at least make the effort to think now?'

'I'm not giving you my baby!'

'Did I ask you to?'

With an obvious effort he adjusted his tone down a degree or two, imposing a ruthless control that calmed his voice, softened its intonation.

'We don't even know if you're pregnant yet—but we have to consider the possibility. All I ask is that you come to Sicily with me so that I can keep an eye on you, at least until things become clear one way or another. You'll be well cared for, looked after.'

'Supervised to make sure that I don't do anything to harm your child, don't you mean? Or, even worse, sleep with someone else and then try to pass off their bastard as a pure-bred Cardella.'

Fury flared in Gio's eyes at her bitter comment, but he didn't even deign to honour it with a reply.

'Call it a free holiday if you like,' he tossed at her. 'You said it was a long time since you had one of those. Perhaps that will make the whole thing more appealing.'

A holiday, Terrie thought longingly. The idea was more than appealing. It sounded *wonderful*. A holiday in Sicily—with sun and the sea, and Gio…

Ten minutes ago, she would have snatched his hand off.

But then ten minutes ago she had still been a poor, blind, deluded fool, lost in the fantasy that he cared—at least enough to want her with him for some time.

Well, he still wanted her with him—but for his own selfish reasons.

'So will you come?'

He had to be joking!

'It seems an eminently sensible solution to me. You can stay in my home for a month—just four short weeks. And if at the end of that time we know you're not pregnant then you can go on your way and there'll be no further complications.'

'And if I *am* pregnant?' Terrie forced herself to ask, willing her insides not to curdle sourly at that 'no further complications'. 'What happens then?'

'We'll decide when we have some facts to act on. Who knows, by then we might find that the answer's taken care of itself?'

'That we get on so well together that we want to stay that way for the baby's sake? Don't bank on it!'

Terrie prayed that the shake in her voice could be taken as having been put there by laughter at just the thought of the two of them ever wanting to decide that. At least that way it might somehow conceal the pain that tore at her inside, the sudden longing to be able to believe that it could happen. That if they had time together they might just grow close, come to feel more for each other.

'Stranger things have happened.'

'But not to me.'

'I'm not looking for another love of my life—I already had that with Lucia, and lightning doesn't strike twice.'

'If you're trying to persuade me that we could have a future together, then you're going exactly the wrong way about it!'

Did he know how much it hurt to know that she would always be second best to his beloved dead wife? That he had wanted Lucia for love, but the only reason he wanted her was because she might be carrying his child?

'What makes you think that this would work?'

'Why not? We get on well enough together in bed. More than well enough. That has to count for something.'

'And sex is the answer to all of this?'

'It's a damned good place to start.'

And the only one, his expression said. The one and only thing she gave him that he couldn't live without. Any dream she had had of finding that there was more to the way he was feeling shrivelled into a microscopic pile of dust on the floor at her feet.

But almost immediately foolish hope reasserted itself. Perhaps there *was* a chance. If she went along with Gio's plan then maybe, just maybe, as they spent the days together they could get to know each other better, grow closer—at least closer on his part. Perhaps they might come to, if not a love relationship, then at least an understanding—and from an understanding something more could grow, given time.

And Gio had offered her time.

Only four weeks, it was true. But it was better than nothing. Better than watching him walk out of here once more and knowing that this time he would never come back.

She could give it a try. She *had* to give it a try. After all, what did she have to lose—how could she come out of it with any less than what she had now? And there might just be the faintest chance that she could end up with more.

'So…' Gio's voice broke into her thoughts. 'What's your answer? Are you coming with me?'

His swift glance at his watch told her that he was already thinking impatiently of leaving and the things he had to do before he got on the plane. She had to make her mind up and she had to do it fast.

'All right,' Terrie said cautiously. 'I'll do it.'

The look in his eyes gave him away. He might have schooled his expression into the cool, noncommittal mask that met her anxious gaze, but he couldn't disguise the flare of triumph, the sexual satisfaction that gleamed in the ebony darkness.

'*Bene!*'

He was taking a step towards her, his intention to kiss her evident. But that was a move too far. Terrie had been caught that way once already. She had no intention of letting it happen again.

Instinctively she held up her hand, bringing him to a reluctant halt.

'One condition!'

His swift sidelong glance told her that she was in no position to go laying down conditions, but to her relief he paused and nodded slowly.

'And that is?'

'While we're in Sicily it's strictly hands off! Is that understood?'

It was clearly the last thing he had expected and the black, arched brows shot up in evident surprise.

'Is that so?'

'Yes!'

She prayed she sounded more confident than she felt. The mocking note in his voice, the devilish look in his eye, both set her nerves on edge and made her wonder just what she had taken on.

'Hands off?'

He was coming towards her with the slow, deliberate prowl of a hunting cat; gleaming eyes fixed on her face.

'Y-yes…'

Definitely not so sure this time. And even though she had taken several hasty steps backwards, his steady advance seemed to be gaining on her.

'Is that a challenge, *cara*?'

A challenge? Now she was totally bemused. How could he take her total rejection of his advances as a challenge to something more?

She soon learned. A moment later her backwards movement was halted as first her foot, and then her shoulders came up against the wall. There was nowhere she could go. And Gio was still coming closer.

'Gio…'

She tried to make his name a sound of warning, but knew she had either failed or was being totally ignored as he came even closer, moving right in front of her, trapping her in the corner with the bulk of his body.

'Hands off, hmm? Well, fine, if that's the way you want it, *carina*. But there are plenty of other ways…'

She could read what was coming from the look in his eyes and frantically turned her face to left and right, trying to avoid him. But Gio imprisoned her by pressing the hard length of his body up against hers—his hands firmly down by his sides, while, as she had anticipated, his mouth sought hers.

And there was no way she could avoid his kiss. Even though she twisted this way and that, she knew he would defeat her soon. In the end it came sooner than she had expected, because when he saw that she was determined to resist him he gave up on the direct approach, and went for a more subtle form of enticement. Terrie's heart jumped in startled reaction as she felt the warmth of his mouth at the base of her neck, lingering softly on the point where her frantic pulse raced. And even as she stilled, unable to do anything but relax into enjoyment of the caress, he started to move, kissing his way slowly up and over her sensitive skin.

'There are more ways to make love to a woman than with your hands, *belleza*,' he murmured against her quivering flesh. 'More ways to caress than by touching…'

And as Terrie froze into immobility, unable to resist, to fight the sensations that were sparking through her, he proceeded to demonstrate exactly what he meant.

He used his mouth like a delicate instrument of pleasure, smoothing, kissing, lapping at her skin. He even made one or two delicate, nipping little bites that had her crying out, in spite of the efforts she made to bite her lip against the betraying sound.

He kissed his way up the slender line of her throat, traced the line of her jaw where a muscle she couldn't control jumped in frantic response. He trailed his tongue around the coils of her ear, sending shivers of reaction through each connecting delicate nerve, and so to every sensitised part of her body. His lips pressed her eyelids shut so that the enforced darkness heightened every sensation she was experiencing, and it was only when she was a pliant, quivering wreck of uncontrolled response that he finally took her mouth in a deep, impassioned and demanding kiss.

'Open to me, *adorata*,' he murmured against her softening lips. 'Open to me and let me show you how a man kisses the woman whose image has haunted his dreams, kept him from sleeping, kept him from eating... The woman who is driving him crazy...'

She *meant* to fight him. Terrie told herself that she wanted to resist...but her body had other ideas. Her bones seemed to melt, her knees buckling weakly in the heat of the desire that seared along every nerve. She could only be grateful for the solidity of the wall at her back, the pressure of Gio's mouth against hers that held her head still and upright.

And still he hadn't touched her; his hands were braced firmly against the paintwork, a couple of feet from her body on either side.

And that was not what she wanted. Her body was aching, yearning, demanding. Her breasts seemed swollen, heavy and full, just wanting—needing the caress of those long, knowing fingers, the heat of his palms against their peaking nipples. But Gio was resolute, ruthless in his control, using only his mouth to pleasure her. And that pleasure, combined with the subtle cruelty of his control, only made her want him all the more desperately.

'Gio...'

His name was a sigh of surrender and a cry of protest all at once, and she strained her hungry body away from the wall, needing the pressure of his against it, the heat and hardness of his strength tight against her hungry flesh. A second, choking cry was torn from her as Gio, with a smile she could feel against her skin, slid his mouth away from her lips, heading down this time. Down to where the low-scooped neckline of her T-shirt just skimmed the top of the curves of her breasts, the faint pressure of his kiss, the tantalising warmth of his breath making her writhe in a tormented frustration of desire.

'Oh, Gio...' she gasped again and felt his smile grow wide, wicked, fiendish.

The next moment his mouth was against her shoulder, his tongue tracing erotic patterns all the way to where the soft pink cotton of her sleeve began. Hard white teeth fixed on the stretchy material, tugging softly, edging it away and down...

And it was too much for her to take any longer. She couldn't bear the sensory deprivation and the seductive torment he was subjecting her to at one and the same time.

'Oh, my...*Gio!*'

Unthinkingly, blindly she reached for him, wanting to close her arms around his neck, tangle her hungry fingers in the coal-black silk of his hair. Needing...

But Gio reacted swiftly and sharply, snapping his head up and twisting himself away from her grasping hands, breaking all physical contact with her, stepping firmly back, well out of reach.

'No touching!' he said, his tone as cold as his eyes. 'Hands off, *belleza*, that's what you said. You made the rules...'

And now she wanted to break them. The agonisingly sharp arousal he had sparked off all over her body was screaming out for appeasement and she felt that she would shatter into a million tiny fragments if he didn't take her back into his arms once more and hold her tight, kiss away the clamouring distress.

She even held out her hands towards him, wanting, needing, hoping to encourage him to come back to her and finish what he had started. But Gio neatly sidestepped her reaching arms, smoothing down his ruffled hair and straightening his clothing with brisk, coolly efficient movements.

'Hands off,' he repeated, his tone cold and clipped, and then to Terrie's total consternation he actually smiled deep into her eyes.

At least, his mouth smiled, but there was no warmth, no trace of humour in it. And his own dark-eyed gaze remained cool and opaque, impenetrable as polished marble.

'Your rules, *cara mia*. That's the way you wanted to play it.'

Terrie could find no words to answer him. None, at least, that she was prepared to give any sort of voice to. If she opened her mouth, she knew that she would be forced to beg. Beg him to come back to her, to hold her, kiss her, caress her. To take her to bed and make sweet, savage, passionate love to her until she was mindless and melting in fulfilment.

And she didn't dare admit that to him. Because it meant admitting the effect he had on her, the power he held over her. She suspected that that was something he knew already. But at least if she didn't actually *say* it then she hadn't put the weapon into his hands, giving him something he could use against her whenever he wanted.

And so she remained stubbornly silent, though her whole body trembled with the effort that it cost her to keep her lips clamped shut, her mouth sealed against the weak words of surrender that struggled to escape her.

For a long, silent moment Gio's dark eyes rested on her face, taking in every inch of her colourless cheeks, her quivering mouth, her over-bright eyes. And then just as she was nerving herself for some other onslaught, one she was afraid her weakened defences would be incapable of repelling, suddenly, shockingly, he smiled again.

'My plane leaves at five,' he said, his tone disturbingly matter-of-fact. 'I'll be here to collect you a couple of hours before that. I expect you to be packed and ready to leave.'

Terrie still could find no reply to give him, but he made it clear that he wasn't expecting one, turning on his heel and striding towards the door. With his fingers on the handle, turning it, he stilled and half turned back to her, dark eyes like lasers probing into her soul.

'You made the rules, *carina*, so you have only yourself to blame if you don't like the way things work out. While I'm gone, perhaps you might like to rethink the way you want to play this.'

A moment later he was gone, and, released at last from the tension that was all that had been holding her upright, Terrie gave a raw, choking gasp and let go, sliding all the way down the wall to collapse in a weak, shaken heap on the floor. Too exhausted, too shattered even to cry, she could only bury her face in her hands and moan aloud as she gave herself up to the pain of her despair.

CHAPTER TEN

'TREEZA! Treeza! Looka me!'

Obedient to Paolo's shrieked command, using his own personal version of her name, Terrie looked across to the opposite side of the swimming pool to where the little boy was poised on the edge of the tiled surround.

'Go on, then!' she encouraged. 'Jump!'

Tanned arms and legs waving frantically, Paolo launched himself into the air and landed, with the maximum amount of splashing, in the cool blue water just a short distance from her. Laughing, Terrie slid back into the cool water and made her way in a leisurely breaststroke to the spot where he had surfaced, spluttering wildly, a wide, brilliant grin on his face.

'See me?' he spluttered, wiping the streaming water away from his eyes and nose. 'See me jump?'

'I saw you,' Terrie told him. 'I don't think anyone could miss you.'

It really wasn't fair, she reflected. Surely nature could have arranged it so that Gio's son hadn't been quite such a perfect replica of his father. His hair, his eyes, his features, all were a smaller, younger copy of his father's, so that even when Gio wasn't actually around at the villa then Paolo was always there to remind her of him, the man faithfully reflected in the boy.

Not that she could ever *forget* what Gio was like, she admitted ruefully. It seemed that he was always in her mind, always at the forefront of her thoughts, and she had only to close her eyes, or simply to think of him, and an image of his dark, stunning features rose before her, clear as life, without a second's hesitation.

'Ride! Ride!'

Paolo was bouncing up and down in the water, sending rippling waves radiating out towards the sides. Gio had insisted that his son be brought up speaking both English and Italian, and he managed to communicate well enough in Terrie's own language when he was with her.

'Treeza—pleeese!'

'A piggyback ride? Again? Oh, OK…'

She couldn't deny this little boy anything. From the first moment that she had been introduced to him, Paolo had stolen a part of her heart away, and she knew she would never get it back. And it seemed that he felt the same about her. Certainly, he loved to be in her company, and after only a moment or two's wary shyness he had taken to her as if he had known her all his life.

She turned her back on him, lowering herself until her shoulders were covered in the water, and he could climb onto her back. When Paolo's arms were tight around her neck, his sturdy legs clamped about her waist, she kicked off and swam, slowly and carefully because of her precious burden, from one side of the pool to another.

From the far side of the terrace, hidden in the shade of the house, Gio stilled on his way to the pool, and watched the scene before him in unmoving silence.

Terrie's blonde hair was slicked wetly against the fine bones of her skull, and her long, slender arms stroked through the water with smooth, powerful movements. Clinging on to her shoulders like a limpet, his son was beaming in total delight, his wide, bright smile as brilliant as the afternoon sunlight.

'Go, Treeza, go, go!'

The little boy's voice, shrill with excitement, echoed all

around the wide, high terrace, and as he heard it something clenched inside Gio's heart, twisting it sharply and painfully.

Madre de Dio, just what was happening to him? Was he jealous of his own son?

And why should it surprise him that the answer was yes? Wasn't it the case that from the moment he had introduced Paolo to Terrie, he had openly envied the little boy's unrestrained ease and uncomplicated friendship with the beautiful blonde?

Face it, he told himself. He was frankly jealous of Terrie's relationship with every member of his family.

She had charmed the entire Cardella clan, effortlessly winning over first his stepfather and then his mother. And even Gio's half-brother Cesare was entranced by her, while Cesare's wife Megan had taken to the newcomer as if they had been sisters separated at birth.

And what made matters so much worse was the fact that since he had brought Teresa to Sicily she had stuck rigidly to her 'hands off' policy. In fact, from the time that he had arrived at her flat to collect her on the start of their journey to Italy, she seemed to have changed into some other woman entirely. A cool-voiced, cool-eyed, cool-natured creature, who forced him to doubt whether the hotly responsive, passionate lover he had taken to bed on their first—their only—night together had ever truly existed or was just a figment of his imagination.

But then as he watched, Terrie reached the far end of the swimming pool, lifted Paolo out, and then hoisted herself onto the white tiled edge beside him. With unconscious grace she tossed back her soaking hair, stretching lightly in the sun, and immediately his senses kicked into overdrive, need clawing at him cruelly.

A week in the warmth of Sicily had brought a light,

golden tone to her skin, drawing out silvery highlights in the blonde of her hair. And the simple, beautifully cut, deep turquoise swimming costume clung in all the right places, smoothing and enhancing the sleek curves of her body and exposing long, long legs and elegantly slender arms. When she bent down to rub at Paolo's hair with the white towel the sight of the delicate line of her neck and shoulder caught on something raw deep inside him, making him clamp his teeth down hard into his bottom lip to hold back the groan of animal response that almost escaped him.

Dannazione, but he was finding this 'hands off' rule impossible to live with!

A week ago it had been a matter of pride for Gio to stick with it absolutely, never once even laying a finger on her. She would come to him, he had vowed. She would break before he did. And he had taken a sort of perverse pleasure in making sure he followed the ruling to the limit. At least as far as his *hands* were concerned.

His arms might brush against hers, his leg came close to the length of her thigh when they sat together. He made sure that he kissed her at each meeting or parting, and his body often brushed against her when they met in a corridor or had to pass in a doorway. But, in all the time since they had left her flat on the journey here, never once had any part of his hands touched any part of her body.

'*Papa!*'

Paolo had caught sight of him, wriggling free from Terrie's gentle restraint and running towards his father, smile wide and brilliant, arms outstretched.

'*Papa! Papa!*'

'*Ciao, bambino!*'

Gio caught the sturdy little body in both hands, lifting his son and swinging him high in the air, his smile as bright as Paolo's as he looked up into the small, laughing face.

'And how is my little one today? What have you been up to?'

'I swim!' Paolo crowed jubilantly. '*Papa*, I swim with Treeza!'

'You sweem?' Gio echoed, laughter bubbling up in his voice as he echoed his son's imperfect English pronunciation. 'Did you indeed? Are you sure you swam...?'

To Terrie's total consternation his gleaming dark eyes slid to her face in a swift, amusement-filled glance that brought her into a joking conspiracy with him, the gesture so warm, so intimate that it made her heart lurch in instant response.

'Because when I saw you it was Teresa who was doing all the sweeming, and you were having a ride!'

'*Papa*—no!'

In his flurry of protest, all Paolo's English deserted him and he subjected his father to a tirade in chirpy Italian that only made Gio's smile widen even more, until at last he threw back his head and laughed out loud, relaxing totally into his feelings in a way that Terrie had rarely seen him do before.

Swamped by a rush of disturbing sensation, a flood of heat that filled her veins from head to toe, making her whole body glow in a way that had nothing to do with the warmth of the sun, Terrie swiftly turned away, unable to watch any longer. Snatching up her towel, she rubbed it fiercely against her face, more as a way of concealing her expression, hiding the betraying colour of her cheeks, than in any attempt to dry her skin. Already the sunny afternoon had made the lingering moisture evaporate, and even the material of her swimming costume was drying so fast that she might never have been in the pool at all.

'OK, so you swam. I believe you.'

The laughter was still there in Gio's voice, sparking off sensations in her thoughts that complicated her already intense reactions to him.

She had to drag her eyes away from the way that Gio's strong hands held his small son so gently yet so securely, long, tanned fingers splayed out against the olive-toned flesh of the small torso. Needed to wipe from her mind the memories of the pleasure just the touch of those hands could bring, the tingling sensation that lingered where they had smoothed her hair, caressed her skin.

When she had agreed to come here to Sicily with him, she had been so sure that she could keep to the crazily impulsive 'hands off' rule that she had flung at him in a temper on that afternoon in her flat. She had had some vague sort of thought that perhaps if Gio found that she wasn't as freely available for sex as he had seemed to expect then he might find other reasons for being with her, other pleasures that her company might bring. She had even hoped that it might just be a case of abstinence making the heart grow fonder.

But she had been sorely disappointed. Gio had seemed worryingly unmoved. He had made none of the sarcastic or critical comments she had anticipated. In fact, he had said nothing at all. And on their arrival here at the villa he had made no attempt to persuade her to share his room, but instead had led her to a totally separate room at the far end of the corridor to his. In fact, she had been forced to wonder whether she had had any effect on him. And, even worse, she had been obliged to ask herself if *she* was the one who was suffering most as a result of her own impetuous edict.

And she had reckoned without the way that the very different climate and way of life that Gio knew in his native land had changed the man himself. In ways that only deepened and dangerously enhanced his already potent sexual attraction until it was positively lethal to any sort of peace of mind she might have hoped for.

Here, in the warmth of the sun, and with the relaxed pace of life enjoyed in his island villa, the sophisticated city lawyer had disappeared, and in his place was a more relaxed, far more casual Giovanni Cardella than she had ever believed existed. Gone were the sleek city suits and in their place were loose T-shirts and shorts that exposed the muscular length of his legs. And several times he had joined Terrie and Paolo for a swim, sending her pulse rate rocketing when he stripped off to reveal the toned lines of a body that the sun had tanned to the shade of dark bronze.

She was desperately afraid that if she stayed in Sicily much longer, he would come to mean more to her than it was safe for her to feel.

Not that she *could* feel any more.

The thought slammed into her mind with the force of a blow to her head, making her reel dizzily.

Where had that come from? And was it true? As soon as she asked herself the question she knew there was only one answer.

She had no way of escape, she told herself. No matter what rational controls she tried to impose on it, her body recognised the personal sexual brand this man had set on it on their single night together. A secret brand that made her as much his possession as if she had been bought and sold in a slave market in days gone by. And she would always be held by that bond, no matter how hard she might struggle to get away.

If she could have done so without provoking suspicion she would have tossed aside the towel and plunged back into the blue depths of the pool, wanting to have them close over her head, conceal her from Gio's prying eyes. She longed for the shock of the cool water against her heated body, dousing and controlling the pounding blood in her veins, the ache of need that was uncoiling low down in the cradle of her pelvis.

'But now it's time for you to go inside,' Gio was saying, lowering his son slowly and setting his small bare feet safely on the ground.

'No!'

Paolo's small face set into stubborn lines that made him look unnervingly like his father. 'I stay with Treeza! I love Treeza! Treeza—love 'oo.'

Teresa sensed rather than saw Gio's sudden stiffening, but she didn't dare to look into his face to see the effect his son's innocent words were having on him. Never before had she felt the ambiguity of her position in Gio's household as strongly as she did now. Admitting to cowardice, she concentrated fiercely on the little boy.

'And I love you, sweetie. But you must do as your daddy says. If he says it's time to go in…'

'And Nonna is here,' Gio added, forestalling the protest Paolo was obviously about to make. 'She's waiting to see you.'

The bribe worked. Paolo adored his paternal grandmother. His smile restored, he set off at a fast pace, heading for the big patio doors into the house.

Gio watched him go, waiting until he saw his son safely indoors before he turned back to Terrie.

'You're a strong swimmer,' he commented, though Terrie had a firm feeling that he was speaking to say anything, fill the silence, with his mind not on the subject he had raised at all. 'Where did you learn?'

'My mother taught me. She loved the water. And then at school I was in the competition team.'

She was hunting for her cover-up as she spoke, finding the loose cotton shirt on a sun-lounger near by. The sense of relief with which she shrugged it on was ridiculous, she knew. The fine weave of the white cotton made the garment almost totally transparent anyway, and at best it was a concession to modesty, nothing more. It certainly wasn't any protection from the dark, assessing gaze that roved over her body in the clinging swimsuit with evident approval.

'Did Lucia like to swim?'

She wouldn't have asked the question if she hadn't already been off balance. Since her arrival at the villa, Lucia Cardella had been a forbidden topic between them. It was impossible to ignore the photographs of the petite, dark-haired woman that were scattered around the large, elegant rooms, but Gio's first wife had never actually been discussed. So now she froze in apprehension, wondering if perhaps she had overstepped some unseen barrier, crossed a line that she didn't even know was there.

'No, she hated it,' he said slowly. 'As a matter of fact, she was terrified of water. Her father was one of those who believed that the way to overcome a nervous fear is to confront it head-on. So, when he saw her hesitating on the side of the pool as a child, he picked her up and threw her in.'

'Oh, poor Lucia. That would just make matters worse!'

'It did.'

Gio's voice was low and flat, dull as his eyes. He seemed to be staring out across the rippling water of the pool, his gaze unfocused, and Terrie had the feeling that he was looking back into his past, reliving some memory. Her heart twisted at the thought of his loss, the loneliness of his life since, and, reacting automatically, she reached out and laid a gentle hand on his arm.

'I'm sorry—I shouldn't have…'

Gio started brusquely at her touch, his hazed eyes going sharply to her face. For a couple of blank seconds it was as if he didn't recognise her, as he stared straight through her, then he blinked hard and came back to himself.

That had never happened before, Gio realised. Terrie had asked him a question about Lucia and it was only when she had that he had realised that his wife, while still so vivid in his memories, had actually not been uppermost in his thoughts. For a second or two he had had to hunt for the facts he wanted to answer her question.

'Non c'e problema,' he muttered automatically. 'It's fine.'

But then he looked down at her hand, small and delicate, as it lay on his arm. In the sunlight the scent of her skin was an evocative perfume, one that stirred his senses to a demanding throb.

'What happened to "hands off"?' he queried softly, lacing the words with a touch of wry amusement.

'Oh, that…'

For the space of a couple of heartbeats, Terrie looked nonplussed, but then swiftly she recovered, even shot him a provocatively challenging glance from the corners of her eyes.

'I only said "hands off" to you! Nowhere is it written that the rule applies to me!'

'You little witch!'

He made it a low, rolling growl, the sound of a dozing tiger, half-roused from sleep, but too lazily contented to bother with pouncing. He was still having trouble adjusting to the discovery he had made about himself just moments before.

'But perhaps it's just as well that there is some contact between us. My mother was starting to wonder just what sort of a couple we are...'

'You told her we are—a couple?'

It was her turn to look disconcerted and she snatched her hand back as if the slight connection between them had burned her, making her flinch away.

'*Naturalmente.*'

'But then—won't she think it's odd that we don't share...that we aren't...?'

'Sleeping together?'

A quick, ironic smile tugged at the corners of his mouth at the memory of his conversation with his mother earlier that week.

'Not at all, *cara mia*. This is Sicily, remember. Mama is still old-fashioned enough to approve of the fact that we have separate rooms. She believes that it is a sign of how serious we are about each other—that I treat you with such respect.'

'And so how will you explain it if I am pregnant?'

'My mother is a realist. She knows that the behaviour she admires here is not necessarily the same everywhere else. Besides, she has always dreamed of having more grandchildren, and now that Cesare and Megan are about to present her with a new member of the family she is hoping to see her dream come true. She would not worry if a baby was conceived before marriage—just as long as it was born into a properly formalised relationship.'

'Marriage?' Terrie looked stunned. 'We didn't discuss marriage.'

'We didn't discuss it, but you must have realised that it was the obvious solution if you should turn out to be carrying my child.'

'Not that obvious to me!'

It was as if a violent thunderstorm was brewing inside her head, making Terrie's thoughts spin.

Marriage. To Gio. How would she feel about that?

The question had knocked her completely off balance, but it was the answer that sent her spinning over the edge and into a freefall of panic-stricken shock.

She couldn't think of anything that she would like better. Couldn't imagine anything more terrifyingly wonderful than the prospect of waking up every day, for the rest of her existence, and knowing that Gio was there, in her life—that this devastating, stunning, sexy man was her *husband*.

'I didn't think—'

'Then *think*!' Gio ordered curtly. 'Any day now we will know. And when we know we will have to act. If you are *incinta*, then the sooner we announce our proposed union the better.'

The spiralling freefall of confusion had ended by dropping her, mentally at least, into an ice-cold pond, sobering her up fast. While she had been thinking of togetherness and a future filled with the time to get to know this man properly, to share his life, his home, his bed, Gio's thoughts had all been of practicalities. Of making public their 'proposed union', for all the world as if it was to be nothing but a legal deal he had thrashed out in court.

But why should that surprise her? It was, after all, the only way Gio actually thought about the possibility of their marriage. He had made that plain before they had left England, telling her in no uncertain terms that he had no heart left to give to her.

'I'm not looking for another love of my life,' he had said. 'I already had that with Lucia, and lightning doesn't strike twice.'

'And how would your mother feel about that?'

'She is delighted that I have a new woman in my life. She believes that it is not good for a man to live alone.'

And any woman was better than none. Any woman would fill the space in his bed, in his house, in his life—but not in his heart. He didn't have to say the words; they were there in his tone, in the opaque look in his eyes.

'It was my mother who sent me out to you here. She is concerned that you and I are not getting any time alone together because of Paolo, and so she has offered to have him all day tomorrow—and all night too. He loves to sleep at her house so he'll see it as a real treat. And we can go out and I can show you the island.'

'That's kind of her.'

Terrie's response was abstracted. Her whirling brain had picked on one phrase and held on to it like a terrier fastening on to a slipper.

'All day…and all night'.

It was crazy to let that fix in her thoughts and mean so much more than the simple phrase deserved, but she couldn't stop herself from doing so. All week, she and Gio had been alone in the house—apart from the small, innocent person of Paolo. A totally empty house, other than the two of them, wouldn't be so very different—would it?

And yet somehow she felt as if it would be completely unlike every other day she had already spent in the villa.

'A full day without any parental responsibilities,' Gio murmured. 'It would be a pity to waste it.'

'Mm.'

It was all that Terrie could manage. She didn't dare to ask him just what he meant by 'waste'. She already had some very strong suspicions as to what was behind the apparently innocent remark. And with her own newly recognised feelings still raw in her mind, she was not at all sure that she would be able to cope with the implications of that.

A full day without any parental responsibilities, Gio reflected. And who knew just how things might stand between them at the end of that day?

Twenty-four hours in which, for the first time in this upside-down relationship, they would actually have a chance to do things the conventional way—follow the usual path that most couples took.

Most male-female relationships started with liking, moved to love, and from there to the deep passion of a committed future together. That was how things had been with Lucia. He had liked her the moment he had seen her; known he loved her in the blink of an eye after that, it had seemed. Had wanted them to be together for the rest of their lives, but it was not to be.

And they had waited what had seemed like an eternity before they slept together.

None of which fitted the way things had developed with Teresa. Instead he had felt as if a tornado had swept into his life, picked him up and whirled him far from anywhere he recognised, losing track of all the familiar landmarks he had ever known. And when he had finally been set down again, he had no idea whether he was on his head or his heels. He only knew that he couldn't get this woman out of his mind. That without her in his life he felt as if he was losing his grip on his sanity.

But when she was with him, he couldn't work out what he wanted with her.

Perhaps tomorrow would give him a chance to get things back under control again. Maybe twenty-four hours from now, he would have some idea of just exactly where he went from here.

And whether Teresa came with him or not.

CHAPTER ELEVEN

THE sun had gone down completely by the time that they returned to the villa late the following evening. After their day out they had had dinner at a wonderful restaurant in Palermo, before making their way back along the winding country roads to Gio's home. Already the heat of the day had chilled to a cool, still evening, and in the darkness the house seemed incredibly silent and empty.

'It seems strange not to have to keep quiet for fear of waking Paolo,' Terrie said as they made their way into the huge lounge. 'Was he always such a light sleeper?'

'Not for the first year.'

Gio tossed his car keys onto the sideboard and went to stand by the patio doors, staring out at the terrace where the pool lay empty and almost still, just a few tiny waves, stirred by a faint wind, lapping lazily at the sides.

'Until he was twelve months old, he slept so deeply that it would have taken an earthquake to waken him. But then things changed. After...'

'After Lucia...' Terrie inserted softly, sensing intuitively the words that had deserted him as his shoulders tensed, and one hand covered his eyes. 'That's what you mean, isn't it? Young as he was, Paolo sensed that someone very special was missing from his life.'

And, from the way that the little boy who had known his mother only such a short time had reacted, she could guess at how deeply his father, who had loved her as much as life itself, had felt her loss.

'Yeah...'

157

It was a long-drawn-out sigh, one that wrenched at her heart, brought the sting of tears to her eyes.

'That's exactly what I mean.'

Abruptly he swung round, turning to face her, and on a shock of surprise Terrie suddenly had the strangest feeling that he was looking at her almost as if for the first time.

'I hope you enjoyed yourself today.'

'I had a wonderful time!' Terrie answered with total honesty, knowing that the gleam in her eyes must speak for itself. 'I've never been that close to the site of a volcano before.'

The circular journey to Etna had been like a pattern of light and shade. In the foothills of the great volcano were the richness of the olive groves, the glistening citrus and the nut plantations. But clinging to the sides of Etna itself had been dark volcanic villages and ruined Norman castles. Further up, seen from a cable car, the setting had seemed like nothing so much as a moonscape.

'It's a scary place.' She gave a shiver just remembering. 'But I'm glad I've seen it. What was that name you said that native Sicilians call Etna?'

'Mongibello. It comes from the Arabic for mountain. Some people just call it *a muntagna*—the mountain—pure and simple.'

Gio's tone was vague and distracted. It was clear that his attention was not on the subject at all.

'Would you like a drink?' Terrie asked, feeling awkward and unsure of herself.

The trip out had gone so well. Gio had seemed relaxed and at ease, a charming and knowledgeable guide to the places they had visited, and an easy, entertaining companion over dinner. But since they had come back into the house it was as if unease had settled round her like a cloak, coming between her and the comfortable mood of the day.

'Some wine?'

'No, nothing alcoholic.'

Gio shook his head. He wanted nothing that might cloud his mind, stop him from thinking clearly. All day he had been plagued by the strangest feelings, ones he didn't know how to handle, and anything intoxicating could only make matters so much worse. It was almost as if he was standing outside himself, watching every move he made, and not understanding it.

He had walked through familiar places, seen familiar sights. He had even eaten in a long-time favourite restaurant. Somewhere where he'd been perhaps a hundred times or more. And everything had seemed new and strangely different.

And he had felt differently too.

The only way he could describe it was that the empty space at his side—the space that he had lived with all day and every day for the last two years—suddenly seemed to be not so empty, not so dark.

It wasn't just that he had had someone with him. He'd lost count of how many times he had gone to some of the special places he had shared with Lucia—alone, with Cesare or Megan, or even the two of them together *and* Paolo. And still he had felt empty, lost and alone.

Today the tall, slender figure of a blonde Englishwoman had gone a long way towards filling that space. And in a way that no one else ever could.

Teresa… He had opened his mouth to say her name, to tell her…but then the realisation that he didn't know *what* to tell her closed his lips again, just as Terrie, enticing, laughed suddenly.

'Well, I'd offer to make you some coffee, if you think

we'd drink it this time. That night in the hotel, and again in my flat, it just got left untouched and went cold. Third time lucky, do you think?'

Gio found that to his surprise the smile that was needed in response came unexpectedly easily, sharing in her amusement.

'So long as we don't risk the brandy as well.'

'No brandy, I promise you.' Terrie laughed again, leading the way out of the lounge and across the tiled hallway.

In the kitchen, Gio leaned against the pale wood cabinets, watching her as she moved around, intent on the simple task. She looked like a pale, exotic flower in a simple sleeveless dress the same shade of turquoise as the swimming costume she had worn yesterday, but so many tones lighter that it looked as if it had faded over time, washed to something very close to white.

Because of the warmth of the day she had caught her hair up in a neat coil at the base of her skull and as she bent her head over the cafetière, concentrating on measuring the right amount of coffee grounds, the delicacy and vulnerability of the curve of her neck affected him strongly.

He felt the clutch of desire deep inside. But at the same time he also felt a rush of gentleness, a fiercely protective rush of emotion that made his head spin with its sheer power.

Unable to stop himself, he moved forward, coming behind her, and dropped a soft, lingering kiss on the exposed skin at the top of her spine.

'Mm…'

Her response was soft and sensual, like a small cat's purr. But then she twisted round to face him, looking deep into his eyes, a faintly puzzled frown creasing the space between her brows.

'What was that for?'

'Because I wanted to. And you can't complain because...'

He lifted both his hands and spread them out on either side of her, bronzed fingers splayed wide.

'See...no hands.'

To Terrie's intense relief there was no darkness in his tone, no underlying thread of anger or reproach. Instead there was a lightness and humour that amazed her, relaxing the strain of muscles held taut with uncertainty.

'I'll let you off, then,' she returned on a matching note, then, drawing in a deep, strengthening breath, she seized the chance his mood had given her. 'Would it help to talk about it? About Lucia?'

She fully expected rejection. Was sure that he would close up, turn against her, or at least tell her it was none of her business. But instead he sighed, flexing his shoulders under the silver-grey silk jacket, and said, 'What do you want to know?'

Terrie swallowed hard, unsure of how to answer that.

'Whatever you want to tell me.'

Gio swung away from her again, but to her relief she saw that it was not to reject her, but so that he could pace up and down the big farmhouse-style kitchen, his restless movements obviously reflecting the unsettled nature of his thoughts.

'We were both only sixteen when we met...'

His voice sounded cracked and rusty, as if it was a long time since it had been used, and he was clearly not finding it easy to use the right words to express his memories. Terrie longed to go to him, to hold him, to help him, but she sensed intuitively that this was not the right moment. Gio needed to handle this on his own. Later, when he had finished, that would be the time to go to him and try to comfort him.

If he would let her.

'I took one look at her and I just *knew*.'

Gio paused in his restless pacing for just a second, pushed both hands through his hair, staring into space as if picturing the scene, then launched into movement once again.

'Cesare always says that the men in our family fall heavily when they fall in love. That it's a once-in-a-lifetime sort of thing…'

Terrie could only be grateful that as the words left his mouth Gio was at the far end of the kitchen, where his long, restless strides had taken him. His back was to her and so he never saw the way that she flinched at his words, the pain that darkened her eyes at that 'once in a lifetime'.

'Certainly, that's how it was with Roberto and my mother. He lost his heart to her when she was still married to my father. So when Papa died he was there to help her through. And Cesare has only ever wanted Megan. He waited for years for her because of a promise to her father.'

'I know. Megan told me.'

And because of that she had known just how much Gio had loved his Lucia. She had understood the lightning-strike of true passion when it had hit. Hadn't she felt something of the same when she had first set eyes on Gio in that hotel bar? She hadn't been able to take her eyes off him then and hadn't been able to put him out of her mind ever since.

'She also said that you and Lucia threatened to run away together if your parents didn't agree to the marriage.'

'The *fuitina*?'

Gio paused in his restless pacing and his mouth quirked up at one corner.

'Yes, we threatened that—both families thought we were far too young to know our own minds. They wanted us to separate—live a little—before we committed ourselves to each other. But we had no doubts.'

'What exactly is a *fuitina*?'

Terrie knew that she was just asking the question to keep the conversation going and because she didn't know what else to say. She had to take a couple of much-needed seconds to pull herself together, adjust to the bruises on her heart where Gio's words had landed, unknowingly wounding her, and the unfamiliar Sicilian term seemed the best possible distraction she could find.

'It's from Sicilian history—but sometimes it still happens today. Basically it just means running away together and it was used as a declaration of how serious your feelings were. It was a way for young lovers to be able to sleep together without moral condemnation.'

'And would you have done it?'

She didn't need the answer. It was there in his face; in his eyes. He would have done that and more if it had been the only way to win his Lucia.

'We both would. But in the end we didn't have to do anything quite so drastic. Our parents agreed to our engagement if I promised to concentrate hard on my studies, work at my training to be a lawyer. We were nineteen when we married.'

'So young.'

'Yeah—but we just couldn't wait any longer…crazy, weren't we?'

'But perhaps you guessed, perhaps you sensed that it wasn't going to be—that you weren't going to be together forever. Perhaps you wanted to grab at what you had while you had it.'

She'd hit a vulnerable point there, Terrie thought, watching his eyes cloud. Wanting to erase the distress, she rushed on.

'Tell me about her—what was she like?'

Did she really want to know this? she wondered as soon as she asked the question. But, strangely, as Gio started to speak she found that, contrary to what she had expected, his memories didn't hurt. Instead she found they intrigued and absorbed her, telling her so much more about the man himself as he told her about the woman he had loved and lost.

She learned what he had been like as an adolescent and a young man. How hard he had worked to become the lawyer his mother wanted him to be—and to be able to support his new young wife in spite of the fact that his family was rich in its own right. She discovered the interests they had shared together, the simple joys that meant so much more than huge, great gestures. The personal, intimate things between a man and his wife.

But she also found out the deepest, most important things about Gio himself. She learned how he loved, why he loved. She learned how he felt about honesty and faithfulness; how he had handled the arguments, the problems and the disappointments that came the way of every marriage. He told her of his joy when he had learned that Lucia was pregnant, the magical moment when his son was born. He told her of his dreams of a large family, dreams that were tragically never to come true.

And she learned how he had suffered and grieved when Lucia had been snatched away from him far, far too soon. He didn't trouble to hide the tears then; clearly felt no shame at the way they filled his eyes, dampened his cheeks and left the lush black lashes clumped together in thick, dark spikes. And Terrie respected him for that. And her heart twisted in sorrow, for both Gio and poor, pretty Lucia, who had not had long enough to share their love together.

She didn't know how long she sat there in the stillness of the night, listening to the words pouring from him. Didn't know whether hours or even days had passed, or simply minutes as she was held absorbed. She only knew that she wouldn't have wanted to lose a single second of them, even though they brought to her the most devastating personal realisation that she had ever known. One that would never leave her, and which could do nothing but change her life once and forever.

Because by the time Gio had finished his tale of love, she recognised just what had happened to her.

She had fallen in love with this man, as hopelessly, desperately and totally as he had been in love with his wife. And, like Gio, hers was a once-in-a-lifetime kind of love. One she would never feel for anyone else.

But Gio had loved and lost another woman. And, as a result, she could never have the true strength of all that his heart was capable of.

'Can I ask you something?' she said at last, when he had stopped speaking, stopped pacing, and was simply standing, one hand resting on the worktop of a cabinet, just within reach of her own.

He looked exhausted, shadows darkening the olive skin of his face, deep lines scored from his nose to his mouth. But the ebony eyes were clear and calm. It was as if he had been through a storm, a violent whirlwind, and come out the other side.

'Anything,' Gio said huskily, rawly.

And strangely enough he sounded as though he meant it.

'That night…'

She knew she didn't have to say which one. That there was only one night she could mean. The night they had met.

'You said once that Lucia died ten days before Paolo's birthday. Was—that night…?'

'That night was the second anniversary of the date she died, yes.'

'Oh, Gio…'

She reached out, touched his hand. And knew from his total stillness how much it meant.

His dark gaze went to where her fingers rested lightly over the top of his and lingered for a moment. Then he looked up again, ebony eyes locking with blue-grey. And holding.

Terrie would never know which one of them moved first. Or whether in fact they both acted in the space of the same heartbeat, heading towards each other on the impulse of almost the same thought.

She was only aware of being on her feet, and needing to be close to him. And finding that was easier than she had ever anticipated because he had halved the short distance between them too. So that all that it needed was a couple of swift, short steps and she was there, with him, his arms closing round her, her face lifting for his kiss.

It was a kiss that seemed to draw her soul out from her body, taking with it every thought of hesitation, of reservation, of second thoughts. She had no time for doubts, no time for anything but the deep-felt need to hold this man, to touch him, kiss him, give him everything that was there in her heart for him.

But most of all to give him herself.

There was a faint, inexplicable awkwardness about the way that Gio was holding her. An unsettled, uncomfortable feeling across her shoulders and back so that she wriggled slightly, trying to adjust, coming briefly out of the haze of need as she heard Gio's faint laughter that warmed her skin with his breath.

'What…?' she asked and looked up, puzzled, into his smiling eyes.

'Hands off,' Gio whispered, his smile a wide, wicked grin. 'You gave me my orders—while we're in Sicily it's strictly—'

'Oh, to hell with hands off!' Terrie exclaimed, but then suddenly she changed her mind. 'On second thoughts…'

His uncertain, slightly wary glance was all that it took to have her mouth curling in teasing mischief as she snuggled closer, rubbing her face against his chin where the rough suggestion of his growth of beard snagged against her delicate skin.

'Perhaps we'll stick to hands off,' she murmured, deliberately pitching her voice as a husky purr. 'But just for you—for me it's definitely hands *on*. I get to touch all I want!'

Slowly, tantalisingly she walked her fingers up the front of his shirt, feeling his quick catch of breath in the first second that she touched. For a moment she lingered, tracing teasing circles around the knot of his tie, round and round, until she saw him swallow, moistening the dryness of his lips.

With another cat-that-got-the-cream smile, she tugged the knot slightly loose. Paused. Tugged again.

'Teresa…'

With a low chuckle deep in her throat, she laid a reproving finger over his mouth, silencing him as she shook her head.

'My turn,' she whispered. 'Mine.'

She drew out the removal of the tie for as long as she dared, fixing her entire concentration on easing the elegant knot open, sliding the burgundy silk free. And it was only when at last it hung loose around his neck that she realised how completely still Gio had become, frozen, hardly breathing, it seemed, all his attention fixed on her.

'Good…'

She caught hold of both ends of the tie, tugged again, drawing his head forward until all she had to do was to reach up and press a long, lingering kiss on his waiting lips. His sigh of response widened the smile on her own mouth.

'You see,' she told him softly. 'Patience is rewarded—in the end.'

It was an effort to ease away from the kiss, decidedly harder to ignore the heated, tingling sensations sparking off all over her body. But she had started on a plan of how to play this and she wanted to carry it through.

The slow, careful unbuttoning of his shirt was accompanied by the heavy, pounding thud of Gio's heart just underneath her fingertips whenever they rested on the heated satin of his skin. Occasionally she paused to trace delicate erotic patterns over the lines of his chest, tangling gently in the dark hair, moving along the curves of his ribcage. When she circled first one and then the second of the dark, tight male nipples with infinite care Gio could not hold back a groan of yearning response.

'Teresa…' he muttered and his voice was thicker, hoarser than before. 'Let me…'

'No.' Her tone was firm. 'Hands off…'

But then, looking into the black pools of his eyes, she weakened, just a little.

'All right,' she conceded. 'You can kiss me…'

It was a kiss that almost broke her resolve, because, forbidden to use his hands, he let his mouth tell her how hungry and aroused he was. How much he wanted her. His hard body strained against hers, awakening the same demanding craving in her own flesh, making her wish that he would just ignore her instructions, her command, and grab for her, haul her into his arms, swing her off the floor and then carry her upstairs to his bed.

But then she risked another glance up into his face, seeing the glaze of desire settle on those brilliant eyes, the tautening of every muscle in the set of burning passion. And she knew that if her resolve to hold to this game she had started was weakening then his had hardened, become immovable. There was no backing out now. And as if to confirm her suspicions, almost, she felt, to indicate that he could read her mind, he smiled straight into her considering eyes.

'Next move, *carina*,' he challenged softly. 'I'm in your hands. But don't you think that, if we're to take this game to its natural conclusion, we might be a little more comfortable in the bedroom?'

But the bedroom was not what Terrie had in mind. The bedroom was the one he had used during his marriage. The one he had shared with Lucia. And so she caught hold of the two sides of his shirt, now gaping wildly over his bronzed chest, and led him by them out of the kitchen and across the hall, into the spacious lounge. Once there, she eased the loosened garment from him, tracing the path of the material as it slid away with her mouth, pressing kisses against his heated skin.

With her hands on the narrow leather belt at his waist, for the first time she lost a little of her confidence, hesitated slightly, but Gio sensed her feelings and shook his head in teasing reproach.

'You can't stop now, *belleza*,' he told her, and the forceful jut of his erection just below her hands gave an added emphasis to the growing urgency in his voice.

An urgency that now infected Terrie as, with rather more haste and rather less finesse, she dealt with the belt, slid off what remained of his clothing and cast them aside onto the nearest chair.

Only then, when he was naked and proudly erect before her, did she turn her attention to her own clothes. The dress was easily pulled up and over her head, the small slivers of silk that were her underwear soon followed, and as she turned back to Gio she heard the harsh, rough-edged breath that hissed in through his clenched teeth. The sound of a man very close to the edge of his control.

'*Teresa!*' he said and it was a groan of desperation. 'Have mercy on me…'

And because it was what she wanted too she nodded slowly, her smile wide and triumphant.

'*Now,*' she said. 'Now you can touch.'

And from the first moment that his hands made contact with her body she was lost, caught up in a whirlwind of sensation such as she had never known before. His fingers woke, teased, tormented, tantalised until she was a screaming mass of awareness and hunger, the need of him like a white-hot pulse at the very core of her being.

With his mouth still on her breast, Gio intuitively ful-filled her fantasy of just moments before, lifting her from her feet and tumbling her down onto the huge, soft cushions of the settee, coming after her in a hungry rush. His long legs nudged hers apart, the heated force of his mas-culinity straining at the juncture of her thighs, his hands sliding under her buttocks, lifting her up, tilting her so that she was perfectly ready for him.

'Now I can touch,' he muttered, more raw and rougher

than ever before. 'Now I can touch—and now I can do *this*…'

The last word was a sound of triumph and the deepest satisfaction all in one as he thrust his hotly aroused body deep into hers, taking, filling, making her his once and for all.

It was only seconds from that moment, only the space of a few, heated, throbbing heartbeats before Terrie felt all trace of control slipping from her, her body curving, arching against his, her senses climbing, peaking, shattering and taking her with him over the edge and into the oblivion of ecstasy.

She had no idea when she surfaced again, how long it had been, what had woken her. But she slowly opened her eyes to find that Gio was awake, his head propped up on one hand, dark eyes watching her with a disturbing intensity.

'Hi!' she murmured, smiling, and felt a twist of apprehension when the smile was not returned but was met with a long, thoughtful stare. 'What…?'

'I've been thinking,' he said slowly. 'About this agreement of ours. How would you feel if I said that I don't want you to go? I want you to stay here?'

'Gio…' Terrie could hardly believe what she was hearing. 'Are you saying that you…?'

She broke off, the swift rush of joy subsiding just as fast as it had come as he closed his eyes, shutting himself off from her.

'Don't, Teresa,' he said with difficulty. 'Don't ask me to give you anything more than I can manage. I'll give you what I can… You mustn't ask for more.'

His eyes opened again, burning straight into her uncertain grey ones.

'All I can…'

And would that be enough? Terrie was forced to ask herself. Feeling as she did about him, could she cope with that?

But then Gio reached for her, his arms closing round her. He kissed her, his hands smoothing down the length of her body, stirring and awakening the heady clamour that drowned out the ability to think straight—to think at all.

And it all began again.

CHAPTER TWELVE

TERRIE walked back into the bedroom slowly and reluctantly, her heart twisting on a painful combination of relief and distress when she realised that the room was empty. Gio had gone downstairs and she was alone. If she listened hard she could hear the sounds of him moving about in the kitchen.

And she could only pray that for the moment at least he would stay there. That he would give her some time to be on her own and think.

Time to adjust to what she had just discovered.

She wasn't pregnant.

She had known it as soon as she had woken up that morning. The familiar aching feeling low down in her body had told its own story. But still she had hoped.

Until now.

Now she knew for certain. Wild and rash as her behaviour with Gio had been on that first night, it had not had any permanent consequences. She was not carrying Gio's baby.

'How would you feel if I said that I don't want you to go? I want you to stay here?'

Gio's words, whispered to her in the dark of the night, came back to haunt her, whirling round and round in her head, impossible to get a grip on.

How had he meant them? Had he really meant them at all?

She knew she didn't dare to put any great reliance on anything that had been said in the heated intensity of the night they had just shared. Adrift on a sea of emotion and passion, she suspected that Gio could have said *anything*, his grip on his tongue lost completely.

But would he still keep to what he had said in the cold light of day?

Especially when he discovered that there was no baby. That the whole reason for her being here at all did not exist.

He would never have asked her to come to Sicily if he hadn't feared she might be pregnant. And she had seen enough of him with Paolo to understand why. He was a wonderful father, loving, devoted, caring. And he would have been the same with any child they had created between them.

But did he care enough about *her* to want her without that child?

'Teresa!'

Gio was calling to her, his voice coming up the stairs from the hallway below.

'Are you coming down? I made coffee—*again*.'

The joke snagged on a raw spot on Terrie's nerves, tugging painfully. She didn't need any reminder of the fact that, once again, they had left their coffee made and poured but growing cold in the mugs as they lost themselves in the inferno of passion that had reached out to swallow them up. She knew already, better than anyone, just how her desire for Gio, the hunger that he could awaken with just a touch, a kiss, a look, could sweep anything and everything else from her mind and leave her incapable of any rational thought.

And it had the same effect on Gio.

So there was no way she could trust the words he had whispered to her. Not until he repeated them to her in totally different circumstances. And when she had told him her news about the baby.

'Teresa!'

'Yes! I'm coming!'

She was already dressed in a pale blue sundress, her hair freshly washed and drying naturally in the warmth of the morning, so she had no excuse to prevaricate any longer. And the note of impatience in Gio's voice told her that if she didn't go down to him then he would come up here to find her.

Gio felt a rush of relief when he finally heard Terrie's footsteps on the stairs and knew she was on her way down at last. She had spent so long delaying upstairs that he had begun to wonder if something was wrong. If there was some reason that she didn't want to face him.

While he couldn't wait to see her. Last night had been a major turning point for him. He hadn't slept so well in a very long time—two years, in fact—and he had woken clear-headed and alert, ready to look at the future in a whole new light.

'Come on, it's getting cold!'

The ring of the doorbell sounded through his shout and with a muttered curse he dumped his own coffee mug down on the table and went to answer it.

Terrie was just reaching the bottom step as he passed in the hall.

'Hi!'

His greeting, like his wave, was swift and offhand. All he was interested in was getting to the door, dealing with whoever was there, and sending them on their way again. He wanted no interruptions, no one else intruding on his plans for Teresa and today.

'Breakfast's in the kitchen. I'll be with you in a minute.'

As he opened the door the sun streamed into the hall, blinding him for a moment, so that he had to blink hard before he could make out the small, stout black-haired woman who stood outside. But when he did, his heart sank.

'Rosa…*buon giorno*…'

Of all the times for Lucia's mother to decide to pay one of her infrequent visits, this had to be the worst she could choose. They had never got on well together, even when her daughter had been alive, and since Lucia's death their relationship had been strained at best, even though he tried to ensure that she saw plenty of Paolo, her grandson. But she only called at the house on very rare occasions. And he knew why she was here this time.

The coming Sunday was the anniversary of Lucia's birthday. And Rosa was here to arrange the trip to the cemetery to leave flowers as they had done each year.

'I…' he began but Rosa clearly wasn't listening. Instead she was staring past him, over his shoulder, her eyes fixed in an expression of disbelief.

'Who…?' she demanded in furious Italian. 'Who is *that*!'

Gio didn't have to turn to look to know who she meant. Clearly Terrie had paused at the bottom of the stairs, not making her way into the kitchen as he had suggested. He groaned inwardly. There never would be a good way for Rosa to meet the new woman in his life. But this was definitely not the best.

Inevitably, it had hit the older woman desperately hard when her daughter had died. Something of her had died with Lucia, and she had never recovered.

Half turning, he glanced to where Terrie stood behind him. She looked pale, he noted in concern. If only Rosa hadn't appeared, then he could find out what was wrong.

'This is Teresa,' he responded, in the same language that his mother-in-law had used, hoping that that would be enough.

It wasn't.

'And *who* is Teresa?' Rosa asked, bristling with antagonism. 'What is she doing here?'

He could answer that very simply and quickly—if only it was *Teresa* he was talking to. But it was Rosa who had asked the question. Rosa, who he knew would never leave until she had had an answer.

And Rosa had no right to be the first to know how he truly felt about Terrie. Certainly not before he had told Terrie herself.

But he had to say something. Anything. Something that would convince Rosa.

It was then that he remembered a conversation he had had with his mother-in-law a couple of months ago, just before he had set off on his trip to England. He snatched at the memory on a rush of relief as he turned back to Rosa.

'She's the person we talked about, remember?'

He kept to Italian, knowing Terrie spoke very little of the language.

'When we discussed getting a nanny for Paolo. An English nanny—someone who could look after him in his own home when I had to be away.'

To his relief he saw a wave of comprehension cross the older woman's face and she nodded almost approvingly.

'Ah, yes, the English governess. A good idea...'

Behind him, Gio heard the faint sound of movement and relaxed slightly. Terrie was obviously heading into the kitchen; he could join her there as soon as possible and they could start the day over again.

Luckily, Rosa didn't want to linger, and it was only

another few minutes before she said her goodbyes and drove away. Shutting the door on a sigh of relief, Gio hurried to the kitchen, a wide smile on his face.

A smile that faltered, died, when he found that the room was empty. Terrie was nowhere to be seen—so where…?

A sound from up above, the creak of floorboards from someone moving about, had him striding swiftly to the stairs.

'Teresa?'

The first tug of real anxiety hit when she didn't respond to his call.

'Teresa!'

Still no response. The tug became a sharply painful twist, some sudden instinct clutching at his guts as he started to climb the stairs, steadily at first, then increasing his pace, taking them two steps at a time as he felt his panic grow.

'*Teresa!* What…?'

The first thing he saw when he pushed open the bedroom door was her case lying open on the bed.

Open and half-filled.

No!

Anxiety became the brutal clutch of fear; the terrible suspicion that everything he had dreamed of during the night, and woken up to wanting today, had all been based on nothing but just that. A dream of wanting. With no foundation in fact.

And fear made him desperate to hide the truth until he knew just what the facts were.

'What's going on here?'

The protective fury in his voice brought Terrie whirling round from where she had been standing beside the open wardrobe. The bundle of coat-hangers and dresses in her hands told their own story, but Gio couldn't believe his eyes. He didn't *want* to believe his eyes.

'What the hell do you think you're doing?'

'I should have thought that it would be obvious just what's going on!' Terrie flung at him, her voice high and tight with hostility. 'And as for what I think I'm doing— I think I'm packing and leaving. What do *you* think?'

'I think that you're damn well not going anywhere. Not without some sort of explanation. Some reason why…'

'A reason?' Terrie echoed cynically. 'You want a reason?'

'I think you owe me one.'

'I owe you nothing. Nothing at all. So you needn't think you can order me around—demanding this and demanding that. I've nothing to give you. I came here and stayed with you because you insisted on it. And now I'm leaving—end of story.'

'No.'

Gio could only shake his head in rejection and confusion. He could almost believe that in the middle of the night, while he had been deep in the sleep of exhaustion created by the after-effects of their passionate lovemaking, someone had crept into the house and taken away the Teresa he knew. Leaving behind a clone of her, someone who was identical in looks, but totally different in personality.

'No. I'm not having that. You know why you're here! You know what our agreement was. That you would stay for four weeks—'

'Or until we were sure that I wasn't pregnant,' Terrie inserted coldly. 'I believe that was what we agreed on.'

'Teresa, what the hell are you talking about? Just what do you mean?'

'Exactly what I said…'

Terrie's hands tightened on the clothes she held, crushing the material convulsively.

'You invited me here to make sure that there was no—repercussion from our night together in the hotel. Well, you can rest assured of that.'

She tossed the dresses down, heedless of the way they fell roughly into the case. The grey eyes blazed like burning stars, brilliant in her pale face. And it was only now that he saw how her cheeks were streaked with the barely dried traces of tears.

'I'm not pregnant,' she declared starkly.

Gio's English totally deserted him.

'*Come?*' he said. '*Come te dice?* Teresa…'

What was happening? How had they come from the glorious, wonderful night they had shared to *this*? And why had she been weeping? If she was as determined to leave him as she seemed, then what in hell had upset her?

'Do you want me to say it again?'

Did she have to repeat it? Terrie thought miserably, blinking back the bitter tears that threatened. Wasn't it bad enough that it was true? She knew that she should be feeling some relief, a sense of gratitude that, now that she knew what his true opinion of her was, at least she wasn't carrying his baby too. At least she could get out, without that cruel reminder of their brief affair.

But the truth was that relief was the opposite of what she felt. That inside she was dying of loss and desolation. And if she could have done she would have welcomed any reminder of the man she loved so desperately. But she had been denied even that.

'My period started this morning. There—is that blunt enough for you? I'm not pregnant with your child, so you have no obligation to me. You don't need to look after me or support me—or—or anything. Four weeks, we said—and if at the end of that time I wasn't pregnant then I could go on my way and there'd be no f-further complications.'

For a terrible second the tears welled up again, almost defeating her. But she swallowed them down fiercely, forcing herself on.

'But in the end you didn't have to wait the full four weeks—isn't that lucky? I'm not pregnant, so you don't have to waste any more time on me. I'm leaving.'

'No!'

'*Yes.*'

She couldn't face him any more so she swung back to the wardrobe, grabbing another handful of dresses. But when she turned to deposit them in her case it was to find that Gio was beside her, reaching for the clothes and wrenching them from her hands.

'I said no. You're not leaving,' he roared, stuffing them back into the cupboard and slamming the door on it. 'At least not like this. What do you think last night was all about?'

'Do you have to ask? If you don't know, then your English mustn't be quite as good as you thought. There's a nice simple word that explains last night perfectly—a nice, simple four-letter word! It's *lust*, Gio—or sex—nothing more, nothing less…'

'No! It was more than that. Much more!'

'Oh, *please*! Don't lie to me! You don't have to pretend! We're both adults.'

'I'm not lying! And I'm not pretending about anything. I don't want you to go. I want you to stay!'

'As what?'

Bitterness overwhelmed her so that she had to force the words out past the hard, tight knot in her throat.

'As a governess for Paolo? Is that it? Is that what you want?'

She saw his face change, saw realisation dawn in the depths of his eyes, and knew that at last the truth had hit home.

'You heard?'

'Of course I heard. And I understood—well, some of it. I may not know very much Italian, so I have to admit that I was a bit fazed by—what was it—*bambin*—something.'

'*Bambinaia*,' Gio supplied, his tone as flat as his expression.

'But I'd have to be pretty thick not to make a guess at *governante*, wouldn't I, Gio? I think even someone with as little Italian as me could have a go at that one. It does mean governess, doesn't it? And I presume that the first one means nanny or something—a nanny for Paolo. An *English* nanny—that's what you were looking for, isn't it?'

She was relieved to see that at least Gio had the grace not to deny it. That he nodded in silent agreement.

'An English nanny for your son—and I fell into your lap at just the right moment. An English nanny for Paolo—an English bedmate for you—and if you were truly, truly lucky, an English mother for your next baby. What was the whole plan, Gio? Did you reckon on marrying me so that I'd do it all for free? So that you didn't even have to find a nanny's wages?'

'No.'

The blazing glare he turned on her would have quelled anyone else. But Terrie was beyond feeling any more pain. Impervious to his anger as a result of her own bitter fury.

'No,' she repeated, injecting every ounce of bite she

could into the words. 'No, of course not. Because you see, *caro mio* Gio, your plan failed. I'm not going to be used as just a nanny for Paolo. And I'm not going to be just a bedmate for you. And, as I've already said, I'm—'

'You're not leaving.'

'Oh, but I am...'

She tried to reach for the wardrobe door to open it again, but Gio moved too quickly for her, ramming his foot hard up against it so that it was impossible to move.

'No you're not! I won't let you! I won't let this happen!'

'You can't stop me!'

'I'll try everything I can. And I warn you I can play dirty if I have to...'

Oh, why wouldn't he give in? Terrie was weakening, reaching the end of her emotional strength. She didn't know how much longer she could keep up this fight.

'Gio—*please*! Don't do this to me! You can't force me to stay. I'm begging you to let me go!'

The change in his face was shocking. All the anger, the furious resistance leeched from it in a rush, leaving him looking dreadfully pale and drained.

'All right,' he said slowly. 'If that's what you want.'

It was the exact opposite of what she wanted but, with the situation as it was, there was nothing else she could do. She couldn't stay here, loving him, and knowing that he had only ever wanted to use her all the time. 'Don't ask me to give you anything more than I can manage,' he had said last night, and now she knew why. He had nothing to give her, emotionally. Nothing at all.

'But I hope you're prepared.'

Terrie had been picking up the dresses he had tossed on the bed, planning on folding them, putting them in her case, but his words froze her hands. Turning, she looked at him frowningly, bruised eyes puzzled and unsure.

'Prepared for what?'

'For the fact that I will be phoning you every single night, without fail.'

'Phoning? But Gio—*why*?'

Gio rubbed the back of his hand across his eyes in a gesture that spoke strangely of exhaustion and defeat.

'Do you remember when I told you about Lucia—how I said that since she died I've never gone to sleep…?'

'Without wishing that you could tell her how much you loved her, just one more time,' Terrie supplied, wonderingly, when his voice cracked embarrassingly, preventing him from finishing the sentence. 'Yes. But I don't see what—'

'I'm *not* going to let it happen again,' Gio told her, his eyes burning into hers, his voice ringing with a harsh desperation. 'I'm not going to let another woman go out of my life and not say how I feel. If you go—if you insist on leaving, Teresa, *amata mia*—then I will do the only thing that I can. Even if you are thousands of miles away, I will have to speak to you. Have to tell you that I love you every night before I can sleep.'

'What?'

The dresses dropped from Terrie's hands and she sank down onto the bed, her legs suddenly unable to support her any more.

'You have to tell me that…'

'That I love you.'

It was low and deep and huskily sincere.

'Is that the truth?' Even though he had said it to her face, she still found it impossible to believe.

'Why else would I say it, *cara mia*?'

'Well—but you said to—to that woman…'

'To Rosa? Lucia's mother? Teresa, *carina*, you have to ignore anything I said to her. Do you truly think that I would tell her that I loved you before I even told you myself?'

'And it's *true*? I thought you would never love anyone the way you loved Lucia.'

'And I thought so too.'

Gio crouched down in front of her, taking both her hands in his, folding his strong fingers tightly over them.

'I thought that with Lucia I'd had my quota of happiness in my lifetime. After all, some people don't even get the ten years we had together. I never thought I'd be lucky enough to have it happen again.'

Lifting her hands to his mouth, he pressed a long, lingering kiss on them, and all the while his eyes locked with hers, never wavering, never hesitating for a second.

'And I thought that, because I'd loved once, if it ever did happen again it would be in exactly the same way as it had been with Lucia. I fell in love with her through liking her, and knowing that I wanted to be with her. With you it was—different.'

'How different?' The words came out jerkily, made uneven by the fast, heavy pounding of her heart.

Gio's smile was wry, slightly self-mocking.

'You knocked me off balance right from the start. I wanted you so badly, I was blind, deaf and dumb to anything else. And at first I felt guilty. I felt as if I'd betrayed Lucia by wanting another woman—as if I'd somehow been unfaithful to her.'

'I'm sure Lucia wouldn't mind. I know she'd want you to be happy.'

Gio nodded his proud, dark head slowly in agreement.

'And now I see that you're right. But I had to come to that in my own time. That's what last night was all about.

Being here, with you, being able talk about her, to share Lucia with you, it helped me to come to terms with my loss at long last. And it helped me to say goodbye to her and be ready to move on to the next stage of my life—with you…if you'll have me.'

'If I'll… Oh, Gio!'

Reaching forward, Terrie laced her hands in the jet silk of his hair, drawing his face towards her for her kiss. His mouth was so tender, so responsive, so giving that she felt tears burn at her eyes once more. But this time they were tears of the purest joy.

'But you didn't say. Even last night…'

'Even last night I was still too much of a coward. Even when I knew how much I wanted this, wanted you in my life, I didn't dare say.'

Gio sighed deeply, lifted a hand to touch her cheek with infinite gentleness.

'My own son is braver than I am. He had no hesitation in telling you that he loved you, while I did everything I could to avoid it.'

Terrie's smile of forgiveness was gentle, filled with understanding.

'He's only a child. He doesn't really understand the pain that love can bring.'

For a moment the shadows of the past clouded Gio's eyes, so that it hurt her to see them.

'I was afraid of that too,' he admitted. 'I'd lost my love once; I was terrified that it would happen again. Then I realised that by being too much of a coward to commit, I was actually creating the situation I was so afraid of. I was driving you to the point where if I didn't say what I felt then you would leave me, and I'd be back in exactly the hell I dreaded most.'

'But you'll never lose me now.'

'Are you sure?'

The intensity in his voice hit home straight to Terrie's heart like an arrow thudding into the gold.

'Are you really sure? Is that what you're saying? Because, *amata*, you…'

He broke off as realisation of what he was saying finally dawned on her, her eyes widening in shock.

'I haven't said it, have I? Oh, Gio—forgive me. Of course that's what I'm saying! I love you. I adore you. I want to spend my life with you.'

'And I you, my darling. I want to make love to you each and every night. To fall asleep in your arms, wake up and find you next to me every morning. And I promise you that each and every day of my life I will tell you how much I love you so that you need never, ever doubt it again.'

'And I'll tell you,' Terrie whispered, her mouth against his for the kiss she so desperately needed.

'We'll tell each other,' Gio vowed, and he took her lips with his to seal his promise for a lifetime.

THE ITALIAN'S MARRIAGE BARGAIN

by

Carol Marinelli

Carol Marinelli recently filled in a form where she was asked for her job title and was thrilled, after all these years, to be able to put down her answer as writer. Then it asked what Carol did for relaxation and after chewing her pen for a moment Carol put down the truth - writing. The third question asked – what are your hobbies? Well, not wanting to look obsessed or, worse still, boring, she crossed the fingers on her free hand and answered swimming and tennis, but, given that the chlorine in the pool does terrible things to her highlights and the closest she's got to a tennis racket in the last couple of years is watching the Australian Open – I'm sure you can guess the real answer!

Look out for Carol Marinelli's exciting new novel, *Italian Boss, Ruthless Revenge,* out in August 2008 from Mills & Boon® Modern™.

CHAPTER ONE

HE WAS beautiful.

Opening her eyes, trying to orientate herself to her surroundings, Felicity knew there should have been a million and one questions buzzing in her mind. Her hazel eyes slowly worked the room, searching for a landmark, a clue as to what exactly she was doing in this elegantly furnished room, in this vast bed and—perhaps more pointedly, as one heavy arm draped more tightly around her—the question should be begged, what on earth was she doing lying in Luca Santanno's arms?

Santanno.

Just thinking that name sent an icy shiver down her spine, a fierce surge of hatred for a man she'd never even met, a man who with one stroke of his expensive pen had changed her family's lives for ever.

But for an indulgent moment before sanity prevailed, before questions demanded answers and the inevitable world rushed in, Felicity gazed across the pillow at her bedfellow, allowing herself a stolen moment of appreciation, a decadent glimpse of a man so exquisitely featured, so picture-perfect it was hard to believe that someone so beautiful could cause so much pain.

Beautiful.

From the jet hair that fanned his chiselled face, the long lashes on full, heavy-lidded eyes, to the wide, sensual mouth, a splash of colour amidst the dark shadow of early-morning growth that dusted his strong, angular jaw, every part of him was exquisite.

An involuntary sigh so small it was barely there escaped Felicity's lips as her eyes worked the length of him. He was tall. His olive-skinned feet, that should be encased in smart Italian shoes to match the dark suit trousers he wore, hung precariously close to the bottom of the bed, and his legs seemed to go on for ever. Felicity's gaze avoided the bit in the middle and moved straight to the white cotton shirt he was wearing.

The dark mascara smudge marring the crisp cotton spoke for itself—she'd been crying.

Worse than that, she'd been crying in Luca's arms.

The realisation truly appalled her. She never cried—never! Never lowered her guard like that. Raking her mind she tried to think of one exception, but none was forthcoming. Even when Joseph had died she'd kept a lid on her grief, refusing to go down that awful path, refusing to let out her pain. Her mind reeled in horror and she mentally fought to slam the window closed, to stop the images not only of last night but of the last few years from flying in, to return to the safe haven she had found, lying in the semi darkness with only beauty on her mind.

But images were starting to flood in—snapshots she didn't want to see, pictures she would rather forget—and the pleasant awakening she had relished for such a brief moment was starting to disperse as cruel reality broke through.

'Good morning.' Even before he spoke Felicity knew his voice—heavily accented, the slow measured cadence making those two simple words strangely erotic. Dragging her attention upwards, she found herself staring directly into the bluest eyes she had ever seen, and she felt the heat of a blush spreading from her chest, up over her neck to her cheeks. She wished she had used those hazy moments earlier to fashion a response to the inevitable questions that would follow.

'Good morning.' Not the wittiest of answers, Felicity realised, and nowhere near as sexy with her mild Australian accent, but it was all the fog where her brain had once been could come up with. He was pulling his arm free from under her, stretching out lazily on the bed, not even bothering to smother a yawn that showed a long pink tongue and very white teeth, as relaxed and at ease with himself as if he woke up with strange women in his bed each and every morning.

He probably did, Felicity thought as those blue eyes landed on her again. With looks like that and... She glanced around the room again, just in case her eyes had been playing tricks, but they hadn't; the heavy mahogany furnishings, the crystalware, the vast golden drapes all reeked of wealth and confirmed the fact that the man who lay beside her could have any woman he wanted—any woman at all.

And for a shameful, terrifying moment Felicity realised she didn't even know if she'd already been added to what was undoubtedly a long list.

'I expect you would like some coffee?' He didn't wait for her response, just picked up the telephone, reciting in Italian what seemed an inordinately complicated order for a simple coffee. Only then did it dawn on Felicity that they were actually in a hotel.

And not just any hotel, if she remembered rightly. She was staying at one of Luca Santanno's luxury hotels.

The question was though, which one?

'We are still in Australia, I assume?' she asked as

he hung up the telephone. 'This isn't the nightmare of the century and I've woken up in Italy?'

He laughed, actually laughed, and to Felicity's surprise she found herself actually smiling back at him, strangely pleased at the response to her vague attempt at humour. 'Yes, Felice, we are still in Australia. Your mystery tour stops here. I spoke in Italian then because Rico, who I was just talking to, is from my home town in Moserallo. There are a lot of Italians on my staff.'

'To remind you of home?'

He laughed again. 'No, my family has a lot of friends and a lot of…' She waited as he paused, and the words that came out made Felicity smile even more. '…a lot of wild cats and dogs backpacking around the world, who all decide to look up Luca for a job.'

At least she was in the right country, but the room she and Matthew had was small—not that it had seemed so at the time, but compared to this…

Matthew!

With a whimper of horror Felicity pulled the counterpane tighter around her, waves of panic threatening to drown her as she began to realise the true horror of her situation.

'I asked for some iced water also,' Luca said, apparently oblivious to her sudden distress. 'I expect you are thirsty.'

That was the understatement of the millennium. Her mouth felt as if someone had emptied a vacuum bag inside it, but even that was small fry compared to the heavy throbbing in her head the small movement had caused.

'Thank you.' Felicity sat up gingerly, pulling the heavy counterpane up and around her, acutely aware that all she was dressed in was some very small panties and a rather sheer bra. 'Thank you,' Felicity said again, clearing her throat with a small cough and wishing her mind would work, throw her some clue, some tiny snippet as to what on earth she was doing here.

'Are you all right?' He sounded concerned, his forehead furrowing as he looked at her closely. The colour drained away from her flushed round face as she sat up, blonde hair starting to escape from the French coil that had held it last night, petite hands moving up to her temples, which she massaged slowly, screwing her eyelids closed tightly.

'Actually, no,' Felicity said, taking a very deep breath and then exhaling out through her full lips, wishing the wretched room would stop moving for a moment so she could gather her thoughts. 'In fact I don't feel very well at all.'

'I'm sure you don't.' The concern had gone from his voice, the sliver of sympathy she could have sworn she'd heard retracted so sharply Felicity opened her eyes abruptly.

'Look, I'm so sorry—' Felicity started, her mind racing, words spilling out of her mouth. 'I really don't know what's happened. I'm staying here with…' she hesitated, unsure what title to give Matthew '…my boyfriend; we were at the award ceremony…'

He was staring at her, one quizzical eyebrow raised, as she struggled to make an excuse and work out how the hell she could get out of here with even a shred of dignity, how she could get back to her and Matthew's room and, more importantly, what possible excuse she could come up with to stop Matthew finding out where she had been…

'I think I must have food poisoning, or the flu or

something. I must have made a mistake and wandered into the wrong room…' Her voice trailed off as his other eyebrow joined its partner in his hairline, and somewhere at about that point Felicity admitted defeat.

'I've got a hangover, haven't I?' she mumbled, completely unable to meet his eyes, pleating the counterpane with her fingers.

'I would suggest so.' He gave a very small nod and she was positive, as his lip twitched slightly, that he was laughing at her, enjoying her utter humiliation. Felicity decided she had had enough. Coiling the counterpane tightly around her, ignoring the million hammers pounding in her head, she stood up. There was no point wasting her time with excuses. Whatever had happened, whatever awful mess she had got into last night, sitting here watching him enjoying her utter misery wasn't going to solve anything.

'I have to go.' How Felicity wished she was one of those sophisticated women she had seen in the movies. How she wished she could manage a mystical smile and sashay off as she blew a kiss. But waking up in a strange man's bedroom—in any man's bedroom, come to that—was uncharted territory for her, and her usually confident demeanour, the slight air of aloofness she generally portrayed, didn't seem to be surfacing this morning.

Tears were threatening now, but Felicity blinked them away. Whatever had possessed her to weep in Luca's arms last night certainly wasn't about to be repeated—and, sniffing none too graciously, she cast her eyes around the room in an attempt to find her clothes.

Skimming the room, she located her shoes and bag and hobbled over. The counterpane—wrapped way too tightly to merit a graceful manoeuvre but Felicity was past caring. She had to get back to Matthew, had to hope to that he was somehow as hungover as her and miraculously would not notice her creeping in at the crack of dawn.

'If you're looking for your dress, Housekeeping will bring it up shortly.'

It was all too much. With a small sob of frustration Felicity lowered herself onto the edge of the bed, resting her head in her hands. Her carefully pinned hair finally collapsed under the strain and unravelled in a blonde curtain around her shoulders tumbling across her face, and for a moment she took refuge under the golden curtain. For a second or two she welcomed its temporary veil as she tried to fathom how she, Felicity Conlon, meticulously organised, completely in control, could have made such an utter mess of things.

Last night had been planned down to the minutest detail. She had attacked it in the same careful way she tackled any job that needed to be done—determinedly pushing emotion aside, looking at every angle, checking and rechecking details until she was sure she had every possible scenario covered.

Last night had been business.

'I didn't just wander in here, did I?' Felicity mumbled, undignified memories not just trickling now, but gushing in with horrible precision. 'You carried me.'

'I did.'

'You were going to sleep on the sofa,' Felicity ventured. 'I didn't want to go downstairs—'

'To be with your *boyfriend*,' Luca broke in, his lips curling somewhat around the word. 'Right again. So I agreed you could stay here, in my bed, and said that I would sleep on the sofa.'

That much made sense. She'd got the four corners

of last night's jigsaw now, and was working on the bottom line, but the rest of it still lay in a higgledy piggledy pile in her cluttered mind.

'So why did I...?' He registered her nervous swallow, the dusting of pink on her far too pale cheeks and fought back a smile. 'Why did I wake up in your arms? Why weren't you on the sofa?'

'You asked me to share the bed.' Luca's voice was slow and measured, every word a scorching indignity as she screwed her eyes more tightly closed. 'I refused at first. Naturally I was concerned, given your...' a small cough, another sting of shame '...given your inebriated state and your lack of attire.'

'But you came over anyway.' Her attempt to discredit him, to exert some control over this hopeless situation, was quickly and skilfully rebuffed.

'You were insistent,' he countered. 'Most insistent.'

'Oh.'

'In fact you became quite hysterical. Rather than slapping you on the cheek, I lay down with you.'

'Oh.' He was speaking the truth. Even if she'd doubted him for a moment, his words had set off a fresh cascade of memories. Luca begging her to be quiet; Luca pouring her water, standing like a protective parent and insisting she drank it; Luca pulling tissues out of a box, wiping away black mascara-laced tears... But through the murky depths of her despair a rather more disturbing image was taking shape. Luca taking her in his arms, holding her not gently, not tenderly, but firmly, clamping his arms around her, that beautiful methodical voice talking over her tears, on and on until...

Felicity took a shaky breath. She could almost feel the hand that had soothed her last night there on the back of her neck, working in small, ever-decreasing circles, massaging away the tension, the pain, working its way along her shoulders, soothing her as one might a child coming out of a nightmare.

But there had been nothing childlike about the response it had triggered, nothing innocent in the way her body had responded to the mastery of his touch. And, sitting there, dejected, embarrassed and utterly, utterly humiliated, Felicity knew there was one final question that really needed to be asked—one awful answer to complete her despair, one more nail to bang into the coffin before she made her way back to her own room and attempted to salvage something from the wreck that last night had turned out to be.

'Did we…?' Felicity swallowed, cleared her throat, looked him in the eye and squared her shoulders, ready to face the world—or, more importantly, her conscience. 'Did we do anything?'

'We talked,' Luca clipped. 'Or rather you talked and I listened.'

'I'm sorry if I bored you.' He didn't reciprocate her tight smile, made no attempt to elaborate further, and it was left to Felicity to pursue this most shameful line of conversation. 'So, if all we did was talk, how did I end up minus a dress?'

'When we first came back to the room I ordered some strong coffee. I was hoping it would sober you up. It might have worked had you not spilled it. Your dress is down with Housekeeping.' He put her out of her misery then, and if Felicity had looked up she'd have seen a surprisingly gentle smile soften his stern features. 'We didn't make love, if that's what is concerning you; though since you choose to bring up the subject…'

'I didn't,' Felicity argued, but of course Luca ignored her.

'Since you bring up the subject,' he repeated, his husky, deep voice halting her protests, 'had we made love, you most certainly wouldn't need to be reminded of the fact. When I make love to a woman I can assure you she has no trouble remembering the occasion!'

Shooting a glimpse from under her eyelashes, Felicity knew, as arrogant and presumptuous as his statement sounded, he was undoubtedly speaking the truth. There was nothing unforgettable about him—not a sliver of him could be labelled dispensable—and, however reluctantly, there and then Felicity had to admit that a night being made love to by a man as effortlessly sensual as Luca Santanno would be a night no woman could even pretend to forget.

'Thank you.'

'For what?'

Felicity swallowed hard. Still she couldn't bring herself to look at him. 'For not taking advantage.'

'Believe me, it wasn't difficult.'

Ouch!

'So we definitely didn't?' Felicity checked unnecessarily, her cheeks positively flaming now.

'We definitely didn't. I happen to prefer my women conscious.'

Felicity chose to ignore that particular little gem and, blinking a couple of times, felt what was suspiciously like relief start to flood her veins.

Things were still salvageable!

Okay, staying out all night wasn't going to go down particularly well with Matthew, and undoubtedly she'd have to omit to mention exactly whose bed she'd awoken in—after all, Luca was effectively Matthew's business partner—but the fact she hadn't slept with Luca offered at least a temporary reprieve. She would get her things and get the hell out, with hopefully no damage done.

Straightening her shoulders, she lifted her hair away from her eyes and flicked it back, forcing a tiny smile as she caught Luca still staring at her, even attempting to inject a flash of humour into this rather unusual situation.

'Whoops!'

He didn't smile back, just rolled over sideways, propping himself on his elbow, and resumed his blatant stare. 'Whoops?' he said in a very low, very sardonic drawl.

'I'm sorry,' Felicity ventured again, the watery voice now replaced by her more confident tones. 'You see, I don't normally drink—well, not spirits. The occasional glass of wine I enjoy…but as for spirits, well I don't even like the taste. I just had a couple for courage, you know.'

He shook his head and Felicity gave a small shrug. 'I'm sure someone like you doesn't need any help in the courage department.'

'I wasn't aware you had been drinking.' His words confused her, and she frowned as he continued, wondering if somewhere along the line she had misinterpreted him, if his English was really less fluent than it first appeared. 'Just how much did you have last night?'

'Two vodka and oranges.' Felicity pulled a face. 'And if this is what it does to me I'm glad that I don't normally drink. How could people do this for pleasure?' She was starting to ramble, the words spilling out from her mouth like a runaway train. She wished

Luca would smile, look away, shrug, even—anything rather than stare at her with that slightly quizzical superior look.

'You really think that two vodka and oranges could have that effect?' he asked finally, but when Felicity opened her mouth to speak Luca got there first, his eyes never leaving her face, watching every flicker of reaction as his words reached her. 'Do you still not realise that your drinks were being spiked?'

'You spiked my drinks?' Startled, she went to stand, but Luca let out a hiss of indignation, flicking one hand in a derisive Latin gesture and muttering something in Italian that Felicity assumed wasn't particularly complimentary, as realisation with the help of a few extremely hazy recollections, finally dawned. 'Matthew spiked them.'

The surge of anger that welled inside her didn't bode very well for the pounding drums in her head, and Felicity screwed her eyes closed as she grappled with this latest vile flaw in Matthew's personality.

Confirmation, if ever she needed it, of just how low Matthew would stoop to get what he wanted. The clanging gates of the prison door banged ever more loudly as she further realised the murky depths of his personality. Proof that the extreme lengths she was taking to curtail him were necessary.

Very necessary.

'My staff alerted me to what was going on,' Luca went on, but Felicity was only half listening—too busy concentrating on her awful predicament to concern herself with small details. 'You will remember I was actually sitting at the next table to you?'

'Mmm.' She gave a small shrug, a vague shake of her head, but as her blush came back for an encore

Felicity knew she wasn't fooling him. The earlier part of the evening was still fairly fresh in her mind, and six-foot-four of Latin good looks at the next table certainly hadn't gone unnoticed—even with a rather over-attentive Matthew at her side. The white-hot look that had passed between them when their eyes had met last night was scorched with aching clarity onto her mind, but she certainly wasn't about to inflate Luca's ego by admitting it.

'You ordered the non-alcoholic summer berry beverage that was on the menu; in fact you ordered three of them.'

'Yes, but like I said I had those wretched vodkas, and then there was wine with dinner…'

'Well, what you actually got was a questionable version of a strawberry daiquiri—and, more pointedly, three of them. Your partner made his way to the bar each time you ordered and told the bar staff you'd changed your mind. He also made very sure that he got a different member of staff each time, and it wasn't until he tried to change your order for the fourth time that one of the other staff overheard him.'

Felicity ran a hand through her hair, furious with Matthew, but more importantly furious with herself for not realising what was going on, for being so naive as to think that the illicit two drinks she'd partaken of earlier could have had such a huge effect. But her fury was starting to take a new direction now. It was all very well for Luca to take the high moral ground, all very well for him to dictate how his guests behaved, to dash in uninvited and play the proverbial knight in shining armour, but he didn't know the circumstances—Luca didn't realise just how significant last night had been for her and, more importantly, her father. She wished Luca had damned well stayed out of it and just let the night run its awful, inevitable course.

At least it would have been over and done with.

'I will be having a few stern words with Matthew this morning. If this is the type of behaviour he indulges in then perhaps he should look for other employment!'

A small groan escaped her lips. 'Please don't,' Felicity begged. It was essential Luca stayed out of it, imperative she persuaded him to leave well alone. 'He really didn't mean it. You know what Matthew can be like.'

'I have no idea what Matthew is like. How can I when I have met him two, maybe three times?' Luca shrugged dismissively but his features sharpened as he saw the question in Felicity's eyes. 'Has Matthew been saying any different?'

Oh, Matthew had been telling another story, all right. According to Matthew, he had a hotline to Luca—a hotline he was more than prepared to use if Felicity didn't toe the line. But that wasn't the issue here, Felicity realised. The issue here was damage control. She simply couldn't risk upsetting Matthew, couldn't risk her parents' stab at, if not eternal happiness, at least some semblance of peace.

Luca just had to believe her.

'Matthew and I—' Felicity started, her blush deepening with each awkward word. 'Well, we were going to…' Her eyes shot up, pleading for Luca to put a halt to this, to raise his hand and say that he didn't need details, that he'd got the message.

But Luca didn't. Instead he stood there haughtily, his lips firmly closed, looking right at her, her obvious discomfort at the subject not bothering him in the least.

Sinking her eyes to the ground, she settled for the less daunting sight of his feet as she mumbled what she hoped would be the conclusion to this embarrassing subject.

'We were going to get engaged...' Her voice was barely audible now, trailing off into a low whisper as she hopefully began to conclude this most difficult conversation. Casting a nervous glance up she saw the confusion in his eyes, listened as he took in a breath, opened his mouth to speak, then changed his mind midway and closed it again. 'That's why I needed a drink. I was nervous,' Felicity explained patiently.

But Luca, it would appear, was having trouble with his own jigsaw. Shaking his head, he opened his mouth again. Only this time the words that came out had none of his usual assured tones; instead he sounded utterly perplexed. 'Why would you be nervous? Why would you be so daunted by something so nice?'

'I just was.' Felicity shrugged. She certainly wasn't about to tell Luca the more personal details, tell him that Matthew had made his intentions very clear. There would be no more reluctant kisses on her doorstep, no more hiding behind her never ending excuses. Matthew was going to claim what he assumed was rightly his.

And there wasn't a single thing she could do about it.

Deciding she'd already said way too much, she stood up and attempted a haughty flick of her hair. 'Let's just leave it there, shall we? Could you please ring Housekeeping and have my dress sent up? I'd really like to get dressed.' She stood for what felt like a full minute, and when Luca made no attempt to reach for the telephone gave a shrug. 'Fine, it that's the way you want to play it then I'll do it myself.' Picking up the receiver, she ran a finger down the numbers before her, ignoring the holes being burnt into her bare shoulder as Luca blatantly stared. She didn't have to justify herself to him. If he wanted to go around playing the hero, he'd better just look for another damsel in distress.

'Okay, I can understand you might have been a little uptight,' Lucas conceded, resuming their discussion as if the most recent part of their conversation hadn't even taken place. Felicity hesitated momentarily, her hand poised over the number nine digit on the telephone. 'But why would Matthew want to get you drunk? What sort of a man would want to propose to a woman when she wouldn't even be able to remember it the next morning?'

She let out a low, hollow laugh, and Luca watched as her cream shoulders stiffened momentarily, her slender hand shaking slightly as it hovered over the telephone. He had to strain to catch the resigned and weary words, imaging those full lips pulled into a taut strained line. 'A determined one.'

The defeat in her voice, the utter exhaustion, stirred something within him. Suddenly his feelings towards Matthew, the so-called man who had annoyed him last night, shifted from distaste to disgust, from scorn to a black churning fury. But not a trace of it was betrayed in his voice. He realised that one misplaced word would have her back on the defensive, would have her marching out of his room and out of his life.

He didn't want her to go.

The realisation astounded him. Last night he had been concerned, as worried as he would have been at seeing any guest, any woman, being taken advantage of, being beguiled in such a way. But it was over now. He had done his moral duty, averted the problem. She was sober now, able to make her own calls. If she wanted her dress, wanted to go back to that snake's room, then why shouldn't she? What could it possibly matter to him what this woman did with her life?

But it did.

'You're not seriously considering going back to Matthew after what he did to you last night?'

'Look,' Felicity snapped, forcing a very standoffish smile as she turned briefly to face him. 'Thank you for your concern. As misguided as it was, I'm sure you meant well, but the truth is I knew what I was doing last night and I certainly didn't need your so-called help.'

'I beg to differ.'

Felicity's eyes widened, her eyebrows shooting up in surprise as his delicious Italian accent was replaced by a rather upper crust English accent.

'That is my London manager's favourite saying,' Luca responded, noting her surprise, but the momentary lapse in proceedings didn't last long. The onslaught continued in thick heavily accented tones that had Felicity scorching with shame right down to her toenails which she stared at in preference to the overbearing ogre that stood over her. 'The only sensible thing you did last night was to beg me for help. Me!' he shouted, cupping her chin with his fingers and forcing her eyes up to him. 'Perhaps you would like me to refresh your memory?'

'Perhaps not.' Felicity cringed, but her humour was entirely wasted on him.

'A colleague diverted Matthew's attention while I took you to one side and told you that your drinks were being spiked. You, Miss Conlon, promptly burst into tears and begged me to get rid of him, begged me for help, left me with no choice but to bring you up here.'

'You didn't have to do it, though!' Felicity interjected, brushing his hand away from her and facing him unaided now, but Luca hadn't finished yet.

'Believe me, I wish I hadn't bothered! Had there been a spare room in the hotel it would have been yours. Do you not think I had better things to do last night than play babysitter to you? Not only did I have a ballroom of guests to take care of, I had the press about to run a story— Damn!'

Without pausing for breath, without further explanation, he marched across the room, flinging open the door, and with her face paling Felicity realised she had pushed him too far, that he was going to throw her out—and what was more, Felicity acknowledged, she completely deserved it. Luca Santanno had behaved like a complete gentleman last night and she in turn had been an utter bitch. If she'd had a tail it would have been between her legs as she attempted to walk wrapped in the counterpane.

'Where are you going?' He didn't exactly haul her back in by the scruff of her neck, but it came pretty close. 'Where the hell do you think you are going?'

'Back to my room,' Felicity yelped. 'I thought you were asking me to leave.'

'I was getting the paper; I was attempting to show you why last night I had better things to do than play nursemaid.' Flicking through the paper, his face hardened, an expletive Felicity could only assume wasn't particularly nice flying from his lips as he hurled the offending paper across the room before redirecting his fury back to her. 'Is this the sort of man you deal with? Men who would throw you out into the corridor dressed in nothing but your underwear and a sheet? Is this how little you think of yourself?' Taking a couple of deep ragged breaths, he relaxed his clenched fists, the taut lines of his features softening, his words coming more softly now. 'Felice, this is surely no way to live?'

His fury she could almost handle—contempt too, come to that. After all, it was nothing she didn't feel about herself. But when his voice softened, the word Felice, almost an endearment, it brought her dangerously close to tears, dangerously close to breaking down. Her teeth were nearly breaking through her bottom lip in an attempt to hold it all in.

'I have to go,' she choked, utterly unable to meet his eyes. 'I'm going to ring Housekeeping to get my dress, borrow your bathroom for two minutes and then I'll be right out of here.'

Pushing the digit, she listened for the ring tone, ready to pounce when her call was answered and get her dress back so she could get the hell out of here, away from Luca and his endless questions. Her life was messy enough right now without this forced introspection.

But Luca hadn't finished yet. Hovering over her like some avenging angel, he held out his hand. 'Shouldn't an engagement be something special?' he asked as something that felt suspiciously like a tear slid down her cheek. 'Shouldn't the night a man proposes be a memory to treasure long into the future? Not some sordid affair, sullied with alcohol and regret?'

'You don't understand,' Felicity said through gritted teeth, wishing he would just stop, just leave her alone!

'I understand this much: if I had been about to propose to you then I would have been ensuring you were having a good time, treating you as a woman deserves to be treated, not sedating you with alcohol. Whatever the reason for last night, it cannot be a good one.'

His hand was on her shoulder now, but she didn't look at him. Reception had picked up, a voice somewhere in the distance was asking how she could help, but the only words she could really hear were Luca's. His words had reached her, and for a second so small it was barely there Felicity imagined herself in Luca's life, imagined being the lucky woman in his arms, imagined the bliss of being made love to by a man like that—those arms around her, that beautiful, expressive mouth exploring hers, his hands caressing her, that husky voice embalming her. The image of perfection only made last night seem even more sullied. The image of such wonder exacerbated the vileness of last night's potential union, and the truth she had chosen to ignore came to the fore as Luca spoke more eloquently than her own conscience.

'I understand you might not be...' He faltered for a second, trying to summon the right word, and Felicity sat rigid, her mind racing with indecision.

She knew she should get back, had to finish what she'd started, but there was something about Luca, something about the surprising gentleness in his voice, his insight, his abhorrence of Matthew's motives that held her there.

'...comfortable.' Now he had found the right word he spoke rapidly, determined to finish, to give her another option—anything rather than see her scuttling back to the excuse of a man downstairs. 'I can see that my presence is making you feel awkward, but that will soon be taken care off. I am due to catch a flight to Rome soon. I will ring Reception, tell them to collect your property and bring it here. They can tell this Matthew you have gone home—ill, perhaps, like you said before. This will give you some space, some time. Please Felice, I know I don't understand what has gone on, but surely you should think carefully before you go back to this man? Last night you were not just upset, you were distraught, and though I do not approve of Matthew's methods maybe he did you a favour.'

'How on earth did you work that one out?' She gave a low, cynical laugh, but it died on her lips as he carried on talking, as Luca once again summed up her innermost feelings in his own direct way.

'Last night you spoke the truth. Matthew's bed is not the place you want to be.'

And when he held out his hand again it only took a moment's hesitation before Felicity handed him the receiver, which he replaced in the cradle.

No matter the hell that followed, no matter the consequences, Luca was right.

Going back to Matthew simply wasn't an option.

CHAPTER TWO

A LOUD knocking at the door heralded breakfast, but, clearly used to staff, Luca carried on talking unfazed, while Felicity, in turn, sat huddled on the edge of the bed, scuffing the floor with her bare foot and burning with shame, appalled at what the waiter must surely be thinking and silently, fruitlessly wishing that Luca would put him right, tell him she wasn't yet another of his conquests, that his latest guest absolutely did not deserve to be the talk of the staffroom this morning, because, quite simply, nothing had happened.

Nothing had happened!

Of course Luca did no such thing. Instead he chattered away to Felicity as the table was laid, oblivious to her discomfort. 'Have something to eat,' he offered, but Felicity shook her head, determined not to accept anything from him. 'A coffee, at least? Or perhaps you would like a shower first?'

If he offered a shower again, if he really insisted, Felicity decided she'd accept; but when Luca merely cocked his head and awaited her reply she finally gave a small reluctant nod. Though it galled her to accept any crumbs from Luca Santanno, the chance of a shower was just too good to pass up.

He dismissed the waiter with a flick of his wrist.

True to form, Felicity thought bitterly; he was as dismissive as Matthew to his workers, but as the waiter left she blinked in surprise when Luca called out thanks in his thick accent, then turned the smile back to her.

'How about I make that call?' He gestured to the bathroom. 'There are robes and toiletries in there. Just help yourself and let me know if there is anything else you need.'

'I'll be fine.'

More than fine, Felicity thought, wandering into the bathroom, glimpsing the rows and rows of glass bottles that heralded a luxury suite—a rather far cry from her own toiletry bag, sitting forlornly in Matthew's room.

With a jolt she looked down at her watch, a mental alarm bell ringing to say that it was time to take her Pill. But with a flood of utter relief she knew at that moment her decision had been made; she didn't need to take the wretched thing, didn't need to worry about it any more.

Now she had finally acknowledged that she couldn't, *wouldn't* sleep with Matthew, the sense of relief was a revelation in itself—an affirmation of the strain she had been under, the turmoil behind the cool façade she'd so determinedly portrayed, the secret agony behind each and every smile.

Eyeing her reflection in the mirror—the wayward hair, the black panda eyes and swollen lids that just about summed up her life—she barely registered a soft knocking at the bathroom door.

'Felice, I'm sorry to disturb you.' Luca stood back as she pulled the door open an inch. 'I just need your surname. Reception want it for the computer.'

'Conlon.' She watched his eyebrows furrow slightly, his eyes narrowing as her surname registered.

'Conlon?' he repeated. 'Why do I know that name? It is familiar, yes?'

'Well, it is to me.' The thin smile didn't reach her eyes, and for the first time since their strange meeting

Luca Santanno didn't look quite the confident man she was rapidly becoming used to.

Snapping his fingers as he raked his mind, it finally registered. 'Richard Conlon?' Another snap of the fingers, another snippet of information. 'He owned the Peninsula Golf Resort.'

'Before you bought it for a pittance.' The acrimony in her voice made his frown deepen. 'I'm Richard Conlon's daughter,' Felicity explained, angry, rebuking eyes finally meeting his. 'I'm the one attempting to pick up the pieces after you destroyed him.'

Luca didn't need to snap his fingers now, details were coming in unaided. The underpriced resort he'd bought a year or so ago, the niggling guilt he'd chosen to ignore at kicking a man when he was down. Okay, Richard Conlon had brought it on himself, though he couldn't remember all the details his new manager Matthew had given him. Gambling, or drinking, or a combination of both? But whatever had caused his hellish debts, whatever had forced his ruin, it had never sat quite right with Luca, and now, as he looked into the face of his predecessor's daughter, the niggling guilt suddenly multiplied.

'It was a business deal,' Luca said, but his voice wasn't quite so assured.

'Sure,' Felicity snapped.

'I'm sorry for what happened, but it's hardly my fault. Your father was a poor businessman. He got himself—'

'My father,' Felicity flared, unbridled anger making her voice tremble as she met her enemy. 'My father was a wonderful businessman. He still is, come to that. The only reason the dump that the resort now is still survives is thanks to the hours my father puts in.'

'He still works there?' Luca answered his own question. 'That's right; I kept him on as a manager.'

'Assistant manager,' Felicity sneered. 'Second in charge to the wonderful Matthew. A man who runs the resort by fear. A man who pumps the profits into his own pockets instead of maintaining the place. A man living off the good will my father nurtured when he was the owner.'

'So why were you about to get engaged to him if he is so awful?' Luca demanded. 'Why did you walk in on his arm last night, half dressed and half drunk?'

His scorching words would under any other circumstances have hurt, would have lacerated her with shame, but in Felicity's present mood they barely touched the surface. Months of unvented fury finally came to the fore, her words so laced with venom she could barely get them out. 'Because your partner made it very clear that unless I slept with him, unless I came up with the goods, my father would be out of a job!'

'He is blackmailing you?'

'Yes.' Her word was sharp, definite—such a contrast to the question in his voice. 'Your partner is blackmailing me.'

'Partner? Matthew is not my partner.' An incredulous laugh was followed by a bewildered shake of his head, but it didn't last for long. Luca Santanno was obviously far more on the ball than Felicity had realized. His expression darkened, those blue eyes narrowing as he let out a long hiss. 'Is that what he has been saying?' When Felicity didn't answer immediately his voice became more demanding. 'Is that how this Matthew operates? How he exerts his authority? By letting the staff think he is the owner?'

'Co-owner,' Felicity corrected.

'Co-owner?' he blasted the word out of his mouth, like two pistol shots, and Felicity flinched with each one. 'He is not a co-owner. I am *the* owner! All the managers of my minor resorts have a five per cent holding; it is good for morale,' Luca explained his voice still angry. 'It ensures profit.'

'Ah, yes, profit.' Felicity found her voice, her hazel eyes flashing with distaste, meeting Luca's full on. 'There it is again! We're all very familiar with your love for that particular word.'

'Scusi?' For the first time Luca's English slipped, but he quickly corrected himself. 'What is that supposed to mean?'

'Profit,' Felicity sneered. There was no point holding back now, she was already in it up to her neck, but at least she could let this jumped-up, haughty, control freak know exactly what she thought of him and his methods—pay him back for the agony he had inflicted on her family. At least the final word in this whole sorry saga would be hers. 'That's the bottom line for you—and the top one, and the bit in the middle. Profit's why you pay your staff a pittance, why they have to stay behind night after night for no extra pay, why a beautiful resort is barely a shadow of what it used to be.'

'Barely a shadow?'

'Don't pretend you don't understand!' Felicity retorted. 'The resort is on its last legs—finished, kaput, *finito*. Now do you get it? Oh, I'm sure it's still returning a healthy *profit*. I'm sure on paper everything looks just fine. But the staff are leaving in droves and it's only a matter of time before the clients follow.'

The silence that followed was awful. Felicity reeled, scarcely able to believe she had admitted the truth, least of all to Luca, and Luca in turn paled, the muscles in his face contorting in fury, his knuckles white as he dug his nails into his palms.

'But what has all this to do with you? Why would you be …?'

'Prepared to get engaged to him?' Felicity finished as Luca's voice trailed off. 'You dare to ask why I would prostitute myself with a man like Matthew?' She watched him flinch at her words and she enjoyed it—enjoyed watching the might that was Luca Santanno squirm. 'Because I'm my father's daughter. I see what needs to be done and I do it.' When he didn't respond she carried on, her small chin jutting defiantly, a stricken dignity in her strained voice. 'My father isn't the poor businessman you make out; he isn't a gambler or a drinker who frittered his money away. My brother was dying…' A tiny pause, a flicker of shadow darkening the gold of her eyes, the only indicator of the depth of her pain. 'The money my father made from selling the resort bought Joseph some time.'

'How much time?'

'Six months. There was a treatment in America—it was never going to be a cure, but selling the resort turned a few agonising weeks into six precious months. It took him to Paris and Rome, gave us time to say all the things that needed to be said, to cram a lifetime of love into six wondrous months, and if he had his time over my father would do it all again.'

'I still don't understand.'

'Death puts things into perspective, but it doesn't stop the bills coming in.' She was almost shouting again. 'Your mortgage doesn't disappear just because in the scheme of things it doesn't really matter. My father has had to start again, now has to work for a pittance for the Santanno chain, has to watch his be-loved resort dissolve into nothing. But he doesn't complain. All my father wants is three more years of work. Three years to pay off his mortgage and get together some funds for his retirement—an honest day's work for an honest day's pay. But then what would the great Santanno empire know about that? All you care about is profit.'

'You are wrong.' Luca waved in abrupt dismissal. 'Yes, I care about profit, I am a businessman after all, but I also care about my staff, and in turn they reward me with absolute devotion. I do not need to check up on them, breathe down their necks while they work, for I know they are giving one hundred per cent.'

'They're giving one hundred percent,' Felicity snarled, 'because they're terrified of losing their jobs.'

'Rubbish.' If she'd seen him angry before then Luca was livid now, a muscle pounding in his cheek, his blue eyes blazing. 'My staff know I look after them. I ensure their birthdays are remembered, their loyalty is rewarded. Take Rico, the man I was speaking with this morning, it is his fortieth wedding anniversary next weekend. He will be staying in this very room with his wife, receiving the same service I demand for myself...'

'With a ten per cent staff discount,' Felicity bit back. 'Matthew reluctantly does the same.'

'There will be no discount,' Luca sneered. 'There will be no bill at all. Rico deserves it.'

For a moment she didn't respond, absorbing his words, his vehement denial confusing her. He certainly didn't sound like a man who mistreated his staff, didn't sound like the ogre she had envisaged. Her initial abhorrence was shifting. The layers of the onion peeled back were revealing a man far removed from the malicious man she had built up in her mind. But suspicion still abounded. The simple facts spoke for themselves—she had seen first-hand the devastation his leadership caused.

'This is Matthew's fault.' His voice was calmer now, but she could hear the hatred behind it, hear the venom behind each word. But his anger at Matthew brought only cold comfort; twelve months of pain were not eradicated that easily. 'I would never treat my staff like that.'

'But you have!' Livid eyes glared at him. 'Don't you understand, Luca, that you've done just that? Matthew may just be your partner—or manager, or co-owner, or whatever it is he calls himself—but it's your name on the headed paper, your signature on the cheques. You're the one destroying my father!'

'*Sei pazza!*' His expletive needed no translation. The hands that had been clenched grabbed at her wrists, pulling her towards him, but the fury she had unleashed didn't scare her, if anything it empowered her. She let her words sink in, gathered her shaking thoughts and took a deep cleansing breath before she continued, her voice calmer now, but still filled with unbridled hatred.

'Matthew has been blackmailing me.' She felt the hands around her wrists tighten, saw the fury burning in his eyes as she continued in low, steady tones, lacing each word with the contempt it deserved. 'He won't just sack my father; he'll destroy him in the process. He's made it very clear to me that he'll accuse my father of embezzlement if things don't go according to his sordid plans. He's already ruined my father's career, and now it would seem he's happy to trash my father's reputation if it will further his cause.'

'Which is?'

The hands weren't just tight around her wrists now, they were like two steel vices, and Felicity wriggled them free.

'Matthew considers it his divine right to have a pretty blonde wife on his arm.' She gave a wry smile. 'And if that sounds conceited I make no apology.'

'It is the truth,' he said simply, his mind temporarily leaving the devastating news she had just imparted and focusing instead on the attractive woman in front of him. 'You make it sound like a curse to be beautiful.'

'I never said I was beautiful,' Felicity corrected matter-of-factly. 'But, yes, looking like a fragile teenager can have its disadvantages, both on the professional and private front.' She stared at him boldly, her back rigid, her eyes defiant. 'Would you take me seriously in the boardroom, Mr Santanno?'

Her question clearly confused him, but he answered her promptly. 'I am not sexist. If your point was valid of course I would listen.'

He almost sounded as if he meant it, but Felicity tried and failed to bite back a scornful laugh.

'You contradict yourself, Felice.' Luca responded. 'You demand to be taken seriously, despite your stunning looks, while on the other hand you are prepared to get engaged to a man who wants you only for a trophy. It doesn't make sense.'

'I thought I could do it.' The scorn was gone from her voice. The directness of his observation was as loud as her own conscience. 'I really thought I could treat this arrangement as a business deal.'

'But in the end you couldn't go through with it.' It was a statement, not a question, but still she gave a tired nod.

'I'm not a romantic, Luca. I don't believe in the pot of gold at the end of the rainbow. I don't think there's a soul mate out there, waiting in the wings for me. Marrying Matthew wasn't saying goodbye to some long-held cherished dream; it was a means to an end, a solution to a problem.'

'For someone so young you have a very jaded view of marriage.' He shook his head in bemusement. 'What if he had wanted children? What if he—?'

'No!' She shook her head vehemently. 'I would never have given him a baby.'

'How can you be sure?' Luca demanded. 'How do you know he wouldn't have upped the stakes, demanded a child?'

'He could have demanded it till he was blue in the face, but that is the one thing I wouldn't have given him—whatever the cost to my father.'

'At least you thought that much through.' His eyes raked her face, searching for a clue in the chameleon pools of her eyes, for insight into this fickle personality.

'That's one thing that wasn't open to negotiation.' For an age her words hung in the air. Escaping his hungry eyes, she stared down, taking in the dark strong hands entwined around her slender wrists. She could almost hear the question in his unspoken words, the expectation in each rapid short breath as he waited for her to elaborate. 'I could never have had his child.' She turned to go, but still he held her.

'Tell me just one thing?' he asked, and as she reluctantly turned to face him he stared into those amber eyes, so wary and fierce. She reminded him of a stray kitten his mother had brought home, hissing and spitting, yet utterly adorable. 'How did you get to be so bitter, Felice?'

For a second she wavered, his harsh judgement searing through her. She wanted to scream at his injustice, to tell him he was wrong, but what possible purpose would that serve?

It was better that he thought her a hard-nosed madam, better just to walk away now.

'Years of practice. Now…' she gave a very thin, very strained smile '…if you'll let me have my wrist back, please, I'd like to have that shower.'

Oh, the bliss of the water as it slid over her body, washing away the caked on make up, the sticky lacquered hair. She allowed the tears she had held back so fiercely to slip unnoticed down her cheeks as she stood trembling under the jets, trying to fathom what she had done, the huge ramifications of the Pandora's box she had opened.

Wrapping herself in a soft white robe, she dragged a comb through her damp blonde hair. She was almost listless now, the unleashed emotions leaving her curiously drained. Staring in the mirror, she gazed at her reflection. The clear amber eyes stared back, for once unsure. The usually stiff upper lip was trembling as she attempted a mental plan of attack, a resolution to her problems.

She had really thought she could do it.

Really thought she could push emotion aside, ignore the awful implications of an empty engagement, do whatever it might take to buy her father some peace. But in the end she had failed him.

She pushed aside the internal ream of excuses that sprang to mind as forcibly as she pushed open the bathroom door.

There was no excuse.

Luca Santanno was right; it all came down to one simple truth: in the end she simply couldn't have gone through with it.

'I'm sorry.'

His words made her start, the sight of him pacing as she walked unannounced out of the bathroom unexpected.

'I am so very sorry for what has happened to you, to your family. I take full responsibility.'

He wasn't looking at her; the pacing had stopped now and he stood like a thundercloud, dark and brooding by the window.

'It's not your fault.' The admission surprised even Felicity. For a year now even the name Luca Santanno had caused her internal abhorrence, a fierce surge of hatred just on hearing it; yet now, standing before him, hearing his words, feeling his guilt, the tide suddenly turned and she knew her hatred had been misdirected.

'But it *is* my fault.' Dragging a deep breath in, he clenched his fists in a strange salute by his sides. 'You were right. It is my name on the notepaper; I am the one who writes the cheques.' His fists tightened more, if that were possible. 'And it is my name this Matthew has sullied. If the coffee is too cold, if the beds are not turned back, the pool too cool, it is *my* responsibility. Sure, I cannot be everywhere; I have to trust my senior staff. But when one of them…' He turned then, his eyes fixing on her; sincerity laced with anger, pride laced with shame 'For him to have treated you like this—' He thumped his chest, balled his fist against his heart. 'He is gone.' The clenched fist opened and he flicked the air dismissively. 'Gone. Dismiss him from your mind.'

'It's not quite that easy. Even if he's exaggerated, Matthew still has—'

'He is gone,' Luca said, with such precision, such a sense of finality Felicity almost believed him.

Almost.

Somewhere along the way she'd given up believing in people. Right here, right now, Luca was probably telling the truth, and Felicity didn't question it, didn't doubt that his apology was genuine, his outrage sincere, that he had every intention of following through. But in a few hours he would be back in Rome, back in his world, a world far removed from hers, and his intentions, however well meant at the time, would fade into insignificance.

She'd seen it all before—too many times.

Promises meant nothing.

'He's got a contract,' Felicity pointed out, her tone businesslike, addressing Luca as she would a client. 'There are unfair dismissal laws in place.'

'Would they have protected your father?' Luca responded quickly, quelling her argument with a stroke of his tongue. 'These are just minor details. My legal staff will take care of them.' He flicked his hand again. 'I promise you this, Felice…you will never have to see him again, never have to worry about that man forcing himself upon you, blackmailing you…'

'It's my father who is the concern here,' Felicity pointed out. 'I can take care of myself.'

'No, Felice, clearly you cannot.' He walked over to her, his eyes never leaving her face. 'Last night anything could have happened to you.'

'You're overreacting.' Her voice remained assured, but she felt rather than heard her conviction waver. Luca was right. Last night she had played a dangerous game, a stupid game, and her only saving grace had been the man who stood before her, the man who had rescued her. Her shift in feelings startled her, unnerved her, triggering a surge of adrenaline as she struggled with the impossibility of her emotions, praying for a voice of reason to descend.

She simply couldn't be attracted to Luca Santanno.

Surely it was a primitive response he had triggered? She was mistaking gratitude for lust. It took a supreme effort to keep her breathing even, to slow down her rapidly accelerating heart-rate as she urged sanity to prevail. It was gratitude she was feeling, nothing else, and it would serve her well to remember the fact. Clearing her throat, she forced conviction into her words. 'I knew what I was getting into.'

'Perhaps.' A muscle flickered in his cheek, but his voice remained soft—weary, even. 'What if it hadn't been my room you ended up in? What if another man…?' The muscle was flickering rapidly now, his mouth set in a grim line. 'What then?'

He searched her face, one hand moving up to her hair, stroking the soft blonde sheen, taking in the wide hazel eyes, so much softer without the sharp black kohl, the full rosebud mouth. The soft woman before him was such a contrast to the sophisticated beauty he had first laid eyes on, and it terrified him, truly terrified him what might have happened. The worst-case scenarios played over and over in his mind, kindling a surge of protectiveness, an immeasurable guilt for the pain he had caused.

'But nothing did happen.' Her voice was strangely high. She was trapped by his eyes, caught in the line of fire and, most surprisingly of all, with no desire to move. 'I ended up here with you.' A ghost of a smile trembled across her lips, but still she held his gaze. 'And you said yourself it wasn't difficult not to take advantage.'

'I lied.'

The simple admission hung in the air between them. He was moving closer now, his hand still on her hair, and the other one was working its way around her slender waist. She had every opportunity to move, every chance to step backwards, to brush away his hand, but instead she stood there, trapped by her own inquisitiveness, overawed and overwhelmed by the feelings he ignited. She could almost taste the thrill of sexual excitement in the air, the tingling awareness of her skin. Every tiny hair, every pore, every cell was saturated by his presence, thrilled and terrified at the same time as his deep voice washed over her.

'It took every ounce of restraint I could muster.'

It had. Closing his eyes for an instant, he remembered holding her, the bliss of her in his arms. He remembered comforting this delicious stranger, the protective feeling she had kindled, and later—when the crying had stopped, when she had curled herself up like a tiny kitten—feeling her hot breath on his hand, the swell of her breasts jutting against him, the tiny grumble as he had tried to move away, one infinitely smooth leg coiling over him, the scent of her, the feel of her. It had taken a super human effort just to lie there, not to respond to the subtle caress of her body. But now, seeing her without make-up, so young, so innocent, he felt the protective feelings that had smouldered, ignite now in a puff. The inevitable sexual awareness of a man and woman sharing a bed magnified. The groomed, sophisticated woman he had first encountered was gone, and in her place was a softer, gentler and infinitely more desirable version.

She could feel the heat of his palm radiating through her robe, pressing into the small of her back, and hazy, half-forgotten memories of the haven she had found last night emerged. The subliminal messages her body had unwittingly sent were more direct now. Her pink tongue bobbed out in a tiny flick to moisten her lips as her pupils dilated, partially eclipsing the golden rays of her amber stare, totality occurring seconds later as the force of his lips against hers obscured everything other than what was here and now.

He made her feel safe.

For the first time in so very long here was a man she could lean on, a man who maybe, just maybe, could make things better. Even if it was only transitory she welcomed the safe haven of his arms, the bliss of oblivion his touch generated. The chance to escape from the world for a while and concentrate on the responses he so easily triggered.

Responses Felicity hadn't known she was capable of.

As his cool tongue slipped between her softly parted lips, as their breath mingled, there was no question in her mind of holding back, no hope of restraint. She felt as if she were falling, freefalling, her body at the elements' mercy. But there was no fear, just a delicious feeling of abandonment, of freedom, of escape from the chains that had bound her for so long now. She kissed him back, her tongue moving with his, tasting him, and pressed her body against his as he scooped her up into his arms and carried her effortlessly across the room. She revelled in the strength of the arms that held her, the eyes that adored her.

At the bedside he paused momentarily, those sapphire eyes questioning, his voice thick with lust but laced with concern.

'You are sure?'

Reason almost stepped in then, sanity almost prevailing. She had never been intimate with a man, but her virginity wasn't borne of fear, nor some hidden desire to wait for the man of her dreams to come along. Relationships had taken a back seat to exams, to her brother's ill health, but now here she was, on the brink of discovery, and reason could go to hell. The need to feel him, to be adored by him, to be made love to by him, was overwhelming her. All she wanted was for Luca to lie her down on the bed they had shared, to make her feel every bit the woman she was, to instigate her into the pleasures of her body.

Oh, she was sure.

More sure than she had ever been in her life!

'Make love to me, Luca.'

The desire in her voice was all the confirmation Luca needed, and he laid her down, his breath coming in heavy gasps as her robe fell open, exposing her body. Her breasts spilled out from the soft white fabric and with a low murmur of approval he knelt over her, capturing one glorious swollen nipple in his lips, tracing the pink of the areola with his tongue as she tore at the buttons on his shirt, wrestled with the zipper of his trousers. She needed his skin against hers, to feel him, see him, all of him, and he registered her need, reluctantly leaving the soft sweetness of her breasts to free himself from the last remnants of his clothes. Turning his attention to her robe, he freed her from this final constraint so there were no barriers between them.

She held him in her hands, marvelling at the strength, and a tiny pocket of fear welled in her throat as he laid her back, slowly parting her legs. The weight of his body above hers was a precursor to the power of his erection. It would hurt, she knew it would hurt, yet she welcomed the pain, welcomed the sting of the first sharp thrust inside her, crying out as he moved deeper, wrapping her legs tightly around his waist, wanting more, more of him, for him to take her higher, deeper.

She could feel herself contract around him, a tight, intimate vice that held him, and the first ripples of her orgasm caught her unaware. The distant pulsing gained in momentum, a flush of heat surged up her breasts, stinging her cheeks, her neck, her ears, then rushed like a mass exodus to her groin. The flickering pulse was more insistent now, each throb a contraction that spasmed her body, feet arching, buttocks lifting. He slipped his hands underneath her, bucking into her, and she dragged him in, each contraction pulling him higher, further inside her, and as he let out a low, guttural groan her body instinctively knew how to respond, moving of its own accord now, drinking from him, sucking him dry, drawing every last precious drop from him, tightening around him as they rode the delicious waves together.

And after, as she lay in his arms, her hair spilling out across his chest, the tempest that had raged was calm. Her body was still tingling from its delicious awakening, and a sigh of contentment whispered from her lips as she revelled in a rare moment of peace and contentment.

Revelled in the solace she had found in his arms.

CHAPTER THREE

'WHAT are you smiling at?'

Closing her eyes for a decadent moment, she basked in the mastery of his touch, scarcely able to believe that one lazy hand gently brushing along the curve of her waist could render her so helpless. Lying beside him, it was easy to smile, easy to know that what had happened was good and right and perfect.

Such a relief to have no regrets.

'How do you know that I'm smiling?' she asked, her smile broadening as her words whispered along the soft ebony mat of his chest.

'I can feel it.'

He probably could, Felicity mused. She felt like an open book, lying in his arms, every page deliciously exposed. He seemed to know what she was thinking, feeling, needing, before she even knew it herself. Their lovemaking had been an utter revelation. Somehow he had known, instinctively *known* what her body unwittingly craved; every touch had been a masterpiece in itself, every delicious stroke an answer to an unvoiced prayer.

'So tell me,' Luca persisted, 'why are you smiling?'

'I can't believe that just an hour ago my one dread was that this had happened, that I might have slept with you, and just look at me now!'

'I am looking.' In one fluid motion he turned, gently flipping her onto her back, those expressive eyes making love to her all over again, scorching her as he dragged them the length of her body. 'No regrets?' he checked, his voice confident, only the tiniest movement of his Adam's apple indicating that her answer really mattered to him.

'Maybe later.' Felicity gave a small laugh. 'Maybe when I'm back at uni on Monday, or at my parents' for dinner tonight I'll have a major panic attack and scarcely be able to believe that I ended up in bed with you. But for the moment I'm just going to enjoy it.'

'You are a student?' She heard the gasp of surprise in his voice. 'Just how old are you?'

'I'm a mature student.' Felicity laughed at his discomfort. 'I know I might look young, but you don't have to worry about that. I'm actually an accountant.'

'Really?' A smile played on his lips and as he lowered his head just a touch, locating the hollow of her stomach with such precision, such skill Felicity found she was holding her breath, holding onto the bedhead for stability as he worked his way upwards. 'I thought accountants were supposed to be serious…'

'Boring, even,' Felicity said, the second word coming out on a gasp as his tongue found her nipples. 'It's a myth, but I'll admit to being serious. My career is important to me.'

'It sounds as if you take great pride in your work?'

'I do.' Felicity squeaked as his hand started to stroke the soft marshmallow of her thighs. 'That's why I'm studying at the moment.' She was trying to concentrate, trying somehow to explain to this wedge of hot flesh pressing against her that she was taking a year off to complete a Masters in Business Administration.

'Why would you bother?'

His question confused her, irritated her, even, and

she pushed his hand away, determined to answer him without distraction.

'Qualifications are important.'

Luca merely shrugged, his hand creeping on a steady march back, determined to finish what he had started, but Felicity was equally determined to have her say.

'Not everyone has the world handed to them on a silver plate, Luca. An MBA might seem irrelevant to you, but it's going to open up a whole new world for me.'

'Perhaps,' Luca conceded, dousing her indignation with one devilish smile, 'but the only world I want to open up is this one.'

His hand was more insistent now, pushing back her thighs he gently nibbled the pink swell of her nipple, flicking it masterfully with his tongue until the only Master Felicity wanted at that moment was one with a major in erogenous zones. But his arrogance still irked her, and this time when she pushed his hand away, when she struggled somewhat breathlessly to sit up, she meant business. The rather stunned look on his face didn't go unnoticed.

'You seem surprised?' Felicity quipped. 'No doubt you're not used to women halting proceedings during such a marvellous overture.'

'Felice…' A smile danced on the edge of his lips, and his body moved towards her to finish what he had started. But, seeing the determined set of her shoulders, the fire in those amber eyes, he thought better of it and instead raised his palms to the air in an insolent gesture of surrender.

'I'm sorry if what I was saying bored you.'

'It didn't,' Luca insisted. 'I can just think of better

things to be doing with our time than discussing your résumé.'

'But if I'd been a man no doubt you'd have paid more attention,' Felicity countered.

'Men don't offer the same distraction.'

'You're so sexist,' Felicity flared, but Luca merely laughed at her fury.

'Felice, you are lying in bed next to me naked; we have just made love. Now, if the fact I want to touch you, to taste you, to make love to you all over again renders me sexist, then I admit it—I am guilty as charged: Luca Santanno is a raging sexist.'

'Okay,' Felicity relented. 'Maybe my timing was a bit off; it's just that my work is important to me. Taking a year off to do my MBA wasn't an easy decision.'

'So why did you do it? Come on,' he insisted as she shot him a suspicious look. 'I really am interested.'

'Why?' she asked rudely. 'Why would you possibly care about my career?'

'I don't know.' The bemusement in his voice was genuine, and a frown crinkled his brow. Felicity found herself smiling as he carried on talking. 'I confess that diminutive talk is not a skill I nurture.'

It was Felicity frowning now—frowning and then smiling at his accent and choice of words.

'It's *small* talk, Luca,' she corrected. 'So, in other words, you generally roll over and pretend to be asleep?'

'Oh, I don't pretend.' Luca laughed. 'If eighteen-hour days have taught me anything, it is how to fall asleep at a second's notice.'

'But not this morning?' There was a slight hesitancy

in her voice, a questioning ring that both confused and excited her.

'Not this morning.' And this time when his hand reached and gently cupped her face she didn't push it away, just rested her cheek there, let him hold her in the palm of his hand as his deep voice washed over her. 'This morning I have no intention of sleeping, so tell me why you have taken a year off a job you clearly enjoy to study. Is your work sponsoring you?'

Felicity shook her head. 'Not financially. I've had to take out a loan to fund it.'

'That sounds expensive?'

'It is,' Felicity agreed, 'but it will be worth it in the long run. I could have done it part time, but this should fast track my career. Once I've finished my studies I'll be in line for a big promotion.'

'Which means more money?'

Felicity nodded. 'It would also have meant goodbye Matthew. You see, I never intended to stay married to him indefinitely. Just long enough to ensure I could take care of my parents—financially, at least.'

'Isn't it their job to take care of you?' Luca suggested gently, ignoring her sharp intake of breath and the fiery response in her eyes. 'Shouldn't it be the other way around? Did they know?' he asked softly. 'About Matthew, I mean? Did they know how much you hated him, the sacrifice you were prepared to make?'

'Of course not.' She shook her head fiercely, blindly, pushing the preposterous truth aside, but again Luca begged to differ. Cupping her face in his strong hands, he left her no choice but to look at him, no choice but to stare into those clear sapphire pools as he asked the question that for so long had haunted her, tapping into her Achilles' heel with such accuracy it had her reeling.

'They knew, Felice. Deep down they must have known.'

She bristled in his hands, bristled at such a cruel portrayal of her parents when there was more to them, so very much more to them. 'You don't understand—'

'No, I don't!' he responded arrogantly. 'I don't understand how they could have let this continue. The second I laid eyes on you last night I could tell that you were not happy. I could tell and I didn't even know you!' he rasped. 'Surely over the months they must have sensed your feelings? When I think of that lizard touching you, making love to you...' She could feel the hatred emanating from him, the anger behind each and every word, and she jumped in quickly, desperate to halt him, to redirect the fury away from the two people she loved most in the world.

'We never made love.' She saw the start of confusion in his eyes, and the hands that had been holding her dropped to his side as she continued. 'Last night would have been the first time—that's why I was so upset. So, you see, my parents really didn't know how much I loathed him.'

'But you were about to get engaged. He was going to propose. And you ask me to believe that you had never made love?'

'I'm not asking you to believe anything,' Felicity replied tartly. 'But it is the truth, Luca. That was how I kept him at arm's length. I told Matthew I wouldn't consider sleeping with a man unless I was engaged to him, and for a while it worked. I could cope with dating him—I didn't enjoy it, of course, but I just treated it as business.' She gave a tight smile. 'With absolutely no trace of pleasure.'

'But Matthew wanted more?' Luca checked slowly, and Felicity gave a resigned nod.

'He made it very clear that the dating game was over.'

'So last night wasn't just about getting engaged? It would have been the first time you'd slept with him…'

'Hence the two vodkas. I needed all the courage I could get!' Her vague attempt at humour passed without comment, and to her dismay she realised he looked far from convinced. He still believed her parents must somehow have known, have turned a blind eye to the appalling facts. 'Look, Luca, my parents really didn't have a clue what was going on. Matthew only made the threats to me, and it's not as if I've spent the past few months walking around in a state of nervous dread. Until last night I really thought I was in control, that I could deal with it, but when it came down to it I just couldn't go through with it. You were right to interfere. The truth is that I'm glad that you did. I may not be the world's most romantic person, but even I can see that losing…' Her voice trailed off as he stared, his eyes widening, a stunned, incredulous look paling the olive of his skin.

'Go on.' His voice was raw, and his hands were back now, but there was nothing similar to the gentle way he had cupped her face. His fingers bit into her, the tension in his body translating until he was practically shaking her, with an urgency in his eyes she had never seen.

'Luca, you're hurting me.' Her wail of protest, the tremble of fear in her voice reached him, and instantly he let her go, but his stance remained the same—blue eyes boring into her, every muscle in his body taut, his breath coming short and rapid, as if he had just finished a morning run. 'Are you telling me that last night wouldn't only have been your first time with Matthew, but your first time full stop? That you had never made love before? That you were a virgin?'

She almost laughed. A hysterical reaction, perhaps, but one that clearly wouldn't have gone down well with Luca in his volatile state. 'You make it sound as I've committed a crime!'

'You might not have, but I have!' Jumping off the bed, he swung around to face her and she reeled back, pulling the sheet around her, confusion drenching her as he gibbered on, fury making his accent more pronounced, tripping over the words in his haste to get them out. 'Where I come from it would be a crime for me to walk away from you now.'

'That's archaic,' Felicity shouted. 'This is the twenty-first century, Luca. You don't have to marry a woman just because you sleep with her. I would have thought you of all people would know that!'

'What is that supposed to mean?'

'Oh, come on, Luca. From the performance you put on this morning, even with my limited experience I'm quite sure that you haven't been saving yourself for marriage.'

'We're talking about you, Felice.'

'So it's different for men?' She gave a disbelieving laugh. 'I was right when I said you were a sexist. Don't worry, Luca, I don't expect you to follow up the morning's events with a proposal. My father's not going to ride up with a shotgun and shoot you at dawn.'

'Don't you see that this is something you should have shared? You should have told me,' he shouted, but his anger only riled her further.

'You make it sound as if I had some terrible disease,'

Felicity responded hotly. How dared he treat her like this? How dared he turn something so beautiful into something so sordid. 'You make it sound as if I've tricked you into you sleeping with me. For God's sake, Luca, you're overreacting!'

'No.' He shook his head firmly, proudly, even, as if she were the mad one! As if it was Felicity who had jumped off the bed in a furious rage for no apparent reason. 'I should have been told that you were…' His voice trailed off, as if he couldn't even bear to say the word, but Felicity had been quiet long enough, and she jumped out of the bed, facing his fury head-on.

'A virgin! You are allowed to say it, Luca.'

'Then why the hell didn't you? Why did you let me make love to you and not even think to tell me?' His lips sneered around each and every word as he practically spat them out. 'Did it not for one minute enter your head that I might want to know? When I lay you down on that bed, when I undressed you, kissed you, held you, did you not even think to tell me that this was your first time, that I was taking your, your…?' Angry fingers were clicking now, only abating when his word of choice finally made itself known. 'Your womanhood?'

Denial surged forth, but the truth beat her to it, and a nervous swallow drowned her lie as Felicity's solemn eyes met his. 'It did enter my head,' she admitted slowly.

'Then why didn't you say something?' he demanded 'Why didn't you tell me?'

'Because I didn't want you to stop.' The raw sincerity in her voice reached him, the painful honesty quelling some of his fury, and he stood there in defeated silence as she slowly continued. 'Luca, I wasn't tricking you. Yes, perhaps I should have told you that I'd never slept with anyone before, but the simple truth is that I didn't want you to stop, and maybe deep down I knew that if I told you you would have.'

For an age he stared at her, for an age he didn't answer, but when finally he spoke his words were gentler, the anger gone. The Luca she almost knew was back now—a touch sulkier, perhaps, definitely moodier, but infinitely more desirable.

'I wouldn't have stopped,' he said slowly, 'because I don't think I could have.' Sitting down on the edge of the bed, he ran a hand through his jet hair, then over his dark unshaven chin, and let out a long ravaged sigh.

'I wasn't trying to trap you,' Felicity said, tentatively joining him.

'I know,' Luca conceded.

'And I know I've got nothing to compare it with, but I'd say as far as first times go it was pretty amazing.'

'Even for a self-confessed unromantic?' Luca checked, a small smile softening his taut lips.

'Luca, I haven't been saving myself for marriage— well, not deliberately anyway. The line I spun Matthew was just that—a line. The truth is, between my studies and Joseph's ill health there really hasn't been much time for relationships. I can't believe I'm discussing this!' She swallowed hard as he turned to face her. Her anger had gone now, and all she felt was embarrassed and shy and utterly unable to look at him. Burying her scorching face in her hands, she kept them clamped there despite his efforts to prise them away. 'I'm so embarrassed.'

'But why?' he asked, perplexed. 'It is me who should be feeling shame.'

'I don't feel shame.' Behind her hands, she couldn't see him, and somehow away from his penetrating gaze it made things easier—easier to be honest, easier to say what she was really feeling. 'Embarrassment and shame are two different things, Luca. I'm embarrassed because…' Suddenly she felt like clicking her own fingers, attempting to summon a word, but instead she cringed as she forced herself to continue. 'I'm a twenty-six-year-old virgin.' She let out a wry laugh. 'Or at least until this morning I was.'

'And my overreaction to the news helped, I'm sure.'

A smile he couldn't see ghosted across her lips, and he saw her shoulders relax slightly, a tumble of blonde curls fall over her forehead, and chose that moment to gently prise her fingers away.

'Surely the very fact that you waited meant that you wanted to be sure, that you wanted it to be right…?'

'And it was.' Her eyes found his then, only this time she didn't jerk them away. What she had to say was too important to hide away from. 'Luca this morning was everything I could have dreamed of and more. Look at this—' she gestured at the room, the vast bed, the elegant surroundings, then her hand came back to his face, tracing his cheekbone with one long slender finger '—and look at you. You made me feel beautiful. You made me feel more like a woman than I've ever felt in my life. Our lovemaking was something I'm never going to forget and it's certainly not something I'm going to regret.'

An impish smile spread across her face. 'There is a down side to that, though. You've probably ruined my love-life for ever; I doubt anyone will ever match up to you, Luca. I'm probably destined to spend the next fifty years or so comparing everything to this one delicious morning and wondering why it doesn't measure up!'

He knew she was joking, knew she was just trying to lighten the mood, but his mind was working overtime. The knowledge that this gorgeous parcel of femininity, this warm, sweet body, was uncharted territory he alone had explored was almost more than he could comprehend. But hearing her speak of the future, imagining another man touching her, loving her, going where only he had been, fired something inside him, something black and churning. To a man who had everything it was so painfully unfamiliar it took a moment or two to register that the emotion assailing him now was jealousy.

'I cannot just walk away, Felice.'

'Then don't.' She was back in businesswoman mode now—back in control, back where she belonged. Pulling on the robe, she shot him a smile as she fastened the belt, flicking her hair from the collar till it tumbled in a golden curtain around her shoulders. 'If you really want to make this morning count all I ask is that you don't forget all about my father when you go back to Rome.'

'I will not let you down, Felice. I am a man of my word.'

'I hope so,' she said softly, heading for the phone again. 'This time I really am going, Luca—and if my dress isn't ready I'll go down and fetch it myself.'

'Why do you have to rush off?' Luca asked. 'Why can't you at least stay and have some breakfast?'

'Because, despite this morning's huge advances in becoming a woman of the world, I'm still a soft touch when it comes to goodbyes.' She flashed a smile but her eyes glittered with tears. 'No regrets, Luca. I really mean that.'

'So that's it?'

Felicity nodded. 'That's all it can be, Luca. You live in Rome, I live in Australia, and that's the smallest of the differences between us. Promising to keep in touch, to stay friends or whatever, would only cheapen things. We both know it isn't going to happen.'

'It could.' His voice was so assured, so positive, for a second or two she almost believed him.

'Let's not kid ourselves, Luca. Let's not make this any more difficult than it already is.' Her voice deliberately brightened. 'Who knows? Next year at the Santanno Hotel Awards it might be the Peninsula Golf Resort getting a plaque for "Most Improved Hotel" with my father on the stage receiving it.'

'Would you come?'

'I guess,' Felicity said thoughtfully. 'But then a year's a long time—who knows where we'll be then? I think some memories are best left, don't you? You get on with your fabulous life and I'll get on with mine. You might even read about me one day in the newspaper, when I make Accountant of the Year. One thing's for sure, though. I'll be reading the social pages with more than a passing interest now.'

She had said the wrong thing! The face that had been almost smiling suddenly darkened, and the mood plummeted around them; her almost dignified exit was disappearing at a rate of knots. 'What's wrong, Luca?'

'You just brought me back to the real world.' He gestured to the discarded pile of newspaper he had hurled across the room earlier. 'There will be a lot of fur flying this morning, and the trouble is I'm the pussycat.'

Felicity broke into peals of giggles. 'What's so funny?' he demanded.

'A pussycat isn't exactly how I'd describe you, Luca.'

'I hate this language.' His hands were back in the air now in a fiery Latin gesture. 'All these *stupidio* phrases you cannot elaborate on without making a fool of yourself. Where is the beauty in that?'

'You do very well, Luca.' Felicity attempted to soothe him but the laughter was still evident in her voice. 'So why's the fur flying this morning?'

'See for yourself.' Retrieving the newspaper, he handed it to her, then sat back down on the bed. After a moment's hesitation Felicity joined him, curiosity finally getting the better of her.

'Come on pussycat.' She giggled, peeling open the pages. 'One cup of coffee and then I'm out of here.'

Lying on his side, propping himself on his elbow, he watched her slowly turn the pages, smiling to himself at her little pink tongue, bobbing out as she forced herself to concentrate.

And it took one huge effort to concentrate! After all, arguably one of the world's most eligible bachelors lay a matter of inches away from her on the bed they had just shared, which made reading the paper just about the last thing Felicity wanted to be doing right now. Still, her interest was raised several hundred degrees as she hit the social pages.

The sight of Luca Santanno with a dark-haired, dark-eyed beauty on his arm shouldn't really have come as that much of a surprise, though. Since the day her father had come home, pale and shaking, and revealed the Santanno chain had made an offer on his property Luca's face had smiled at her from the newspapers, malicious and superior, the cat with the cream, but her hatred had gone now, and all Felicity felt as she stared was a curious surge of jealousy at the raven-headed beauty smiling seductively.

'I stand corrected.' Taking a nervous lick of her lips Felicity fought to keep her voice even. 'There I was, thinking you were only *arguably* one of the world's most eligible bachelors, but it says right here in black and white that you're in the top one hundred.'

'What else does it say?' His voice was gruff, and, shooting a look from under her eyelashes, she watched him wince as she spoke—even with the benefit of her hastily edited version.

'Oh, the usual sort of thing.' Felicity shrugged. 'A few choice words about your legendary playboy status, a couple of comments on your latest choice of date's impeccable fashion sense.'

'What else?' His words were like two pistol shots, the tension in the room rising as Felicity struggled to dilute the venom of the article.

'Not much.' She tried to keep her voice light, tried to sound impassive as she carried on talking. 'It just begs the question what were you doing in the arms of the newly married Anna Giordano while her husband is sick in Moserallo?'

'This is exactly what I was trying to prevent,' Luca hissed. 'My lawyers spent all of yesterday trying to prevent the paper running with this story.'

'Is this my fault?' Her voice caught in her throat. 'If you hadn't had to deal with me would you have been able to stop this?'

'That was my temper talking,' Luca said magnanimously. 'The first edition would have already hit the stands by then.'

She watched as he lay back on the bed, cupping his hands behind his head and giving an exaggerated sigh. Felicity wrestled her mind back to the article, trying to ignore the fact that even Luca's underarm hair managed to look sexy.

'The fact I blacked the photographer's eye after he took that picture probably didn't help my case. The best lawyers in the world can't stop the press when they've got the bit between their teeth—just ask the royal family.'

From anyone else his comment would have sounded conceited at worst, far-fetched at best, but there and then Felicity felt the gulf between them widen irretrievably.

Luca didn't just move in different circles; he inhabited a different world altogether.

Felicity deliberately didn't look up, not at all sure what he expected from her here. His hand had moved from behind his head now, and from the incessant drumming of his fingers on the bedside table Felicity knew he wasn't nearly as laid back as he appeared.

'Anna and I were lovers. In fact we were together for a couple of years. The papers didn't give a damn then, of course. She was Signorina Anna Ritonni then, so there really wasn't much for them to get excited about. Our mutual families were delighted, though, sure a wedding was just around the corner.' He watched for her reaction, but Felicity deliberately kept her face impassive.

'But there wasn't?'

'Not the one our families had in mind. Anna got married six months ago.'

'So it says here.' She made her voice light. The fact Luca Santanno hadn't held onto his virginity until

Felicity came along was hardly a shock—and what right did she have to make demands now over something that had taken place before they had even met? But even so her jealousy was curiously tinged with disappointment that a man like Luca, a man about whom she had only so very recently revised her opinion, would have run true to the form Felicity had previously predicted and committed adultery with his ex-lover.

'We didn't sleep together.' His voice was clear, his words measured, and the surge of relief that swept through her as she finally looked at him was inexplicable even to Felicity. 'And to avoid the confusion of earlier I will qualify that by adding "this time".' His dry humour didn't shift the tension an inch. 'Since Anna and Ricardo married I haven't slept with her—though not for the want of trying on Anna's part. The only problem is no one is going to believe me.'

'I believe you.' Felicity gave a small smile as Luca blinked in surprise. 'But why does this article matter to you so much? I hate to state the obvious, but you're in the papers every other week with some stunning woman on your arm; surely no one is going to bat an eyelid?'

'They will this time.' He let out a long, low sigh, one dark-skinned hand coming up and raking his short hair, then dragging over his unshaven chin before finally he spoke. 'As I said, we *were* lovers. Anna is my public relations manager—although—' he gave a tiny wry smile '—I think on these grounds I wouldn't have much problem dismissing her.'

'Careful.' Felicity wagged a playful finger across the bed. 'I think she might have a bit of a claim for sexual harassment there.'

He gave a low laugh, but then shook his head, and Felicity knew the time for joking was over. 'We are from the same village.'

'In Moserallo?'

Luca nodded. 'We both still base ourselves there. It's just a small village, but every time I go home I wonder how I ever left in the first place. It's nestled in the Italian Alps, and everywhere you look there's a view to die for, especially now, with the snow on the mountains.'

'It sounds wonderful.'

'It is.' Luca nodded. 'Of course the fact it's a three-hour drive to Rome means I don't get there often enough, and spend most of the week staying in one of my hotels. Though sometimes, if I'm feeling really homesick, I use a helicopter, which makes the journey almost manageable. No matter how luxurious the hotel, it can get too much. Sometimes it is nice to come home.'

'I can understand that.' Felicity shrugged. 'I can't imagine it, but I think I can understand it.'

He paused for a moment, those beautiful eyes narrowing as he looked at her thoughtfully, weighing up whether to go on or not. Felicity realised she was holding her breath, desperate to pass this imaginary test, to glean whatever she could about this difficult, complicated man.

'Anna was crazy about me,' Luca said, his words coming slowly, 'and I was crazy about her, but we didn't love each other. As much as she denies that, I know it to be true. Anna loved money, riches, the lifestyle. Not me.'

'Maybe she loved both,' Felicity said thoughtfully. 'The money and you?'

'No.' Luca shook his head firmly. 'A few months ago there were some financial problems—nothing huge, I had already foreseen them and taken care of things, but I didn't tell Anna that.'

'You were testing her?' Felicity, asked her eyes widening.

'Not at first.' He shook his head, but she could hear the hint of discomfort in his voice. 'I honestly didn't want to worry her, and as you have seen for yourself I don't really like discussing work when I am in bed. Still, she became more insistent, more…' Felicity waited, half smiling as again he snapped his fingers. 'More nervous. I realised she was worried I might lose my money, and even though it wasn't even a vague possibility I chose not to put her mind at rest, so, yes, I suppose in the end I was testing her.'

'I assume she failed.'

'She married Ricardo Giordano two weeks later. He is also from my town.' Luca's voice suddenly dropped and she saw his Adam's apple bob up and down a couple of times before he continued. 'Ricardo is also the closest thing I have to a father.'

Suddenly things seemed rather more sordid than complicated, and Felicity felt her mouth open slightly, her intention to remain impassive diminishing with every word.

'He is not in a relationship with my mother.' Luca grinned, realising in an instant the path her mind had taken. 'My own *papà* died when I was eight, and Ricardo has been the man I turn to for advice—I guess he is the father figure in my life. Apart from being a wonderful man, he is also exceptionally rich. He made his fortune in wine. Ricardo makes me look like a poor church mouse, which is why she married him.'

'You don't know that,' Felicity argued, though why she was defending Anna she had no idea—but given that she was tucked up in Luca's luxury suite maybe she could afford to be generous. 'Perhaps they just fell in love.'

'He is sixty years old.'

'Oh.'

'With a poor heart.'

'Oh.' Glancing down at the picture, Felicity shook her head. 'What a waste,' she said slowly. 'Poor Anna.'

'Hardly poor,' Luca pointed out, but Felicity shook her head more firmly.

'She is poor, Luca. Money can't buy happiness.'

'Anna thinks it can,' Luca argued. 'After all, it bought her a first-class ticket to Melbourne when her husband thought she was doing business at the Singapore hotel. She wanted to pick up where we left off, wanted us to still be lovers. I told her no, of course. I neither need nor want to sleep with another man's wife. The trouble is, this picture will be in the Italian papers now and any minute my mother will ring.'

'So tell her what you told me.'

Luca shook his head.

'It is not that simple.'

'Of course it is,' Felicity argued. 'If you really didn't sleep with her, your mother will know you are telling the truth.'

'My mother wouldn't mind if I was sleeping with her,' Luca responded, to Felicity's utter bemusement. 'My mother probably expects it! What will upset her is our lack of discretion.'

'Hold on a minute.' Felicity shook her head, sure she must have misheard. 'Your mother wouldn't mind you sleeping with a married woman?'

'Why would she? A lot of men have mistresses. It is our indiscretion she will not forgive. Shaming Ricardo so publicly—that is what is unforgivable. Even this so-called article—' he picked up the paper and tossed it across the room as Felicity sat there, blinking rapidly '—is better than the real truth. The fact that Anna cannot bear to be with Ricardo, does not want him near her and that still I rejected her, would bring the ultimate shame to all our families. Whatever way I look at it, it is a mess.'

'Goodness.' Nibbling the skin around her thumbnail, Felicity stared at the picture, scarcely able to believe that someone so beautiful could make such a mess of things. 'Is Anna worried?'

'She will be when she sees this,' Luca said darkly. 'I told her yesterday that she needs to respect her husband, her family. That it is definitely over between us.'

'And what did she say?'

'She agreed. She was embarrassed, a bit upset. And when I spoke to her, told her how I felt, she begged me not to let anyone find out. I think she finally realised she must work at her marriage.'

Felicity doubted that. Being rejected by Luca would hurt like hell. She had only spent one night in his arms and already she was out of her depth. To have known such perfection for two years and then have it snatched away—well, it defied rational thought.

Picking up the paper, Felicity stared at the picture once more. Anna's dark calculating eyes sent a shiver of mistrust through her.

Anna had more than saving her marriage on her mind.

'I tell you, when my mother reads this she will go crazy.' Luca's worried voice broke into her thoughts and Felicity smothered a smile. But it was too late for Luca's sharp eyes. 'What is so funny?' he demanded.

'You just don't seem like the sort of man who'd be worried about what his mother would think.'

'Why? Do you think a man can only be macho if he disregards the people he loves?' Luca snapped as Felicity swallowed her response. 'That I should not care if I shame my mother, if I disappoint her? These press don't know the hell they create. You are not the only one who cares about their parents, Felice. My mother is older now, she wants her son married, settled, yet she turns a blind eye, accepts I am not ready to settle down. But when she thinks I am sleeping with a family friend's wife and not even bothering to be discreet, then…' He stood up, and this time he did pull on a robe, tying the belt in fury. The incessant pacing started again as Felicity looked on. 'Then I hurt her.'

'It's night time in Italy.' Her small voice stopped him in his tracks. Swinging around, he shot her an incredulous look.

'What the hell has that got to do with it?'

'The papers won't be out yet. You've got a few hours to come up with something—something to tell your family.'

'I don't need a few hours.' The haughty face softened then, an almost apologetic smile brushing over lips. 'Because I already have a solution.'

'You do?' Smiling, Felicity sat straighter, perking up with interest. 'Well, why didn't you say so?'

He didn't answer, just walked over and sat down, one hand pulling hers across the bed, those dark blue eyes staring intently now. The bob of his Adam's apple as he cleared his throat made Felicity suddenly awash with the strangest sense of foreboding, the weirdest feeling that his solution wasn't a simple one.

'Anna and I could be just friends,' he started, and Felicity's eyes darted nervously. 'Perhaps if I had fallen head over heels in love, it wouldn't be out of the question for her to have flown over for a bit of feminine insight.'

'Insight?' Felicity squeaked, her mind working overtime, his calculated words coming too fast at her.

'Insight,' Luca repeated. 'I'm hopeless with jewellery, things like that, and with something as important as an engagement ring I'd want to get it right.'

Alarm bells weren't just ringing now, they were clanging. Her eyes widened as she shrank back on the bed, shaking her head wildly as Luca sweetened his words with the softest of smiles. 'Oh, no. Absolutely no.'

'But it would solve everything,' Luca said, his voice completely calm, as if he had suggested they pop out to the shops or perhaps call down for some cake. 'And in the meantime we could have some fun.'

'And exactly how long is this "fun" supposed to last?' Before the inevitable shrug had even left his shoulders Felicity broke in. 'It's a reasonable question, Luca.'

'You could do your studies by correspondence, see the world with me. We get on so well together.'

'We've only been together one night, and for most of that we were asleep!'

'At least you can read the newspaper in silence. Have you any idea what an impossible feat that is for some women?' A poor imitation of a female voice followed. '"Luca, wasn't last night special? Luca, what shall we do today? Luca, what would you like for dinner?''

A tiny laugh softened her strained features. 'That's called insecurity, Luca; they were probably trying to make sure there would be another night, that you were actually coming back.'

'I probably would have, if they'd just let me read in peace.'

'And I suppose that would be one of the rules?' Her voice was sharp, to the point, and Luca frowned as Felicity carried on talking. 'That I'd have to eat my breakfast in silence? That I mustn't ask about the master's plans for the day—'

'You are twisting my words,' Luca broke in. 'You are making me out as some sort of monster. I would treat you wonderfully—better than that *bastardo* Matthew. You would want for nothing.' He gave a devilish smile that had her insides doing somersaults. 'Particularly in bed.'

'I'd be a glorified mistress,' Felicity responded, distaste curling her lips, but Luca merely smiled.

'A mistress with a ring, though. Have you any idea the power that would wield? Have you any idea the doors that would open for you?'

'I don't want doors to open for me, I'm happy turning the handles myself, Luca.' She knew she had confused him, but Felicity was past caring, her mind focused instead on telling this spoilt playboy in no uncertain terms that for once in his life the answer was most definitely no! 'I don't mind working for a living. I don't mind staying up all night studying if I have to. I happen to like my life.'

'It didn't look that way last night.' Luca's voice stilled her outburst. 'In fact last night you'd have given just about anything to change it. And now you can,' he said simply. 'Marry me and I'll sign the resort back over to your father. Marry me and your parents will have the peace they crave.'

He paused, and for the first time Felicity didn't jump in to fill it. Instead she sat in stunned silence, scarcely able to fathom she was even considering this outrageous request, scarcely able to believe she was seriously contemplating it.

'Marry me,' he said softly.

'Is this because we slept together?' Felicity asked. 'Is this some misguided sense of honour…?'

'There is nothing misguided about honour,' Luca said smartly. 'I took your womanhood; it is right that I marry you.'

'It's archaic,' Felicity retorted, 'and it is also completely unnecessary.'

'Just think about it for a moment.' His voice was still soft, but there was a power she couldn't identify behind it, a note of absolute determination that told Felicity that the power Luca yielded wasn't just confined to the boardroom. For despite her initial abhorrence, despite the abundance of questions flooding her usually ordered mind, a flutter of excitement welled in the pit of her stomach. The prospect of lying next to Luca each night, seeing the world through his sophisticated eyes, holding him, adoring him, being made love to by him again and again…

'I'm not asking for forever here—just long enough to put things right, for both of us,' he added softly. 'You will save not only my family, but Ricardo too from being shamed. Now, that doesn't mean a thing to you and I understand that completely, but I would be indebted to you—I will make your father owner of the resort again; I'll get my lawyers on to it first thing on Monday. And as for honour…' He drew a deep, ragged breath, his eyes holding hers with a sincerity that reached for her soul. 'Call it archaic, call it what you will, but I cannot just walk away now…'

'But you will walk away one day, Luca,' Felicity pointed out, ignoring the icy fingers of fear that wrapped around her heart at the prospect. 'What does that do to your argument? Where's the honour in being divorced?'

'You will have slept only with one man,' Luca responded swiftly. 'And that man will have been your husband. I would say there's plenty of honour in that.'

He held her at arm's length then, his eyes searing her with their clarity. 'You would come into this marriage with no hidden threats, no secret agenda…' He was like a runaway train, gaining momentum with each and every forward motion. The germ of an idea that had emerged was taking shape, crystal-clear shape, and seeing her sitting on his bed, so cute, so utterly, utterly adorable, all Luca knew was that he couldn't let her go, couldn't let this blonde beauty walk out of the room and out of his life.

Nothing else mattered. Nothing else made any sense.

'There will be no false declarations of love, no babies clouding the issue, no promises of for ever— just a mutual respect and understanding. Felice, I will be strong for you. I *will* make this work.'

Suspicious eyes turned up to him then, but his strength, his quiet dignity were more of an aphrodisiac than the love he had so skilfully made.

Sensing weakness, he let a teasing smile creep over his face, and his low, sexy voice almost masked the humour behind his words. 'And I don't doubt for a second that I am far better in bed than Matthew would ever have been.'

Of all the pompous— The words were on the tip of her tongue, but so was Luca, his lips forcing hers apart, the hand that had been holding hers dragging her forward, into his arms and into his life—and every eloquent argument that had formed in her mind was reduced to a quivering mass of jelly as she landed on his lap.

Her gown fell open as his hands greedily claimed the rising swell of her breasts, the velvet steel of his erection parting the robe, nudging its way in uninvited but terribly, shamefully welcome. Her head flailed backwards as his lips moved down, blazing a trail over her neck, and his fingers worked their magic further down, causing her to cry out in reluctant ecstasy as he located the flickering swollen nub of her womanhood.

'Is that a yes?'

The genius of his lovemaking, the mastery of his touch awoke so much more than passion in her. Here was a man who made the terribly complicated straightforward all of sudden, propelled her into a stratosphere where rules didn't matter, where surely all could be conquered. She had always been passionate about Luca, however misdirected, and though the hate she had felt had shifted now, the passion remained; only this time it looked something suspiciously like love.

'Is that a yes?' he demanded again, his voice hoarse, his manhood swollen at her entrance, awaiting her answer.

She felt as if she were falling again, freefalling into dangerous, forbidden but decadently tempting territory, and she waited for her mental safety chute to open, for sanity to prevail, for her usually meticulous and ordered mind to register its protest, to tell her she was falling out of the frying pan into the fire.

Oh, but what a fire.

Luca was the man who could put things to right, the man who had saved her from herself, the man who could give her family the peace they deserved. And as she stared into his eyes the world seemed suddenly to make sense.

Luca held all the answers.

'Yes.'

The single word simultaneously excited and terrified her. Reeling from her boldness, she made a mental dash for the safety rope, for the back-up chute that must surely be there. But something in his eyes pulled her back, something in the way he held her kept her there, until all she cared about was here and now and not letting this moment end.

And as he thrust inside her, as she welcomed him shamelessly into her sweet oiled warmth, her words were a needless affirmation, her consent already irretrievably delivered.

'Yes, Luca, I'll marry you.'

CHAPTER FOUR

'HAVE a drink.' Luca smiled, his hand resting on Felicity's thigh as she gazed out of the window. A lump surely as big as the book she'd been pretending to read swelled in her throat as the plane lifted up into the sky, the dimmed cabin lights providing a welcome moment of privacy as she contemplated all she had left behind. 'I'm sure they can rustle up a couple of vodka and oranges—even a strawberry daiquiri…' His voice trailed off as the cabin lights flicked on, and he started in concern as he saw her stricken face. 'I was joking,' he said. 'Just trying to make you smile.'

'I know,' Felicity admitted, picking up a serviette to blow her nose and then changing her mind. Gone were the days of economy class and paper napkins. Settling for the heavy silk handkerchief Luca pressed into her hand, Felicity blew rather loudly. Luca's rather startled look caused a reluctant smile to shine through her pain. 'It's just hard, leaving them behind.'

'But you are not leaving your family behind. You can fly back tomorrow—next week if you choose. The world's a tiny place; you're only a day and night away.' His voice grew more solemn. 'I'm not going to keep you from your family, Felice. I know how important they are.' She nodded, but tears were too close to permit words, and the last thing she wanted to do was cry in front of Luca again.

'As soon as I am back at work I will speak with my

lawyers and arrange for the resort to be transferred back to your father. It might take a while, though.'

Felicity looked up sharply. Eternally suspicious, she narrowed her eyes as Luca, for the first time since their meeting, seemed to be stalling for time. But Luca moved quickly to reassure her.

'You know what lawyers can be like. Nothing happens quickly these days. Surely you know my intentions are true? I have given you my word.'

But was his word enough? She had nothing in writing, just pillow talk and promises. How would that stand up in a court of law?

A shrill, mirthless laugh rang out in her mind.

What court of law?

Her tiny nail scissors weren't up to Luca's red tape.

'That's not all that's upsetting you, is it?'

Felicity shrug was non-committal, as his voice dragged her out of her introspection. 'Isn't the fact I'm effectively emigrating enough to be going on with?'

'I guess,' Luca said gently. The hand that had been resting on her thigh was still there, but, turning to face her, he softly located her lashes with his free hand, his thumb brushing away a salty tear that hovered there. 'Are you remembering your brother Joseph and when you came to Rome with him?'

How did he know? How could he have known? The agony of his words was a small price to pay for the reward of his insight, but still she held back, quelled her pain and forced a tight smile. 'It's silly even comparing it; it's nothing like back then.'

'Why do you always do that?' Luca asked, his voice serious, eyes questioning. 'Why do you always push me away?'

'I'm not.' Felicity shook her head firmly, willing him

to change the subject. It was a bone of contention between them lately. Luca, now he had a ring on her
finger, assumed he should be privy to her innermost
thoughts, but Felicity consistently refused to go there.

Her innermost thoughts were not really up to an open
inspection from Luca.

'You never let me in—never let me know what goes
on in that ordered mind of yours,' Luca pushed.
'You're so damned independent. You never let me
know what you are really thinking.'

'I'm not holding back from you,' Felicity said
firmly. 'Believe me, there's really nothing very exciting
going on in there.' Tapping the side of her head, she
gave a tight shrug, picking up the menu the steward
had handed her and pretending to read. She tried to
immerse herself in the delicious delicacies on offer but
it was all to no avail when the only delicacy she craved
sat not a breath away. 'It's just hard saying goodbye
to my family…'

'Am I not your family now?' Still his hand was on
her cheek, hot and warm and infinitely strong. 'Can't
I make you happy?'

Oh, how she wanted to lean against him, to bury her
head in that strong, strong shoulder.

How badly she wanted to believe him.

But how could she?

Every push for information, every attempt to ration-
alise things, to draw up some sort of guideline, a blue-
print for their marriage, had been rebuked with a familiar flick of his wrist. Every attempt to work out
where she stood shrugged off.

'Details?' Luca would say. 'I'll take care of all that.
Just enjoy now.'

But now wasn't enough. A taste of paradise had left her hungry for more.

The questions were becoming more insistent now. Oh, Luca had been true to his word—since the night of the awards she hadn't even laid eyes on Matthew, just heard the excited chatter of the hotel staff about his undignified exit, and even though it was what she had wanted, secretly dreamed of, still it unnerved her.

Matthew had had a contract, shares, a token holding in the company—yet it had proved nothing against the might of Luca.

What did she have?

She glanced down at the massive diamond of her ring, glinting back at her, soothing her momentarily, distracting her from the impossible conundrums that taunted her mind. For all Luca's supposed poor taste, the ring he had chosen for her was just exquisite, a massive single pear-shaped diamond set high on a claw setting. The simple fine gold wedding band was almost obliterated by the sparkle of the stone.

Surely it counted for something?

'Talk to me, Felice,' Luca grumbled. 'I hate flying.'

'I'm tired, Luca.' Felicity sighed, resting back in her seat and closing her eyes, desperate for two minutes' peace, for a chance to gather her thoughts into some semblance of a shape, to wade through the mass of emotions that seemed to be suffocating her.

Being married to Luca was exhausting.

Wonderful, exciting, exhilarating—yes.

But still exhausting.

Life with Luca was a constant rollercoaster ride, his volatile nature unreadable at times, but Felicity was slowly working it out. Sulking moods culminated in huge rows which invariably ended up in bed. He simply couldn't comprehend that Felicity might actually like her own company now and then, might need ten minutes in the bath without him joining her, might want to read a book without discussing the entire plot along the way.

It was like living with a spoilt two-year-old, Felicity thought with a surge of spite that surprised even herself. Yes, like trying to cope with a spoilt two-year-old *and* a demanding newborn, if you factored in his rather impressive manhood, that awoke at all hours waiting for attention and very loudly making it known that until it was satisfied no one in the room was going to get any sleep!

Her spite was short-lived. As his hand lazily stroked her thigh it took all the restraint she could muster to hold her relaxed pose, to quell the bubbling cauldron of emotions that Luca so easily aroused.

Luca wanted no more than she did.

She didn't want her own company right now, didn't want to lie in the bath alone when Luca was just a room away—and what was the point of reading when Luca was the book she lived by, when he was her beginning, middle and end?

'You've never told me what happened to Joseph.'

Flicking her eyes open, Felicity let out a weary sigh and again focused her attention on the menu. But when he took it out of her hands she realised Luca wasn't going to be brushed off. He carried on with this most painful subject. 'It would seem to be a no go area with your father?'

Felicity nodded. 'He gets upset if we talk about it. He says talking won't bring him back.'

'Talking is good,' Luca said gently. 'Why don't you try?'

Automatically she went to shake her head, to retrieve her menu and dismiss his offer. But when she briefly looked up the eyes that met hers were so steeped in concern, so infinitely understanding, her dismissal died on her lips. Despite her initial annoyance, deep down she was grateful. Grateful for Luca's insight, for his persistence.

Grateful to have someone to lean on, however fleetingly.

'He died in Rome.' The silence that followed wasn't uncomfortable and, Luca held her hand as she struggled to find words to sum up the most difficult part of her life. 'Joseph had a melanoma.' She registered his frown. 'A form of skin cancer. He'd had it for a while, but things seemed to be going well—the doctors said he was in remission, said that he was over the worst. They were wrong.'

She swallowed hard, taking a moment to sip her water before carrying on. 'There really wasn't much they could do for him. We tried everywhere, but each time the answer was the same: enjoy what time he's got. Then I found out about this treatment in America—but, like I said, it was never about curing him.'

'This is why your father sold the resort?'

Felicity nodded, but, registering the guilt flickering across his face, she knew more needed to be said. 'You weren't to know, Luca,' she said softly.

'Maybe, but the truth is it never felt right. When it came on the market Matthew brought it to my attention. He was an assistant manager at my Melbourne hotel, and when he first suggested I look at it I had this idea that business clients who were staying for a few weeks in Australia could go there at weekends—have a bit of a break from a formal hotel, take in some golf and tennis. It was just a germ of an idea, I wasn't even really sure I wanted to take on the resort, so I put in a ridiculously low offer—expecting, of course, some negotiation—but when my first offer was accepted, naturally I went ahead.'

'It was business.' There was no bitterness in her voice now, just a weary acceptance of the facts. 'Dad should have held out for more, but he was desperate to free up some money. It had been on the market for months without a single offer.'

'If only I'd known.'

Felicity shook her head. 'You're a businessman, Luca, not a charity. You did nothing wrong—I can see that now.' She was speaking the truth. The benefit of hindsight, hearing Luca's take on things, watching the way he ran his business, had cleared up so many of her misgivings. 'Anyway, Joseph went to America with his girlfriend and had the treatment, and when he came back we barely recognised him.'

'He was worse?'

'Oh, no.' He watched a smile break over her face like the morning sun rising above the mountains in his beloved village, and he found himself smiling back as she spoke. 'It was like getting him back. He went to America so weak and ill, a shadow of the man we all loved, but when he came back... Oh, Luca, he'd put on weight and he had this energy, this vitality, this thirst for life. It was so wonderful to see. Dad was right to sell; it was worth every last cent to get Joseph back for a while. He used every moment, lived each day as if it was his last. Kate, his girlfriend, took him to Paris...'

He watched the smile fade from her face and ached to put his arms around her, to somehow shield her from the pain to come. But a deeper instinct told him to wait and he sat quietly, holding her hand as she told her story and the plane sliced through the night sky, trapped in their own time capsule, happy to escape from the world awhile.

'Kate had to get back to work. It was supposed to be a short holiday, but Joseph got it into his head he wanted to see Rome. He was very artistic.'

'Are you?'

Felicity gave a soft laugh. 'Not in the slightest. I wish I was, but even with the best will in the world "artistic" isn't a word that would describe me.'

'Doesn't matter. Perhaps you're more…' Smiling, he shook his head, willing the word that would describe her to come to him. But somewhere high over the hot red earth of central Australia everything stilled for a second, and the low hum of the engines was the only sound as he realised his lack of eloquence had nothing to do with the language barrier that sometimes thwarted him, and everything to do with Felicity. Nothing about her could be summed up in a single word; nothing about her could be relegated to a single sentence.

'You're just you,' he finished lamely. 'So—you came to Roma with Joseph?'

Felicity nodded. 'It was wonderful. We visited the galleries, the Colosseum, the Vatican.' Her eyes shone as she spoke. 'We sat out on the pavements drinking coffee…'

Luca gave a tight smile. 'It might be a bit cold for that at the moment. What else did you do?'

'All the touristy things—ate gelato, threw coins in the Trevi Fountain.' Her smile faded, pain clouding her eyes as she carried on talking. 'Joseph wouldn't throw one in. Our guide said that if you throw in a coin…'

'You will return to the eternal city,' Luca finished softly.

'Joseph said it was a wasted wish.'

'But you obviously did?' Luca smiled.

'I threw in three. The guide said, "One to return, two to marry an Italian…"' A blush crept up her cheeks and she shook her head in bewilderment, the innocent gesture taking on an entirely new slant now. '"Three to live happily ever after."'

Luca gave a low laugh. 'There are many different versions of the legend. The one my mother always told us was "one to return, two to marry, three for a divorce."'

He always did that, Felicity thought with a pang of clarity. Every step forward that they took together Luca instantly depleted with two rapid steps back. Every glimmer of intimacy was shrouded by their inevitable departure—almost as if he'd changed his mind midway, as if suddenly she bored him.

'What happened then?'

She dragged her mind back, forced herself to the conversation, but the see-saw of emotions he provoked was too much for her now, his thoughtless comments, his deliberate withdrawal shattering any bridges they might have built.

'He died, Luca.' Retrieving the menu, she ran her eyes down it, painfully aware of his bemused eyes scorching into her cheeks. 'That's all you need to know.'

'Once we get there you will feel better.' His attempt to comfort her had an almost patronising ring, and Felicity bit back a smart reply as he carried on assuredly. 'When we arrive in Rome my driver will collect us and take us to my village. Everyone is very excited to meet you.'

'You've got two sisters and two brothers?' Felicity checked, glad of the change of subject and doing a quick mental calculation to work out the size of the entourage that would surely greet them.

'And their children, of course. And then there will be my cousins and aunts and uncles.' He managed a nervous swallow before continuing. 'And I think my mother has invited a few family friends.'

'Anna?'

Luca nodded. 'With Ricardo.'

'Not exactly an intimate dinner party, then?'

'Not exactly,' Luca conceded. 'But we won't have to stay too long. Once we have had a few drinks and said hello I will take you to our home.'

Our home.

He made it sound so simple, as if they really were two normal newlyweds crossing the threshold of their new lives together, sharing a home, dreams, aspirations.

'I'm looking forward to that,' Felicity admitted. 'Maybe once we're there it will seem more real. The hotel was nice and everything, but it will be lovely to finally be just the two of us. I can't believe I'm actually looking forward to doing housework again!'

'*Scusi?*' Luca gave her a horrified look. 'You won't have to lift a finger. There are staff to take care of all that.'

Sinking back in her seat, Felicity let out a low sigh. She was sick of staff—sick of being taken care of. She wanted Luca to herself, wanted time alone with the man she loved.

Loved.

How easily the word popped into her mind, but how terrifying the consequences.

She had loved him from the moment she met him, had recited her vows with an honesty that petrified her, but Luca didn't want her love. Luca wanted a temporary solution, with honour the only vow they had privately agreed to keep. Luca wanted a wife he could eventually discard with ease, and love simply didn't factor into their marriage.

That secret was hers to keep.

'Rosa might be a bit of a problem.' Luca broke into her tortured thoughts and gave a half-laugh, more to himself than to Felicity. 'She is my housekeeper; she has been in the family years. She always gives...' His voice trailed off and he looked uncomfortable as Felicity finished his sentence for him.

'Your girlfriends a hard time? You can say it, Luca, I know full well I'm not the first woman to share your bed.'

'I'm sorry,' he mumbled. 'Anyway, she'll come around in the end. Although tact isn't her strong point. If you think I put my foot in it often, just wait till you meet Rosa.' He winced slightly as he looked over. 'She'll probably call you Anna. She won't mean it, it's just that she gets mixed up. She's getting older.'

'I get the picture, Luca.' Felicity sighed. 'This isn't going to be as easy as I thought.'

'Nonsense,' Luca said quickly. 'Felice you will be wonderful—they are all going to love you!'

'I don't even speak Italian,' Felicity pointed out unnecessarily. 'And you've told me that hardly anyone speaks English.'

'Anna and Ricardo do.' Luca's attempt to soothe her didn't fare particularly well, and the involuntary look she shot at him had even Luca shrinking back in his seat a touch.

'Surely you can manage a few words of Italian by now?' Luca nudged her. 'You must have picked up some in our two weeks together.'

'A few, I guess.' Her lips twisted into a devilish smile. 'But I'm sure they shouldn't be repeated.'

He actually blushed. Leaning over, he whispered into her ear, his hot breath causing a shiver to ripple through her. 'That, *bella*, is for your ears only.'

'I hope so.' The words were out before she could stop them; she watched him frown, heard his intake of breath and wished she could take them back.

'What is that supposed to mean?'

'Nothing.' Felicity shrugged, keeping her voice deliberately light. 'Anyway, the only two Italian words I really know are *caffè* and *latte*, which is exactly what I fancy right now!' Pushing the call button, she ignored the tightening of his hand on hers, the hurt questioning look in his eyes. But Luca refused to be fobbed off.

'Felice, I would never deliberately hurt you. Surely you know that much?'

The flight attendant was there, smiling her pussycat smile as she moved the blanket an inch tighter around Luca's knees. As naturally as breathing he moved forward, giving her room to plump his pillow, and it dawned on Felicity then that it wasn't just the fact he was a first-class passenger that instigated this response. Hell, *her* blanket was somewhere mid-calf right now, and no one seemed to care! It wasn't even Luca's rather arrogant assumption that every whim would be catered to; there was an aura about him, an intrinsic appeal not easily defined, and it unnerved her.

She felt as if she were emerging from a cocoon. The

last few weeks had been a whirlwind, yes, but somehow she had felt cosseted, wrapped in a safe Santanno blanket, protected from the elements by the impressive, ordered wheels of the hotel. Cars appearing from nowhere, taking them to her family. Luca taking care of every last detail. Even her own wedding had been easily arranged; all Felicity had had to do was slip on a dress and admire her image.

But now…

The safe cocoon was gone, and her first glimpse at the sun—or, more pointedly, the camera lens of a photographer at the airport—had truly terrified her. She was in Luca's world now. Very soon it would be *her* filling the social pages of the newspapers, and no doubt her unlikely status would cause more than a few caustic comments from the reporters.

Luca's world was one in which she simply didn't belong.

'Could I have a *caffè latte* please?'

'Right away.' The stewardess's smile didn't move an inch. She didn't point out that dinner would be served soon, or that there was a whole bar on offer, but the warmth reserved for Luca was noticeably absent, the feminine smile gone now. Felicity realised there and then that the curious stares directed their way all morning, the inevitable mordant words of the journalists, hadn't really been aimed at her. Her adulation for Luca wasn't exclusive; his irrefutable grace and charm didn't only work their magic on her.

It could be Audrey Hepburn sitting next to Luca, and still she wouldn't be deemed good enough!

Retrieving her own blanket, Felicity leant back in her vast seat, the glint of her diamond offering little reassurance now.

'Felice, you didn't answer me.' Luca's voice was more insistent now. 'I said I'd never deliberately hurt you.'

'Not deliberately, perhaps…'

Her coffee appeared like magic, with a couple of chocolates and some tiny almond *biscotti*—and, of course, a good splash of whisky for her favourite client's glass and another fluff of his pillow.

Felicity choked back the nauseating waft of perfume that lingered in the stewardess's wake. Staring out of the window, watching everything familiar disappear before her eyes, she felt the biggest wave of home-sickness threaten to choke her, and she wasn't sure if she even voiced the words that came next. 'I've a feeling you just can't help yourself…'

CHAPTER FIVE

WALKING into the Santanno family home was, Felicity decided, rather like pressing the wrong button on the remote control and plunging, utterly unprepared, into some very exotic, extremely loud foreign movie.

Without the aid of subtitles, though!

From every angle raven or silver-haired beauties descended upon her, kissing the air around her cheeks then holding her at arm's length, running their eyes, even their hands, over her, as if she were some fabulous dress in a shop and, Felicity gathered, asking their friend, sister, cousin or mother what they thought! Thrusting plates piled with food at her, they filled her glass with a deep rich red wine which was the last thing Felicity fancied right now, but her attempts to put her hand over her glass were countered by them prising her hand away. *'Cincin,'* a very glamorous grandmother insisted, when Felicity attempted to stop them but she shook her head.

'Could I have some water, please? Water?' she repeated, in what she hoped was a friendly voice. But her patience turned to exasperation as she was met with another nonplussed look.

'She doesn't have a clue what you're going on about.'

That deep, low voice relaxed her in an instant. A glass of iced water was being pressed into her hands and Felicity took a grateful sip. 'All I wanted was a glass of water.' ·

'And all they want is a piece of you. I think you've proved rather a hit, Felice. They're going to monopolise you all night, I'm afraid.'

'That's fine.' Felicity smiled, and the most amazing part of it all was that she didn't mind a bit. They were loud, colourful, overbearing—but, Felicity realised almost instantaneously, just gorgeous.

'The only trouble is, if they don't even understand "water" how on earth are we supposed to communicate?'

'It has its advantages. We can talk about anything!' Luca winked. 'Just keep on smiling and they'll keep right on smiling back.'

'What's happening?' The crowd was gathering again, and a knife or spoon was clinking on the edge of every glass in the room—everyone seemed to be joining in! Her glittering eyes turned questioningly to Luca, who had never been more than an arm's length away, surveying his family with a slightly bemused smile on his face.

'It's an Italian tradition.'

'What is?'

'Every time someone chinks their glass we're expected to kiss. It will go on all night.'

'All night?'

His arms were around her, his face bearing down, and Felicity looked up shyly, expecting a brief kiss, a polite retort to the demands of the room. But as Luca's lips met hers he pulled her in so tight her breath came out in a quick, surprised gasp, instantly smothered by the weight of his lips.

As the appreciative cheers of the room faded into the distance the rough scratch of his chin surely cut her face to shreds. He moulded her body into his and claimed her in the most blatant, possessive, public display of affection.

'All night,' he said, pulling away slightly, his voice rough, his eyes dilated with lust. The scent of him was hot and sexy, his touch almost more than she could bear and still stay within the bounds of decency.

'Don't I deserve an introduction? After all, I did choose the ring!' A heaving, throbbing purr broke the moment, and with the sudden tension in Luca Felicity didn't even have to guess who the voice belonged to.

Turning, a smile painted on, she faced her predecessor, determined to play it cool, to accept Luca's past as easily as he had accepted hers. But nothing had prepared Felicity for the sheer, stunning opulence of Anna. The newspaper photo hadn't even begun to capture the magnificent curves, the ripple of black curls that cascaded down her long neck, the magnificent bosom that spilled out of her black velvet dress, the tiny waist flowing into curvaceous buttocks, mocking Felicity's own less voluptuous offerings. She felt like a pale, washed-out shadow beside this utterly ravishing creature.

'Felicity, this is Anna...' Luca didn't miss a beat, his voice didn't waver and his smile stayed fixed, but as his hand slipped from her shoulders and came to rest in the small of her back, pushing her gently forward for the awful introduction, she could feel the ball of tension in his fist. From the sudden hush in the room, Felicity knew she had every reason to be nervous.

'Pleased to meet you.'

'And Ricardo—' Luca carried on with the formalities '—Anna's husband and my very dear friend.'

'Pleased to meet you.' Felicity blinked in surprise as Ricardo Giordano stepped forward, her vision of some geriatric playboy vanishing. In his sixties he might well be, but Ricardo was one of those men who aged beautifully. His hair was for the most part silver, but superbly cut, and there was barely a line on his swarthy face. He was almost as tall as Luca, and had a deep, steady voice and come-to-bed eyes that had probably been winning women over for years.

'*Bella!*' There was no formal handshake this time, not even the customary air kisses Felicity was getting used to. Instead Ricardo took his time, kissing her none too discreetly on both cheeks and then her lips as Luca's fist practically indented into her back.

'You 'ave excellent taste, Luca.'

'So do I,' Anna purred, picking up Felicity's hand and taking her time to examine the ring. 'We had such a fun afternoon choosing it—didn't we, Luca?'

Her voice dropped so low it was almost baritone, and Felicity stood there bristling with indignation as Anna surveyed the diamond, a malicious smile curving her full mouth as she shot a black look for Felicity's eyes only.

'Of course Luca wanted to rush things,' she murmured. 'You know what men can be like. But I said, "No, darling, we have to take our time. I know what women want, and this is something we really should get right." And we did!' The note of triumph in her voice didn't go unnoticed, and neither did her sexual innuendo.

'Yes, you did,' Felicity said calmly, slipping closer to Luca, eternally grateful when he reciprocated with a possessive squeeze of her bare arm. 'So, thanks for your input in choosing the ring.' Placing her glass on a tray, Felicity shot Anna her own black smile. 'I'm having such fun *wearing* it!'

*   *   *

It should have been a wonderful night. Luca's family had pulled out all the stops, opening up their impressive home and welcoming her into the expensively scented bosom of their family, but Felicity felt as if she were trapped on a merry-go-round. The lights and the colours were all merging into one, with only one constant remaining: Anna's black eyes, mercilessly trained on her.

She wanted to push the stop button, to get off, for Luca to take her home—wherever that was—to get back some order, to establish some sort of routine. She wanted some sort of normality to prevail.

'It is hard work, yes?'

Ricardo caught her in an unguarded moment, blowing her blonde fringe skywards as she blew an exhausted sigh heavenwards.

'They're all charming,' Felicity countered, her smile snapping back into place. After all, Luca had played the part of devoted fiancé and newlywed for her family's benefit; it was only fair to return the favour. 'I'm just tired after such a long flight—although I have to admit I feel guilty complaining; we slept most of the way. I can't believe that those chairs turned into beds.'

Realising how gauche and unsophisticated she must sound, describing the wonders of first-class flying to this sophisticate, Felicity gave a helpless shrug, blushing to her roots. Ricardo merely smiled.

'Ah, but there is nothing like your own bed. Especially when you get to my age.' He flashed her a very endearing smile. 'You are not used to flying?'

Felicity shook her head, deciding there and then that she liked Ricardo. 'The occasional family holiday from

Melbourne to Queensland and one trip to Europe doesn't really compare.'

'You can soon get used to it—that is if you want to, of course.'

Ricardo read Felicity's frown, his distinguished features breaking into another smile. 'Our partners lead a jet-set existence, and it can be a bit exhausting keeping up sometimes. Me, I like to stay here, with my grapes.'

'Your grapes?'

Ricardo grinned more widely. 'They are my babies.'

He was nice, Felicity realised, and maybe—just maybe—she had got it all wrong. Ricardo was no idiot, and he was certainly a good-looking, sexy man in his own right. Maybe Anna was in love with him. But just as she relaxed, just as the night didn't seem so bad after all, every nerve shot into overdrive. Ricardo had carried on talking, his voice so casual it took a moment to register exactly what he was saying.

'I am sorry Anna upset you earlier, flirting with Luca like that. It was most inappropriate.'

'She didn't—she wasn't—' Felicity stammered. 'I mean she didn't upset me.'

'She did and she was.' He spoke with the same heavy accent as Luca, but his English was also spot-on, and Felicity lowered her eyes, unsure what to say. After all, this was Anna's husband. 'I will speak to her the second we get home. You are a nice lady, Felicity, I don't want to see you embarrassed. Anna and Luca will just have to learn to be more discreet.'

'Discreet?' Felicity shook her head in bewilderment. 'There's nothing going on.'

'Oh, Felicity...'

Recoiling from the pity she saw in his eyes, she shook her head more firmly this time. 'You've got it all wrong,' she insisted, but the doubt in her voice was audible even to herself. 'Nothing happened at the hotel—nothing at all.'

'Did Anna choose your ring?' Black eyes were testing her now, watching her every move. 'Of course she didn't. You know it and so do I. Anna's performance before was just part of the charade—the charade we all live by. But Luca is a good man, Felicity, he will never dishonour you, never cause you shame. You are his wife after all.'

Ricardo was smiling, trying to comfort her, to reassure her, but there was no comfort to be had. She felt like putting her hands up to her ears, to block out the fateful words he was uttering, to shield herself from a truth she couldn't bear to admit.

'You will have to learn to look the other way.'

'There you are.' Luca was back, only this time the sight of him did nothing to soothe her. She desperately wanted some space to think things through. 'You look tired.'

She could see the snowflakes dusting his hair, and the cool of the night air he had brought in with him made her shiver slightly. His eyes were loaded with concern, and one tender hand brushed a stray curl from her face, capturing her chin and holding it there for all the world as if he truly cared.

'I am.' Her voice was high, her heart pounding so loudly she was sure he must be able to hear it. 'Where were you?'

'Talking to my mother.' He shot her a quizzical look. 'Where did you think I was?'

'You left your drink on the balcony, darling.' Anna joined them, her deep throbbing voice grating now, and even if she had wanted to Felicity couldn't ignore the snowflakes on Anna's hair, the intimate way she handed Luca his drink and worse, far worse, the compassion in Ricardo's eyes as he flashed a wry, sympathetic smile at her.

The merry-go-round was slowing now, the colours and the lights separating. the world was coming back into sharp focus and Felicity didn't like what she saw. 'Take me home, Luca.' Her voice was a mere croak, and if the floor hadn't still been spinning under her she'd have refused the arm Luca offered her, refused the shred of support he offered and walked out of the room unaided.

'Ricardo says that you and Anna need to be more discreet.' They were driving up and up. The winding roads were carved into the mountainside, the precarious drop visible in the pale moonlight. But even driving on the 'wrong' side of the road at a seemingly alarming speed didn't faze her. Her mind was still reeling from the little gem Ricardo had so readily imparted, wondering how best to play this. Stealing a look sideways, she drank in the haughty profile that still made her catch her breath, the straight roman nose, the sculpted cheekbones accentuating his almond-shaped eyes, and wished, now more than ever, that his beauty didn't touch her so.

'Ricardo doesn't know what he's talking about.' Shifting gear, he fiddled with the radio, obviously not remotely bothered by the conversation. But Felicity badly wanted answers.

'He seems pretty sure. Look, Luca, I know this isn't a conventional marriage, and I know this isn't going to last for ever, but I will not be made a fool. I can't bear the thought of you leaving her bed and coming to mine.'

The idle drumming of his fingers on the steering wheel only incensed her further.

'Luca, will you damn well listen to me?'

'When you have something relevant to say, then I will listen,' he responded haughtily.

'Oh, this is extremely relevant. ' Her hand shot to the radio, flicking off the opera. She was determined to force his attention. 'Do you intend to carry on as before with Anna?'

'Before what?' he asked rudely.

'Before we were married,' Felicity said through gritted teeth. 'Do you intend to have her as your mistress?'

'Why would I need a mistress?' His hands flew off the wheel, his outstretched palms gesticulating wildly in the air, and Felicity's hands gripped tighter on the seat as she debated the wisdom of confronting him as the car hugged the mountainside. 'As long as I'm with you there is no need.'

'Is that a threat?'

A long hiss of breath was the only answer forthcoming.

'Do you mean that as long as I keep coming up with the goods you'll stay away from Anna? That the second I don't toe the line and fall into your arms you'll find solace in Anna's?'

'You are twisting my words.'

'Oh, I don't think so, Luca. You told me you were talking to your mother.' She could hear a needy note creeping into her voice and fought quickly to check it. 'Instead you were out on the balcony in the freezing snow doing heaven knows what with Anna.'

He didn't answer, just carried on driving, his face set in a grim line.

'I will not be made a fool of, Luca. If something is going on between you two then I want to hear it from you. Anna said—'

'"Anna said!"' He spat the words out '"Ricardo said!"' The car swerved momentarily but he quickly controlled it, the lapse in concentration doing nothing to improve his temper. 'I am your husband, for God's sake,' Luca shouted. 'Doesn't what *I* say surely count for more? Why do you listen to them? Why do you believe them and not me?'

'Because…' She tore her eyes away. The sheer drop outside her window was preferable to the torture of looking at him, seeing his charitable smile if she dared tell him the truth. That this was not nor had it ever been a mere solution. That this marriage wasn't one of convenience, in fact it was a terrible inconvenience. It had turned her world upside down. She'd follow him to the other side of the earth just to be near him. All that sustained her was the blissful thought of being made love to by him, held by him, cherished by him.

The car was crunching along gravel now, then screeching to a halt outside a massive stone building. Lights flicked on as Luca pulled on the handbrake, his ragged breaths growing more angry now.

'My father smokes; my mother does not like him to do it indoors.' His voice had a patronising ring to it, as if she were suffering from some sort of delusional paranoia that he refused to go along with. 'That is why we were outside; there is nothing more sinister to it than that. And,' he added nastily, 'if you'd bothered to come out and join your husband, instead of sulking inside and hanging onto Ricardo's every word, we wouldn't even be having this discussion.'

'So I've got it all wrong?' Felicity retorted with a sarcastic sneer. 'Or perhaps I've got it all right. I just didn't "look the other way" quickly enough.'

An elderly couple was bearing down on them now, the man pulling open the boot, the woman shivering expectantly in the snow like a dog greeting its master after a long separation.

'I suppose this is the infamous Rosa?'

'She will be looking forward to meeting you.'

'I must remember that when she calls me Anna,' Felicity snapped. 'And I expect you want me to switch into dewy-eyed newlywed mode now—after all, it wouldn't do to disappoint the staff.'

Luca let out a low hiss. Wrenching open the car door, he walked around the front, forcing a greeting to the elderly couple who rushed over to greet them, his breath white in the cold mountain air. Felicity sat shivering, the icy cold air blasting in through the open door preferable to the cold black stare that greeted her as Luca wrenched her own car door open.

'Come on, darling.' His voice was like a caress, but Felicity was privy to the blind fury in his eyes. 'I can't wait to get you inside.' In one lithe movement, ignoring her indignant wail of protest, he scooped her into his arms, angrily kicking the door closed with one very well-shod foot and fixing his bride with a menacing smile as he bundled her against him. He carried her up the steps with barely a breath, and through the front door for her first glimpse of her marital home, barely in focus as Luca marched purposefully through the hallway and the line of staff looked on with wide smiles.

'Put me down, Luca.' Her voice was soft, her forced smile staying in place but her eyes letting it be known she meant business.

'When I am ready. As you said, we must not disappoint the staff.'

'Luca—' Still her voice was calm, but her anger was starting to mount; she utterly refused to be intimidated by him. 'If you don't put me down this instant I'll blow this little charade out of the water.' She knew she wasn't going to win, knew the arms wrapped tightly around her would only let her go when he was good and ready, and she also knew that the delicious wide mouth would silence her in a second if she registered her protest.

Well, two could play at that game!

Boldly she pressed her mouth against his, registering his gasp of surprise as her tongue edged his lips apart. As their mouths entwined his grip tightened, his breath coming faster at her audacious response, his eyes closing involuntarily as he soaked in her delicious scent, but opening abruptly when Felicity pulled away.

'Now will you put me down?'

For once he did as requested, but as he gently lowered her she almost wished he hadn't, secretly missing the strength he had imbued her with as she faced the suspicious, curious looks of the gathered entourage, and beating back a beastly blush as Luca introduced her in rapid Italian.

'This is Rosa and Marco.' He guided her forward, and even as she put out her hand to shake Rosa's she instantly regretted her rather formal greeting.

'You're supposed to kiss her on the cheeks,' Luca said in a low voice, but his warning came too late, and as the elderly woman's hand reluctantly shook

Felicity's she realised there and then that she had already lost a few Brownie points, that the rather proprietary Rosa wasn't the sweet old lady Luca had so happily described.

'Come.' With something akin to a sniff she led them through to what Felicity assumed was the lounge, though the high walls and dark leather furniture, the cool marble of the floor and the ornate antiques that lined the massive occasional tables were a million miles from the soft, welcoming lounge of her parents.

Through heavily lidded eyes he watched her, something akin to a smile softening his features as she hesitantly worked the room.

The kitten was gone. Instead she reminded him of a cat now, Luca thought. Some gracious elegant feline, with suspicious, mistrusting eyes, a proud aloofness belying her fear, choosing her seat with the utmost caution, ready to pounce, to up and leave at the slightest provocation.

'Here.' As Rosa pressed a glass into her hands Felicity eyed the pale lemon drink with caution.

'Limoncello.' Luca smiled. 'It's sweet and warm—just the thing for a cold night.'

Taking a grateful sip, Felicity nearly spat out the revolting mixture, screwing up her face and swallowing the strong sweet liquor as if she were forcing down medicine—to Rosa's obvious annoyance.

'You no like?' she asked accusingly, and Felicity shrugged helplessly.

'I'm sure it's lovely, but I would think it's an acquired taste.'

'A simple yes or no would have done.' Luca laughed as Rosa took the drink, returning almost immediately with a glass of water which Felicity accepted gratefully.

'I am sorry.' Rosa shrugged, but the smile of acceptance died on Felicity's lips as the elderly woman continued. 'It is just that Signorina Anna always likes a glass of *limoncello* before she goes to bed.'

'Ignore her.' Luca laughed again as Rosa left the room. 'She hates change, but she'll soon come around. Anna let her get away with murder, which is why she misses her so much.'

'What sort of murder?' Felicity asked, curious despite herself, her ears still ringing from Rosa's spiteful words.

'Rosa likes the *limoncello* too. When Anna was around no one really noticed the ever-decreasing bottles. I think she misses her ally.'

'And you don't mind?' Felicity asked, smiling now despite herself. 'Most people would hate their staff helping themselves to the drinks.'

'It is no big deal to turn a blind eye. Rosa is a good woman; you'll see that for yourself soon enough.'

'Well, I won't hold my breath! I'm sure Rosa's adorable where you're concerned, Luca, but I doubt that goodwill is going to extend to your wife.'

'I'm sorry for what Ricardo said.'

Felicity gave a tight shrug.

'He judges everyone by his own rules.'

'Does he have a mistress?' Felicity asked, wide-eyed, but Luca shook his head.

'Ricardo is in poor health now. I expect he has enough trouble keeping up with Anna, let alone a mistress. But with his last wife he did.'

Felicity gave a weary sigh; it was all too damned complicated for her.

'You are exhausted,' Luca said gently. 'Come, I will take you upstairs.'

She went to stand, only Luca beat her to it, and this time when he swooped her up in his arms she offered no resistance. This time she let her body curve into him, rested her head on his strong chest as he carried her up the impressive staircase, kicking open the bedroom door with his foot and gently lowering her onto a massive wooden bed.

'Poor Felice,' he whispered tenderly as with infinite tenderness he undressed her, caressing her aching feet as he pulled off her heels. 'My poor baby, it is all so confusing for you.' Massaging her shoulders, he slipped the straps of her dress down and removed her bra with all the skill and precision of a man who knew what women wanted. And while it was reassurance Felicity craved, not endearments, and though the row still resonated in her mind, it was so much easier to take the comfort Luca offered, to drown in the only succour available, to die a little in his arms as he held her.

To silence her fears with his touch.

CHAPTER SIX

'WHAT are you doing today?'

'Studying,' Felicity said determinedly, ignoring the black look Rosa flashed at her as she wandered into the kitchen in her short robe, her blonde hair tumbling. Luca rushed around, gulping down impossibly strong coffee and trying to load his briefcase at the same time. 'I'm already seriously behind. What time do you think you'll be back?'

'Late.' Luca pulled a face. 'I shouldn't ask you to wait up for me, really, but if you knew how adorable you looked this morning you'd understand why I am being so selfish.'

'Luca,' Felicity admonished, rolling her eyes towards Rosa and brushing aside his intimate observation. Luca, used to servants, didn't give a damn who was in the room, didn't lower his voice or alter his comments one iota, while Felicity felt as if she were in a perpetual restaurant—lowering her voice each and every time a waiter appeared, pausing in conversation when a napkin was placed in her lap.

And it irritated the hell out of Luca.

'Why don't you come?' he suggested 'Come on— you could do some shopping and meet me for lunch. You must be sick of being cooped up here.'

'I need to study, Luca.' Selecting a pastry from the plate Rosa pushed towards her, she took a half-hearted bite. A sickly sweet pastry was the last thing she felt like right now, but it was that or choosing from the massive tray of salami and ham Rosa always prepared, and the sight of it this morning literally turned her stomach.

'You no like?' Rosa asked accusingly.

'It's lovely,' Felicity said brightly, taking what she hoped was a more enthusiastic bite, determined to hit the local shops and find the Italian equivalent to cornflakes. A cup of tea wouldn't go amiss either, she thought, taking a sip of the strong, sweet coffee that Italians seemed to survive on.

'Can't you give the books a miss for once?' Luca pushed, but Felicity shook her head.

'I have to work, Luca; I've got an assignment due in next week. You know how important my studies are.'

Or had been, Felicity mentally corrected. The assignments that waited for her upstairs were nowhere near as inviting as a shopping spree in Rome, but she hadn't been lying when she'd said her studies were falling seriously behind and it unnerved her. She missed the safety net of lectures, the rigid timetable of university. Studying by correspondence, it was all too easy to put things off—particularly with a distraction as gorgeous as Luca. Night after night he would arrive home late, uncork a bottle of red wine and sigh with impatience as she tapped away on the computer, or run himself a long bath and then invite her to join him...

A date with her books was long overdue.

'You could bring your laptop.' Luca's voice was more insistent now. 'There's nothing you can do here that can't be done there. Come on, Felice. We could stay overnight; I'll finish work around six and we can actually have an evening together.'

The phone was ringing in the hall, and though she'd

clearly rather have stayed Rosa reluctantly went to answer it as Luca grew more insistent.

'Go and grab your books and computer and get dressed.' He gave a low laugh. 'Or on second thoughts come just as you are.'

His hand toyed with edge of her robe, melting her resistance like ice cream in the sun. Taking a deep breath, she nodded, rewarded tenfold by the smile he returned.

'It will be nice to have some time together at last.'

'We're going to be working,' Felicity pointed out, but she knew what he meant. The prospect of lunch, dinner and breakfast with him caused a bubble to well in her stomach just at the thought. Her abhorrence of hotel life seemed to have vanished after a fortnight practically alone in the house with Rosa. Moserallo was beautiful, but tiny. She'd explored every last street, walked for hours along the winding paths, attempted to chat with the locals, but without Luca she always felt as if she were just killing time, filling in the long empty hours between dawn and midnight, and the prospect of a full evening alone with him stretched before her like a delicious treat. A night in his arms with no beastly helicopter swooping out of the sky and plucking him away at some ungodly hour in the morning. 'Still, I'm sure we can squeeze in a lunch break.'

'Morning coffee too,' he whispered, his sensual mouth nuzzling the edge of her ear. 'And how about afternoon tea?'

'That's English.' Felicity giggled. 'I thought the Italians had siestas.'

'Even better.'

'*Signore.*' Rosa was back from the telephone and Felicity pulled away hastily, her cheeks scorching as the elderly woman eyed her disapprovingly. *'Signorina Anna e al telefono, desidera parlare con Lei.'*

'Anna is ringing from the hotel?' Even with her non-existent Italian, the combined words of 'Anna' and 'hotel' made the message pretty clear. The fact that Anna was on the telephone at this ridiculous hour had all Felicity's senses on high alert, but she watched Luca's reaction with relief—he rolled his eyes.

'Ricardo is only letting her stay there two or three days a week now,' he offered by way of explanation. 'She will already be working.'

'She sleeps at the hotel?'

'Of course.' Again he rolled his eyes. 'I am the only fool making the journey each day. We leave in fifteen minutes.' Luca smiled, grazing her cheek with a kiss before calmly following Rosa down the hall, completely unaware of the utter chaos about to let rip in his ordered, tidy bedroom.

Felicity's reflexes were like lightning. Taking the stairs two at a time and entering the room, she flicked on her heated rollers, then made a vague attempt to gather up her books. But good as her intentions were, Felicity knew there wasn't a hope in hell of getting any work done. With Luca in the same building, concentrating on the finer points of Strategic Management or trying to wrestle with Organisational Analysis would no doubt prove an impossible feat. But, perhaps more to the point, never when she had accepted his offer had it even entered her head that she might be seeing Anna. God, she wished she had hours to tart herself up. Images of sleek Italian beauties, brimming with fashion sense, sent her into a momentary spin of panic as she waded through her wardrobe, praying for some sort of divine intervention—or at the very least a good hair day.

A smart navy trouser suit normally reserved for interviews was the best she could come up with. A touch too formal for studying, perhaps, but Felicity consoled herself that she was going to one of the most glamorous hotels in Rome—she could hardly rock up in jeans. Slipping on some heels while simultaneously brushing her hair, she abandoned all hope of a meeting with her rollers as she heard the sound of the chopper revving up in the distance—no respecter of the fashion crisis going on just a stone's throw away. The best she could hope for now was a massive squirt of gel and a prayer that the slicked-back look wasn't a complete fashion *faux pas*.

'Felice.'

She heard her summons, but ignored it, scrabbling instead in her bag for some eyeliner, pinching some colour into her pale cheeks, then rougeing her full lips.

'Felice!' She heard impatience in his tone now; standing back, she caught her reflection in the full-length mirror, admiring her handiwork as she stared at the sleek, sophisticated woman that smiled back at her.

'Felice!'

Picking up her bag, she stood at the stop of the stairwell, watching quietly for a second as he paced up and down the impressive hallway, glancing furiously at his watch as he shouted into his mobile phone.

'Was that the third and final call?'

He turned, glancing up impatiently and beckoning her with his free hand, but somewhere mid-gesture he stopped, the rapid Italian fading as he bade a hasty goodbye. Clicking off the mobile, he stood perfectly still, engulfing her with the intensity of his stare, a mus-

cle twitching in his face as she slowly walked down
the stairs towards him.

'You look…' He swallowed hard as she joined him,
the heady fragrance of her perfume reaching him before she did, a precursor of the delicious parcel of sophisticated femininity that tentatively joined him. 'You
look beautiful,' he said simply, taking her hand as they
stepped out into the crisp morning air.

'*Signora.*' Rosa ran up behind them and Felicity
turned in surprise, the elderly lady initiating a conversation was something of a novelty. 'You no finish your
pastry.'

'Oh.' Felicity glanced down at the curling pastry
Rosa had wrapped in a serviette, the yellow custard
oozing out of the sides, and felt her stomach tighten.
'Thank you, Rosa.'

'Breakfast on the go,' Luca said dryly. 'Come on,
Felice.'

Felicity had never been on a helicopter before, and
as Luca took her hand she gave a gurgle of excited
laughter. They ducked, running under the blades, the
false wind catching in her throat, and Luca noncha-
lantly climbed in, then took her hand and hauled her
none too gallantly inside.

It would have been too obvious to get out her mirror,
but as it was still dark outside she managed a quick
check of her reflection in the window as the helicopter
lifted off the lawn, glad to see the hair gel she had used
really was as long-lasting as the label had promised
and her hair hadn't reached manic proportions yet.

'You look fine,' Luca mouthed, catching her eye as
she turned from the window and making her blush as
she realised she'd been caught.

But she didn't want to look fine. She wanted to look

divine, stunning, to knock everyone's fabulously expensive silk stockings off as she gracefully swept into the building.

To show Luca's world that she wasn't a complete hick.

The noise of the rotors didn't allow for much more than amicable silence, but as the sun rose over the Italian Alps and the chopper buzzed through the sky, hugging the mountain so close Felicity was sure if she opened a window and reached out she could have plucked a handful of snow from the side, the true beauty of Luca's country finally hit her.

She could see Moserallo fading in the distance—acre after acre of neatly rowed vineyards surrounding the knot of winding roads that all led to the war memorial, standing tall and proud, gazing down on the delicious landscape, a true meeting place where old men gossiped and teenagers kissed. She could see too the stone villas, nestled in the hillsides, and the white church so small now it looked like a model. She craned her neck for a final glimpse as it ebbed out of sight, finally understanding just why Luca made the journey each day, how bland a hotel must seem beside this rich, inspiring land.

'How long till we get there?' Felicity shouted, but Luca shook his head. Fiddling in the chair, he handed her a pair of headphones.

'Far more civilised than shouting.' His voice was so low and clear when she put them on that Felicity blinked in surprise as he spoke, a grin spreading across her face. There was a certain comfort to be had, a delicious sense of intimacy, as his deliciously accented voice filled her, low and rich and for her ears only. She adored hearing him speak, lived for the telephone calls he made during the day, when she would lie on the bed as his deep, sexy voice surrounded her, only this was better. So much better, she could see him, stretched before her in his leather seat, a safety belt slung around his thighs, dark and brooding and infinitely desirable.

'Say something,' she grumbled, wanting to hear him again, wanting his lyrical voice to wash over her, wanting to hear a hint of suggestion, to see the excitement in his eyes as she responded. 'Talk to me, Luca.' He must have sensed the shift in her, the gentle throb of suggestion as her eyes met his, his bold invitation to join in the game.

He flashed her a decadent smile, stabbing her with his eyes, rolling his tongue in his cheek as he looked at her thoughtfully.

'Quanto tempo finché arriviamo?'

She loved it when he spoke in Italian to her, loved the way he lowered his voice and made love to her with his eyes. She could feel her toes curling in her smart shoes, a flush of colour warming her rouged cheeks, and her tongue bobbed out on her full painted lips.

'Circa quarantacinque minuti.'

Practically jumping out of her seat as a voice that definitely wasn't Luca's filled her ears, Felicity clapped her hand to her mouth, stifling a nervous giggle as Luca grinned wickedly at her.

'According to Leo, we'll be there in about forty-five minutes. Now…' a tiny wink shuttered his eye momentarily '…what was it that you wanted me to talk about?'

Stinging with embarrassment, utterly unable to meet

his eyes, she took a hasty bite of the pastry warming in her hot hands.

Big mistake.

Suddenly the snow-capped mountains didn't look so gentle any more, and rather more alarmingly even Luca's liquid gold voice was doing nothing to soothe her as the cabin seemed to close in around her. She could feel beads of sweat trickling between her breasts, and the stuffy confines of the helicopter were positively claustrophobic as Luca's voice droned on mercilessly about air speed and wind direction.

'Luca!' Her voice was barely a croak. Running her tongue over her lips, she struggled to take deep breaths, dragging air into her lungs, forcing herself to keep her breathing even as she begged for his attention. But Luca wasn't looking at her now; instead he was busy pointing out landmarks, as if he were a tour guide. She rummaged in her bag—for what, she didn't know— and was sure that the paltry tissue she finally produced would prove woefully inadequate.

'Luca!' Her voice was more urgent now, forcing his attention, and his mouth opened in shock as he saw the state she was in. In one movement he pushed her head between her legs, calling in rapid Italian to Leo, who mercifully produced a bag as, reeling with mortification, burning with the indignity of it all, Felicity discovered at the rather late stage of twenty-six years that she didn't like heights after all!

To add to her utter humiliation, Luca completely overreacted. Gone was the smooth businessman. In a second he had snapped into over-protective parent mode, rubbing her back enthusiastically when she wished he'd let her just die quietly—in fact, if Felicity hadn't put her rather pale and shaking foot down, she was sure he'd have arranged an ambulance to meet them.

'Why didn't you tell me?' he demanded as he led her, pale and trembling, across the landing pad. The relative safety of solid ground was still unappealing, given they were on the roof of the hotel. 'Why didn't you tell me you hated heights?'

'I only just found out.' She managed a very thin, very watery smile. 'Is there anywhere I can freshen up—before we go to your office, I mean?'

But Luca wouldn't hear of it. Assuring her she looked just fine, he swept her down the hallway, determined to get her to the comfort of his suite, barely acknowledging the lift boy as he wrenched open the massive old-fashioned gates, holding her tightly as the lift took a plunge and Felicity's stomach did the same.

It wasn't the best way to meet one's nemesis.

Anna, dressed in a blood-red suit, the skirt impossibly short, showing a massive expanse of bronzed thigh, gaped in open-mouthed astonishment as Luca led her into the massive suite, thankfully bypassing the massive mahogany desk and array of leather seats and taking her through a wooden door where—heaven of heavens—a giant four-poster bed begged her to lie down. Not wanting to argue, Felicity sank gratefully into the fluffy eiderdown, willing the room to stop moving as Anna moved in for a closer inspection.

'*Che c'è?*'

'We will speak in English,' Luca responded tartly, which should have made Felicity cheer, but for the first time since landing in the country she would have been grateful to have him hang politeness and just talk about her in Italian. There was absolutely no desire on her part to hear in graphic detail this morning's embarrassing tale.

They nattered on for a moment and slowly the world came back into focus. Taking a grateful sip of the water Luca had poured, she sank back into the pillows, scarcely able to believe something as simple as fear of heights could have had such a devastating effect.

Utterly and completely worn out, she watched as Anna sat down beside the bed, and to Felicity's eternal disgust not even a single globule of cellulite marred those thighs as she crossed her legs and addressed Luca in a formal voice.

'I wish you'd told me you were bringing Felicity.'

Luca didn't even look up. Pulling a handkerchief from his pocket, he gently dabbed at a wayward river of mascara before responding. 'We only decided this morning.'

'Still, it would have been better if you'd told me.' Sighing deeply, Anna raked a hand through her impressive dark curls, chewing on the end of her pen with her ruby-red lips till Luca finally turned to her. 'The reason I asked you to come directly is because we've got some dignitaries from Saudi flying in. They want you to show them around the city and meet them for lunch.'

'Deal with them,' Luca said dismissively.

'They'd rather see you, Luca. They're talking about taking out a permanent rental on a couple of the penthouse suites.'

'My wife is sick and you are asking me to play chaperone to these people? Tell them to give more notice next time—tell them I am unavailable. Tell them what the hell you like. That is what I pay you for, is it not?

Now, if you would give us some privacy, I would like to see for myself that my wife is okay.'

'Can I at least say that you'll be meeting us for coffee? Perhaps we could…' Anna began, but her voice trailed off as Luca let out an acid hiss.

'When I know what is wrong with Felice,' he snapped, 'then I will decide. Engage the red light on your way out!'

Anna didn't slam the door exactly, but at the way she tossed her hair and marched across the room Felicity found she was bracing herself for a bang.

The tension in the air lifted once they were alone.

'Engage the red light?' A smile dusted her pale lips. 'What on earth does that mean?'

'That I do not want to be disturbed,' he explained. 'Which I don't.'

Struggling to sit up, Felicity took a couple of steadying breaths, realising with relief that the room had finally stopped moving. 'It's not quite your standard office, is it?' she said dryly, taking in her surroundings. 'Was the four-poster bed an optional extra?'

'Felice…' Luca sighed. 'Until I married you I practically lived here. You could hardly expect me to sleep at my desk.'

'I guess not,' she mumbled, realising how churlish she must sound, but it wasn't the grandeur of the surroundings that was eating at her now. Anna had followed them into this bedroom without a moment's hesitation, and it irked Felicity, but, pushing her misgivings to one side, she forced a smile. 'I'm feeling a lot better, Luca. If you need to meet with these people I'll be fine. I'm just going to lie here and do some reading.'

'I'm not meeting with anyone, and *you* are not going

to be reading,' Luca said tartly. 'You are not even going to open those books of yours. First you will lie here and rest awhile, and then if you do feel better you will take a gentle walk, get some fresh air. Is there anything I can get you?'

Felicity shook her head. 'You get on with your work. I'm just going to lie here.'

'No studying,' Luca warned. 'I'll pull the curtains and let you sleep. In fact, I'm going to keep your books and computer at my desk to make sure that you rest.' After pulling the curtains he fussed a couple of moments more, tucking a rug around her and collecting her bags.

'I'm sorry, Luca,' she mumbled as he headed for the door, her eyes heavy with sleep but not wanting him to go.

'For what?

'Being sick like that. Ruining our day.'

'Who said it was ruined?' he asked softly. 'It's just nice having you here. And don't worry about being sick, I'm used to it; Bonita, my secretary, is expecting, and she takes dictation with her head between her knees at the moment, whipping out little plastic bags at the most inopportune times. Still, at least that's one thing we don't have to worry about.'

Shutting the door, he left her frowning into the darkness.

Frowning into the darkness and praying it wasn't so.

CHAPTER SEVEN

'YOU look better!' Smiling as she tentatively pushed open the bedroom door, Luca clicked off his Dictaphone and came around the desk to join her.

'I feel better,' Felicity said brightly, and she was speaking the truth. An hour lying in the dark had done wonders, and after a quick freshen-up in the bathroom she was desperate to get out and do some exploring. 'In fact so much so I think I'm going to take your advice and get a bit of fresh air.'

'Good idea.' Pulling out his wallet, he selected a credit card. 'I would love to come, but I really do have to meet with these people. Just for a short while,' he added quickly. 'You could do a bit of shopping while I am tied up. I could arrange for someone to go with you.'

'Someone to go with me?' Felicity asked, bewildered.

'Katrina can take you to the shops on the Via Condotti. All the best fashion houses are there, but they won't know your face yet, and without an appointment they can make things difficult. Katrina can deal with all that. She will introduce you to them, let them know you are my wife; she can help you plan your wardrobe.'

'But I've *got* a wardrobe,' Felicity replied indignantly. 'Are you not happy with the way I dress, Luca? Are you trying to tell me that I embarrass you?'

'Of course not,' he answered, irritated. 'But you

have just come from an Australian summer to an Italian winter, and I don't recall too many woollen coats hanging in the wardrobe, or boots or gloves. Take it,' he urged, pressing the gold card into her hand. 'What is it that women say? Go and "shop till you drop".'

'Shop till I droop, more likely.' Felicity sighed. 'Look, Luca, the last thing I feel like doing now is shopping, and when—if—I decide that a new coat or new boots are in order I'll buy them myself, thank you. I certainly don't need some wardrobe consultant telling me what colours suit me best; I worked that out long ago.'

'Why do you always have to be so stubborn?' Luca admonished. 'You are the only woman I can think of who could start a row because I tell her to go clothes-shopping! Most women—'

'I'm not most women,' Felicity broke in, popping the card into his top pocket and dousing his anger with a bright smile. 'But thank you for the offer.'

'I suppose you're going to insist on paying half for lunch,' he said broodingly, which only made her smile wider.

'Stop sulking, Luca. Look, you really ought to eat lunch with these people; you know that as well as I do. Turning down that sort of clientele is hardly a wise move. And you would be turning them down,' she said quickly as he opened his mouth to argue. 'A quick morning coffee isn't really the way to do business.'

'I guess,' he muttered. 'But come with us at least. I can't just leave you on your own on your first day in Rome.'

'Why not? I'm not a baby, Luca; I can brave the streets without an escort. Anyway, after this morning's episode a heavy long lunch really isn't at the top of my agenda—and it isn't my first day in Rome. I was here with Joseph, remember?'

'Okay,' he said resignedly. 'But if you need anything, if you run into any problems and I am not here, you ring the hotel and ask to speak with Rafaello.'

'Rafaello? Is that your personal assistant?'

'No, he is far more useful than that. Rafaello is the chief concierge. There is nothing he cannot organise.'

'I'll bear it in mind.'

'So when will I see you?' Luca grumbled. 'When can you squeeze me in?'

'Tonight,' Felicity said brightly, refusing to be drawn by his sulking. 'I'll arrange dinner; just meet me back here around six.' And, kissing him briefly on the cheek, she headed out of the door.

Wincing slightly as she worked out the exchange rate, for a while Felicity wished she had taken Luca up on his offer and pocketed his little gold credit card.

'No, you don't,' she said firmly, forging her way slowly through the crowded streets, gaping in open-mouthed admiration at the ravishing women and well-groomed men, their beautiful coats trailing massive bright scarves, immaculate shoes clicking along as they shouted in their exuberant language, blowing white clouds of air as they sipped their hot coffee or chatted noisily into their mobiles.

Rome was everything she remembered and more. Somehow shopping and art melted into one. Every turn of a corner heralded a building steeped in history, hundreds of churches, each one deserving so much more than the awe-inspired glances she gave as she teetered past, her high heels no match for the cobbled streets.

Luca, as insensitive as he might have been in his

delivery, certainly had a point. Her suit, appropriate as it might be for Australia, was no match for the icy weather here. The cold literally bit into her, and she could hear her teeth chattering involuntarily as she walked along. Bypassing elegant shops with only one or two garments tastefully displayed and not a hint of a pricetag in sight, she settled for some of the rather less imposing boutiques. They might not have been Luca's idea of heaven, but for Felicity it was like stepping into paradise. It was so easy to waste the day, wandering from shop to shop, and after an age of running her hand over fine wools and beautifully cut suits she finally threw caution to the wind and took her rather less impressive navy blue credit card out of its mothballs and gave it a long-overdue workout. After all, she would be needing the clothes soon, she consoled herself. Once she had her MBA it would be Felicity taking clients out for lunch.

If she got down and did some work for the blessed thing.

Paying for her purchases, weighed down with endless bags, she pushed her pang of guilt aside. It had been ages since she'd spent a cent on clothes, ages since she'd treated herself. Anyway, she didn't have to worry about money now her parents were taken care of.

Or would be if Luca ever spoke to his lawyer.

Catching sight of a row of ties, she ran her hands over them. The silk was so heavy the ties barely moved, but one in particular caught her eye, standing out amongst the heavy checks and bold stripes, the deep sapphire-blue an almost perfect match for Luca's eyes. Its simplicity was its beauty, and on impulse she bought it, berating herself for not looking at the pricetag as the assistant boxed it, then further wrapped it in endless wads of tissue paper before placing it in small silver bag, using practically half a forest for one simple garment. For that much paper it had to be expensive.

It was.

The slightly startled look of the hotel staff as she staggered through Reception brought a rueful smile to her lips; no doubt they expected the wife of the great Signor Santanno to arrive with an entourage of assistants weighed down with the fruits of her labours.

'Signor Santanno should be back shortly,' Rafaello greeted her warmly. 'In the meantime he has asked that I ensure you are taken care of. Would you like me to send the head chef up to you, *signora*? He can take you through the menu personally; Signor Santanno mentioned you have been finding the food rather rich.'

'That won't be necessary, Rafaello,' Felicity said assuredly. 'I've got everything I need right here.'

Even the eternally impassive mask of the concierge slipped momentarily as he relieved Felicity of a bag while simultaneously clicking his fingers to summon assistance. Undoubtedly the aroma of fresh-baked bread and the chinking of bottles were out of place anywhere other than in the impressive dining room here, but Rafaello recovered quickly.

'Is there anything I can get you, *signora*? Anything at all?'

'A picnic blanket?' Felicity asked, watching his reaction closely, but this time Rafaello never turned a hair.

'Certainly, *signora*. I will have it sent to your room immediately.'

As good as his word, a picnic blanket arrived before

she had even peeled off her shoes. Shooing out the staff, insisting she was more than capable of putting away her own purchases, she set about preparing the room, laying out the blanket, buttering the bread into thick mounds, arranging the cheeses and dried fruits temptingly, and smiling to herself at Rafaello's foresight when two chambermaids discreetly knocked, buckling under the weight of a massive silver ice bucket and huge candelabra.

Rafaello was obviously a romantic!

'What's all this?' Blinking in the semi-darkness, Luca eyed the room slowly before turning his rather bemused face to Felicity.

'Dinner in Italy,' she said softly. 'Conlon-style.' Taking the lead, she sat on the rug, and after a moment's hesitation Luca pulled off his jacket and shoes and joined her. He was uncomfortable and awkward at first, but finally—along with his tie—he loosened up, accepting the cheap red wine Felicity handed him as she sipped on some sparkling mineral water.

'Tastes like mouthwash.' He grimaced. 'Where on earth did you get it?'

'At my usual deli,' Felicity laughed. 'This is what Joseph and I used to eat when we came to Rome. We couldn't afford to go to fancy restaurants for every meal, so instead we found this wonderful deli. We'd go off and have a picnic lunch somewhere wonderful—though I admit the wine is rather an acquired taste; I just stuck to mineral water.'

'Happy times?'

'Very,' Felicity said softly. Looking up, she saw him staring at her, his face softer in the candlelight, those beautiful heavy-lidded eyes loaded with surprising tenderness. 'And so is this.'

And even though the whole meal probably cost as much as a bowl of soup in Luca's dining room, if ever there was a moment of perfection in their marriage this was it. No waiters hovering, no staff wringing their hands in an effort to help. Just her and Luca and an entire evening stretching before them. Oh, she knew they had a lot to talk about, knew there was a lot of difficult ground to cover. The stalemate with the lawyers, his refusal to give her a timeline, but for a while she put the questions on hold, determined not to mar this rare moment of togetherness.

'I bought you a present.' Handing him the parcel, she watched the question in his eyes as he accepted it. 'It isn't much,' she ventured. 'I just saw it and liked it. I thought it matched…' She swallowed hard, grateful for the candlelight to soften the furious blush that scorched her cheeks. 'It matches your eyes.'

She watched as he turned it over in his hands and then slowly peeled back the mountains of paper, pulling the tie out of its box and running his fingers over it for a moment before speaking.

'It's lovely.' His voice was thick, and when he looked up Felicity was almost knocked sideways by the raw emotion in his proud, expressive eyes. 'I shall wear it tomorrow.'

'You—you don't have to,' she stammered. 'I know it's probably nothing like the quality you're used to—'

'It's perfect,' Luca broke in. 'In fact, it is the nicest present I've ever had.'

'It's just a tie, Luca,' Felicity pointed out, startled by his reaction. 'You don't have to go over the top.'

But Luca begged to differ. 'Do you realise this is the first real present a woman has ever given me?'

'Oh, come on.' Felicity laughed nervously. 'Your dressing table at home is weighed down with Tiffany cufflinks and little one-offs that only a woman could choose. I'm sure a tie is way down on your list of memorable gifts.'

'This is the only one I will remember,' Luca said fiercely. 'Yes, women have given me *gifts*, and undoubtedly they have agonised over the choice of precious metal or the wording of an engraving, and for a while maybe I was touched. But the sentiment behind the gift tends to wane when it appears on your own credit card statement.'

His voice trailed off, his gaze returning to the fabric he held in his hands, and for the first time since their meeting Felicity felt something akin to pity for him. Something in his voice, his stance, throbbed with loneliness, and she realised there and then how hard it must be for Luca at times. How hard it must be when every friendship, every relationship, both professional and personal, was dictated by his bank balance. The price he paid for adulation.

'And this is a night I will remember too.' His gaze drifted around the blanket, the foods she had so carefully chosen, each tiny jar, each taste loaded with memories, both new and old. 'Felice, there is something I need to tell you—something we need to talk through.'

Her breath seemed to be coming in hot, short bursts, trapped in her lungs as her throat constricted, her fight or flight response triggered as his hand inched over the rug to hers. She could feel it hot and dry over hers, hear the hesitancy in his voice as he spoke.

'I have not been strictly honest with you.'

It was like the executioner's axe falling. Her heart was banging in her ribcage so loudly she was sure he must hear it. The confrontation she had sought was here now, but suddenly the truth was something she wasn't sure she wanted to hear—not if it spelt the end, not if it involved the one thing she simply couldn't forget or forgive.

'Anna!'

The word that pounded in her mind spilled from his lips, and it took a second to register that Luca wasn't confirming her worst fears, that in fact Anna had pushed open the door and was standing just a few feet in front of them.

'What are you doing here?' Standing angrily, he walked over to her, running an impatient hand through his hair. 'Haven't you heard of knocking?'

'Since when did I need to knock?' Anna drawled, then, taking in the picnic blanket, formed a mocking smile on her heavily made-up lips. With one scathing look she managed to sully all Felicity had lovingly created. 'Oh, am I breaking up a little tea party? Or have the kitchen staff all gone on strike?' Not waiting for an answer, she flicked on the lights, handing Luca a small card to sign. 'I need your signature on this, darling. I'm sending Ahmett a basket of Italian delicacies.' She gave a low laugh. 'Perhaps I should order two and have one sent up here; I didn't realise people actually drank that stuff!'

Without a word Luca took the card and scribbled a message, though from the look on his face Felicity wasn't sure it would be usable.

'Ricardo just telephoned,' Anna carried on airily, not remotely fazed by the sudden drop in temperature. 'He would like you to come for dinner on Saturday.'

Luca opened his mouth to respond, but Felicity beat him to it. 'We're busy on Saturday,' she responded curtly, and if the ambience had been cool before it was positively arctic now, as Anna took the card without a word and turned on her razor-sharp stiletto. Only this time her temper didn't stay quite so well in check, and she slammed the door loudly on her way out.

Only when she'd safely gone did Felicity let out a large sigh. 'That was pleasant.' Turning, she expected an apologetic smile or at the very least a mutual sigh of relief from Luca, but if he had been annoyed before he was livid now. His mouth was set in a grim line, every muscle in his face straining as his blazing eyes turned to her.

'What the hell did you say that for?' he demanded. 'How dare you turn down a dinner invitation from Ricardo without consulting me first?'

'I *dare* because I have no desire for a night in Anna's company,' Felicity answered tartly, but her conviction wavered as Luca's fury erupted.

'So you refuse his invitation?' Luca roared. 'Ricardo is my family's oldest friend and you refuse to eat at his table?'

'I refuse to eat at his wife's table,' Felicity responded hotly. 'I refuse to be humiliated by Anna! I refuse to allow her to laugh in my face at the mockery of this so-called marriage.'

'Is that what all this is about?' He swung around, his eyes blazing. 'Are you demanding we change the rules all of a sudden? Do you want me to say I love you, Felice? Do you want me to tell you that this is for ever?' Each word was like a knife plunging into her heart; each word lacerated her with its emptiness.

She shook her head, her hands flying to her ears. Oh,

she wanted him to love her, wanted him to tell her, but not like this, never like this—some enforced declaration, a platitude to keep her quiet, a crumb to sustain her.

'Have I ever for one moment treated you with anything other than respect? Have I ever for even a second given you reason to doubt me?' He didn't give her time to answer, his fury gaining momentum with each and every elaborate gesture. 'I told you the day we met that Anna and I were finished, and you looked me in the eye and said you believed me...'

'It was easy to believe you then.' She had found her voice, shaky as it was. 'I didn't have to see her then, pawing you, making innuendoes. The red light is on, Luca. You said yourself that meant you were not to be disturbed! But it would seem those rules don't apply to Anna. Why, even Ricardo—'

'So you are listening to Ricardo now? Listening to some *puttana's* husband? A man who would rather let people think I had slept with his wife than rejected her!' The shock on her face wasn't missed, and Luca gave a haughty nod. 'That is right. These are the people you choose to listen to over your husband.'

'You're talking as if our marriage is real!' As he let out a furious hiss she retreated somewhat, shaking her head and turning to go—to where, she wasn't sure, but she had no desire to continue this explosive argument, no wish to upturn stones and expose the horrible lies that bound them. But Luca had other ideas. Pulling her back, he swung her around none too gently, forcing her attention, stabbing her with his eyes.

'Don't you walk out on me! Come and finish what you started, Felice.'

Her eyes darted nervously; she could feel the sweat

trickling between her breasts as he moved closer, his face menacing. 'I'm just pointing out that you're talking as if we're a real husband and wife, as if…' She was swallowing hard now. She'd been pushing for this confrontation but now that it was here she didn't want it—didn't want to hear the mirth in his voice, the pity when he realised she loved him, that this wasn't nor had ever been a game to her, a solution to a problem.

That it was the real thing.

'As if what?' His voice was like a whip cracking, every word so well articulated, so measured the Italian accent almost melted away.

'As if we love each other,' Felicity whispered. 'As if it's imperative that I believe you; as if you care what I think of you.'

'And just what do *you* think, Felice?' His voice was deathly quiet, but it didn't mask the danger behind it. 'What goes on in that pretty head of yours? I've tried asking nicely, tried treading carefully, but it's got me nowhere. Well, I'm through being nice. I'm through treading gently. If you've got something to say, then now would be a good time.'

'I want you to talk to the solicitor, Luca! I want you to deliver on your promise and sort out the title at the resort, and I want you to stop sabotaging any attempt I make to study.'

Letting her go, he picked up his glass, then with a howl of anger hurled it at the wall before carefully selecting another glass from the silver tray and pouring a large whisky. 'Have you finished?' Turning, he let his eyes blaze a trail across the room, his words biting her with their savagery. 'Is that all you want from me, Felice? Is that it?'

'Not quite.'

His knuckles were white around the glass, his face deathly pale and menacing as she calmly walked towards him, every calm, measured word she spoke exacerbating the tension in the room.

'There is another thing I want from you, Luca.' She was in front of him now, her stance confrontational, utterly refusing to be intimidated by this insufferable man, refusing to let him even glimpse the agony in her soul. 'I want some respect. If you can't keep your lover quiet then at least keep her at a respectable distance.'

If Felicity had possessed such a thing no doubt she would have dressed for bed buttoned up to the neck in some Victorian cotton nightdress. Certainly, from the bristling indignation emanating from Luca, had he possessed a pair of pyjamas they'd have been on also.

Instead they had to settle for opposite sides of the bed, with Felicity practically hanging onto the mattress-edge in an effort not to touch him, concentrating on keeping her breathing even as he blew out the candles and flicked off the light, utterly determined to be the first to fall asleep.

She lost by a mile.

However much Felicity wanted to believe he was pretending, somewhere between his turning off the light and his head hitting the pillow Luca fell into the deepest of sleeps, each gentle snore rippling through her, catapulting her into a fury. She wanted to dig him in the ribs, kick him, even, demand how the hell he could go and fall asleep when there were so many questions to be answered, so much unsaid.

His hand sliding across the bed, sleepily snaking around her hips, was like being branded with a red-hot poker. She didn't want him to touch her, didn't want to lose herself in his touch. The row that had blown in needed to be faced head-on, not made up in bed. He pulled her towards him, even in sleep the attraction they generated so palpable, the sexual awareness so real it was impossible to deny it. He tucked his body into hers, pulling his knees up behind her, and she lay frozen, unyielding, wondering how to explain to this impossible, difficult man what she didn't even understand herself. That her body ached for him, that even as she lay there as still as stone he moved her, that every fibre of her being screamed for him—for all of him, not this half-life they had engineered, not this shell of a marriage without commitment.

His tumid warmth was nudging her thigh now; she could feel him responding to her. One lazy hand was almost distractedly circling her stomach, then with a low grumble he pulled her closer, snaking his fingers up and cupping her breast in his hot, dry hand.

It hurt.

Wriggling slightly, she heard his low moan of protest, but the horrible nagging question that had been plaguing her was back, and no matter how she tried to ignore it, no matter how she tried to suppress it, it was here with force now, demanding she face it, stop ignoring things and deal with the problem.

'Felice?' His low sleepy moan caused her to pause momentarily as she crept out of the bed, missing the safety of his caress already.

'I'm just going to the bathroom,' she whispered. 'Go back to sleep.'

'Let's not fight.' He didn't even open his eyes, and she stood and stared at him in the darkness for a moment, wishing it was all that simple, wishing it was all so easy.

Wishing his beauty didn't touch her so.

'Come back to bed, Felice. Don't keep pushing me away.' His hand flicked out from the sheets, warm and strong, his grip possessive, pulling her towards him. His eyes had opened, and even in the darkness she could see the desire burning there.

But she couldn't do it—couldn't slip back between the sheets, into his arms, and make love as if everything was okay, when everything around her seemed to be falling apart. When the charade she was half of was unravelling at the seams.

'I need to go to the bathroom…'

'Felice…' His hand snaked around her waist and the sheet slipped away from his dark, toned body. The full beauty of his arousal caused her breath to catch in her throat, a million wrongs righted with just a fleeting glimpse of his naked splendour. 'Come back to bed.' It was an order, not a request, but delivered with such silken promise that she felt her insides turn to liquid. His hot lips nuzzled her pale stomach, his devilish tongue working its way downwards, and her eyes closed with the agony of indecision.

Oh, she wanted him, *how* she wanted him. To lie on the bed, for his skilful lovemaking to work its undeniable magic, for him to take her to that special place he had shown her, quieting the impossible conundrums stamping through her mind, for the aftermath of her orgasm to obliterate the hopeless questions that taunted her, more soothing than a pill, more toxic than any drink and more addictive than any drug.

But what then?

'Luca, no!' Felicity's words came out more harshly than intended, and her body tensed as he instantly pulled away. She was missing him already, wishing she could somehow take back those two little words, or at the very least the ferocity with which she had expelled them. 'I mean…' Her voice tailed off, the hurt in his eyes surprised even Felicity. 'I really do need to go to the bathroom.'

'I get the message, Felice. My English might not be perfect, but you've made yourself pretty clear.'

Sitting on the bath-edge, she pulled the tiny folded paper from the Pill packet, opening it up and scanning the tiny writing. How many times in the last few days had she done this? Felicity had lost count. Each time the words had offered some assurance, some ray of hope that she wasn't pregnant.

Tender breasts, labile moods, nausea; Felicity gave a rueful laugh. Three out of three so far—*of course* it was the Pill making her feel this way; according to this it might even account for her being so late.

But…

God, she hated the bold print, the thick black letters that warned missing even one tiny pill could cause pregnancy, to take extra precautions for the next couple of weeks, oh, and by the way, could she please see a doctor if symptoms persisted!

Screwing up the flimsy paper in her fist, she threw the tiny ball into the bin and then clasped her fingers to her temples. The truth was too terrifying to contemplate.

How could she tell him, when babies weren't part of the deal?

Babies had never been on her agenda.

Ever.

A whimper of fear escaped into the still night air, echoing around the high walls of the bathroom, the impossibility of the situation overwhelming her.

Suppose she could do it—suppose she could push aside her own fears, embrace the future, however unplanned. How could she possibly tell Luca when even at a stretch, this could only be called a tenuous relationship? Looking down at her flat pale stomach, she tried to imagine it rounded and swollen, heavy with a child, with Luca Santanno's child, her breasts heavy with milk. Whatever way Felicity looked she couldn't see it—couldn't see his hand there, touching their unborn baby, revelling in every little kick, facing every milestone together.

It was all too much, too soon, and just so very terrifying.

Creeping back into the bed beside him, she lay staring into the darkness. Never had she felt more alone, more scared, and never had she needed him more.

One small hand crept across the pillow, trying to turn his rigid cheek, to force him to look at her, honesty just a breath away. 'I'm sorry for before, Luca. Of course I want you; I always have.' Still he wouldn't look at her, his face set in stone, his eyes staring at the ceiling, and she did the only thing she could, to show how much she wanted him.

Pushing her face to his, she kissed his unmoving mouth, her tongue forcing his lips apart, willing him to respond, but he lay rigid beneath her. She knew she had hurt him, rejected him, and suddenly it seemed imperative she put things right, restore their closeness with the only language Luca seemed to want to speak. Her hand moved down, her boldness terrifying her. Yes, he was her husband, yes, they had made love over and over, but never had she instigated it, never in her life had she been the one calling the shots.

Inching down, she felt the soft scratch of his chest

hair thin out; she imagined the delicious snaky line of hair over his abdomen and her nervous fingers dusted it, following the trail, her breath on hold as she tentatively lowered her head, tasting the salty warmth of his skin as her tongue worked down. She could feel his arousal against her cheek, nudging, soft and hard and warm all at the same time, and instinctively she turned, ready to take him, to taste him, to revel in him. But in one swift movement his hands shot to her shoulders, pushing her back, his dark eyes blazing with contempt.

'Are you worried when pay-day comes you won't get your bonus?' he spat as Felicity reeled backwards, her cheeks stinging, every nerve burning with mortification at his brutal rejection. 'Worried if you don't sleep with the boss, he'll renege on the contract? Well, let me tell you this, Felice. I've never had to beg for sex and I don't intend to start now. I suggest you do the same.'

Reeling with humiliation, stunned by the venom in his attack, she stared into the darkness, blinking away the lonely tears as she listened to Luca's rhythmic breathing. Trying to fathom what on earth she had done and worse, far worse, what Luca was going to say when he found out.

CHAPTER EIGHT

SOMEHOW they limped along, the endless army of staff at least ensuring their rows were confined to the bedroom.

Luca, used to a multitude of people swarming around, tending to his every whim, still sucked in his breath in indignation when Felicity stopped talking mid-sentence or dropped her voice to whisper whenever Rosa the housekeeper appeared.

'She barely speaks English,' Luca hissed one morning as they glared over their coffee cups at each other. 'Yet you carry on as if you were at a funeral.'

'I feel like I'm at a funeral,' Felicity retorted. 'Have you any idea how boring it is here? It's okay for you, swanning off to work every day.'

'I thought you were busy with your precious studies.'

'My studies are important,' Felicity flared, but Luca most annoyingly just flicked his newspaper and carried on reading. 'Just because you consider women should be barefoot and pregnant in the kitchen...'

'Heaven forbid.' Luca visibly shuddered, angry eyes peering over the top of the paper. 'Could you imagine the hell a baby would add to this supposed domestic bliss?'

It wasn't a point Felicity cared to dwell on, but she was saved from answering as Rosa appeared, with the inevitable coffeepot in hand, filling his cup without waiting to be asked. Suddenly Felicity had had enough.

If Luca wanted her to carry on as normal around the staff, to say what was on her mind, then she damn well would.

'Do you realise I don't know how many sugars you have in your coffee?'

'What the hell has that got to do with anything?'

'Everything,' Felicity flared. 'You're my husband, yet I've never even made you so much as a drink. It's not just room service with you, Luca; it's a butler and waitress to boot. I've never ironed you a shirt, never cooked you dinner…'

'You're contradicting yourself,' Luca drawled. 'You were just saying before how important your studies were; now you're complaining there's not enough domestic drudgery for you. I could have a word with Rosa,' he offered sarcastically. 'I'm sure she can rustle you up a pile of dirty laundry if that's what you so desire.'

'Oh, you're impossible.' Flinging down her napkin, Felicity forced back the sting of tears in her eyes. God, he was loathsome, conceited and difficult—but she loved him. And, as boring and pathetic as it sounded, she wanted all of him, not this tiny slice she was being offered, but Luca just couldn't see it.

'I have to go to Florence today.' He was sitting reading his paper, not a care in the world, turning the pages slowly as he demolished a pastry and three impossibly strong short black coffees.

Felicity surveyed the gleaming quiet kitchen and tried to fathom Luca's take on it with a baby sitting in a high chair, throwing egg around and disrupting his much loved morning peace.

'Florence?' Felicity took a nervous sip of her *latte*, praying she could keep it down till Luca had left for work at least. She was used to the helicopter revving up around seven a.m. now, whisking him off to the Rome hotel as easily as pulling the car out of the drive, but Florence was hardly a hop and a skip away.

'I might stay the night; it depends how much work there is to do.'

'Fine.'

She could hear the chopper revving up in the distance, knew the routine already so well it hurt, but as Luca glanced at his watch and downed the last of his coffee, the very last thing she wanted was him to leave.

He gave her a vague kiss on the cheek and then, because Rosa came in, he kissed her more thoroughly, but the heavy scent of his aftershave was too much in her fragile state. As she flinched slightly she saw the start of confusion in his eyes. 'I'll ring when I get there. I'll know more then.'

'Luca?' He was at the door now, gorgeous in a dark suit, the crisp white shirt accentuating his strong olive neck, his haughty face cleanshaven, a black briefcase in his manicured hand. He looked angry and restless and confused, but infinitely beautiful. 'Have a safe trip.'

How paltry her words sounded, how utterly empty and meaningless, when the fact that she loved him was at the tip of her tongue, that she had never been more scared in her life, that today was the day she found out for sure if she was carrying his child.

He gave a stiff nod, a tight smile, but didn't say anything, and all that was left to do was sit and drink her *latte*, sit and listen to the helicopter lift into the gently rising morning sun, the whirring blades humming their own tune as he flew away.

*   *   *

The feel of snow crunching under her new boots was as unfamiliar as everything else, but Felicity liked it. Liked the sinking feeling as she walked along, her face hidden behind a massive wrap, her shoulders hunched in the camel-coloured coat she had bought.

She'd been offered a driver, a car, even, but to the staff's bemusement she had refused, determined to have some time to herself, to wander into the village alone and come back when she was good and ready. The mountains were amazing, everywhere she turned a picture postcard in the making—blues, greens and purples capped with snow, villages dotted like models—and Felicity took her time, stopping at the war memorial, waving to curious onlookers as they salted their paths and rushed to catch the bread van. Walking past a tiny graveyard, on impulse she wandered in. Brushing the snow off the stones with her gloved hands, she read the inscriptions. Santanno, Giordano and Ritonni appeared with alarming regularity, staring back at her like a mocking taunt again and again.

Luca, Ricardo and Anna.

Each carefully worded inscription confirmed the futility of the love triangle she had entered. Every one alienated her further, ramming home the incestuous ties that bound this town, the impossible hand she had been dealt.

This truly was Luca's territory, and never in a million years would she belong.

Even with her non-existent Italian, the word *farmacia* was pretty universal, and Felicity took a tentative step inside, relaxing as she saw the white-coated uniform of the staff. The rows of items were touchingly familiar, and she was sure she would have no trouble locating the pregnancy testing kits.

A pretty assistant smiled, offering her help, but Felicity politely declined, far happier to wander than explain what she was here for.

There they were. Congratulating herself, she surveyed the kits, looking for what she hoped would be a simple one.

'Do you know what you're looking for?'

Pulling her hand back as if she were touching hot coals, Felicity swung round aghast. 'Anna! I'm just trying to find some paracetamol. I couldn't get the staff to understand me.'

Anna frowned. 'I thought Cara spoke some English. No problem—I will show you.' She gave a low laugh. 'I hope for your sake you won't need one of these for a while. I'd hate to be the unlucky girl who tries to tell Luca he is about to become a father.'

She looked more closely at Felicity's shocked expression, thankfully misinterpreting it. 'These are pregnancy testing kits,' she explained with a throaty chuckle. 'Now do you understand what I am saying? Can you imagine Luca Santanno a father? Believe me, I know from experience it's not on his list of must-haves.' A wistful look flashed over Anna's face, and a smile bordering on sympathy flickered on her lips as she caught Felicity staring at her. 'I thought I was pregnant by the great man himself once.'

'What did he say?' Her voice was a croak. The answer was one she really didn't want to hear, but she knew deep down it was imperative she at least found out what she was up against.

'A lot.' Anna sighed, rolling her eyes dramatically.

'You know Luca; his life revolves around his work—heaven help the woman who tries to change him.'

'But what did he say about the baby?' Felicity pushed, fingers of fear wrapping around her heart as Anna's cold black eyes met hers.

'Lucky for me there was no baby, it was a false alarm. But Luca made it very clear he had no intention of becoming a father, even an estranged one. He wanted me to have an abortion,' Anna finished watching as the colour drained out of Felicity's cheeks. 'But thankfully there was no need. Let's get these tablets for you. Nothing seriously wrong, I hope?'

Felicity shook her head, still reeling from Anna's words, forcing her voice to come out even. 'I've just got a bit of a headache.'

'Oh, a headache!' The malicious smile was back. 'That's what wives get, isn't it? I must try that one on Ricardo!'

A crushing reply was on the tip of Felicity's tongue, but Anna seemed to change her mind all of a sudden, and the malicious smile was replaced by the first genuinely friendly one Felicity had seen.

'I'm joking. Come, let's get your paracetamol and I will get Ricardo's antacid. He was complaining of chest pain this morning. For a minute I thought my luck was in, but it was only indigestion.' Seeing Felicity's shocked expression, she flashed that bewitching smile again. 'You are very easy to tease, Felicity. You must toughen up a bit.'

A rapid exchange in Italian followed, and Ricardo's antacid was smothered in Anna's basket as the assistant loaded in hair conditioners, face packs and various items of make-up.

'It is so boring here.' Anna shrugged. 'Now that

Ricardo is insisting I give up work there is nothing for me to do except have facials. I understand that you and Luca were tied up last Saturday, but at the very least we should go and have a coffee—be friends. It will be nice having someone young to play with.'

Even Felicity smiled at Anna's terminology. *Playing* with Anna was way down on her list of priorities; it would only end in tears, after all! 'Maybe some other time. I really do have to get back; I'm supposed to be studying.'

'I will hold you to it. *Ciao.*' Kissing Felicity's rather taut cheeks, Anna sauntered out, spraying every perfume on display as she did so.

Only when she had gone did Felicity make her way over to where Anna had disturbed her. At least she knew she was buying the right thing now. Blushing furiously, she made her purchase, frantically trying to avoid the assistant's eyes and praying that *farmacia* staff had the same moral code as doctors, or Luca would know the answer before she did!

It was the longest two minutes of her life. Sitting in the bathroom, staring at the piece of paper, her coat discarded on the floor, her scarf still draped around her shoulders, her need to know, to be absolutely sure, surpassed everything. She was strangely calm as she awaited her fate, and the pink cross slowly appearing was not even a surprise—more a confirmation of what she already knew.

'We'll be all right.' Instinctively Felicity's hand moved to her stomach, massaging the tiny scrap of life that so clearly was meant to be. Catching sight of herself in the mirror, she wondered how she could still look the same when so much had changed. She was going to be a mother and Luca was going to be a father.

She was having Luca's baby.

It was scary and overwhelming, and everything she hadn't planned, but even in the midst of her internal chaos she could sense the beauty of the moment. Whether it was maternal instinct or just the chains of love Luca had trapped her in, she could never regret this infant for a moment, never resent a baby borne of love.

Love.

But did Luca love her?

Anna's words came back like a mocking taunt, the demons that had snapped at her heels awakening now. Her mind whirred as she played out different scenarios, tried to imagine Luca's ordered, busy life with a baby on board, a child born to a woman who was supposed to be a temporary solution.

Making her way out of the bathroom, she lay on the bed, staring dry-eyed at the small plastic indicator and the tiny pink cross that signified what she truly did not know. The beginning or the end?

'*Signora?*'

Even though the knock on the door was firm Felicity barely heard it, and she stuffed the indicator under the pillow, hardly even bothering to look up as Rosa finally peered around.

'Signor Luca, he *telefono* while you out. He will be back tonight.'

'Thank you, Rosa.'

The elderly lady turned to go, but midway she changed her mind. Crossing the room, she nervously perched herself on the edge of the bed, one bony hand touching Felicity's in a surprising gesture of warmth.

'You were right this morning,' she started, as Felicity looked up sharply, eternally suspicious of the other woman. 'You need some time alone with him. Tonight you cook, and me, Rosa, will go out. Come.' She gave Felicity the benefit of a very rare smile. 'I will show you how.'

Considering the internal bombshell that had just been dropped, Felicity found a strange sense of calm as she worked with Rosa in the kitchen. Old Italian music played on Rosa's equally ancient radio, the wood stove was warm and womblike, and the two woman worked quietly together, Felicity listing intently as Rosa indoctrinated her into the finer points of Italian cuisine.

Real Italian cuisine, Felicity realised, not the plastic-wrapped bags of pasta and jars of spicy sauce she was used to, or the tiny bottle of smelly parmesan that stayed in her cupboard gathering dust. Instead, under Rosa's patient guidance, Felicity turned a mountain of potatoes into tiny balls of *gnocchi*, rubbing the little bundles in flour, each one a labour of love in itself. She chopped onions and mushrooms, whisked eggs and fried bacon, until all that would be needed that night was a two-minute whisk in the saucepan while the gnocchi rose to the top of boiling water. And she learnt at twenty-six years of age that *real* parmesan cheese didn't smell at all, biting into the sharp, tiny curls Rosa shaved off, and suddenly discovering another vice to add to her list, along with chocolate and ice cream.

'*Grazie*, Rosa.' Felicity smiled as Rosa pulled on her coat, calling to her husband in rapid Italian.

'You are a good student.' Rosa shrugged. 'I hope you both have a nice night.'

As she turned to go Felicity felt a surge of panic.

For weeks now she had wanted this, a night alone with Luca, but now it was finally here she balked at the final hurdle, terrified of his reaction to the news she had to tell him. She wanted to call Rosa back, wanted the relative safety of an audience, but deep down Felicity knew she needed to face this alone.

She was having a baby.

And tonight Luca was going to find out.

CHAPTER NINE

LUCA'S methods of transport had some advantages.

The low throb of rotors nearing gave Felicity time for a final check. Lighting the candles, she flicked the switch on the CD player, hoping that the fact Puccini's *La Bohème* was at the top of the pile meant it was one of Luca's favourites. Standing at the fireplace, she checked her reflection for maybe the hundredth time.

A warm bath and the crackling fire she had lit brought a warmth to her pale cheeks that was so unfamiliar these days. Her blonde hair gleamed, piled high on her head and twisted into a coil, tendrils escaping around her face and neck, and a flash of lipstick accentuated her curvy mouth. The pale pink cashmere dress, another of her fabulous purchases, scooped low, her creamy décolletage for once filled something, and the soft pink hugged her swollen breasts, tapering into her waist. As the flash of helicopter lights flooded the lounge room she caught the reflection of her own glittering golden eyes. The nausea, so ever-present these days, was pleasantly absent—just the military march of her heart thumped as she struggled with her news.

Tried to fathom Luca's response.

'Where's Rosa?'

It wasn't exactly the most romantic of greetings, but given the frostiness of the morning's departure Felicity couldn't blame Luca. Barely dusting her cheeks with his lips he marched through the hallway and she clipped behind him in her heels. If anything his restless, brooding mood only made him more desirable, made it more imperative that she tell him the truth.

'I gave her the night off,' Felicity said in a falsely cheerful voice as Luca tossed his jacket in the vague direction of the couch. 'I thought it would be nice to spend some time together.'

'That wasn't the impression you gave this morning.' The sarcastic edge to his voice didn't go unnoticed. 'In fact this morning you gave the impression that some time *alone* was exactly what you wanted.'

Despite his aloofness Felicity knew he was hurt, knew that he was confused. After all, since their arrival in Italy she had hardly been the loving, giving wife he had so recently married. Constant nausea had put paid to that, but soon it would all be behind them. Once Luca understood the reason behind her distance they could finally move on, alone or together.

Now all she had to do was tell him.

'I did need some time alone this morning,' Felicity admitted slowly, bracing herself—but it was too soon; she wanted them to be sitting down, a meal between them, not this hostile confrontation. 'But now—'

'Oh, you've changed you mind,' Luca broke in, and Felicity snapped her mouth closed. 'Just like that.' He clicked his fingers so loudly, so close she jumped back. 'Never mind that I wanted to talk at the hotel. Never mind that you've pushed me away in bed for a full week. Now you've decided you want some quality time! Does it not enter your head that I might have had a bad day? That the very last thing I need right now is an in-depth discussion? That all I want to do is come home and have dinner?'

'I can understand you're upset, and I know it seems as if I've been pushing you away...' Felicity ventured as Luca pulled off his tie and simultaneously filled a whisky glass.

'You understand, do you?' Gulping his drink, he tore at his tie, cursing himself for his weakness. For weeks now she had pushed him away, the mere touch of him making her recoil. This morning's exchange had churned his stomach all day, and he wanted to hold that thought, to stay angry, to let her feel some of the pain he had, but he hadn't reckoned on this. Hadn't even contemplated coming home to her so sweet and warm, the effort she had gone to, the genuine appeal in her eyes—and that dress!

That body, wrapped, bathed in the softest pink, her breasts jutting out, her nipples swelling like berries... The need to touch, to possess was so strong he wanted to grab at those pins that held her hair, to feel it spill through his fingers, but more appealing, more utterly endearing, was seeing the fire in her eyes. The feisty woman he had first met seemed back now, the lethargic, tearful stranger had happily disappeared, but he couldn't let it go—couldn't just walk in and carry on as if nothing had happened, jump to her tune. There was too much pride and too much pain.

'I've cooked.'

'Why?' he asked rudely. 'I didn't bring you to the other side of the world to cook for me. Rosa is the cook; I employ her to cook for me.' An angry hand tossed at the air and Felicity felt her goodwill evaporate. Gorgeous he might be, but she damned well wasn't going to just stand there and let him walk over her...

'Oh, and I suppose a wife has other duties?' Felicity bit back.

'Exactly.' Downing his drink in one gulp, he turned

his fiery eyes to hers. 'So now I have a housekeeper who doesn't cook and a wife who doesn't like sex!'

His words were like a slap, but instead of defusing her mounting anger they only fired it. 'Well, maybe you should take more care with who you employ, Mr. Santanno,' Felicity retorted, her angry eyes a match for his, her chin jutting defiantly, five-foot-three of bristling indignation rising on her high heels. 'So far you don't appear to have a very good track record.'

'I assume by that you're referring to Matthew?' His voice was like ice, a muscle pounded in his cheek, and Felicity knew their argument had overstepped the mark, gone into uncharted territory. The festering boil needed to be lanced, but not like this; never like this. 'Do you really think he would have put up with this? His wife mooching around the house, barely talking, pretending to be asleep in bed at night?' He saw the colour rise on her cheek and gave a malevolent smile. 'You think I don't know when you pretend?'

'At least I knew where I stood with him!' Even as the words came out Felicity regretted them. There was no comparison in her relationships to Matthew and Luca. He was livid now, his olive skin tinged with grey, his eyes glinting dangerously as they narrowed, his hand so tight around the glass Felicity half expected it to shatter.

'Do I have to remind you that excuse of a man not only drugged you, he was blackmailing you also?' He slammed the glass down, and Felicity flinched as the verbal attack continued. 'I have never treated you with anything other than respect. Have I forced myself upon you? Have I pushed when it was clear you didn't want to sleep with me?' And you have the—the...' his fingers were snapping furiously, his mouth contorting in furious rage as he tried to fashion the word '…you have the—'

'Audacity, I think is the word you're looking for, Luca,' Felicity shouted, anger blurring her senses, crossing the invisible line they had drawn, pushing for a confrontation she wasn't sure she really wanted. But she was too fired up to care now. Tonight should have been so perfect. Tonight she had been going to tell him. And instead they were nose to nose, pouring out insults that could never be taken back. 'Yes, Luca, I have the audacity to expect my husband to understand that maybe I don't feel well, maybe there is a reason I'm not swinging off the chandeliers at the moment, and respect that, not rush off to another women's bed!'

He closed his eyes, every muscle in his face rigid as he raked his fingers through his hair. Dark, angry eyes finally opened, and for the briefest second the flash of pain she read in them cut her to the core. But the words that followed were more damning, more agonising than Felicity could ever have imagined.

'At least I know she wants me.'

How long they stood in stunned silence, Felicity didn't know. The spitting fire, the ticking clock, the low music were no match for the pounding in her temples, the vile taste of bile in her throat as she digested his words.

'Felice.' His voice came out in a low, weary moan, his head shaking as he tried to touch her, one hand reaching for her arm, but she shrugged it off, her face utterly white as she tried to fathom what he had just said. 'I shouldn't have said that.'

'Why not.' Her voice was a croak, her throat felt as if it had been sanded, and despite the heat of the fire, her raging pulse, she had never felt so icy-cold. 'It's hardly a State secret.'

'I should never have said it,' he said again, 'because it simply isn't true.'

'Isn't it?' Tears were now coursing, unchecked down her pale cheeks, but her voice was angry and strained. 'I'm sorry if I'm not very good at this—sorry if I'm not one of the sophisticated lovers you're used to. I don't know the rules, Luca, because I've never played before. I don't know what's real and what's imagined; I don't know how I'm supposed to react when half the village assumes that you're sleeping with Anna. And if your words were meant to give me some sort of cruel bedroom kick, then they worked, because you've hurt me.' A pale, trembling hand thumped at her chest, the fury lighting in her eyes again. 'You've hurt me and you promised you never would!'

A mass of flesh bore down on her, crushing her face with his kiss, quieting her protests, her doubts, her fury, her fears with the weight of his adoration. Hungry hands ravished her body, possessing it. Lowering her to the floor, he pulled at the dress. The tiny row of buttons at the back were too much to take in, the need to be inside her overwhelming both of them, and he pushed the soft fabric up over her thighs, ripping the tiny lace panties and tossing them aside, revelling in the sweet taste of her. She gasped beneath him, shocked and unsure at first, unable to believe he could be enjoying this, but his groans of approval were the confirmation she needed.

His closed eyes and rapt concentration allowed her a brief interlude to take in the feeling of him there, his probing tongue flicking at her swollen bud, her thighs tightening in spasms as her stomach tensed not with nerves, not with embarrassment or shame, but with the delicious trembling of her orgasm, deep, rapid contractions, that made her back arch. His strong hands held the peach of her trembling buttocks as she quivered under the mastery of his touch, tiny gasping sobs coming out of her parted lips, her body a delicious ball of tension, down to her curling toenails.

He had to stop, had to let her catch her breath, had to let the world stop spinning for a moment—only just as she thought it was over, just as he knelt back on his heels and the flickering pulse of her womanhood abated slightly, he pulled her dress higher, the sight of her engorged pink breasts meriting a slow kiss as he pulled down his zipper, as she moaned beneath him, exhausted, sure she had left that magical place he had taken her to, sure it was over for now.

The sight of him so swollen and virile stirred something in her almost akin to fear, her eyes widening with a thrill of sexual terror as he slowly parted her legs, dragging her along the cool tiles, every movement measured now, his eyes locking on hers, his voice a distant drum in the swirling fog of passion.

And he revelled in it, revelled in her innocence, in the feel of her gasping for him and him alone, adored the sound of strangled gasps that filled the vast room, the satin of her skin beneath his touch. He wanted so much to hold this moment for ever, to bathe in the beauty of her gaze, to treasure the feel of her, swollen and ready and welcome at his engorged tip, but he couldn't. The need to be inside her, to feel her wrapped around him, to plant his seed high in her womanhood was utterly overwhelming now, and he plunged inside her, simultaneously exploding as she gripped like a velvet vice.

'Felice.' His single word was more a moan, a gasp, as lay beside her, pulling her into the crook of his arm, his fingers making idle circles along her arms. The tiny, almost invisible hairs shivered as her nerves twitched, her body slowly winding down, ever down, and the world came back into focus. It took a moment to register that the phone was ringing, and they lay there for a silent moment, refusing to let a stranger intrude, relaxing when it stopped, when only the crackling fire and the sound of their breathing filled the room.

Now.

Closing her eyes, she took in a heady breath of the musky, citrus tang of his aftershave, the solid chest beneath her cheek, and for a moment in time she felt safe, sure that their lovemaking, the deeper union they had forged tonight, would sustain this onslaught.

'Luca…' Her voice was barely a whisper, her eyes still screwed closed as the dice started to roll, but the phone was ringing again, and Felicity froze in his arms as he cursed at the intrusion.

'It might be important,' he said, reluctantly untangling himself, quickly sorting his clothes. She fumbled on the floor, pulling down her dress as he picked up the phone. *'Pronto?'*

As Luca's voice became more urgent, her forehead creased. He spoke loudly, but she tried to convince herself that nothing was wrong. Italians always shouted into the telephone, she'd learnt, always sounded as if World War III had broken out or the family was about to be ripped to shreds by marauding wolves, when all they were discussing was the weather.

'It's Ricardo.' As Luca replaced the receiver the reassuring smile didn't come, his face paling as he walked over. 'He has had a heart attack.'

'Oh, my God.' Sinking to the couch, Felicity shook her head. 'I saw Anna just this morning. She said he had chest pain, but they thought it was just indigestion.'

'It was his heart. They've taken him to a hospital in Rome, the best, but he nearly died on the way. They managed to revive him, but he is very sick. Anna is very upset.'

A smart retort that was absolutely out of place bobbed on Felicity's tongue, but she bit it back. Ricardo was a close friend of Luca; the last thing he needed was a sarcastic comment from his wife. Still, Felicity wasn't quite convinced Anna really was that upset. Her dismissive words about her husband this morning still reeled in Felicity's mind. If she'd called a doctor, taken him to the hospital then, instead of buying indigestion liquid, surely this could have been avoided, surely…

'I have to go.'

'To Anna?' Felicity gasped, unable to comprehend what he was saying and praying she'd somehow misheard.

'She's upset; she's alone at the *infermeria*. I couldn't say no to her. Come with me.'

Instantly she shook her head. The word *infirmeria* had sent an icy chill through her spine, memories of Joseph's death too utterly painful even to tentatively explore. 'I can't.'

'Can't or won't?' His words were sneering, but seeing the pain in her eyes he stopped, one hand tentatively catching her cheek.

'That's where Joseph died.'

'Oh, Felice.' His words were gentler now, her palpable pain reaching him. 'I am so sorry for your pain. But you of all people must realise how Anna is feeling;

surely you can understand why she needs me to go to her?'

But Felicity *didn't* understand; the part of helpless female was one she had never played before. Her mind whizzed back a year, to here in this very city, sitting on a hard-backed chair as Joseph neared his painful end, her parents, exhausted from their mercy flight, grabbing a few hours' sleep back at the hotel.

My God, she didn't even speak the language, but it had never even entered her head to wake her father in the middle of the night, to call him to fetch her. Why the hell couldn't Anna get a taxi? 'Surely she's got family, friends? Why does it have to be you?'

'Because it's always me!' Luca's words were sharp—bitter, even. 'Anything happens in this village, it is me they call.' His voice softened then, and taking both her hands, he looked at her, imploring her to understand. 'If it was you alone at the hospital Ricardo would do the same. I wouldn't expect any less from him, and I cannot let him down.'

'But you can let *me* down?' She could hear the jealous edge to her voice, see the weary resignation in his eyes as he shook his head, but still she couldn't stop herself. Tonight meant everything; tonight there was so much she wanted—no, needed to say. But Anna clicked her fingers and Luca ran. 'We've just made love, Luca. There are things I need to talk about.'

'Me, me me!' He shook his head, his eyes blazing. 'You know, I almost feel sorry for you! You're like a jealous two-year-old. Again and again I tell you it is over. It has been for years between Anna and me...'

'She tried to make love to you the other week,' Felicity retorted, but still Luca wouldn't relent.

'She made a mistake! She knows it is all over between us. I am married to you and Anna respects that! Has she not tried to be friends with you? Has she not rung you several times and tried to go for coffee? You moan you are lonely, that there is no one to talk to, yet when someone extends the hand of friendship you pull away.'

'She used to be your lover!' She was shouting now, utterly perplexed that he couldn't see her point of view. 'How can I be friends with someone you slept with? Mind you, maybe I'd better get used to it—after all, if you lined up all your ex-lovers half the female population would be ruled out.' Bitching was something Felicity wasn't used to, something she'd never done, but then again she'd never been in love before, never ridden the rollercoaster of emotions that came when you gave away your heart to a lousy playboy. The words that tumbled from her lips, and the scoffing laugh that followed were so alien Felicity almost didn't recognise her own voice.

His finger razored her cheek, his head shaking with almost weary resignation. 'You know, I thought you were so gentle, so sweet—that underneath that harsh exterior there was a warm loving woman inside. I guess even I get things wrong sometimes.'

She watched him go, and her heart didn't feel as if it was beating any more. She watched his car snake down the mountainside with dry eyes that couldn't even expend a tear.

Had she really got things so wrong?

Looking around, she saw the telltale remnants of their passionate encounter, the candle wicks spitting in the puddles of wax. She blew them out with pale lips, picking up her discarded shoes and underpants and making her way up the stairs to the vast lonely bed.

She tried and failed not to imagine Anna in Luca's arms, that beautiful, calculating raven head resting on his chest, tried to believe the comfort Luca imparted to her would be as innocent as he swore.

The cotton sheets were cool on her body, and her hand moved down to the hollow of her stomach, resting naturally on the tiny life within.

Luca's child.

She lay there for an age, staring at the ceiling. The heavy snow of the mountains muffled sound, creating an eerie silence, paving the way for her own self-doubts to voice themselves loudly. The moon drifting past gobbled up minutes, turning them into hours as she waited for the master to return, waited for Anna to have her fill.

And finally, when dawn was breaking, when a million taunting questions had made a mockery of each and every platitude she'd attempted to deliver, it was with hurt, jealous eyes that she turned to Luca as he crept into the bedroom, the cool night air following him in, sending a shiver across the bed as he pulled off his coat.

'How is he?'

'No change.' Luca shrugged. 'I only got to see him for a moment; the doctor said he should rest.'

'But…'

She sat up, confused eyes locking on his. Never had he looked more beautiful. The early-morning five o'clock shadow darkened his chin, accentuating the razor-sharp lines of his cheekbones, his black hair was laced with snowflakes, and she ached, physically ached to put her hand up, to let her fingers massage, capture that face in the palm of her hand, to pull that cold tired body into the warm bed, to kiss away the stern taut flexion of his lips. But, as beautiful as he might look, never had he seemed more unobtainable.

Trying and failing to keep her voice even, to eloquently put forward her point without lacing each word with the bitter sound of jealousy, she spoke again. 'You've been gone six hours.'

'Anna was upset.' His eyes locked on hers, defiant, angry eyes, without a hint of contrition.

'And naturally you had to comfort her,' Felicity sneered.

Tonight should have been so special. Tonight should have been about babies and plans and moving forward. Instead Anna had yet again impinged on them. Anna's shadow had again darkened the door of their relationship. Frankly, Felicity was sick of it.

'Actually—' his eyes were like ice, his words laced with scorn, '—as it turned out, Anna ended up comforting me. Ricardo has been like a father to me since my own died. Seeing him lying there, so old and so feeble all of a sudden, hit me in a way I didn't expect and Anna understood. I never really expected my wife to.'

CHAPTER TEN

'YOU'VE both been wonderful.'

Anna's deep, throbbing voice still set Felicity's teeth on edge, but, bracing herself, she poured Anna's third *limoncello* into a glass and offered it to the pale woman sitting on the sofa, her raven hair cascading down her shoulders, her unbuttoned coat slipping enough to show a mocking curve of voluptuous creamy bosom.

To say she had seen more of Anna than Luca in the last few days since Ricardo's heart attack would be the understatement of the millennium. Anna would appear in the kitchen, draped in cashmere or fur, as Felicity struggled to focus, then disappeared with Luca in a waft of nauseating perfume, only to return at some ungodly hour and regale Felicity with snippets of Ricardo's progress while Luca disappeared into the study to make a few international calls, surfacing to drive his ex-mistress the short journey home.

Their marriage, if you could call it that, had eclipsed the rowing stage, bypassed the acrimonious one, and seemed to have slipped into the rather more terminal state of weary resignedness.

'Where's Rosa?' Anna asked, taking a hefty sip of her drink.

'Felice gave her the night off. Again,' Luca added, with a hint of an edge to his voice that Anna instantly picked up on.

'She wants her husband to herself, darling,' she drawled. 'And frankly I don't blame her.' Felicity was just about to come up with a withering reply, but her response faded on her lips as Anna continued. 'She really is a most difficult woman. I don't know why you still employ her, Luca.'

'But you get on with her,' Felicity pointed out.

'Only because I'm out of her precious Luca's life. She treated me like dirt on a shoe when I was here, but now that I am gone she has exalted me to saint-like status. I don't blame you for wanting rid of her and to have the house to yourself. I know that when I get Ricardo home I am going to do everything for him. The hospital has organised nurses to come to the house but I don't want them. I am going to take care of him myself. This has been a big...'

'Wake-up call?' Felicity's voice was barely a croak as she finished Anna's sentence.

'That's what I am trying to say.' Anna smiled gratefully. 'Seeing him so ill, so frail and being able to do nothing.' She closed her eyes and a tear slid down her cheek. 'That night when I called, I am sorry I disturbed you, but the nurse was saying I had to go home, to find his medication and bring it back, to get some rest. My tears were upsetting Ricardo. I shouldn't have disturbed you... '

'Nonsense.' Sitting beside Anna on the couch, Felicity took the other woman's cold hand and gave it a small squeeze, offering her first genuine response to Anna. 'Of course you should have rung; we're friends.'

Looking up, she saw the start in Luca's expression, registered the tiny grateful smile he gave her, and the guilt that had been niggling at her for the past week suddenly multiplied.

Anna wasn't just upset; she was genuinely distraught. The brash, man-eating vixen Felicity had imagined seemed far removed from the pale, wan woman sitting trembling on the sofa.

'I'd better go.' Standing, she buttoned her coat, gesturing for Luca to sit down as he rummaged for his car keys. 'I can walk. It is only a few minutes, and the fresh air will do me good.'

'You mustn't walk.' It was Felicity who was insisting now, Felicity, handing Luca his keys. 'It's been snowing again; Luca will drive you.'

Standing in the lounge, she wiped the fog from the steamed-up window, watching as Luca opened the passenger door, gently guiding Anna into the seat. His hand on the small of her back was a simple action that only a few moments ago would have spun her into a frenzy of jealousy, but Anna's grief had touched her.

When Luca returned he was tired, pale and tense.

'Was I too long for you?' he snapped as he walked in, tossing his coat over the pale sofa and kicking off his shoes. 'Did you expect me to just drop her off at the gates?'

'Of course not.'

'She offered me a coffee,' Luca volunteered, unmoved by her response. 'But naturally I declined. I wouldn't want to give you more ammunition.'

'Luca, please, I don't want to fight.'

'Neither do I.' Suddenly all the fight seemed to go out of him. Lines she had never seen before were grooved beside his eyes, and Felicity realised there and then how much the last few days had taken their toll. The last few weeks, come to that.

Horrified by what had happened at the golf resort, Luca had been springing surprise visits on every hotel he owned, calling meetings, leaving at the crack of dawn and not returning until late at night in an effort to ensure no one else would suffer the way her family had.

And what had she done in return?

Moaned she was lonely, carried on like a spoilt two-year-old, devoid of attention.

And now his dear friend was sick, and he was stuck with a jealous wife, questioning his every move.

Well, no more.

'I don't want to fight either. Luca, I'm sorry for doubting you. Seeing Anna tonight has made me realise how selfish I've been—not just to her, but to you as well. It can't have been easy for you these past few weeks.' Swallowing hard, she tried to plan her words, but nothing came. What was more disturbing was the noticeable absence of Luca's response to her attempt at an apology. 'Luca, what I'm trying to say is—'

'Save it.' He didn't snap, there wasn't even a trace of malice in his voice, but right now Felicity would have preferred it. Their passionate rows, volatile encounters left her spinning and reeling, but this lethargic response to her heartfelt apology was far more worrying, and her eyes widened with anxiety as Luca shrugged her hand off his arm and headed for the stairs.

'Luca, please.'

He turned briefly, his face so jaded, so utterly, utterly exhausted it momentarily stopped Felicity in her tracks.

'I'm tired, Felice. I've been getting up at five every morning, not getting home till after midnight. Surely you can understand that even I need to sleep occasionally?'

'It's not Anna that I want to speak about, Luca,' Felicity implored. 'It's us.'

A tight smile twitched his grim lips. 'I'm sure the row will keep till morning.'

The abyss between them as she lay in the massive bed seemed to stretch for ever. She mentally willed Luca to roll over, to reach for her in his sleep as he always had…

Till now.

A tentative hand reached for one broad shoulder. Even in sleep she could feel his tension, feel the taut muscles under her hands. A tiny shrug as he subconsciously dismissed her had her hand pulling back as if she had touched hot coal, and an awful sense of foreboding filled her, her stomach spasming simultaneously with her heart as Luca rolled further to his edge of the bed and further out of her life.

He awoke at the first ring of his alarm, jumping out of bed with military control when surely his body must be aching for a few more hours of undisturbed rest, and she watched him through sleep-deprived eyes. Her whole night had been spent tossing and turning, and the pain in her stomach was one she didn't want to acknowledge, but one she couldn't ignore.

'You look terrible.' He was knotting his tie, fresh-shaven now, utterly in control.

Utterly out of reach.

'I didn't get much sleep,' Felicity admitted, pulling her knees up to her stomach and wishing the pain would abate, wishing he would just go so she could deal with whatever her body was dishing out. Privacy was something she craved now.

'Maybe this will make you feel better.' Reaching into his briefcase, he handed her a bundle of papers, watching with questioning eyes as Felicity struggled to sit up, noting her flushed cheeks as she slowly turned the mountain of pages. 'It is the deeds for the golf resort. You will see your father is the owner now.' A tiny pause, a tiny hesitation—and, though Felicity couldn't be sure, a tiny tinge of sadness before he carried on talking. 'It is watertight, Felice. My lawyers have been working on it all week; I cannot suddenly change my mind.'

Tears pricked her eyes as she felt the mattress indent, watched one large, dark-skinned hand move across the sheet and take hers.

'We haven't made each other very happy, have we? I'm tired of fighting, and seeing you so sad, like a prisoner here—well, it isn't what I intended.' His hand tightened around hers, and Felicity had to bite through her bottom lip to stop herself from crying out as Luca went on. 'You've got what you wanted. Matthew's out of your life and your father has his resort back, which is no less than he deserves.'

'But what about you?' Her voice was a mere croak as cruel reality hit.

'Me?' He gave a low laugh. 'With your permission, of course, I'll tell my mother that my one attempt at marriage has put me off for life. It should keep her off my back for a couple of years at least—so, you see, it hasn't been a total waste of time.'

It was over, over, over, and if anything Luca was relieved.

'What I said about Anna...' Felicity started, but Luca just shook his head.

'It isn't just about Anna, Felice; you know that deep down. It is as much my fault. You wanted details and I refused to give them, but I didn't think I should have to spell everything out.'

Bemused, she stole a look from under tear-laden eyelashes, her lips parting, longing to stop him, to halt the horrible end, but Luca carried on relentlessly, his fare-well speech obviously well rehearsed—no questions from the back of the room, please!

'I didn't just want *fun*, a mistress with a ring on her finger. I wanted a wife.'

'I want to be your wife,' Felicity begged, but Luca just shook his head.

'Ricardo is like my second father—you know that, I have told you again and again, but have you come to the hospital with me? Have you held my hand, been there for me? I know that the hospital has bad mem-ories for you, I know about Joseph, and I would have supported you through that, been there to help you if only you had met me halfway. Shown me you cared.'

'I do care,' Felicity insisted, but it fell on deaf ears.

'Anna is not my lover, not my mistress. Over and over I have told you, yet you steadfastly refuse to be-lieve me. Felice I cannot live like this, cannot face the accusation in your eyes every time I am home ten minutes late. I explained on my first day with you how things were; I thought you would trust me. I admit I have said some hurtful things, but that was in the heat of a row—a row you continually instigated.' He let his words sink in for a moment before continuing, more gently this time. 'You are holding back from me. Every day I feel I know you a bit less; every day I feel you distance yourself a bit more.'

Standing, he stared at her for an age, before depos-iting a soft kiss on her cheek and heading for the door.

'We both deserve better, Felice; you know that as well as I do.'

Watching him leave, watching him turn and walk away, was like seeing the coffin lowered. She wanted to fling herself on him, to beg for a second chance, for the hands of time to pull back, for the powers that be to breathe life into all she had lost. But, battling with nausea and grief, all she could do was stumble from the bed. The heavy door closed and the tears finally came, the pain in her stomach a dull ache compared to the loss in her heart.

She had lost him, lost the only man she had ever loved, and her nausea trebled. Hearing the chopper thudding overhead, pulling him away with every swoop of its rotors, she was literally overwhelmed by grief. Beads of sweat rose on her brow, and the pain in her stomach ripped through her like a gunshot. Felicity felt as if her world had been ripped apart at the seams.

She only just made it to the bathroom in time.

CHAPTER ELEVEN

SOMETHING was wrong.

Rinsing her mouth at the sink, Felicity caught sight of her ashen face in the mirror. Only two spots of color flamed, but her skin felt as if it were on fire. Resting her cheek against the cool mirror, she closed her eyes, begging the room to stop spinning, for her breathing to even out, for the pain in her stomach to abate somewhat.

She couldn't be losing the baby. Felicity battled with a tidal wave of emotions. The little life she had felt so equivocal about suddenly took on momentous proportions. Telling Luca she loved him would be so much easier without a baby on board, so less complicated without a pregnancy to comprehend, but Mother Nature was playing her cards now, signing Felicity up for a crash course in maternal instinct, and she sank to the floor, hugging her knees to her chest, trying to somehow protect the tiny life within as gradually, mercifully, the pain lessened.

With or without Luca, this baby was everything to her.

It wasn't just a Santanno, it was her child, and losing it now would be like losing her soul.

'*Signora!*' Rosa was tapping on the door, her voice annoyingly loud, and Felicity struggled into a robe and pulled open the bedroom door. 'Signor Santanno just telephone—he forget his briefcase. He needs some papers for a lunchtime meeting, so my husband is going to drive it to Rome for him and drop it into Reception.'

'Okay.' Her voice sounded amazingly normal as she retrieved the case from the floor.

'Signora Felicity!' Rosa did a double-take as she took the case and made to go. 'You look terrible.'

'So everyone keeps telling me,' Felicity said dryly, then forced a smile. 'I'm fine, Rosa; I've got a stomach upset, that's all.' She was about to blame it on something she'd eaten, but, anticipating the hysterics that would send the elderly woman into, Felicity quickly changed tack. 'A bit of gastric flu or something.'

'Do you want me to send for the doctor?'

Felicity hesitated. A doctor was exactly what she needed, but not with Rosa hovering anxiously downstairs. Luca deserved to hear the news from her first.

'Rosa, could you ask Marco to wait? I'll only be five minutes. I want to go into Rome myself; if he wouldn't mind giving me a lift that would be great.'

'But you are sick.'

Oh, she was sick, Felicity thought sadly. Sick of the lies, sick of putting everything off, sick of avoiding confrontation.

'I need to see my husband,' Felicity said firmly, and Rosa gave a heavy shrug. 'I'll get dressed now.'

The journey seemed to take for ever. Battling with nausea, forcing a smile as the questioning eyes of Marco surveyed her from the rearview mirror. All she knew was that she had to see Luca, tell him the truth and then take it from there. Together they would go to the hospital. Together they would face the truth about their unborn child.

Gradually the lush mountains gave way to the oc- casional village, soon joining into one mass of streets, and the coiling, writhing city came to life before her eyes as they battled the heavy traffic. The inevitable horns, the beautiful women and handsome men rushing along the streets, the pavement cafés littered with lovers and smart businessmen, backpackers and tourists, all descending on this most beautiful city.

Just as she had left it a year ago.

A sign for the Trevi Fountain came into view as the car slowed, and for a moment so did Felicity's heart.

'One coin means you'll come back, two to marry an Italian, three to live happily ever after.' Joseph's voice echoed through her mind. The last precious days of Joseph's life, those poignant final days, days that had been too painful for recollection until now.

God, she missed him so.

'*Ére.*' Marco's voice snapped her mind to attention as they drew up outside the hotel, the door opening before the car had even come to a halt, and as the green-uniformed man realised who she was he called for the concierge, Rafaello.

'*Bongiorno*, Signora Felicity,' Rafaello called as he flew down the steps to greet her, a beaming smile splitting his face as he tried to relieve her of the briefcase. 'This is a pleasant surprise! Allow me to take Signor Santanno's case for you; I will take it to him directly.'

'*Bongiorno*, Rafaello.' Felicity returned the warm greeting as he walked towards the revolving doors. 'But there's really no need. I'll take it to Luca myself.'

'It is no problem, *signora*.' Suddenly the beaming smile didn't seem quite so natural, and Felicity felt her eyes narrow as her fingers tightened around the handle. 'I will arrange some morning tea for you. Signor Santanno is in a meeting.'

They were crossing the courtyard now, and Felicity

felt every last vestige of hope, of trust disappear as Rafaello carried on talking, the beautiful, lyrical accent grating now as the ream of excuses pounded in her ears.

'I will let him know you are here, and no doubt he will come down directly, but he made it very clear he didn't want to be disturbed.'

'Did he, now?' Felicity's voice was quiet, but strong. She had come here to face the truth, but it would seem from the staff's reaction that the truth might be a touch more complicated than she had envisaged.

Her eyes met Rafaello's head-on. 'I don't want morning tea—thank you for asking. And I most certainly don't want to sit and wait. My husband wants his case, and I intend to take it up to him.'

'But *signora*…'

'Please.' Putting up a slightly trembling hand, Felicity stopped Rafaello mid-flow. Whatever life was about to throw at her, it needed to be faced. She was tired of following Luca's golden path, tired of the staff that smoothed over the cracks, tired of Luca's refusal to follow life's simple moral code. 'This isn't your problem.'

Cheeks burning, she strode through the golden re-volving doors, barely acknowledging the grandeur of her surroundings as she spun through the massive foyer, ignoring the agonised looks from the concierge as he gestured to one of his staff to pick up the tele-phone. It was an old-fashioned lift, and as the gates pulled closed she felt as if she were being imprisoned, locked in her own eternal hell. She braced herself for what was to come as she rummaged in her purse for her swipe card.

Poor Rafaello would be joining Ricardo in the coronary care unit, Felicity thought ruefully as he burst through the stairwell door, admitting defeat with a sorry shrug as she determinedly swiped her card and pushed open the heavy door.

She'd thought she had prepared herself for the sight that might greet her, but the pain that seared through her as she took in the scene told Felicity that nothing ever truly prepared a person for loss.

Anticipation was no antidote for confirmation.

'Felice!'

She couldn't look at him, couldn't bring herself to face the man who had just broken her heart. Instead her eyes worked the room, taking in the massive floral bouquets, the champagne cooling in a silver bucket, the candles burning, *La Bohème* throbbing through the heavy air, and finally she dragged her eyes to where Luca stood, Anna just a foot away, her raven curls still falling from being hastily pushed away by him—but not hastily enough.

The image of her in his arms, of that beautiful face resting on that strong chest in this most beautiful of surroundings was etched on Felicity's mind for ever.

'Ho provato a telefonare, il signore.'

The Italian was rapid, but it didn't take Einstein to work out what Rafaello was saying, and with a strange surge of confidence Felicity watched their stunned faces as she managed a translation.

'Which might have helped—' Felicity gave a thin smile as she crossed the room to the bedside table '—if the telephone hadn't been taken off the hook. You were right, Rafaello; Signor Santanno really didn't want to be disturbed after all.'

'Felice, please.' Tossing Anna to one side, Luca was next to her in a second, grabbing at her arm, swinging her around and forcing her to face him. 'This is not how it seems. Tell her Anna.' His pleading eyes hardened as he turned to his smirking mistress. 'Tell her how you planned this, tell her I knew nothing about it...'

'Come now, Luca.' The smirk widened to a malicious grin as she sidled over, her rounded hips sashaying across the room, tossing her mane of hair, not a trace of contrition as she faced Felicity. And for a second, for a horrible moment, Felicity swore she saw pity in those beautiful almond eyes. 'Felicity had to find out about us sooner or later. I'm sure given time she'll come to understand.'

'Understand this!' Her words were like pistol-shots, the pity in Anna's eyes neither wanted nor needed. 'You can have him, Anna—all of him. And I didn't *just* find out; I've known all along. The only mistake I made was believing Luca when he told me how much he thought you'd changed, but I think his first assessment of you was rather more correct.'

'And what was that?' A flicker of doubt flashed in her eyes, and a muscle was pounding in her smooth olive cheek as she turned questioningly to Luca, but it was Felicity who answered her.

'Well, you'll have to forgive my rather poor Italian, and I'm sure you'll understand if my pronunciation isn't quite correct, but the word *puttana* is the one that springs to mind.' And, turning on her heel, she left the room, ignoring Luca's calls, even managing a hollow laugh at Anna's emerging hysterics.

He caught up with her at the lift, blocking the gap with his shoulder as she slammed the heavy iron gates. Even though it must have been agony, he barely winced as she struggled to close them. 'Felicity, you have it all wrong.'

'No, I don't,' she shouted. 'You told me she'd changed, told me you were taking her to the hospital every morning, told me she was sitting at her husband's bedside, willing him to live—and look what was really going on. God, I even insisted you drove her home last night; you must have been laughing yourselves sick in the car. Poor, blind Felicity. Poor, trusting Felicity. I trusted, you Luca; I trusted you and look where that got me.'

'You've never trusted me!' His voice was a roar, and the urgency in it, the sheer volume behind it startled her.

A surge of nervousness had her forcing the lift gate closed as she wrestled to keep him out. Like a keeper slamming the gate on a deranged animal. Only when the gate was firmly shut did she look at him again, but her hand was on the button, pushing for the ground floor as she prayed for the beastly lift to move.

'You never trusted me,' he shouted again, 'not for a single moment, but you have to trust me now.'

'Why? So you can humiliate me again? So you can carry on your sordid little affair with an air of respectability? Well, forget it, Luca. A mistress with a ring is something I'll never be.'

'Come out of this lift this instant.' His voice was still loud, still packed its usual authoritarian punch, but there was such raw urgency in it, such an air of desperation that Felicity almost did as he begged. But this bitter end was just too painful to face. The lift was starting to move, beginning its slow descent, and maybe it was for the best, she decided. What was the point in hearing more lies, shovelling hurt onto hurt?

But there was one more thing she needed to say, three little words that would prove the magnitude of her pain, so he clearly knew just what he had flicked away.

'I loved you, Luca—loved you all along. And just look where it got me!' Her words echoed upwards as she shouted to the walls.

Slamming at the gate, wrestling with the weight of iron, if he could have put his hand through the metalwork and grabbed the thick oily chain, somehow held onto her, Luca would have. Instead he gripped onto the gate, gripped for a second or two as her final words washed over him, screwing his eyes closed as the truth finally dawned.

That surly, moody chameleon who had shared his bed, who had teetered into his life on too-high heels in a too-tight dress, had really, truly loved him.

'Luca?' Anna was coming over, but he barely even recognised her, didn't even have it in him to be angry with her at this moment. Nothing seemed to matter now. Nothing except what he had lost. 'It is for the best. Felicity is too soft for you—too soft to be a Santanno. She will be okay.'

But as Luca turned, as Anna saw his broken, shattered face, heard that usually strong voice so hoarse, so bereft, for the first time in her life she felt an alien sting of guilt, a rumble of shame, and she watched the man she adored dissolve before her eyes.

'She probably will,' he mumbled, speaking in English, the only thread he had left that bound him to Felice. 'But will I?'

CHAPTER TWELVE

THROUGH the tiny steep backstreets she ran, slipping, stumbling, but not caring, immune to the curious looks of the locals as she ran sobbing by. There was no master plan, no direction or purpose to her journey, just an overwhelming need for space, for distance. Gulping air into her lungs, she felt the cool rain on her burning face and only then did she register where she was.

The Trevi Fountain. Neptune standing proud and tall, just as she had left him a year ago, water cascading, the glitter of coins at the bottom, tossed in the eternal hope that the world would keep on turning, that life would go on and that one day in the future you surely would return. But all Felicity felt as she stared into the water was agony, and wonder at how a city so beautiful could have caused so much pain, how she could be holding a place responsible for taking away so much that was dear.

Her brother.

Her husband.

And as her hands moved to her stomach, as the pain that had engulfed her through the night returned with a vengeance, Felicity knew the city had staked its final claim, that the baby she had only just begun to hold dear was surely about to be its final victim.

It was Joseph's voice ringing in her ears as she sank to the floor, Joseph's voice playing over and over as she registered the horror in the onlookers' eyes, heard in the distance their chaotic shouting, the distant wail of sirens drawing closer.

'I should ask for a refund.'

The paramedics didn't get it. Instead they mumbled about her being delirious as they loaded her into the ambulance.

Drifting in and out of consciousness she lay there still; nothing more could hurt her now. Even the overhead signs for *Emergenza* as they raced her through the stark tiled corridors of the hospital barely touched her. The oxygen mask smelt funny, and the drip maybe stung a bit, but such was her grief, such was her loss it didn't really matter.

Nothing mattered any more.

CHAPTER THIRTEEN

HE WAS beautiful.

It was the first thought that popped into Felicity's mind as her heavy eyes opened. She battled an overwhelming urge to close them again, to let the drug-induced oblivion descend on her once again.

He lay dozing in the chair beside her bed, but even sleep didn't seem to relax him. His weary features were ravaged with lines, the shadow dusting his chin as dark as night, as dark as the hollows smudged under his eyes. Looking down, she saw his dark hand clasped over hers, his fingers carefully avoiding the drip that seeped into her thin vein, the flash of his heavy gold watch.

The hospital tape over her wedding ring seemed fitting somehow.

Masking the union that should never have been.

He was as beautiful as he had been when she had first laid eyes on him, just a few short weeks ago, only now there was so much more between them than ships that passed in the night. A marriage in smithereens, an aching, gaping void where her heart had once been.

Yet she couldn't regret it.

Somewhere deep inside she still attempted to justify the pain that had been inflicted. The bliss she had found in his arms, the warmth that had bathed her when those mocking, calculating eyes had occasionally lowered their guard, when those strong arms had held her as a man should hold a woman, the childlike belief that Luca really could make everything all right.

'Felice?' His concerned face hovered over hers. His jacket had been discarded, and as her eyes flicked down she saw the savage smear of Anna's lipstick on his collar—an awful reminder of what had taken place if ever she'd needed one. Wincing, she tore her eyes away, and he misinterpreted her agony. 'Here—' Pushing a tiny cord into her hand, he wrapped her fingers over a switch. 'Push this. It takes away the pain.'

Nothing will take away my pain. She nearly said it, drugs and emotion were a dangerous cocktail, but somewhere within she still had pride, still had a piece of her left that Luca Santanno could never destroy. Instead of looking at him she turned her face to the bland curtains, worked her tired eyes around the room, its familiarity doing nothing to soothe her.

The rooms were undoubtedly all the same here, so why should she think that this was the same one where Joseph had died? That the beige curtains and rickety bedside table were exclusive to her loss?

Losses.

The baby bobbed into her consciousness then, the tiny scrap of life she had never really met, never consciously desired. But now it was gone Felicity realised with a piercing sense of loss just how desperately it had been wanted.

Her baby.

Tears squeezed out of her eyes, salty heavy tears, each one loaded with agony for the loss of a little life so precious. As Luca pressed the button deeper into her hand she resolutely pushed it away. Somehow she wanted, *needed* to feel the pain, needed the physical agony. Her body demanded this memorial to all she had lost.

'I'm sorry.'

How meaningless his words were, how utterly utterly, empty his apology when their child was dead.

'I should have listened to you.' Gently, so as not to hurt her further, he lowered himself onto the bed, the mattress indenting, the scent of him filling her. Yet still her face stayed turned away; still she couldn't bring herself to look at him. 'I couldn't understand why you didn't trust me, why you insisted that there was something between Anna and I.'

'You couldn't understand?' They were the first words she had spoken, and when they came her voice was hoarse with emotion. 'How can you say that when all the time you were lying to me? Was I supposed to just melt into a corner? To turn a blind eye when you slept with your mistress? Is that the language you understand?'

'Since Anna and I parted I have never slept with her.'

'Oh, save it, Luca.' Her hand was working the tiny button now, pushing the switch furiously, listening to the tiny bleeps that meant a cure was being delivered. But this was a pain no drug could deal with; this was an agony modern medicine would never cure. The cure for a broken heart was as elusive as the cure for the common cold, and the disease probably just as prevalent. 'I saw you; I caught you, don't try and deny it now. Your staff knew, Rafaello nearly had a coronary racing to warn you your little wife was on her way up, and yet you have the gall to sit here and tell me that you're not sleeping together.'

For the first time he didn't rise, didn't match her

fury. Instead he pulled the switch from her, then tightened his hand around her cold, trembling fingers. 'You need to be awake for this, Felice. You are going to listen to me and you are going to believe me. I have been naïve.'

To hear such a strong, assured man make this admission had her turning momentarily to him, her forehead puckering as he falteringly continued. 'Till I met you I had never been jealous in my life. It is an emotion I have never encountered, and then you came along.'

His hand tightened on hers, only this time it wasn't tenderly. 'When I thought about you and Matthew, when I imagined him making love to you, I felt this sick, churning loathing and I didn't even recognise it. Didn't understand that the emotion I was experiencing was jealousy. The same jealousy Anna was feeling. And, from my brief encounter with it, I am starting to understand how it can make you do strange things.

'That first day when you were in my room, demanding your dress, heading back to him, all I knew was that I had to stop you. I would have done anything to stop you, *anything*, and that is what Anna was doing. In her mind she believed if she told everyone we were still together, if enough people—you included— thought it was happening, then perhaps it really would. She engineered things right down to the last detail. She drove enough of a wedge between us to ensure that doubt was there, and then stepped in like a vulture swooping on her prey. But I would never have slept with her. *Never.*

'Walking into the hotel room, I was furious. I finally realised how right you had been to be suspicious, just how calculating Anna had been all along. I told her to get out; she just refused to accept it, kept on throwing herself on me, begging me to reconsider. That was when you walked in.'

Oh, she wanted to believe him, wanted to so badly it hurt, but she was too raw, too scared to just accept his story, to believe it could all be so straightforward.

'I should hate Anna, but I don't,' Luca said more softly. 'I pity her—and, more pointedly, I can understand her motives. Understand how jealousy can make you do the strangest things. How it can strike at the strangest times. How it can toss aside reason and make you act on impulse.'

'Like asking a stranger to marry you?' Felicity ventured, and Luca gave a tired nod.

'In my mind I really believed that if I married you, loved you, told the world you were my wife, somehow one day you might end up loving me back. I love you Felice.'

'No false declarations, remember?' Pulling her hand away, she stared at the bland wall. His pity was the one thing she couldn't take. But Luca's hands were cupping her face, turning her to face him.

'How can it be a false declaration when I am speaking from my heart? I love you. I have done from the second you fell into my arms, from the moment I held you and you wept. When you called out in your sleep and I came to lie beside you, I knew there and then that I never wanted to let you go again. I barely knew you and yet I would have done anything to keep you. You were right. I did sabotage your plans to study, did put off talking to the lawyer—but only because I couldn't bear the thought of losing you. Couldn't stand to see you walking out of my life before we'd even started.'

She lay there, his words washing over her, utterly

floored as he carried on in that delicious faltering voice. This strong, beautiful man was telling her the one thing she needed to hear.

Luca Santanno loved her.

And it should have helped; only it didn't. The omission of any declaration of love in their relationship had cost the life of their child.

The hope that had briefly invaded her war torn body dispersed then. Lying back on the starched white pillow, she closed her eyes, retrieving her hand from his grasp.

Love seemed small compensation for such an overwhelming loss.

'You knew about the baby, didn't you?' His voice was soft, thick, and laced with uncertainty. Slowly she nodded, the tears sliding down her cheeks into her hair. 'That is why you were so sick, why you were so—so...'

'Difficult?' Felicity finished for him. 'I've never been so scared in my life, never felt so sick, and I just didn't know what to do—how to tell you.'

'I wish you had,' he said, but with not a hint of reproach in his voice. 'Surely I'm not that unapproachable?'

'You are.' Felicity sighed. 'But not enough to keep me from loving you. And you made it very clear from the start that you didn't want babies.'

'I *didn't* want babies,' Luca agreed. 'Frankly, I couldn't see what all the fuss was about. I'd watched friends and family turn from competent professionals to neurotic parents, discussing unmentionable things at the dinner table, debating for hours the merits of breast-feeding versus bottles, then you came along and suddenly there I was wondering if we'd have blonde or dark-haired children, children with your reserve or my fiery temper. But how could I tell you that? I was sure you would run away, laugh in my face. I had to be so very careful not to scare you off.'

The nub of his thumb was wiping her tears away, but it couldn't keep up with her inexhaustible supply. His soft lips were shushing her now, dusting her cheeks like velvet paws, and she ached to press her cheek into his hand, to take the comfort he was imparting, but still she couldn't.

'We understand each other now; that is all that matters.'

'No, Luca.' Her words were strangled in her throat, and he fought to reassure her.

'From this we will learn, move forward together. It might not seem like it now, it might seem scary and overwhelming, but in time you will see it is surely for the best.'

'For the best!' Her eyes opened to a stranger. 'How can you say that it's for the best? How can you just dismiss our baby? But then I guess you've had some practice. Anna told me how you demanded she have an abortion when she thought she was pregnant...'

His face darkened. The hand on her cheek stilled as he let out a low hiss.

'Never!'

'*Signora?*' A pretty nurse was at the bedside, her eyes smiling, her surprise at Felicity's sudden re-entry to the world evident as she blew up a blood pressure cuff around her arm.

Felicity lay there, feeling the impatience emanating from Luca, the tension in the room as the nurse chatted away, checking her temperature, her pulse, oblivious to Luca's increasingly mounting irritation.

'Never,' he repeated, once they were alone again. 'She could never have been pregnant by me. I took care of that—made sure it would never happen!''

'You weren't so careful with me!' Felicity retorted. 'You didn't stop to think of the consequences when *we* made love.'

'Because making love and having sex are two different things.'

His simple explanation halted her; his summing up of the magic they had once shared took some of the fight out of her response, allowing him a small window to continue.

'Anna has done so much damage, told so many lies. If there is to be any hope for the three of us we must ignore every last vile thing she has said. We must—'

'Two of us,' Felicity choked. Correcting Luca was second nature, but his inadvertent slip seemed rather insensitive, and her tears seemed to be coming back for an encore.

'The three of us.' Luca sat back down, his eyes never leaving her, one strong, warm hand moving so very gently down to her tender bruised stomach below the starched white blanket. Its warmth, its quiet strength didn't cause the pain she'd anticipated. Instead came a sense of security and support, and the muscles that had tensed as he'd moved relaxed under his hand, moulded into the soft comfort of his touch.

'It's too soon, Luca,' Felicity sobbed. 'Too soon to be making promises we can't keep. Too soon to be talking about other babies when all I want is this one.'

'It is all I want too.'

His hand was still on her stomach, gentle, protective and infinitely safe, and as a small smile rose on his face, more breathtaking than the morning sun rising over Moserallo, the bleeping of her heart-rate on the monitor picked up. Somewhere deep inside hope flared, a tiny fluttering, stretching its wings, as Luca softly spoke.

'What do you think is wrong with you, Felice?'

'A miscarriage.' She struggled with the word, struggled with the images so hazy in her mind. 'When I came in the doctor said...' Her mind searched its recesses, dragging the painful memory to the fore. *"Gravidanza ectopica probabile."* I didn't need a translation dictionary to work out that it was an ectopic pregnancy, that my tube had ruptured. I signed the consent form...'

'Probabile.' He was smiling so widely she almost joined him, almost dared to believe that Luca really could do everything—Luca really could put this right. 'It means probably,' he said softly. 'The one little word that is every doctor's escape clause. Only in this case they were only too happy to be proved wrong. You had a ruptured appendix, Felice. Yes you were sick. Yes, we have been worried about you and the baby, of course, but that was all it was. The baby is safe.'

He knew what she'd been through, understood that her doubt in no way reflected on her love for him, understood that the rivers of her pain ran deep, and that sometimes his word simply wouldn't be quite enough.

'Wait there,' he whispered, kissing her softly on the cheek.

'I don't exactly have much choice.'

He was back in a moment, back with the nurse, who smiled kindly and gently lifted her gown, squirting jelly onto her stomach as Luca held her hand.

'Now do you believe me?'

She would have answered, would have said yes, but

tears were streaming unchecked now as one shaking hand touched the screen, trying somehow to capture the future, all her hopes and dreams, right there before her eyes.

'It's so tiny,' Luca said gruffly, and there was a definite catch in his throat as he stared in wonder at the monitor.

'"From little acorns…"' Glancing across the pillow, she stared at his profile, stared at the man who loved her gazing upon the child they would love together.

Come whatever.

EPILOGUE

'Jo's getting very spoilt.'

As they ambled along, their hands entwined, the early-evening sun casting an amber glow around them, catching the sprinklers jetting in to life and watering the lush green golf course, Felicity was grateful to the glare for the excuse to wear her sunglasses and hide the inevitable tears that came each and every time they left Australia. Not that she was complaining—Luca didn't turn a hair whenever a wave of homesickness hit, and the air path between Italy and Australia was a rather frayed carpet.

'I don't think you can spoil a six-month-old.' Felicity smiled. 'Dad's just enjoying having him around.' Luca's hand tightened around hers and she squeezed it back gratefully.

'I wish I wasn't so badly handicapped.' Luca sighed. 'Your dad just laughed at me when I said that, but I'm going to work on it. I'm going to improve my game if it's the last thing I do.'

She didn't even bother to correct him, but a smile chased away her threatening tears at the image of Luca and her father on the golf course. Richard, a true-blue Aussie in every sense of the word, still scratched his head in bemusement at some of Luca's odd ways. Still, *gnocchi* with carbonara sauce Santanno-style was proving a big hit on the menu, and it was nice to see Richard smiling again after so many difficult years— getting to know his son-in-law over a game of golf, and bypassing beer for a glass of good Italian red and chatting long into the night about football and golf and all the things men strangely held so dear.

'You know, after Joseph died I never thought my parents would be happy again—I mean really happy. Content was the best I could hope for. But seeing them with Jo…'

'They're happy,' Luca said softly. 'Of course there will always be sadness there, always be a big piece of their lives missing, but Jo has been a gift in so many more ways than we could ever have imagined.'

He was right, of course. The purgatory of morning sickness had seemingly been left behind with her appendix, and Felicity had enjoyed the final six months of her pregnancy being spoiled, loved and adored by her doting husband. Jo had burst into their lives two weeks late after a trouble-free labour, and had been making up for lost time ever since—smiling at the world, charming everyone who came near with his dribbling smile and mass of dark curls, his dark, dimpled olive skin and eyes that melted even the hardest heart.

'Let's meet the neighbours.'

Felicity frowned as Luca started to walk more purposefully now, turning into the driveway of a massive sprawling property that adjoined the resort. The field was laden with vineyards, the huge rambling home in desperate need of some TLC, but the elderly couple who owned it were too old and too tired to get around to it. She bit back her irritation. This was supposed to be a romantic walk, time to take five before Jo's evening bath and her parents' farewell dinner, not a get-to-know-you session with the neighbours.

'Doesn't seem like anyone's at home.' Luca frowned,

knocking on the massive doors and peering through the dusty window.

'Maybe they're at the resort.' Felicity shrugged. 'A lot of the locals are going there for dinner now that the place has picked up. Oh, look…' A small sigh escaped her lips as she eyed the table on the veranda, the clean white tablecloth and breathtaking flower arrangement out of place amongst the clutter. Two long-stemmed glasses just begged to be filled from the bottle of red wine open beside them. 'I hope we're that romantic when we're in our eighties.'

'We will be,' Luca said assuredly, smiling unseen as she fingered the petals on the flowers.

'Imagine sitting here in fifty years, drinking our own wine, watching our grandchildren and great-grand-children running around.'

'Careful what you wish for…'

Felicity looked up. 'I didn't mean here,' she said quickly. 'I'm happy in Moserallo. I just didn't realise the Murrays had it in them, that's all.'

'Oh, the Murrays are romantic all right,' Luca said, picking up the bottle and pouring two deep glasses. 'They've decided to sell up and move to a resort in Queensland. They want a pool they don't have to worry about cleaning, wine they don't have to worry about bottling, and a house they don't need to think about cleaning. They just want to enjoy each other.'

He looked at her bemused face, handing her a glass. After a moment's hesitation Felicity took it, colour mounting in her cheeks as Luca led her to a chair.

'I'm handing the hotel chain over to my brother.' For an age he didn't elaborate, just stared at the view— the sun bobbing on the horizon, shadows stretching across the vineyard, a cooling welcome breeze soothing the dry hot land. 'I can't do it any more. Can't fire up like I used to, can't leave for work at six and not get home till ten any more, when the only place I want to be is with you and Jo. I know how hard it is for you, leaving your parents, and I know you've never once complained about the hours I put in. But I know it hurts you.'

Finally he dared to look at her, relief flooding his features when he saw that she was smiling. 'We won't starve. I'll still be on the board of directors. But it's too much for one person—things were starting to get missed, look what happened to your father…'

'Luca.' Her soft voice cut into his well-rehearsed speech. 'You don't have to keep apologising for that. It wasn't your fault, and anyway it's over now. My father is happier than I dared imagine he could be. You don't have to justify cutting back to me, and you certainly don't have to give up your career to keep me happy. I'm not so reliant on you I can't amuse myself.'

'I know you're not,' Luca grumbled. 'Sometimes I wish you were.'

'Well, I'm not. I love you, Luca. I love being with you, being married to you, but I'm not going to collapse in a heap if you're not home by five each night.'

'You miss your parents, though?'

'Yes,' Felicity admitted. 'But it's not as if I don't see them.'

'Remember when we got married? Remember sitting on that plane when I said I'd never hurt you?'

Felicity nodded.

'Leaving here hurts you each and every time, and in turn it hurts me. I understand where you're coming from, Felice. There's no shame in wanting your family near—it's what we Italians do best.'

'What about your family, though? If we relocate here, aren't yours going to be just as upset as mine?'

Luca shrugged. 'We'll go home and see my mother all the time. Anyway, there're hundreds of Santannos—countless grandchildren vying for her attention. It's kind of nice here when Jo's the only one. We can make this work, Felice, with my business sense and your accounting skills. Ricardo has taught me a lot about wine over the years. I have discussed it with him and he's happy to offer advice. From what the doctors said at his last check-up,' Luca said with a teasing smile, 'he'll be around to offer advice for the next twenty years or so.'

'Anna's going to have a long wait for that inheritance.' Felicity grinned back, her smile fading as Luca's expression grew more serious.

'I really believe we can make a go of this.'

'So do I,' Felicity murmured, dreams and plans dancing in her mind. She surveyed the familiar land with new eyes now, imagining Jo and his brothers and sisters yet to come running along the veranda, Luca beside her each and every day…

Facing the future together.

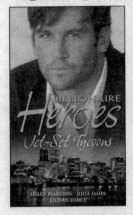 

This proud man must learn to love again

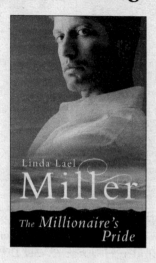

Successful, rich widower Rance McKettrick is determined that nothing is going to get in the way of his new start in life.

But after meeting the sweet, beautiful Echo Wells, Rance finds her straightforward honesty is challenging everything he thought he knew about himself. Both Rance and Echo must come to grips with who they really are to find a once-in-a-lifetime happiness.

Available 18th July 2008

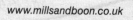

Queens of Romance

Bedding His Virgin Mistress

Ricardo Salvatore planned to take over Carly's company, so
why not have her as well? But Ricardo was stunned when in
the heat of passion he learned of Carly's innocence…

Expecting the Playboy's Heir

American billionaire and heir to an earldom, Silas Carter is
one of the world's most eligible men. Beautiful Julia Fellowes
is perfect wife material. And she's pregnant!

Blackmailing the Society Bride

When millionaire banker Marcus Canning decides it's time
to get an heir, debt-ridden Lucy becomes a convenient wife.
Their sexual chemistry is purely a bonus…

Available 5th September 2008

Collect all 10 superb books in the collection!